THE WOMANIZER

THE WOMANIZER

a man of his time

RICK SALUTIN

DOUBLEDAY CANADA

Copyright © Rick Salutin 2002

Doubleday Canada and colophon are trademarks.

National Library of Canada Cataloguing in Publication Data

Salutin, Rick, 1942–
The womanizer : a man of his time / Rick Salutin.

ISBN 0–385–25946–8

I. Title.
PS8587.A355W64 2002   C813.'54   C2002–901552–9
PR9199.3.S18W64 2002

Jacket image: Patrick Morgan/Artville
Jacket and text design: Daniel Cullen
Printed and bound in the USA

Published in Canada by Doubleday Canada, a division of
Random House of Canada Limited

Visit Random House of Canada Limited's website: www.randomhouse.ca

BVG 10 9 8 7 6 5 4 3 2 1

For Theresa and Gideon

And we are put on earth a little space
That we may learn to bear the beams of love.
—WILLIAM BLAKE

Part I

TRIGGER HAD
A HARD-ON

L et's consider the little Casanova at age eight, he thinks, as he steps from the last stair of the porch onto the pavement. Yes, that will do for a start. Amazing how sometimes all it takes is that moment when your foot hits the street for thought to flow, the muddle clears and the problem resolves. It's a good enough reason to walk, as he always has. Same walk, same route, only the years have passed. Many years to be sure. Sometimes you think you've got it right at last, so why not try a different route, which he occasionally does; on the other hand, there's always more to learn from where you've already been.

He guesstimates he's walked this route ten thousand times and the returns might be diminishing, though he hasn't done a cost-benefit analysis. Sometimes he varies it, but never for long. Does that mean he lacks imagination? No one ever accused people in his field of being creative. But human beings take the same walk because they're repetitive and obsessive, it's their nature and has its reasons. You travel the same block because you haven't solved its puzzle yet. Walk it again once more and it may finally yield its secret. Then you can move on to another route, different problem. Once he thought the sole purpose of these walks was to meet somebody, and often he did. Now, he thinks it's to solve the puzzle, whatever it is. So keep walking.

Of course now he's walking mainly for cardiac purposes, and with care, nitro puffer in his pocket, just in case. After the operation he'll get down to serous cardiac walking, maybe buy a treadmill, though everyone says they end up as storage space for files and knickknacks. A tall woman with long brown hair strides toward him on the other side. In the past he'd have crossed over, casually, to pass nearer, maybe say hi, see if there's a response. Something reminds him of the girl in the rain. Her carriage. She walks haughtily, shoulders back, head up, hair flowing. The hair has a life of its own. *I don't need anyone*, it all says, along with: *I am making contact by the mere way I walk and look, and inviting others to contact me back.* Then she is gone. *Who was that woman?* people could ask, the way they used to say, *Who was that masked man?* until someone solved it by saying, *That was the Lone Ranger.*

There are traffic calmers on the road beside him. They used to be called traffic bumps but apparently it was provocative, or just accurate, and the bumps made many drivers angrier and more aggressive even without the term, so now they call them calmers, to the same effect or worse. Traffic flow holds the secret to many mysteries, in his view. It's a totally scientific matter of physics and math, yet it's one hundred per cent about psychology and choice. It is, in other words, like economics. He turns onto Bloor Street, a main, ahem, artery, and not a side street, yet notoriously narrow and clogged. He remembers when there were streetcar tracks, restricting the flow even further. Two lanes expanded to four, and the traffic wound up going slower and being more crowded than before. It's a metaphor for the standard notion of growth in economics: a great thing to have, except when it makes everything worse, which it generally does.

He passes Amanda, closing the dry cleaner's. Since her teens she's been entrancing the men of the city. She calls his name and waves. She knows every customer she's ever had. She's smart and funny and he'd sleep easier than he does if she was prime minister of the country and secretary-general of the UN too. He told her that, back when she was in her teens. "Dry cleaning is my life," she replied, saying nothing much as if it was everything there is to say. Why is there such intimacy between sexy and smart? He's still working on that.

The bypass will be routine of course, as everyone says, almost as routine as a filling these days. Of course a bypass probably isn't quite so routine if you're the one going to have it. They saw open your chest and wrench it apart and, well, who knows? Then there's the valve job, just slightly less routine. Means they go right into your heart, the way they did when they snaked the little tube up for the angio, after which he got the bad news. Or good, as some say: catch it, fix it, done. Still, he's anxious to get on with this little tale, the one he's formulating as he walks. Lay it out and set it down. Just in case. Not because he's pessimistic or angry, and definitely not because he's bitter and feeling cheated. He doesn't. He isn't. He has met his wonderful child, at a time in his life when he had given up on such a thing happening, and he has known true love. When your life has turned out all right, it sprinkles a little healing dust back over the past. Except—his boy has not known him. That's the only sore spot. It will be a while before the son can know the dad back. We are the repositories of our children's experience, till they can serve as their own. What would this child want to know from this parent, if he could ask? What should his parent pass on, if he must do it immediately? The two of them still haven't had the conversations he's been hearing in his head since before the kid arrived. The ones about fishing and the night sky. And above all, of course, the solemn futile duty every dad owes his son: to talk to him about sex.

Futile because it is the historic mission of each generation to surpass, antiquate, minimize, and trivialize all the heroic sexual advances and breakthroughs made by the generation before it. So any discussion is already superceded by events, by history, you could say. History always triumphs, so far. Yet unavoidable as well because, well, because you have nothing else to give. It's the only way to justify your own lucky slot in the parade of generations, which you, through this child, had the fortune to join. You must offer your meagre experience and the pathetic tidbits of wisdom gleaned from it to those who are about to succeed you, roll their eyes as they may and probably must. That's the solemn, futile duty of every dad to every son. Especially if the dad is not quite certain how long he'll be around; and his son, coming up to big birthday number one, is still too small to understand words, much less the components of a sex life. There's a need to gather it somehow so it will be available whenever he, in the future, has the will and leisure to dip into it. Or not, as he chooses. The obligation, at least, will have been discharged. So let's consider the little Casanova. And let's call him—well, why call him anything?

Because this is not a study (economic, econometric, statistical, or historical) like the work he normally does. It is a *story*, an exemplary tale and a cautionary one. The "true" record is something else and is ample, as much as those ever are: documents, recollections, photos, debris. But the figure in this tale is not the typically messy human reality who doesn't quite fit his or any context just right; he must be somebody tailored to the tale, to fill the need, an ideal type of the sort concocted by Max Weber, that sociologist of economies, or economist of societies, who sought to exemplify, not replicate. He will not belong to any actual reality but will illuminate many. And besides, embarking on a story of some uncertainty and pain, for the sake of a person you don't really know yet, it won't hurt to create a little distance. So let's call him Max.

It is winter, 1950. The hapless twentieth century has finally clambered over a series of shames and horrors which it has only begun to grasp, and reached the little pinnacle of its midpoint. It's looking forward to a well-deserved slide down the other side.

Max's parents are away. They are in Miami Beach. It's their first and only trip south for Christmas. They drove there in the DeSoto, leaving him to the care of a stern Slavic woman, or maybe she's Scottish. At eight, those distinctions aren't easy. His folks phone every few days, which isn't easy either, in the current state of telephone technology.

The woman speaks to him a lot about her nephew, Scotty, or perhaps Sasha, who's a bad kid. That's her point, her only point, about this kid. He and his pals sit in a restaurant and sweep the dregs from the tables and ashtrays around them into a glass. They swish it about and then Scotty—or Sasha—drains it dry. She doesn't say what's bad about this. The only truly grisly content in the concoction is the butts and ashes. And the kid isn't forcing it on anyone else. He drinks it himself. He takes some crap from the world and pours it down his hatch. Maybe her point is: he's transforming himself, from the inside out, into a force for evil. He is the opposite—could be the thing she means to say—of what you must become. But beware: he may lurk inside you just the way all that tabletop junk now resides in him.

He's sitting on the sofa beside little Marta from next door.

Their legs protrude out over the edge of the cushions. They're alone and they're smooching, in the argot of the forties, the swing era. This is their practice. He's always done this stuff with little girls in the neighbourhood, at least as long as he's had a memory. Since he was, oh, three? Two? Rolling around on his parents' big lumpy bed with the headboard, among whichever of the neighbours' daughters happen to be over. Usually more than one, it seems a group kind of thing to do. It's part of his natural exuberance, like running up and down the aisle shooting off his toy six-guns when his mother takes him on the streetcar, or rocking madly back and forth on his rocking horse. You can hardly tell the difference between exuberance and sex in a little guy. It could be called sexuberance.

With Marta it's just more convenient than it is with his other little partners in passion, since their two apartments connect via a back porch, called by the landlord a "balcony." He puts his arm around Marta's head, it barely makes it to the other side of her neck, as if they're *necking* at a movie in the balcony, the way he pictures Uncle Ansel, his bachelor uncle, doing on one of his dates when he borrows the car from Max's dad. Then, suddenly, an ear-splitting whine erupts from the direction of the dining room.

"Aha—that's what I thought you were doing!" It's the Slavic Scot, or Celtic Slav, bursting on them like a V-2 rocket hitting London without warning during the last days of the war. Or a Jap Zero bearing down straight out of the sun so they can't see her and react till she's bang on top of them. Vengeance is hers. He goes a profound red. Radical red, which would be apt, since Marta's dad is a Communist party organizer. Sometimes her dad rushes out of their next-door apartment in the middle of the night and barricades himself in with some unemployed worker's family that's been evicted by a bloodsucking landlord. Marta more or less vapourizes, he has no thoughts for her at this moment and just one impulse: flight. He cannot bear his shame, and certainly wouldn't think of defending it. The rampaging sitter's howling accusation fills the apartment, the air in it has become unbreathable. He bounds—or bails, like a fighter pilot ejecting—to the floor. He streaks for the door, going by a little Johnson and Johnson Band-Aid box in which he banks his allowance and other assets. It's his stash. Maybe he's saving it for university or retirement but he needs it now. He skids like a cartoon character as he passes the box, snatches a silver dollar he knows is inside, and rushes out the door onto Shaw. Breathe now. Steady, steady. Good. It's gone—that . . . palpable stifling reproach—but it might follow him out, like the rubber arm of a comic book supervillain, if he lingers in front of the door.

He dashes up to Bloor and hails a passing taxi, as if cab-hailing is a native human instinct, the way lambs get up and walk moments after they're born. He climbs in back and mutters, "One hundred Margaretta." The cabby flips down the meter and heads off as if this is all normal. Eight-year-old in a big rush. Max knows the address on Margaretta because it's where Uncle Ansel and Grandpa live. He's never been there but he knows the number. His dad and Uncle Ansel work together at 100 King Street and Uncle Ansel and Grandpa live at 100 Margaretta. It's like their reserved family number. He hands the driver the silver dollar and gets out as if tipping—"Keep the change"—is also genetically encoded.

He asks for Uncle Ansel and the desk clerk motions toward the hall. It's a tidy three-storey building of single rooms, men only, bath and toilet midway down the corridor on each floor. The clerk says Uncle Ansel is out but Grandpa isn't, and tells him the room number. Grandpa doesn't seem surprised to see him but Grandpa, according to family lore, was never much of a stay-at-home guy himself in his younger days. He rambled and he gambolled. Like Grandpa, like grandson. They wait silently for Ansel to return from his date. Max has never had much to say to the old guy. They take a weekly trip together to the corner store where Grandpa pays for six comic books he chooses from the racks: mainly realistic ones like Red Ryder and Tarzan rather than the funnies like Bugs Bunny or Scrooge McDuck, or the weirdies about rubber-limbed guys. On one of their outings, Grandpa slipped him the silver dollar, as if he had foreseen the ugly possibilities of the near future. They could duck out for comics now, except they might miss Uncle Ansel, and they both agree, in their silent way, that Ansel should handle this one. Who knows, by now that vindictive judge of a caregiver could have reported him to the police as lost or a runaway smoocher. There might be a dragnet out for him. (DUM DA DUM DUM. *My name's Max. I'm a kid.*)

When Ansel returns from his date, he listens and says nothing. He was in the war and has a plate in his head. He has no kids yet and may not know what to say. But it's an era in which adults don't talk a lot to kids anyway, at most they talk to each other about kids. He drives Max back to Shaw Street and speaks to the person who drove his nephew from the boy's own home. Their conversation has a serious timbre but they're in the other room and Max can't make out the words. She doesn't sound worried and it never occurred to him she would be. She opened the door to them as if they'd been keeping her awake, or dragged her from a good book. Why would she care where the little wastrel was once he'd swung over to the public ashtray side of the moral universe?

Marta of course is nowhere to be seen. Perhaps she's been eaten, but even in his distressed state, he knows that's unlikely.

After that, he avoids the back porch, though it means neglecting a fava bean experiment he set up out there with his mum's help. He gets through the coming days—or months or decades, it's all so indeterminate at eight, and in such a state—in the same house with *her*. She acts as if nothing momentous has passed between them. She prepares meals and reads to him at bedtime. Six months later, on his birthday, she even sends a book with a card and a note. But all this is reconstruction. In specific terms, he recalls nothing; the only thought in his mind, like a shepherd boy's simple prayer, is his parents' return and her departure.

Then they are back, she is gone, and nothing is said. Weeks later—as he remembers, but who really knows—his mother sits down beside him on the folding cot which serves as his bed, the kind everyone picked up after the war in army surplus stores. He's been waiting for this moment. Oh, how he's waited. She tells him she heard what happened. He says nothing. He just waits for her to say that she knows it must have been hard for him. She says it. He is relieved and more: eased, allayed, just this side of exonerated. He waits for her to add, "because you didn't do anything wrong." Like a pardon from the governor. But she doesn't say it.

Had she done so, perhaps the past, and therefore his future, would have been washed away. Or not. Maybe the peculiar way he came to be—not the womanizing, which wasn't notably strange, but the part that preceded it, which surely was—had nothing to do with anything that others said or did to him, including his mum. Maybe his emotional membrane just got stretched too damn thin somewhere along the way—before he was born? or sometime after? or during?—and things reverberated inside him too damn much—who knows why? So what if the hired help came swooping and whooping down on him and he got dragged back to her like a runaway slave who didn't quite make it up the Freedom Road to Canada? It's hardly Auschwitz. It's not even Sarajevo, if anybody remembers that. Never mind, causes are overrated. So are explanations.

He doesn't abandon his mother, as she seemed to abandon him. He continues to find his way to her in the middle of each night. He'll wake up to pee and take a savvy wrong turn coming out of the bathroom. Or just pad down the hall and slip up into their bed, alongside her, as she turns to cradle him, spoon in spoon, making sure he doesn't slip down to the floor. He backs into her, luxuriates and stretches in her shade. Meanwhile, far away over her shoulder, like the dark outline of the cordillera by night, looms his dad, back to them both.

As a family, they continue to go places together in their DeSoto, them in the front, him in back. When the car stops—for a red light, an accident, a backup on the long ride to the lake every summer—his dad's right hand invariably lifts from the steering wheel and snakes slowly across the top of the front seat (those couch-like seats of automotive prehistory), thumb and forefinger arched like a cobra's jaw, till it settles round his mother's ear, which it dandles, outlining the shape of the ear, testing its feel, moving it around. It's amazing how many ways you can touch a human ear, how patient and searching and gratifying it can look to a little guy in the back. It continues as long as the stop. It doesn't progress, doesn't end. Eventually the line of cars moves and the hand returns to the wheel, or gearstick. Neither of them looks to the side or behind. It's as if they aren't there and he's not either. Just hand and ear, snake and ear. It's their family version of the primal scene. It's as breathy as the Kama Sutra. Who decreed it all had to happen in a bedroom?

Gradually, a change sets in, a kind of targeted blindness on his part. A couple of years later, when he's ten or eleven, he goes off to the Royal Winter Fair with his buddy, Noel. It is the first thing they ever do together and they will stay pals through all the decades to come, till death do them part, one day. Noel is a rich little guy, the only kid Max knows with his own credit cards and taxi chits—in the 1950s, when those things scarcely exist, even for grown-ups. Noel has his own phone too, in a time when it is a rare family who own an extension. He is prone to answering it, "Yeah," as if he is a bookie. Their home fronts on two separate streets, it is that grand. Noel wanders through it like the Little King, in ermine and fur.

At the fair, Max and Noel stray into the stalls behind the show-jumping arena. There you can see the Guernseys and prize pigs, the Budweiser Lippizaners, beribboned sheep, jittery jumpers, and Trigger, the Wonder Horse. Trigger is still alive, it's long before he got stuffed and mounted in Roy Rogers' museum in California. He's a guest star from the States, the way Aunt Jemima always appears nearby at the Pure Food Building of the Canadian National Exhibition in the summers, dishing up her pancakes. Trigger has a hard-on. Noel nudges Max and points. Max looks but he sees—nothing. Nothing he considers worthy of comment. There's a thing you could take for a stunted fifth leg, between Trigger's hindquarters. But for him, it's an oddity he can easily discount, like seeing a gorilla drive a convertible through downtown. (*Somebody must be shooting a commercial. Or a frat pledge on a dare. Whatever.*) He asks what Noel's looking at. "Trigger's got a boner," says Noel. This mundane technical term known to all young boys of the era as if it's distributed somewhere along the birth canal hardly registers for Max—he reacts as if he might not have heard it. Just as he first drew a near blank on the visual, now he does so on the audio. Yet there it juts directly before him. He's had boners, surely. How can he miss, pardon the expression, the point? It's not that he doesn't see it; it's that he doesn't, pardon the expression, inhabit it, inhabit Trigger's boner just as he does not inhabit his own, that is, sexually. A boner is not something he associates with sexual feeling, believe it or not. It's a thing that may happen, but if you had never touched it, how would you know it can make you tingle, and wish to stroke it, and then . . . But why would you never have touched it and so found these things out, all the way to ejaculation, and, inevitably, wanting to repeat the same: intensely, elatedly, compulsively? Yet why would you touch, if you didn't know? It's a marvellous closed circle. Ignorance is *the* superb tool for repressing an activity, far more effective than threat and prohibition, which have rarely worked down through the millennia of human sexual history, and every other branch of human history too. There is no royal road to womanizing, and if there is a customary route, which Max was perhaps on at an earlier point, he has now veered from it. He has begun a unique and lengthy detour. This is not your average womanizer.

But ignorance, like simplicity, is expensive to maintain. What can he do, for instance, with wet dreams, which will occur with normal frequency in coming years? They aren't like masturbation; they happen on their own, you don't have to *know* a thing about them. Not the word, nor its definition. When wet dreams come in the middle of a night, he will contrive to drift swiftly back into sleep. As if he'd merely failed to get to the bathroom for a pee. By the time he wakes again, he will think of the stain on the sheet as the result of having wet his bed at a relatively late age—embarrassing but not existentially destabilizing—or fail to notice it at all; it's a small thing, a semen stain. Thus he will not need to know anything about ejaculation either. In the case of wet dreams, there's no necessity to distinguish between urine and semen. They both come out of the same spout. Why would a guy suspect that two different pipes were laid in there, especially if he's never had a waking experience of ejaculation?

Does that mean he doesn't think about sex? Well, he thinks about girls, in a fraught and gothic way. They are tied to chairs in a windowless room. They are blindfolded, or he is masked, like Zorro. He caresses them and kisses them. The contact is confined to kissing. No breasts, no orifices except mouths. Or he's the commander of a crack military team in a jungle war in the Far East. He walks into the luxurious dining room of a colonial hotel, fresh from a decisive victory over the rebels, still wearing his fatigues and weapons, and a couple of them are there, on some kind of tour; they were cheerleaders when he saw them last, back in school. They gasp to recognize him in this role, they practically swoon. He swaggers over (modestly) and joins them. You could say these are thoughts about sex, in a distant way. There is no object, no goal, no consummation, and most of all, most of the time, no physical relation. They are thoughts about romance more than they are about sex. They are like the musings girls have, or used to.

How long can a guy launched into puberty and beyond maintain a state of ignorance about such matters? You would be astounded.

"We won't be discussing masturbation this term," Mr. Bryans says to the boys in health class, who are separated from the girls for this course only, "because we've dealt with it already." Max doesn't remember discussing it. He draws the customary blank. All his classmates seem sanguine. Maybe he was away the day they discussed masturbation, whatever it is. Maybe he went into a trance and shipped out to Neptune. This time, perhaps because it *isn't* going to be discussed, its mention slips through to the threshold of his awareness. He is a conscientious scholar. After class he climbs the stairs stealthily, making sure he isn't being tailed, to the library on the third floor—this is before they categorized libraries as frills—and looks the word up in the encyclopedia. Nothing. He pads over to the giant dictionary on the revolving stand. And there it is: "sexual self-gratification." As good as nothing. He heaves the volume shut with relief. He still knows as little as ever, but no one can blame him for not trying. That summer, his parents send him to summer camp.

He's been to day camp but this is hard core: overnight for three weeks. It will be their first long separation since the Florida catastrophe. His dad drives him to Lawrence Plaza to join a bus convoy to the wilds of Haliburton; but when they arrive, they find the buses have broken down, like the snafus of D-Day. (Transport problems are still automatically assimilated to wartime mode.) He and his dad go off to Little Jack's for a little breakfast. They sit at the counter. Tears pour down his face and into his orange juice. Men his dad knows pass to and fro behind them, he can see them in the mirror. "What's the matter?" one asks. "Doesn't he want to go to camp?" His dad claps him hard on the back like a fellow salesman from the Commercial Travellers' Association, smiles his famous smile, and says in the jovial, hollow way of dads through the ages, "Oh, he's dying to go!"

He writes home each day and always reminds them when and where they're to pick him up on the day his sentence ends: Lawrence Plaza, of all places! In order not to sound scared and little, he includes grown-up phrases like, "Give my regards to

Auntie Belle and Uncle Monte." Some days he gets letters from them; this makes him wild with missing home. On others, and hellish hellish days they are, he receives nothing. One such day, after mail call, his counsellor, Rex, asks him to come for a walk during rest hour. The other guys are sprawled on their bunks, reading comic books and, sob, letters from home. They sit under a tree, Rex and Max. Rex chews on a stalk of grass; he looks about a million years old to Max. "How are things at home?" says Rex. "Fine," says the little guy, successfully stifling a sob. "Except you're not there," says Rex kindly, and the dam bursts. Rex pats his back as he heaves; it feels . . . *great*—to have somebody know what you're feeling, and say it! As they walk back to the cabin, Rex changes the subject, as if it's possible to be all broken up over one thing and still be coherent about something else. They discuss the great comic book caper; all over camp, comics have been vanishing during lunchtime. It took a while to recognize the pattern, as with most innovative crimes—train or bank robberies, for example, in the Old West; or holding up the buses taking gamblers to Casino Rama in our own time—but a plan is in place now and a suspects' list is forming. When they re-enter the cabin, the guys are talking about the big social at the end of their stint.

Oh God, isn't it always thus—just when you've learned to survive one mighty hammer blow, another falls. A social means dancing! It means girls. It means, uh-oh, touching them. *And what will he wear?* He carefully packed only jeans and shorts, plus bathing trunks, with his name tag sewn carefully in by his mum. Who expected socials? They never had those at day camp. He's allowed a call home and his mother says she'll send some dressy pants up. Camp seemed to him a vast and almost unbridgeable distance away, yet the pants arrive with amazing speed.

It is the dancing that truly cows him. It contains the same combo of known and unknown as sex itself—another term, like boner, which he would squint at dumbly. The unknown is how you actually dance: what goes where, when, and how. The known is girls and touching them, which he did with joy and abandon, till he learned how unbelievably *risky* that could be. Rex, with his wizardly foreknowledge, takes charge again. He conscripts Elaine, another counsellor. One night the rest of the camp disappears. Maybe they went on a hayride and got lost. Max pulls on his dressy pants, the ones that came by pony express, and goes to meet Elaine, as Rex instructed him to, in the empty rec hall, just the two of them. It's eerie and kind of intimate, also a word he doesn't know. She puts a record on a turntable, a slow one. Then she asks him to put his feet on top of hers, and she moves around to the music. She's taller than he is, so it works just fine. They glide across the floor. "Feel the music," she says, "and how we're moving to it." This can hardly be all there is, he thinks, as she gently slides out from under his feet and they keep . . . dancing.

Surely there is more. His parents take lessons to learn the mambo and the cha-cha. They descend into Uncle Monte's rec room once a week with some other couples and two dance instructors they've hired who are from South America, or say so. Maybe they just bused down from Sudbury or Kapuskasing, bought a few billowy frocks in Eaton's Annex, and plastered their hair with Wildroot Cream Oil. His community cares to learn very little about Latin America in those years beyond the mambo and cha-cha; for them, south stops at Miami Beach. Not till Castro descends from the Sierra Maestre and takes Havana will those other nations register much beyond the Latin beat in the rumpus rooms. At any rate, those are not dances you just stand on each other's feet for and wait to feel the music. You need instruction and information; you have to concentrate your mind. That winter he himself will don his charcoal grey jacket and take Saturday morning classes at Mambo Italiano Dance Studio on the Danforth. The teacher there compliments him on how firmly and instinctively he holds his partner's waist with his right hand while "leading" her with his left. Well, if you gotta touch, you might as well clutch. He seems to have a natural sense for it, says the teacher. It worries him. He wonders if anyone else has noticed. As always, for the rest of his life, the acquisition of sought-for knowledge comes with a dollop of danger; it brings him closer to the peril which his ignorance has shielded him from.

It would have been easier for him had dancing been decoupled from sex as it historically was. Dancing has always been mainly about movement, and little Max loved to move. At camp that summer, his favourite game was soccer because you could run wild. Give the ball a big boot, then skitter madly after it; it didn't require the control and minute adjustment that hockey or baseball needed and the playing area wasn't hemmed in tight, as basketball is. Dancing—from its primitive forms till early modern days—was a lot like running around when you play soccer, plus a rhythmic accompaniment. Sexual partnering as an essential element of the dance came late—or recently, in terms of Max's own small place in history. The prissy minuets and gavottes of European court life, then at the turn of the last century, Strauss's waltzes, denounced in Vienna as savage, licentious, immoral, and foreign. Followed by variations like the tango; the Americanization of partnered dance embodied in the foxtrot, and so on. As Max grew older the model reversed again, dancing began to decouple once more; the parties of his grad school years were decomposing toward the anarchic group movement that used to happen around the ancestral— as opposed to the summer camp—fires. It was too late for him by then.

But on the evidence, you'd have to say that he wasn't just abandoned on the lonely road of sexual perplexity. Folks seemed willing to help: Rex, Elaine, the teacher at Mambo Italiano. The question isn't so much how he got lost out there; it's how, with the help offered, he managed not to get back on track for such a long time.

Noel, his best friend, is probably trying to help too, even if he often seems to be setting traps for his good buddy Max. One day that winter, they are sent home early due to a snowstorm. They slog over to Noel's huge house. Noel's parents are out and they are planning a major raid on the fridge, but the Jamaican maid is in the kitchen. Noel leers at her as they pass through and continue to the den. They'll watch TV instead, Noel says, knowing Max's family still don't own a set. There's this new after-school show called "The Mickey Mouse Club." They both feel superior to anything with a name like that, it's obviously meant for little kids, but one of the Mouseketeers has rivetting tits, says Noel. "Tits" registers on Max marginally more than boner, of the year before, which didn't register at all. You have to give Noel marks for persistence. Then suddenly he whirls away from the TV, pulls a book from the shelves behind it with a swishing sound, and begins to read. "Listen to this," he hisses, as if there's no need to justify the switch in media, from screen to page.

"She walked toward me. She was tall. Her dark luxurious hair hung down across her dark face and tumbled over her pendulous breasts. Her nipples were engorged. They surged toward me like mountains on the moon." He starts moving toward Max like one of the monsters in *It Came from Outer Space*, like the same fearsome female in the book he is reading from. By doing so, he blocks the way to the door. Anyway, what excuse would Max have for bolting? It is snowy chaos outside. That's why they're in here. "Her breasts undulated back and forth,'" he continues, "'the nipples a tawny brown deeper than the hue of the massive globes. Cracks riddled them and a whitish fluid oozed from them temptingly. She cupped and offered them to me. I raised my hands to receive them. My palms sank under their ominous weight. 'Lift them to your lips,' she said, 'and suck until you are sated . . .'"

"Noel! Get out here and shovel the snow off these groceries and off me!" shrieks his mother from one of the front doors on either side of the house. "Never mind, Mildred has them." Then she is in the den with them, but Noel is quicker, the book is back in its place on the shelves, the TV is droning. Annette, the chesty one Noel mentioned, is just coming into shot for her part of the Mouseketeers' roll call off the top of the show, or maybe it's already their farewell, with Mouseke-waves to the kids at home. Max is dazed. He can't even tell the difference between entrance and sign-off. If Annette's tits are rivetting, you couldn't prove it by his reaction or lack of. Noel's mother glances around and withdraws. He finds himself scanning the shelf where Noel just replaced the book. But there's nothing on those shelves except a Great Books series edited by some guy from the University of Chicago, thirty of them, or sixty, anyway all the Great Books that exist, bound in exactly the same way. Nearby are some *Reader's Digest* condensed bestsellers, four titles to the volume. He's sure *Reader's Digest* doesn't compress novels like the one Noel just assaulted him with, and if they do, that's exactly the passage they'd excise to save space.

That spring, he pastes a photo of Annette the Mouseketeer on the ceiling of his room, directly over his bed. He found it in a magazine. He doesn't think about her breasts, the way Noel and other boys his age do. I mean, she wears that tight white sweater with her name on it, so how would a guy *know* if she had big breasts under it or not? Because breasts don't exist unless you actually see them, right, or have them implacably described by a book like the one Noel claimed to be reading from. Otherwise, where's the evidence? One day he barged mistakenly into the bathroom in a rush to get to school, and there was his mum with her breasts hanging right off her chest, with his dad shaving just behind her. They both turned their heads to look at him as he looked at . . . *them*. He slapped that door shut and did his best to forget the memorable sight. He just likes Annette. That's why he glued her up there.

Next summer he stays home, no more summer camp, no more devilish surprises. It is the summer the local kids start going down into the ravine each evening in pairs or groups; then they come back up mussed and flushed. It is Ravine U, a great place to learn about sex, but he hangs back. He wanders over each night after supper but lingers at the lip of the ravine, watching them descend and return, wiping the knowledge they've gained off their faces. An observer, already, talking as he watches, with Clarence, an older, university-age guy who, looking back, might have been a bit off mentally, but enjoyed making conversation with the bright kid. It worked well, this hanging-back and commenting-on, rather than being part of it. Almost as if he preferred that role, you might even conclude he'd deliberately chosen it, instead of not having a clue how to cross the space from up here to down there and what to do once you'd done it.

In the last year of junior high, he scores a part in the school play—teenage son of an immigrant family in turn-of-the-century America. The family has a cat they call Betty. But one day their son—Max's character—informs them that *she* is a he. His parents ask how he knows and his line, which Max can tell is meant to be a sure-fire laugh line, goes, "Because I looked." Yet it never quite works. Each time they run this scene in rehearsal he can see the staff advisers huddle at the back of the auditorium. An air of consternation. Finally Loney, his English teacher, is delegated to take him aside. "Do you know what that line means?" she says delicately. As if she'd told the others he might not get it and they said, Oh c'mon, what thirteen-year-old Canadian male doesn't understand kindergarten-level anatomy? *Pre*-kindergarten? She was reluctant, perhaps sensing the strength of his need not to know—but better her than the rest. So she asks. He doesn't exactly reply that he understands the line, but he intimates it. In truth, it's as opaque to him as masturbation and Trigger's boner. It completes a set in his array of incomprehension: Max's trilogy. It's not that he isn't aware that boys have penises and girls don't, including boy and girl animals. But from his careful point of view, those are what you pee out of. He has managed to desexualize the genital regions, no mean feat, even in one so young. He can't really see why the line should be a big source of amusement, or even a few giggles. And there may be more. He knows cats have furry bottoms, and to ascertain whether a little penis is hiding there, you might have to stick your fingers in and dig around. You would have to touch the area, the avoidance of which is precisely what has allowed him to remain in blissless ignorance of its possibilities. Or maybe he's just repelled by the whole messy swamp down there, the way he was when he walked in on his mother's breasts in the bathroom. Whoops, shut that door fast.

Loney, prudent as a sapper in a minefield, says no more and backs away. All his young life people will sense this kind of danger in him, and give him space. (Except Noel, most of the time.) As if a warning ran across his forehead like a weather alert crawling along the bottom of a TV show. Without their collusion, he couldn't have pulled it off.

Far later, down the corridors of young adulthood, well after he became the Womanizer, he could still play the clueless novice. He had perfected the role; it was no trouble to alter the content. He would sit on a bench in a parkette at ten-thirty on a summer night, or a front lawn, just out of sprinkler range—a bit like Adam in the garden, come to think of it, who also denied any knowledge when the Lord came to inquire who ate that apple—and he would watch the couples pass, arm in arm, on their way to Mac's Milk; then he'd see them return minutes later with a carton of milk for their morning coffee, softly chatting. To and fro, to and fro. What secret information, he would wonder, were they born with that he would never have? So was his bogus ignorance—about the cat, about the couples, any of it—sincere? Definitely, no doubt about it. He'd have passed a polygraph. You can't say that about Adam.

Onto the stage of his excruciating, unacknowledged (by him) effort, steps Elvis, who will look to later generations as Bing Crosby or Rudy Vallee did to Max. Bing who? Rudy who? Each era is issued a permit: to be mesmerized, no explanation required or available, by a voice. Not transferrable between generations. Max alone was excluded, the way others failed their driving test. Who decided he and he alone would not participate in his demographic's mania? Is there a committee that issues exemptions? Can a guy appeal the decision? Elvis came by radio. His song was called

"Heartbreak Hotel." Max listened hard as he could, his attention rivetted, yet all he heard was "Awbeebuhsawloadeebaybay," over and over. The rest of the kids talked about this "song" and bought stacks of 45s. Then they bought everything else by Elvis. What did they hear that Max couldn't? You can't just say to other kids, *'Scuse me, but I don't get it. 'Scuse me, please, but the King has no clothes. Pardon me, he's mumbling, did you happen to catch what it is he's—?*

The music Max grew up with on radio till then—Your Hit Parade and its vile spawn—was audible and comprehensible. The audio technology wasn't always precise; it often sounded, in his early years, as if high-pitched pixies were jammed inside the radio on the window ledge in the kitchen. But if you didn't catch the words, you knew you were meant to: "Memories are made of this," etc. It was their fault for singing indistinctly, or that boxy little radio's, not your own. Your Hit Parade didn't divide its listeners into two groups: everybody and then Max. If even those songs were really about sex, like most pop music since forever, they were so in the bowdlerized style of the age: evasive, sentimental mush. ("Love and marriage/ They go together like a horse and carriage.") If there were codes (candy equals sex, of which you'll get some if you come on over to see me), you could miss them and still get by on the plain sense. In truth, there were also codes in the rock 'n' roll and blues traditions which Elvis pilfered (astutely) from the world of black music, but that mumbly inaudibility, the moaning and suggestion, the slurring as an effect of being sexually overcome as you . . . as you *came*—that wasn't solvable with any key available to Max. He couldn't dig out his Captain Midnight secret decoder that he mailed away for to the radio station a couple of years back when life was simpler, and use it on an encrypted message at the end of the episode.

This was about sex. You got it or you didn't. Max didn't, he achingly, embarrassingly didn't—no more than he got the thrusting of Elvis's pelvis, which you saw on TV if the networks allowed the cameras, as they sometimes did and sometimes didn't, to shoot below waist level. What was *that* about? To him, it was a thing the guy did, who knows why? It was like Trigger's boner.

Of course, none of the other kids knew the blues tradition from which Elvis sprang. But when they heard him mutter and slur, they felt a tingling in their crotch or nipples or both. Max erred only in thinking they had a language he hadn't, that it was all there in the damn lyrics, and *ergo* they possessed information he lacked—maybe he could find it in a book somewhere. He spent a lot of time reading.

So imagine the impact, during the first year of high school, when it was three guys he *knew* singing one of those mystifying songs, including, naturally, Noel. They didn't even sing, they lip-synched, at the Epsilon Kappa pledge show. The EKK. Max wasn't pledging the frat, but Noel invited him to the show and pledge party. *"Mostly Martha,"* they mouthed. *"What has she got? She's got the most."* He was stymied, yet again. The most *what?* But they strutted and curled their lips, as Elvis did, and the girls besieged them after the show. He'd been born without the code. He hadn't found it in any of the books yet but he was still checking. He would persevere.

And his sexuberance, the calling card of his youngest years? What became of that? Now those manic giggles, his mouth drooping lopsided from exhaustion because of *grinning* so much, his arms pumping like the manic leader of a marching band while he stomped up and down the aisle of a streetcar to the discomfiture and dismay of his mother—all gone now, long gone, you've never seen anything so gone, no trace, no remnant. By high school, what he's known for is a remarkable ability to keep a straight face, *to not laugh*, even in the presence of Mr. Snetsinger's (the name itself a provocation) howlers, which have cracked up generations of grade-ten science students. Now when Snetsinger uncorks a pun, or pulls a sight gag with his pointer, or mimes hanging himself on the cord of the venetian blind, there's a burst of teen hilarity, then all eyes swivel onto Max at the back of the room, where he slouches behind his desk, leaning back and looking down his nose at the rest of them with "a supercilious, Olympian sneer," as a covertly admiring math teacher of his described it in the staff room—everyone looks to see if he alone can suppress his amusement. He summons a mighty self-discipline and responds—by not responding. The muscles in his jaw clench. Neither sound nor smile escapes. What is he proving? Who is he proving it to? (In the Bible, laughing is one of the words for sexual activity. "Will you come and laugh with me?" says Potiphar's wife when she tries to seduce the chaste Joseph.)

Girls, of course, are such a problem. Here. Have a look in his room. There in the corner is a kind of junior file cabinet. The key to open it is hidden behind *He Shoots, He Scores!*, by Foster Hewitt, up on the bookshelf. No one would look there. That book—today it would be called a juvenile novel—is just for little kids, hasn't been read in years. In the lower part of the cabinet, at the bottom of a small pile, is the source of Max's deepest dread: *that* prom photo. The girl in it is indescribably *cute*, lofty accolade of an epoch. Her ponytail sweeps up perkily, frozen in mid-bounce. How does she get it to do that—bouncy hair will remain a mystery on into the next century—same as it does when she runs precise circles with the other cheerleaders in the gym? Her pert smile, just this side of sassy. A modest area of chest, framed by her silvery gown, and the corsage he gave her in a daze when she opened the door to him. He stands beside her, crimson. Not with pleasure but something else. Terror. Confusion. More, but it's unnameable, the term hasn't been invented. The photo is black yet crimson suffuses it, like an old movie that got colourized and is for that reason even more dated. Those colourizations never have worked. In the photo, his eyes dart, his arm dangles, not even daring to think about a move toward her lovely shoulder, or her neck . . .

She more or less asked him. Noel came up one day in the boys' and said, "Edna told me to say she laks you." *Laks* was Noel's take on the fact Edna had transferred from the American South. Jackson, Miss. Her mom—as they'd surely say down there, not mummy or mum—had died and her dad came home to Canada with her, hoping for some family support in raising his exquisite daughter, um, kinfolk. There's something so languid and sexual in that way of talking—*laks* . . . *haaaiii darlin'*—even when you don't know what sexual is.

Because she was perfect, it never occurred to him she might lak him. So he relaxed and was funny around her. Like a sexuberant little guy. The way he'd be if he was alone, or with Noel. "I have to go to the john," he said in the hall before class, "or do you call it the Jane?" The gods had thrown him a line. She bounced the ponytail a couple of times and laughed with perfect pitch. They were flirting. Then she sent the message via Noel.

He bought the corsage, put on his charcoal grey sport coat, picked her up, passed through a long dark night at the prom like St. John of the Cross, uttering no word. Not that he could remember after anyway. As if he'd taken a vow of silence for a *date.* In the Chinese restaurant, his buddies performed for their companions. He was stiffer than his chopstick and as inarticulate. The muter he sat, the muter he grew. At least when it was over, it was done. Then, weeks later, the photo was delivered. He'd forgotten that part. It embalmed his humiliation for all time.

He's less caught in the shot than trapped. By her skin, ponytail, smile, her affection maybe, the prospect even of her high school love. There ought to be a trap door as part of the film-development process that you pay extra for to drop yourself out of a moment you don't want to recall, like the one Stalin had for May Day pictures of comrades with whom he'd grown weary. That would leave her alone in the frame. It would be a sin to waste a look so adorable. But as it stands, what can you do with such a thing? Bury it like radioactive waste underground to glow, tick, radiate, whatever deadly rubbish does, and dwindle away through its interminable half-lives.

After he picked it up, he dropped a copy at her door, fast and dirty, like Secret Agent X-9 from the comics; then went home and interred his in the junior file cabinet, beneath envelopes, folders, his "journal," his dreams diary, his lapsed membership in the Captain Midnight Radio Club. Why not destroy it? Shred or burn it? Shred *and* burn it? I guess, because it was him, he was all he had. Poor lad. He thinks he alone is all alone, out there in the land of adolescence.

He becomes a teenage intellectual, of course. Where else can he go? He wants to know what they know, whatever it is, and have acquired without apparent effort. Since he doesn't possess it as they do—innately, by birthright—he turns to reading, research, study, scholarship, cultivation of the masters—the whole ponderous life of the mind. He will earn what they inherited. He tears through the history and biography sections at the local library. He reads the lives of the Fathers of Confederation and Sandburg's volumes on Lincoln; historical novels by Kenneth Roberts with their stubborn, contrarian view of American history (Benedict Arnold as hero!); and book after book on U.S. politics and the Civil War. Under the influence of his secret admirer in the staff room, his math teacher, he devours, concealed within the covers of their text during French or Latin, H. G. Wells's *Outline of History*, and Hendrik Willem Van Loon's *Story of Mankind*, with its kooky pencil drawings; also the socially intense novels of Dickens, Steinbeck, Somerset Maugham—novels are okay, so long as they cover some serious historical ground; plus Gandhi, Bernard Baruch, and Morgenthau on foreign policy. He is the perplexed in search of a guide.

But guide to take him where? What destination does he need to reach? What is the point of all the history and biography he devours? One day he picks up a book called *The Hidden Persuaders* by some guy named Vance Packard. Cool name. Could be a private eye. He likes the idea of hidden, he resonates to it like the tuning fork in music class, something that's hidden is persuading us about something. The title reminds him of one of the few songs popular among the other kids that he gets, "The Great Pretender." He's pleased to learn the book is merely about economics and why people buy what they do and need what they need: he likes finding out what's really going on behind what seems to be happening. He moves on to other books on economics. He reads *The Theory of the Leisure Class*, by Thorstein Veblen. He loves the phrase "conspicuous consumption," he rolls it around in his mouth.

A journalist comes to his high school researching an article on today's teens and interviews him in the guidance office. The journalist asks what books he is reading and Max says: *Growing*

Up Absurd by Paul Goodman; *The Affluent Society* by John Kenneth Galbraith; and *The Lonely Crowd* by David Reisman. He asks what magazines Max reads and Max says: *Reader's Digest*, *Foreign Affairs*, and *Mad Magazine*. The reporter's pencil pauses at the mention of *Mad*, as if in prayer. He is thinking: Thank you, God, maybe there's hope for this bewildered youth.

The other kids decide not to mind, because he isn't using his smarts to suck up to teachers or ace his exams. He is on some kind of weird quest for its own sake. Being smart is like his hobby, the way others collect stamps or work on cars. Noel decides it's neat and wants to join his old pal part-time, as an associate member in Max's one-man mind club. It will balance the earthy antics at the frat and give him cachet. He does a little research on his own and one day explains to Max what dialectical materialism is. ("Dialectical as in conflict leads to revolution; materialism as in the laws of science, not the laws of God.") It's a bit heady for Noel but Max prefers it to the passage on tawny breasts. By a lot. Encouraged, Noel guides him downtown to a seedy little bookstore run by the Communist party, or some split-off from it, on Yonge Street. So this is where he got his definitions. He pulls a number of texts off the shelves and presents them to Max as a gift. One is called *Man's Worldly Goods*, about the history of economics. It has little line drawings like the ones in Van Loon's book. It's exciting when pieces you discovered in different places come together.

Of course none of what Max reads is about sex (except accidentally, like the clandestine handholding scene in the coach, in Maugham's *Of Human Bondage*; which came on him unexpectedly, before he could plot an escape). But entire books on sex would be too direct; they'd resolve some of his riddles, and in turn, uh-oh, might reveal the questions lurking behind. It is as though, while he tears frantically through libraries and bookstores, the title that truly motivates his search, the treasure under the *X* on the map, is taped to the back of his shirt like a practical joke, so no matter where he lunges and whirls in high hopes, his eye will never light on it.

What happens, of course, down the line, is that his intellect becomes a sexual asset. Think Marilyn Monroe and Arthur Miller, in that decade of the 1950s; think all the profs and their grad students in the decade which followed: he gets a body, she gets a mind. (*Doo da, doo da.*) Each winds up with what they think they lack. A lot of good that does him *now*.

Near the end of high school, Noel suggests they take in a foreign film—it will be more proof of their intellectual superiority to the mob, there's never enough evidence of that—called *Two Women*. The two women turn out to be a mother and daughter wandering the Italian countryside near the end of the Second World War. They are liberated by North African troops whom they greet and who, of course, rape them. Gritty so far, as advertised. But to Max, the rape scene that unfolds on the screen is a virtual manual not on rape but on the fundamentals of sex and intercourse. Whoops. He had been expecting the mayhem, violence, horror: yes, of course. But the birds and the bees, the sex talk you got from your camp counsellor when the guys had told one too many dirty jokes, the earnest talk with your dad, or even your first visit to a hooker—all the stuff he'd remarkably avoided till now by wit and luck—no, never, anything but that. (Avoided how? Well, the sex talk at camp consisted of diagrams—male organ here on the chalkboard, female on the far side, but no picture of one contacting the other, so the mystery remained; as for his dad, they never had an earnest talk about anything.) And now this damn scene in an art movie. It's the revenge of sex ed.

The soldiers hold down the daughter and hoist one of their comrades onto her. Shot from the girl's POV. Then shot from the POV of the soldiers lowering their mate onto her. Threatening to snuff out all Max's hard-won ignorance. He tries to concentrate on the violence and degradation—he's up for that, he has no illusions about the depravity of the human animal; he's a teen existentialist, isn't he? It's the damn mechanics of sex that panic him: she spreads her legs (or has them spread against her will) and the guy starts to descend. What's a desperate moviegoer to do, trapped before an art-house screen as he'd once been trapped in Noel's den? He can't say he needs to pee, he just did that; or go for popcorn, they still have lots. But wait, there may be a way out. The film doesn't actually show the diagrammatic completion of the rape, at least not in its North American version, and probably not in Europe either. It's so close to that, any audience simply fills in the act. *Thunk*, coupling completed. That's how imagination works, you don't show everything, there's no need: Close-up of penis entering vagina, *in your mind*. This leaves Max his escape hatch: Long shot scanning countryside; or: Pan of leering, bestial soldiers; or: Close-up of horrified mother, *in Max's mind*. You do what you can and work your little butt off to block awareness, hoping all the while that the moment will pass, as it finally does. Then you pretend it never happened.

He has been on the road to repression for a substantial time. It now feels like his life. Sex happens in the lives of other people: Noel, Edna, Elvis, even his parents. That ear thing in the front seat of the car with his mum and dad has never ceased.

It didn't happen when she learned to drive. But then their positions were reversed. She was in the driver's seat, literally (and only literally), just as Max has been recently now that he too, at sixteen, is learning. So his dad shouted at her, just as he yells, bellows, and barks while teaching Max. Both mother and son find it oddly undisturbing. Perhaps because, in a rare case, the fury is coming from a clear source. The rest of the time, which is all the time, it comes from everywhere and nowhere. He erupts at her in the morning as he is selecting his tie; when she dawdles on the way to a family event; when he wants to leave that event and she dawdles some more; most of all when they are all leaving on a trip, even a short one to the lake or a longer one to the States. He derides her stupidity, her incompetence, her mere existence. Then he subsides, like Vesuvius. He slumps in a chair, depleted, relieved, post-orgasmic. He looks almost grateful. It's not fair, observes Max. This becomes his model for everything that isn't fair in the world, like colonialism and underdevelopment.

His eruptions have always affected Max the way seismic events do: by chance. He lives in anticipation and wariness, like people in earthquake zones or flood plains. It feels impersonal. It's almost always his mum who's the target. What a different experience it must be to stand at the centre as she does, knowing you are the cause and the objective. It may even be satisfying. She often looks chuffed in the midst of it. Distress is strikingly absent, at least on her surface. Max, on the other hand, is more like a hamlet—the village, not the prince—who gets wiped out (repeatedly) because the river must burst its banks; its sole goal is its own release, not his destruction; nevertheless, he perishes, as it were, a little each time.

Once, around this time, that is not the case. He is asleep, and suddenly the light on the ceiling, right beside the Mouseketeer cut-out he put up there, bursts on and his dad's face is over him, blocking Annette and screaming at him, that it's *his* fault, only his, they're going to be thrown out of their apartment onto the street tomorrow with nowhere to go and it's all due to him. Then his dad is gone. He straggles over to the switch and turns it off. Yes indeed, it was almost satisfying, even thrilling, to be the centre of your dad's attention.

It must be about money, he thinks, drifting back to sleep. Some mornings, while his mum is occupied with breakfast, his dad pads in and says, "Max, have you got a hundred dollars?" Max almost always does, or fifty—from his paper route, or delivering orders on his bike for old man Mickelburg at the pharmacy, or slinging sodas at Little Jack's, where he now works part-time. It happens often, his little trips down to the bank to withdraw whatever amount he's managed to build up. One day Noel comments on it. Noel is the only kid he knows who would ask to examine his pal's bank book. It engrosses Noel in the same way the book about tawny breasts did. "This is a *very* active account," he says with admiration. Max never asks what the money is for, his dad obviously needs help, and he likes the idea of giving it. It makes them seem like a family. He assigns it a meaning when it's more like a mystery. He doesn't wonder why his mum is never involved in their transactions. The one time he refers to them with her around, his dad acts as if he doesn't know what the heck the kid is jabbering about. Money, or its absence, sits there at the centre of their lives, unacknowledged and undiscussed. Its lurking mystery will become the model for his fascination with the economy.

Sex tends to find its way back, no matter where it has been banished, like Odysseus making his long way home, like Ivanhoe (a favourite of his) strumming his way through medieval Europe, serenading each prison tower in case it might hold his beloved King Richard. It pops out, sex does, oozes through, pushes up, or just dribbles down eventually. The psychohydraulics of sex, a professor of economics Max will soon encounter likes to say. At any rate, enter Olivia.

They share a table during biology, because the course includes dissections, its climax is the frog. Her best friend, red-headed Arlene, sits with them, as does Noel. It's Arlene who Max yearns for, in his fashion. It's her he pictures in Singapore, at that balmy hotel (The Imperial), as he emerges from the jungle after hunting down the guerrillas. He pauses at the entrance to the bar—it looks a lot like the Georgian Room in Eaton's at tea time—pulls the bush hat from his tanned brow, glances round the room . . .

Arlene and Olivia see him. (Arlene takes Olivia, her best friend, wherever she goes.) They recognize him from the days back in bio during the final year of high school; now he's this famous jungle fighter, lightly swinging a . . . Sten gun. They hadn't quite grasped that the guy from high school was . . . this other one, whom everyone has heard about. They're kind of . . . awestruck. He saunters to their table and sits. Nothing to prove now. This ain't the prom no more, no sir. He and Arlene, who he'd sometimes cha-cha with at school parties till the record ended and he was lost for words, they can begin again now from somewhere else.

Yet it's Olivia who becomes his best friend, as she'd been Arlene's. There's no pressure with Olivia since he isn't enchanted by her. Absence of attraction equals the asexual kiss of the frog that releases the inner prince. He can be himself with Olivia, as he was briefly with Edna, before the thunderous news that she lakked him. They talk about everything, all the time, Max and Olivia, Olivia and Max. They are always there for each other, and it goes without saying, given the seriousness of their discussions, they always will be. They take long night walks on pavement-less suburban streets, sit on the curb under street lights, and converse. If he reads Jane Jacobs' book on the life and death of cities, he tells her about it, chapter by chapter. She is as enraptured by his excitement as he was by the book. Her interest energizes him. She tells him in turn about a novel she just read, it's called *Marjorie Morningstar*, a lot of it takes place at a summer camp, and it just happens that he's going off to work in one at the end of the school year. It's astounding how things fall in place between them when they talk: who they are, what they read, what they plan to do next summer. It's sheer electric. Surely no one has ever connected like this. They work together on the annual high school Christmas show. They sit together in the rumpus room, a.k.a. basement, of her home, writing the script and songs. They take tunes from movies and broadway shows they have the LPs of, but make up their own lyrics—like Rodgers and Hammerstein or Lerner and Loewe. They've read about some tricks of the musical-writing trade and share them with each other; you sometimes find them in the liner notes of the albums. *South Pacific. The Pajama Game. My Fair Lady. West Side Story* too, though you gotta admit it's in another league altogether, it's so *serious*. Directly above them, in the living room, Noel and the other kids rehearse the verses to the songs as they get sent upstairs via Olivia's kid brother. The plot of the show has the devil kidnapping Santa right before Christmas. It owes a lot to *Damn Yankees*. The show is a big hit. They take more walks, talk more talk.

On a Sunday afternoon that spring he and Noel are sitting on a picnic table in the park, yakking. Around them, on the grass, immigrant families picnic. Immigrants use parks the way everyone they know uses backyards. Noel was in Buffalo with his frat brothers this weekend, he just got back. Their Buffalo trips always include a visit to the whorehouse. In fact, it's the purpose of the trips to Buffalo by the brothers—and of having a Buffalo branch of the frat. Even Noel avoids mentioning this part, about the whores. It isn't sensitivity; it's that distant early warning system that surrounds Max and protects him, just like the one that saved us from Russian missiles and bombers during those years, we're told. But once, when he was squatting in a cubicle in the boys', he heard Noel tell some guys at the sinks about the first trip to Buffalo he ever made with the frat, while he was still a pledge, and his first whore too. "I guess she gave me a blow job," said Noel. Max stayed in the cubicle till they'd left. Of course he didn't know what a blow job was, part of the standard lack of sexual awareness which he'd been issued. He wondered about it though, and tried to picture it. No luck of course. Some picnic debris flutters by. He kind of wishes Noel would talk about Buffalo and the whorehouse. Maybe he should just ask what a blow job is.

Noel says, "Olivia and I made out."

"Oh?" says Max.

"She really wanted to," says Noel. "Afterward," he goes on, skipping the details, "I went home and threw up." This is offered as proof of friendship. Or Noel's sensitivity. Or maybe he's being provocative, always a possibility. Or showing how crashingly male he is. That he threw up is mere "fact"; it requires interpretation.

That evening Max strides, head down, along the tree-lined street that leads to Olivia's house, under a blue and gentle sky—where storm clouds ought to lower, like a pathetic fallacy in the novels of Thomas Hardy which they've been studying together for the English final. He taps the knocker above the little leaded window in the door of her house, a Snow White and the dwarves house, gables-and-vines kind of thing, there are lots on her street. He's never come here, till now, without calling. She opens the door, sees his pale visage, and gasps—*gasps*—as if they're in a novel too, something from the Brontës or Austen. "He told you!" she says on the exhale. There's a little person inside him, like one of the dwarves, who wants to pipe up, *So what, don't hit yourself over your own head about it, little lady, it's only sex, we're all just human.* But that would be a voice from another galaxy, to which he may or may not some day travel. For now, there's another script they must play. So they sit in silence on the living-room couch, shades of him and Marta long ago. Her parents are out—or waiting silently in the bedroom upstairs the way he sat in the cubicle, till the scene about Buffalo he wasn't meant to hear ended. Maybe they get bored partway through and let themselves down on bedsheets so they can pad over to Eglinton Avenue for coffee and a Danish at the Greek's without disturbing their daughter and her odd "friend." Because this one goes on a long time.

She mutters some broad phrases from the catalogue of remorse: *I wanted to* not . . . *Like someone was behind me, pushing* . . . *It's ruined, I destroyed it* . . . He grunts back as best he can: *Hmm . . . Mmm . . . Ahhmm*—with such frozen effort he might as well be delivering a eulogy—one of those experiences where you're paralyzed because if you get it wrong, you won't ever have another chance to do it right. Now they're back where he came in, from entrance to exit, the script has been covered, she's looking through the pane onto the street, ready to see him out, he's behind her. This is where everything important happens: standing at the door, nothing more to say because it's all been said, everything has been decided. (That's what sociologists and journalists learn: when the interview is *over* and your notes are in your case and your pen back in your pocket and you're on the way out: *that's when you must remember every word.*)

She leans her head on the leaded bits, as if for moral support, sighs, and starts to lean back, open the door for him as she always does after one of their walk-talks. But she's weary and battered and doesn't carry through. Her hair backs into his face, ravishes the skin on his face lightly. Very lightly. He has no responsibility, it's being done to him, you can't even say for sure it's occurring. Hair to face, and time feeling quite . . . elastic, not pushy. Respectful, waiting to know when to pick up the pace or draw it out. Hair, firmer touch of the back of her head, maybe the shoulder blades? With glacial slowness, eventually she turns. There is no time, and no sense of time, involved. Each instant, each hair in contact with surface of face, seems as discreet as a snapshot. His ignorance works for him, finally: he doesn't know there is anywhere to go, or arrive. Each separate millisecond is like an end in itself, a final destination, though at last, she turns her face up, just the way they do in the romance comics, which he never bought, and they kiss. So this is it—kissing. It doesn't seem as external as he'd pictured. Surely if there is a destination, this is it—yet it too seems aimless. How different this all would be had he ever masturbated. The ignorance about climax is what makes it bottomless.

The following night he returns for another doorway moment. And in the months after. Then in the same unhappening way, they move to sitting, lying, on the couch in the living room, or in the den upstairs, where the TV is. His penis—ah, *that's* a hard-on—gets involved on its own, as it were, like an independent, self-governing state, determining its destiny the way new countries you hear about when they join the UN, such as Ghana, do. When he starts to come one night—a damn unexpected event, you better believe it, *another* one—it's in his pant leg, pressing against her. He shifts a little, as if to get out of the way of whatever's coming, the intensity peaks gently and a little wetness spurts around; it has pretty much dried inside his pants by the time she lets him out the door and he heads home down the leafy, well-watered suburban street. It's as though his dick chose to take a modest initiative of its own, he's just a bystander. He and Olivia never talk about it and he doesn't muse over it when he's alone. As far as he knows it's just more of the same stuff that comes out of your penis, though in a different, more thrilling way than when you pee, which isn't pleasurable unless you've been holding it in a long time, and even then . . . no, it's not really the same, but enough said. He's managed to preserve his ignorance about anatomy and sexuality while expanding his experience of them. He's doing but not knowing, the way you catch a ball without thinking it through. As for Olivia, doubtless she knows what's going on; there's no reason to think she's abnormal for her generation. She assumes he gets it too.

For months after those first nights in the hallway, they remain "friends" to the outside world. He tells no one, not even Noel. As if those who like him would like him less if they felt he was happy in his life, and getting some. The truth is his friends like him *in spite of* his gloom and sad eyes. If he had a good time—and said so—it would fill them with delight, in part because they could stop grieving for him. If only he knew. What he knows is this: all his experience of orgasm and ejaculation so far has happened with her. His pleasure is tied to his gratitude to her. Sexual pleasure occurs only in relation to a woman. So let us now praise ignorance. What a lovely, lingering supposition to haul into the coming phases of his sex life.

By first-year university, he may have set a world record for non-masturbating. The situation is not static, things have moved along. He has a dawning sense of what an ejaculation is, he may even know its name, and occasional orgasms, courtesy of Olivia. But the pace remains stately. Nothing like intercourse yet. He would still say, and pass the polygraph, that he doesn't *know* how that works: where his thing goes, what you do when it gets near her thing. The relationship has not moved beyond Olivia's thigh. She seems content to leave it there, as if he must know what he is doing, whatever the hell it is; or at least, be respectful of his reticence. The mysteries abide, and he would find it embarrassing to request a little basic info at this point. Who is he going to ask? Everybody thinks of *him* as the well-rounded intellectual you can pose questions to. And still no masturbation. You could say he hasn't even declared his sexual independence yet. Among women such a thing is less rare. Or used to be. He is a man as repressed as women once were.

It is his economics professor, Sorstad, who broaches the possibility of a record. Sorstad grew up in the Weimar Republic, "opening for the Third Reich," as he puts it. His parents, both Swedish academics, moved there to participate in the construction of democratic socialism in post-war Germany. They named their baby boy Adolph, in honour of solidarity between the Swedish and German peoples. He refuses to change it—though many an Adolph morphed into an Arnold or an Edward while crossing the Atlantic—because he will not give "that little Austrian shite" (he says it as they do in England, where he picked up his doctorate while learning English) any more victories now that he is dead than he won while alive. "You people in the West pay too little attention to the Swedish model," he tells his mad Maoist students of the 1960s, who smile on the idea indulgently.

Imagine: mild Sweden as your inspiration when you can choose among the roaring pyres of China, Cuba, Vietnam, even the Soviet Union—Sorstad takes these rejections with aplomb. He in turn tells them that he rejects the Faustian bargains which Marxists everywhere have made, leaving his students to check the reference—Faust, that is, not Marx.

For he always has a quote from Goethe to go with the point he is making. "It impresses the hell out of you North Americans," he says, "even though it's stuff every German kid gets in grade school, the way Canadians get Bliss Carman and Archibald Lampman." By the time Max is taking Sorstad's Major Trends in Economic Thought in the 1960s, the names Carman and Lampman mean nothing to the students. They gape at the sounds. "Never mind," Sorstad says, "but if any of you become scholars, be sure to drop a German book or article into every bibliography." The students like to mimic the way he says Hayek, as if he is drawing up sputum, in order to expectorate contempt for the founder of neoliberal economics and progenitor of über-conservative Milton Friedman. Sorstad always refers to him by first name only and pronounces it "Mil-*ton*," somehow implying that Friedman himself was embarrassed by having such a common, goofy name, same as the crass TV comic called Uncle Miltie, so he tried to Frenchify and dignify it. Sometimes Sorstad just calls Friedman Uncle Miltie. But he reserves his greatest scorn for what he calls the Robinson Crusoe school of economic analysis: the notion that humans can be reduced to isolated individuals, and all their material behaviour then deduced from that model, as if human existence is not ineluctably social. "Reduce it and deduce it," he'd say, with a cascade of Germanic sounds. His students like imitating that too.

It was the Robinson Crusoe lecture that led to the topic of masturbation. "Economic behaviour can no more be reduced to an isolated individual's activity than sexual behaviour can," he said near the end. "Ah, the two great mysteries of life," he digressed, "money and sex." Like a Shavian aside. He had wandered over near the door of the classroom. He looked like a marginal note. No one took him up on it for a moment. Then somebody asked, "What about masturbation?" *Aha*, said Sorstad, as if his purpose had been to provoke exactly this challenge. "Masturbation is inconceivable without its social and economic context. In masturbation, you always fantasize an other." Someone else asked, "Can't you fantasize yourself when you masturbate?" Sorstad hesitated not a millisecond. "Then you'd be separating yourself in two," he said, "which proves that genuinely individual activity in this realm is not conceivable, much less achievable. The human being, precisely here, in his apparently most isolated act, is irrepressibly social-minded! Be sure to read Polanyi on this. Not Marx. Polanyi!" The class seemed impressed but unpersuaded. Max seized the moment. "What if you never masturbated at all?" he said, hoping he sounded casual.

"In that case, you'd be the proud holder," said Sorstad gravely, "of a Guinness world record," and the class cracked up.

On their walk to the pub afterward with everybody else, Sorstad said to Max, as if the discussion in class had never ended, "If you simply stopped yourself from jerking off, then it would still be social and interactional, in a Freudian sense: because you'd have split yourself into the cop and the potential perp." Sorstad watched a lot of American TV, especially cop shows. Max said nothing. He tried to look as if he was thinking. Sorstad seemed to be monitoring him—his aura, his little cartoon-balloon thoughts—from the side. "On the other hand," Sorstad continued, "if you had never thought about masturbating at all, or"—here he slowed almost to a stop—"you didn't even know what jerking off was"—it sounded odd in that accent: *dee dunt know vot jairkeen awf wuss*. Max cocked his head and nodded as if duplicating the behaviour of someone with a sprightly but strictly theoretical interest—"then it wouldn't be much of an achievement," Sorstad finished. "Setting the record, that is." You could tell even Sorstad had his doubts: could one really reach such an age and not even *know* of masturbation? The *repressio ad absurdum*. He had an open mind, but this one tested his limits.

Ta–da

It is the end of first-year university. He has a job at Frontier College for the summer. The "campus" he's assigned to is a logging oper- ation north of Timmins. He works in the woods during the day and teaches the loggers (cooks, drivers, etc.) English in the evenings. They told him he'd be bunking in with the workers, which sounded worthy. But when he arrived they said there was a separate cabin for him and Norman, the other teacher. They'll use the washroom that's in the bunkhouse where the men sleep.

Norman is taciturn though he volunteers that he was named after Norman Bethune, the legendary communist doctor of the 1930s, by his parents, a left-wing accountant and a den- tal assistant. Norman says little during the first two weeks, then announces he's moving nearby, to one of those inexplicable farms on the hard Canadian Shield of Northern Ontario, where there is indoor running water, electricity, and he'll have his own room. Max is welcome to keep their cabin by himself; there are no plans to move anyone else in. Max reacts bizarrely.

He says Norman doesn't need to go. Norman agrees. He's leaving because he wants to. Then Max begs Norman to stay. Norman looks puzzled. They aren't close. They've roomed together for a brief period. They rarely converse. They haven't

45

put any posters on the walls. There's nothing to divvy. They share an occasional discussion of teaching techniques, but have no interests in common. Max is more interested in Norman Bethune than Norman is. But Max is suddenly desperate for Norman not to leave.

He says he feels Norman has a troubled soul and they can talk, if he'll just stay in their good ol' cabin instead of moving to some farm where no one knows or cares what he's going through. He'll listen to Norman, listen so that he really hears what Norman is saying, as opposed to the casual way he's paid less than full attention till now, he's certain they'll make progress at getting closer. This is seriously inappropriate, verging on weird. Norman stares back, amiable and unresponsive. He's going to a farm, that's all. It's a nice place and he'll have his own room. The food may be better, it could hardly be worse. Max asks if it's anonymity he's seeking, the escape from being known. He himself has felt that temptation, he confesses. Norman says no, the farmer is there and probably a family too, he's not sure, but at least he can hope the guy won't yammer at him like the abbot in a monastery talking down to a novice. Norman has never said anything before that indicated a knack for sarcasm. It's his first and only self-revelation. Then he leaves.

He walks out and shuts the door as if no drama is involved, as if coming and going and changing your room are normal things on a summer job. As he closes the door, a calm descends on Max. A sense of reverence—as if he's in a sanctuary! The tension drains swiftly out of the drama he had, just a moment ago, laboured to generate. What a blessed relief. Yet something has changed, all things aren't as they were. This has become *his* place, not merely his room in someone else's, like his folks'.

He looks at the closed door and the walls as if they weren't there until now. Whatever it is, happened as Norman shut the door behind him. There is one way out and one way in. Max controls it. No one can enter unless he admits them. And no one has a reason to be there but him. So what? Does it matter? He finds out later, after class, when he returns.

There's his cot, and there's Norman's—used to be. He's tosses his Frontier College guide to teaching literacy on it, and his wind-breaker. Right of possession. Tosses self on his own cot. He lies on his back, reading. His left leg is crooked up, right calf resting on left knee. His hands hold a book, Harold Innis's *The Fur Trade in Canada*, and a pencil to make notes in the margins. Students always make notes in pencil, as if they borrowed the book from the author and plan to return it. It seemed an apt read to bring to a rough-hewn Canadian job site, and anyway, they say Innis too worked at Frontier College during his student years. Almost everyone did, it appears. Even Bethune, according to Norman, in one of his rare slips into chit-chat.

His penis lies small, soft and slack—not worth a mention except for the miracle about to happen—tucked between his thighs, in such a way they can rub it lightly. He does nothing intentionally, nor is he aware of it happening. He's absent-mindedly, lightly kneading this non-erection with his thighs, akin, say, to making a little circle with your forefinger on a table-top. Aimless and a tad compulsive.

It's only happening because he's alone in a room—his room in his place—to which he controls access exclusively. It proceeds. Pleasant. He has no idea where it's going. Just around in circles. A trip for its own sake.

His thighs, large relative to the nub they're encircling, press hardly at all, just enough to mobilize a slight sensitivity up the shaft and down toward his anus, shunting the little tingle along an arc toward whatever the penis connects to there. So the stimulation diffuses, sort of the way women describe orgasm—spreads rather than narrowing. And since the pressure is happening at the base of his penis rather than up farther along where things get touchier, it's very slow and strangely nonspecific. Different in some way from what occurs between him and Olivia. Anyway, he doesn't know what's going on, doesn't know anything that should, could, or might happen, so there's no anticipation, no direction. Just a gradual increase—of pleasure. His hands uninvolved. They're making notes. The first chapter is called "The Beaver." Good start. Something playful about it, in an economic history. Thighs aren't directive and flexible like hands and fingers, so they aren't responsible, at least not the kind of responsibility that hands and fingers have. Hands are for sex. But they're not involved here. Whatever minimal direction he may provide is only by way of generalized pressure and release of thighs. This could go on a long time. It could go nowhere in all that time. Just round and round.

Yet it intensifies, in minimal increments. It does seem to be going somewhere, maybe. But he doesn't know where. A destination is implied, as he keeps lightly pressing and relaxing and making notes in the margins. It rises and lowers, the pleasure, up a bit, dips back. Then, what does he do as, one last time, it rises, rises some more, and starts to crescendo? In a fit of creativity and instinct he squeezes his legs together and a muted climax happens. (He thinks this word spontaneously rather than applying it as the standard term. It's definitely not a standard climax.) And for some reason—luck? intuition? divine oversight?—when he squeezes this last time he doesn't release—it's like snapping a ring around the base of the penis which seals off, or shuttles back, whatever is making its way from the gonads to the tip. It seems to reverse course inside him and retrace its path, as it were, whence it came. So, after the feeling hits that understated peak and subsides, there is no ejaculate, no evidence. It's coming without come. *Nothing has really happened.* Look, Ma, no hands.

It goes on this way through the Frontier College summer and for several years after. Two, maybe three years. Gradually it occurs to him: you could use your hands to do this thing. He knows masturbating is generally associated with hands. But for a long time, using his hands feels clumsy and difficult; nowhere near as fluid as the technique he stumbled on, invented, you might say, and then, over time, refined. It's like the difference between strumming and frailing the banjo—a popular instrument on campuses in those years; the former seems much simpler, till you truly master the latter. Perhaps not as satisfying either. There was something about doing it without the control hands and fingers made possible. As if it came from a deeper, more instinctual place, on its own. As if he was calling on the ineffable source of pleasure, asking it to join him if it chose. And how fine and unimperious that it arrived in his life *after* those initial ejaculations with Olivia, so that pride of place, orgasmically speaking, went to sex in the presence of an Other, as Sorstad would likely, delightedly, point out. From then on, it was doubtless only a matter of time. If we lived long enough, everything would sort itself out. There would be no missed chances, no regrets.

That summer he finds himself thinking a lot about economics. Maybe he'll make it his major. That's why he has Innis's study of the fur trade in his hands when the big event happens. Could it be that he owes his unique masturbatory technique to the fact his hands were occupied with a book at the moment of discovery—not just any book but one which engaged him sufficiently that he wouldn't put it down? His curiosity about economics seems much like his general curiosity, that restless urge he feels to understand everything but what he really needs to know. If he is blocked from inquiring about one thing, the *mysterium tremendum*, as the mystics say, then he'll inquire conscientiously about all others. Maybe he'll get there by indirection, filling in the blanks till he surrounds it. One day he asked Noel, "So how does money work?" since Noel has so much of it around. Noel practically swims in the stuff, like Scrooge McDuck in his pool filled with dollar bills. "You take the stuff, paper or coin, and turn it into things you can eat or read or wear. It's like the best trick in the world. What's the secret?" Noel didn't seem interested by the question. "When you have a *lot* of money," he sort of yawned, "you realize the point of having money is to make more money." It sounded smart and Max filed it for future mulling. But he didn't get over the trick part. He pictured economists as reverse magicians: guys who can reveal the secret of the trick. Unmagicians.

It sounded better than the trick itself. One day when he was four, the big kids on the street were picking on him. He ran home and made his mum call his big cousin Herb. Herb was eight and Herb's mum said she'd send him down on the TTC. Kids used to traipse around the city on their own in those days. Max stood on Bloor Street back from the streetcar stop (so the drivers wouldn't mistake him for a waiting fare), and called as loud as he could, "Shaw Street," each time he saw one of the red rockets coming. Eventually Herb arrived and Max led him down the street to where the big kids hung out. Most of them had gone in for dinner but one girl was on her way home as they crossed paths and said cheerily, "Hi, Max," as if *nothing* awful had just happened between them. Was she faking it? Backing off in the face of the formidable Herb threat? He never knew. Human ways are inscrutable, therefore enthralling. There's no chance your fascination will wane, because the answers will never be known, most of the tricks will remain veiled. He liked it that way; it felt safe. Who truly wants to know, deep deep down? No wonder he went into the social, not the "hard," sciences.

The summer after Frontier College, he's working at a camp for culturally deprived kids—that year's word for poor—a few hours north of the city. Olivia has a job in a bookstore near the university. By now others know their relationship has . . . changed. Max has a gal, not just a pal. He hitchhikes down to see her every day off. His devotion amazes her. It stuns her parents. It surprises everyone he knows, including himself.

He leaves camp early, catches a ride on a delivery truck or a local milk-and-bread run, then perhaps with a salesman the rest of the way. He gets there about noon, meets her at the bookstore, and they go straight to a local park, or parkette, or construction site. They find a bush or hoarding and lie down behind it. They sink into the rubbing-and-kissing thing they have. It's still fresh, it hasn't been replaced by his discovery of masturbation. It always feels as if it could go on and on, though sooner or later, and more and more it's sooner, he comes inside his pant leg and they talk and walk back to the bookstore. After one such day, he gets on the phone and persuades Noel, who's selling penny stocks out of a boiler room for the summer, to drive him back, in his Corvette—Noel gets one new Corvette a year from his dad, whether he needs it or not—at least part of the way to camp, so

Olivia can ride along too. Noel and Olivia are friendly again. They've surmounted the nauseating experience of making out together. Halfway there, he and Olivia persuade Noel to drive the rest of the way. It wasn't hard since there's this girl working at the camp—her name is Nolah, it truly is—who Noel has a hard-on for (they both use this term now). She's been making out with another counsellor. (This is still the era when making out was what having sex would soon become.) When Noel learns about the other guy, you couldn't stop him from finishing the drive if you washed out the highway. As the Corvette glides quietly up the dirt road into the camp lot, Max points the way to Nolah's cabin. Noel heads off like a man about to make an important takeover offer.

He and Olivia go to the arts and crafts shed. The screen door to it is open, there's no one inside, just twine and scissors, glue and tempra paints all over the floor, among which they clear space. The sign on the wall says: Art Is for Everyone. She undoes her skirt and they lie on it. He has his shorts off. He rolls here, she rolls there, it lasts a while, longer than usual, then the lovely shudder and he comes on some coloured contruction paper. They rise to go. As they're heading toward the lot to meet Noel for the ride home, she looks back. "Did you leave something there?" he says. "Almost," she says, with a smirk.

She never smirks. She laughs and smiles and sometimes makes jokes but this is the only smirk he'll ever see on her. It rattles him. He knows roughly what she means, but not . . . really. He doesn't know the details, the specifics, of virginity and how you ditch it. When they were brushing themselves off in the parkette on his last day off, some kids went by on their bikes and one yelled, "Give her a fuck." He flushed with anger and made as if to go after them and pound them, but in truth, he was upset because he wouldn't have known how to do it. (Fuck her, not pound them.) Those little kids did and he didn't. He'd heard, like rumours from a foreign country, all the details over the years, but not how they came together. Still, after all this time and all the, um, progress he's made, sexually. Sometimes he tries to picture it, fleetingly and dauntingly: there is no obvious way. On the A & C floor, Olivia had probably spread her thighs and swivelled her hips to a position where she knew it was just *pop* and they'd be having intercourse and Bob's your uncle. She could likely have taken him by his hips and just dropped him in like her dad inserting the last piece of their backyard barbecue grill from Canadian Tire, no manual required. Others, even Olivia, knew such things. He knew things they didn't, and they knew this, which he *still* didn't. He read books they didn't and they read this one, or had a Platonic recall of it without ever needing to read the thing. Is it possible he already had the information and it just wasn't registering? Anything's possible. Once, he asked Sorstad if you could know something and not know you knew it. Sorstad said, "Sure. It would be like a blind man could be the world expert in optics. He'd know everything about it. He just wouldn't know what the hell he was talking about."

When he returns to school that fall for his final year, he has Sorstad again, this time one on one. He's doing Independent Study on Economy and Society. Three years ago, when Sorstad gave back Max's term paper for Major Trends in Economic Thought, there were 148 pencilled numbers scattered over its twenty-two pages and a sheaf at the back, with thickly typed comments for each footnote. It felt like a scholarly journal. And that was a mere term paper. Sorstad has that knack: he can make you feel special. The time he mentioned the non-masturbation record, Max actually felt proud. If it was easy, why hadn't others done it?

They're discussing a topic for his honours thesis. Sorstad proposes the economy of sex. He doesn't mean pimps and hookers; he means the *political* economy of sex. Max wiggles a little in the chair. He guesses Sorstad is talking about Wilhelm Reich, who's become a minor fad among left-wing students, less than Fanon, more than Trotsky. Reich was Freud's student and a Marxist, who lived in Nazi Germany, analyzed the rise of Hitler in connection, somehow or other, with sex and—"*Ay yay yay,*" shrieks Sorstad. "It always comes back to Marxism these days!" He says he was thinking about Sweden now, not Nazi Germany then. Sweden has what would be considered in the rest of the West highly unorthodox public practices on sex education, pornography, prostitution, and these are actual national policies, not just airy-fairy (rolling his r's) disputations in the *rrrrrealm* of theory. But it's the height of the sixties—he rrrants on—and everything has to be "relevant," which means more or less that the student gets a veto: if they want Reich, they get Reich. He's not unsympathetic. He dimly recalls his own manic student days. So he proposes a compromise: an examination of Reich's theory of sex economy, particularly the functions of the orgasm, Reich's main interest, against actual experiments in policy that have taken place in Sweden. Max is still squirming. He'd rather veto the whole thing. It isn't what he had in mind. Perhaps that's why Sorstad, always alert to twitching, mentions Olivia.

He knows her—she took one of his courses. She's such an "integrated" person, he says in passing, as if this will help Max deal with the political economy of sex. Max realizes—Ay yay yay—that the assumption behind Sorstad's whole approach is that Max has already covered the course on sex himself, including the basic act, with Olivia, probably among many others. That's why he suggested this topic: to give his student a chance to unite subjective awareness with objective theory. Max stammers that he and Olivia haven't actually done, er, had the full sexual experience. Not because it's unimportant, of course, he ploughs on, but because it may be *too* important. Ugh. What a prissy thing to say. He feels like he's writing a column on teen advice in a church magazine. He cringes. He didn't even mean to mention this, this—humiliating vacuum in his character and experience (he doesn't think).

Sorstad pauses, as if to check with himself, perhaps cross-reference to the earlier exchange, the one on masturbation, which he hadn't forgotten—just archived. This isn't quite the level of intellectual exchange he expected on this topic. He asks Max to return to his office at the same time tomorrow and they'll discuss it further, whatever "it" is.

Next day when they meet again, Sorstad talks amiably and academically, making clear his respect for Max as his student. They pin down an entirely different thesis topic. Max starts to go and Sorstad says, "Oh, I picked up something you might like to read." He slides a slim brown paper bag across his desk. Inside is a little pocketbook manual on sex, with the male and female symbols on the cover. It looks straighforward, instructive, as unmenacing as a cookbook. You could buy it at any drugstore newsstand.

Max devours it that night. It has everything, in one little book: plain language, diagrams. All he really needed was an authorized delivery. As if it had been couriered to Max, but left in the care of his neighbour who happened to be Sorstad, so Sorstad signed for it and brought it over when Max got home. Sorstad was an ideal intermediary. He had already revealed some of the great secrets of money. He was a revealer.

Then he goes to the university library and starts to read everything in the stacks that doesn't require putting in a traceable request: medicine, sexology, anthropology. *Lots* of anthro, back there in the stacks, with many accounts of sexual initiation rites. If he likes what he sees, he takes the book into the bathroom, to a stall.

Ta–da (2)

It happens under the dining-room table at her house, a floor below her parents' bed. Their pants are off, he's rubbing on her thigh, as usual. But he's read the book. He knows where hers is and where his goes. *I'm in!* he thinks, in the phrase a generation twenty-five years later will trumpet when they hack into a computer. They have the codes, and so does he, he found it in a book. Who wouldn't esteem the life of the mind, if this is its power?

He lies there as you do on the taxi ride home from the airport after a hard business trip, thinking how fine it would be if someone met you at the door, offered you a cup of tea, and said you did well, all things considered. Or like a kid straggling home late under the street lights after playing hockey on the rink till you can't even see the puck, and when you get there, your mum makes a hot chocolate and takes all your soaked stuff away to deal with it. Hockey is a funny game, you can't really have a strategy for it, the way you can for basketball or football, where you handle the ball and control where it's going, more or less. In hockey, everything is slips and slides and slaps with your stick. You don't have a strategy, you have a wish list. The best hockey strategy is probably—have no strategy. But *stay positive.* He turns over, slips into her again, and slides about. Each little slide tickles and tingles.

Was it worth that long wait? Well, you can say this: He has been groping about in this cave for so long, trying without knowing it to find his way to the day outside, that once he does, the brilliance never fades. He doubted it would ever happen at all; he never dreamed what the world out here could be like; or that it would be his. Now it exists, to be entered and re-entered, daily if he will. It's as though you spent your lifetime in the city, where the night sky is barely noticeable, with a dim array of Christmassy lights strung above, pretty but hardly worth craning your neck for. Then you're up north, camped on a lonely lake, you awaken at midnight and step outside the tent to pee and the stars are so close and bright you actually duck to get out of their way.

"So now we can get married," he says, shortly after the Big Event. He doesn't put it as a question, or raise it as a topic for one of their famous talks. The apparent reason: he has won a fellowship for graduate studies at the London School of Economics. He presents it as a non sequitur: marriage following the academic award like a syllogism. No one he knows thinks to question it because he sounds so certain, he must have thought it through, even if Noel, among others, doesn't quite catch the connection. Olivia will get a job there, no problem, she has British citizenship as well as Canadian. Her dad came from Birmingham to Canada as a kid in the dirty thirties, more or less indentured to a Canadian farmer by his parents, in return for sending money home. He was so intimidated when the farmer asked his name that he said "J- J- J-" trying to get Johnny out, till the farmer barked, "All right then, George it is!" He's been George ever since.

One night, just days before the wedding, he takes a walk along the boardwalk in the east end with Rosemary. She was a

colleague of Olivia's at the summer bookstore job. She went in
one day looking for a book about a woman jockey, the one who
married Fred Astaire, and noticed a Help Wanted sign. She'd like
to be a riding instructor, but the way there is murky; bookselling
probably isn't it. He likes her unacademic quality, the sense of
the stable. Olivia told him Rosemary once said that when she
kisses a guy, he stays kissed. It sounded terrific. Kissing had a
special force for him, all that time when he didn't know what
intercourse was—sort of the way it functioned in Hollywood
movies of the fifties as a substitute for sex. She's been on his
mind since he crossed the frontier recently under the table at
Olivia's. He showed up at Rosemary's place this evening and
suggested a walk. They swerve off the boardwalk to avoid some
cyclists. They're in the shadows, on the park and trees side, not
the beach and lake part. He takes her hand without looking over
or saying anything. She says nothing. They walk. He presses it,
in what could be just friendly. She smiles without looking or
pressing back. He takes her arm. He still hasn't said anything. He
wonders if this is how it's done, or if he's inventing something
new. She leans toward him. A few steps and they kiss, still walking, then stop and kiss. He mentions the thing about staying
kissed. "She told you that, eh?" says Rosemary.

They sidle toward a picnic table, sit there a while, then slide
to the ground. They're under a big oak. People continue passing
on the boardwalk. The two of them can't be seen, or only a
lumpy double outline. When he moves his hand toward her
breasts—well, toward where they'd be: she has fried-egg kind of
breasts, almost flat. He finds them appealing, though he also
finds large breasts appealing. He wonders if this means he's
undeveloped in his tastes, or just likes breasts. She resists. "I don't
want to," she says. To tell the truth, he feels relieved. He doesn't

even ask why. It's her business, right? "I'd like to," she volunteers, "but I can't." He doesn't know if it's because she has a boyfriend, or is saving herself, or because she knows Olivia, or maybe doesn't find him attractive enough to have full-blown sex with. "That's okay," he says, and to his surprise, he means it. It satisfies him mightily that she'd like to go farther—it hardly matters that they aren't actually going to, the main thing seems achieved, now that he could if she would. It's almost better this way.

They continue, approaching the same point, her pushing him back from it again. Then again. In between, they chat. "Doesn't it bother you?" she says. "What?" he says. "That you're getting married next week."

"Oh no," he says. She asks why. She expects him to say: *I won't do this kind of thing any more.* You know, the usual: sowing his last crop of wild oats, what you'd anticipate from a guy about to get hitched. It's traditional. Instead he says, "Because once I'm married, I won't want this any more."

You gotta be kidding, she thinks.

The morning set for his marriage he goes to Tony's barbershop and sits in Tony's chair as he has since he was a kid. Tony greets him: So long since I saw you, etc. Your *wedding* day? What an honour for me! This haircut is free, it's a wedding present. When Tony finishes the cut he holds up the mirror. Max explodes like a landmine. He curses Tony with language he didn't know he had. Tony, befuddled, asks what's wrong. "You made it too short, you idiot!" Tony says he'll fix it. "No, you idiot, it's too late for that." The awful thing about short is it can't be undone. You can't wash it out and do it it over—"*You idiot!*" He looks round the shop, he wants to wreck everything, starting with those mocking mirrors, which reflect his intention, and that will have to suffice. He's lost everything, at least everything that matters, like Samson. Then he goes to his wedding.

The ceremony is modest, as if he is hoping no one will notice. They do it in city hall, at noon on a weekday. The small wedding party will move from there to lunch in the classy dining room of an excellent hotel. Then the two of them will drive to a lodge up north for several days. You could think of it as economic, just right for an economist.

After the ceremony, they sit in back of the hired limo, waiting for the small line of cars to rev up for the short drive to lunch. Olivia, in a white satin gown with long sleeves, oh so slightly brocaded, sobs into his shoulder. She is happy, he is what she always wanted. She feels as if he is what she wanted even before she met him, then he came and filled in the blank. He looks straight ahead, almost at attention, like a soldier in dress uniform. Into his view moves the face of the limo driver, arm on the front seat, looking back to see if it's time to start. The kind of guy who could be a mover when he's not driving limo, or on the phys ed faculty. But under the cap, as his gaze crosses Max's face, he looks surprised. Then puzzled. Reading that face like a mirror of his own, Max knows what the driver sees: a guy in a tux thinking, I have made a terrible mistake.

So marriage isn't the beginning of his life as a womanizer, nor even the end of his abstemious, bizarre pre-life. It is a futile, doomed attempt to prolong things as they were, and avoid his destiny.

Here he is then, our fine young swain, much like his own favourite character in fiction, Huck Finn, preparing to light out for the territories, sexually speaking, though he continues to procrastinate. In absolute terms, it has been just a handful of years since the roust from the couch. Relative to an average lifespan, it may not seem long. But if we take that moment as a starting point, then in his own terms he idled in sexual oblivion for the equivalent of *more than a lifetime*. Now, at long last, he has arrived. Will it take him *another* lifetime to make up the ground? As they used to say on the radio during that golden era: *Return with us now, to those thrilling days of yesteryear. The Womanizer rides again . . .*

Part II

THE HUCK
FINN OF SEX

Jenny's Version

~

I was the only one he slept with while he was still married,
before he supposedly became such a womanizer. I'm pretty
sure. I was the *first* anyway. I came down to London from
Cambridge one weekday to take in Ralph Miliband's seminar
on Capitalism and Underdevelopment. They were still pounding the drum of Marxist economics there, though it was
already on life-support, you could sense it. The class had begun
and he came in late and scanned the room and his face just
illuminated when he saw mine, and quick as a whip, he ges-
tured as if to ask if the seat beside me was taken. And before I
knew it, he was there, writing notes to me about the class.
They were cute and witty. *Who are you?* I wrote on the pad and
he wrote back, *Aarrgghh!* Like he had an identity crisis right
there on the notepad. Bright but not cocky. Vulnerable. Women
like me love vulnerable, don't ask me why. Add humour and
I'm helpless. He walked me to the tube after, and before I knew

it, we arranged to have lunch later in the week when, I quickly decided, I had to be in London again. So I came back and after that lunch we walked around and somehow ended up at his flat. Olivia was out at her job, what was it—some architectural firm for a public housing project. And very quickly there he was close to me, both of us standing still. I guess he had his shoes off and he was kind of placing his feet over mine as he faced me, like one of those dolls people can learn to ballroom dance with. It was very urgent yet not aggressive. I was surprised because I suspected this might come and I'd deliberately made myself what I thought of as unattractive for the date. My hair was up in a pretty slovenly ponytail. No makeup, not to speak of. Eyeliner doesn't count. Ugly slacks and blouse. I wanted to feel I hadn't *provoked* this married young man. I guess another way to put that is to say I wanted him to really want me, want *me*, not the look I knew how to put on and the sex that went with it. Hair and tits. But I think he'd already made up his mind to desire me desperately as soon as he saw me in the seminar. I told him to come visit me in Cambridge, when he could. I had the impression if I'd said Lapland, he'd have been there just as fast.

So Monday a week, just after noon, the phone rang and here he was. Some subterfuge about taking the train up to consult an expert on short-term interest rates in Third World nations. He came straight to the flat. My roommate was out. I took him into my bedroom and stuck a book in the door—it was a signal my roommate and I used when we had men in. And he started the same thing as in London. Not the feet on top of mine, but similar. Touching, moving closer, with that urgent, importuning quality. I said, "Hey, you don't have to seduce me." He looked not hurt but confused, as if he wouldn't know how to seduce a girl to save his life. It wasn't in his repertoire, cross his heart and hope to die. From his stricken look, I'd have testified for him myself: *This fellow don't know the meaning of seduction, your Lordship.* Then we were in bed and he looked so *relieved.* Almost like you feel when you finally lose your virginity. We met for sex often after that. We didn't do much else, but I always felt he was there, you know, the person. He seemed to relax once he knew the sex part was, sort of, covered. Out of the way. We'd have great conversations then. Or go out to eat and yap. That part took me by surprise. When he showed up the first time, I asked if he wanted to get lunch and he said, "Let's do that after." And I said, "Oh, sure. That's what everyone says." And he got the stricken look. But we did go for tandoori when we were done, he was good as his word, I was surprised, I'll tell you, and so animated in conversation. We talked about *anything,* as if he wanted me to know who he was, which was not just some desperate-for-sex fellow. As though the sex once done stimulated every other quality and interest that was him, including the sexual urge itself again. And again, I might add.

I never had an orgasm with him. Come to think of it, he may have been the only one of my lovers about whom I can say that. Yet it didn't bother me. The one thing I ever demanded was that he sleep with me frequently. Hard to explain, I suppose. He was just so damn . . . *grateful.*

That's what I told my friends when we talked about how men we knew were in bed. In our book group or, before that, in consciousness-raising discussions. That was back when you could use the phrase without having to put quotation marks around it in your voice. *I don't really mind how it goes*—I used to tell my "sisters"—*so long as they're grateful.*

It led me to give some thought to the category, which was very taken for granted at the time, like, say, imperialism, liberation, revolution. The category, womanizing, I mean. I researched it, and I can tell you with some assurance that the phenomenon is entirely relative. Casanova himself, according to his memoirs, seduced thirty-five women. Georges Simenon, creator of Inspector Maigret, says he slept with ten thousand. Wilt Chamberlain, an American athlete, claims twenty thousand. But no one calls Casanova a Simenon or, for that matter, Wilt. With regard to originating factors, his own weird background, which he alluded to sometimes, proves you can start from almost anywhere. The term implies an unbridled sexual practice but doesn't even include, say, sex with other men. That would be *man*izing, or might not be if you preferred to reserve that term for a female equivalent to womanizer, an interesting concept, interesting particularly in that it has never developed. Womanizing might or might not include varied races and ages and a wide spread of activities. It's vague and imprecise, much like promiscuity, the only even approximately comparable word normally applied to women at the time. He told me that when he began his life as a womanizer in earnest, he often met women who said, "It's a shame I didn't run into you a little while ago when I was in my promiscuous phase." He said he found this a cruel fate. It happened often enough that he began asking when their promiscuous period had been and how long it lasted. Usually, they replied, it was three or four weeks during which they slept with two to four men. As I say, everything in the area is relative. "If I was a woman, I guess I'd be called a nymphomaniac," he concluded. But he was wrong. If he had been a woman, he'd have been called a slut.

Francie's Version

~

He was so different from the other boys I dated. When they got up from the bed to go to the bathroom, they had these little washboard tummies they held in. It made me tense. Would they manage to keep it tucked in or would something slide out of place? He had a pot. He wasn't obese, not even fat, but he had a pot like a normal person, and he didn't seem to know it. I found it a relief.

He didn't dress like them either. The English boys mostly had tight little bums and clothes that matched. He wore this loose stuff, as if he stepped into his closet each morning and just let some things fall on him. He called it "the lumberjack effect." I'd guess it worked on the English; it made them think of him as some kind of North American force of nature. I imagine if he went back to Canada and wore ascots, got his hair styled, you know, layered or moussed, he could pull the reverse thing on Canadians. He liked french fries and fast food; we went to Wimpy's a lot. I don't remember us going to the kind of restaurants that had been normal for me on dates. Though he made an exception for tandoori and Chinese. He once told me that "good" shops and cafés intimidated him, but I didn't take it seriously. I just assumed it was something he didn't care enough about to get good at. Anyone willing to put in the time can master that stuff. You don't need to be a genius to act a little snooty. Believe me.

He was the same way about sex. I don't mean like a lumberjack. It wasn't meat-and-potatoes sex. But it wasn't showy, like those boys who toss you up in the air and make you do

three and a half flips before you land again, perfectly posi-
tioned for another display of their . . . swordsmanship. It was
very direct. He didn't talk about it much, he just liked doing it.
There was a lot of talking about sex in those days. It was supposed to be frank and "upfront." Man. But it wasn't, usually.
It was flirty and coy and irritating, like too much foreplay. He
just did what he wanted. It was refreshing, like his little pot.

What touched me even more was his idealism. He said that
was my word for Keynesianism. I never knew what it meant,
although I did know Keynes had been a lord. But whatever it
meant, his goals were very modest. People used to posture a lot
back then. They were always talking about the Revolution, as if
it was a club or a group, you know, as if you could look up its
address in the London directory. Nobody else was ever radical
enough, everyone else was a sellout or a bourgeois. You could
feel the anger and superiority, especially when they were supposed to be doing it all out of love for the workers or the
wretched of the earth, none of whom they ever had over. If a
person just wanted the world to be slightly kinder, they were
dismissed as *mere* liberals. Or fucking liberals. You wouldn't
even give them the simple respect of arguing with them. To me,
it was like the tight bums and flat tummies. Showing off. Boys
being boys. His ideas seemed different. He wanted the world to
be just a bit better for people in it, and it had nothing to do
with proving how revolutionary he was. He could care less. You
know it's funny, when you think about it: because that kind of
made him *more* radical than all the radicals. There were so many
of them, saying the same things, striking similar poses. Being
sort of moderate, for those times, almost conservative, made
him stand out as different and daring to be so. Put it together
with the sex and clothes and fast food—it was a great combo.

That's why I couldn't believe it when he pulled back. Everything had been so direct and honest. Then it's gone. Does that mean it was false? Can it just vanish? He opened something up in me. Maybe it was the Canadian element. God, I never expected that would undo me. So then when he took it away—I expect it might have driven anybody bonkers.

Francie

Oh God, if you'll let me have her, just once, I swear I won't ever ask you for anything else.

This was his prayer. He prayed it with an ancient fervour down those decades—morning and night, like a devout Jew or Moslem—and often in between, as the piety fanatics do for extra points. He sometimes felt he'd prayed it in an earlier life, even before Sorstad slid the Little Book of Intercourse across the desk. Yet each time he prayed, there was a miracle. It felt fresh and new, as if he'd created it on the spot at that moment—which is the unattainable goal of all ritual: to be utterly familiar yet totally fresh. Plato, whom Innis adored for combining the oral and written traditions and thus dominating the West for two thousand years, believed you never learned anything new; you just recalled what you'd forgotten. Maybe Max had always known about sex and women; he just forgot, and then it came back. Maybe he prayed his prayer each day back in grade two when he passed the little girl with silky blonde hair who held the door open to the yard at recess. It stands to reason. He's never forgotten *her*, just his prayer *about* her.

The one peering in a bookstore window half a block down Oxford Street is also blonde, and golden, with tumbling curls. Does she know the power of those tumbles? How can she not?

At some age you have to grasp such things. When you're holding the door for recess and see the little guys gasp? Or in your teens: one day you stroll past a group of guys standing on a sunny corner and the talk stops cold. It hits you: you can actually halt their conversation. Just you, walking. This one nods as she darts into the bookstore. He follows. She's in back, among the social sciences. "Find anything?" he says, across a couple of tables, as if they're part of a joint search team on either side of a valley; a dig, a police hunt or, this being England, a mushroom trek. The micologists' picnic. "I'm looking for something in the area of industrial archeology," she replies. "It's a quite new field." She has the plummiest Oxbridge accent he's ever heard. "Where in England are you from?" he asks in his flat Canadian voice. He knows he sounds American to most locals. She'll ask where *he's* from, he'll say Canada to her mild surprise, and so on. "I'm not actually from here," she says. "I'm from Canada." "Go on," he says. "From where?" "Toronto actually," she says. "No shit," he blurts. "What high school did you go to?" Not the smoothest line you'll find in the pickup books, which of course he doesn't pick up, but it will locate her, fast. "Leaside," she says, still sounding like the Queen. Leaside is the blandest suburb in Toronto. Kids from Leaside had first names like Dot and last names like Johnson. They lived on streets called Parkwood Circle. It wasn't crass like the suburbs that get savaged in sociological studies and sitcoms, it was just . . . Leaside.

Her name's Francie and she's a consultant. He has no idea what that means. Consultants have tried to tell him what they do. They've taken him on tours of their offices, introduced him to their colleagues—he still doesn't get it. Maybe he has dyslexia about job categories. Economists tend to be weak on things like the work people actually do or how to figure out the tip. He tells her there's a party at his flat tonight and she's welcome to drop by. It's his standard low-key invitation: you ask someone over and see if they stay; it's a way to get a response from her, soon as he can, and establish at the same time that he doesn't care much. He wants *her* to commit, he's not putting himself on the line. She of course senses the vulnerability behind his defensive posture, and is moved.

To his amazement, she's at the door that night. The party is underway. He asks her in, dropping her coat on the cot in the hall with the others, and starts dancing with her. An hour later, when she says she's leaving he walks her to the street and tells her he'd like to ask her to stay for the night, but he has no idea when people will leave. She looks at him sweetly, as if she doesn't believe anyone can be this direct and hapless. There's a party tomorrow in Hampstead, she says, professionals in her field mainly. Would he care to come? Like a mirror image of his invitation, the onus shifted back. Basic baseline play. *Thunk, thunk, thunk.* Stand your ground and return the shot. She gives him the address.

It's the most English environment he's ever been in. Everybody talks like her. There's even a guy in cricket whites: the V-neck sweater, the trousers. As the evening passes, they take him aside one by one and confess that, well, actually they're Canadian too. Every damn one. It's like a collection point for transnationals: people who were born inside Canadian bodies in freezing places like Sioux Lookout but always felt there was an English person trapped far beneath, struggling to get to the tidy countryside south of London. Francie leaves early, he can't tell if she's with one of the transnationals or not. It's hard to get away because they keep confessing. Last is the guy in cricket whites. He says he admires anyone as honestly Canadian as Max, making him sound like a coureur de bois.

Next day he phones her and she comes by his place. He didn't say why and she didn't ask. She walks in, they get halfway across the living room to the couch, he puts his hands on her shoulders, turns her, and they kiss. They skip the couch and angle toward the bedroom. He has an erection as they undress and thinks, as he often does in the early days of his womanizing, Better get it in, in case there's trouble. Pushing, he starts to wilt. This can happen when you have sex several times a day, often with several different women, each more than once. He knows there are those who would call this compulsive. But with his training in the social sciences, he's not impressed by technical terms. Maybe he's just trying to make up for what he missed when he didn't even know what was missing. That's rational. Sometimes it even happens when he's skipped sex for a day or two. Then he notices a whitish strand of hair circling down beside her ear, hanging in front of the golden curls like a tassel, like the drawstring on drapes. He's touched by it. And he's in.

After, she says she likes his approach. He says he didn't think he had an approach. She says that's what she likes. They lie a while and chat. Then she puts her hand between his legs. "I don't think your friend is finished," she says. This time she's above, but he swivels her and somehow winds up over and behind. He doesn't recall doing this manoeuvre before yet it seems familiar, as if he covered it in a course. Like the prayer. Later, they lie on their sides, her back against his front. He's touched again, this time by her shoulder blade. He leans toward it. "Mickey," she says in wonder—no one has ever called him that, he doesn't know if it's an English short form for Maxwell or she just didn't get his name right—"you kissed my back!"

They never schedule in advance. He calls or she does, miraculously the other is there, available. They have sex and watch TV or watch TV and have sex. Go for tandoori, usually after. One night John and Yoko come into their regular Indian restaurant. No one looks at John and Yoko. Instead they all check around the room to make sure no other diners are gawking. It's about sophistication. No, actually it's about politics. People are people, you don't have to be a Marxist with a rustproof class analysis to swallow that. You can be a rock-ribbed Keynesian like Max and buy into the argument that some human beings do not count more than others, never mind their fame or money. It's a thing everyone feels, it's in the air of the era.

One Friday night she drops by to leave a note on his door. (It is an age in which people have phones, but there is no way to leave a message. If someone is out, you call back.) The note says she won't be around tonight, in case he calls. There's a farewell party for a bloke she works with. It's innocent. Still, she hopes it will worry him a little. She finds a note already there for her, in case she comes by: he's away for the weekend with, well, he doesn't say. When he returns on Sunday, her original note is stroked out and beneath it: "You win again. You always win. Love, F." There is this kind of edginess to their relationship, a trace of worry on both sides, an attempt not to be vulnerable. It works for them.

With her, within her to be precise, he learns to yell. They've gone up to the north, a rare case in which they had to do advance planning. They're in Leeds to see the cathedral or something. Sid Amram has a flat there, he's down in London, he and Max have traded apartments for the weekend. Sid is post-doc in the cool new field of law and economics, and a playwright, for purposes of exorcising his Jewish past. Sid spent his early years in parochial school, mastering oversize folio pages of the Talmud. One day he showed Max a volume of those centrifugal pools of Hebraic text, and Max felt he was staring at a perfect example of the Innisian claim that you can combine oral and written traditions: the backs and forths of rabbinic debate embodied in distinct typefaces and layouts on the very same pages. As if Socrates and his interlocutors got a chunk of print each, cheek by jowl, plus space for the kibitzers in the cheap seats. Then Sid did law at Oxford, standing first in his class in every course, since he found the intricacies of British jurisprudence frightfully simple compared to the terse legal style of his ancient rabbis. ("Two grasp a scarf. To which?" Translation of translation: two people come upon a garment left lying in the road and each seizes one end. How is ownership to be determined?) Sid claims the Talmud was also excellent training for work in the theatre, because dialogue—as opposed to the prose of the novel or the economic treatise—is compact and allusive, leaving out far more than it explicitly states, and depends on actors and staging to fill the vast unsaid. As a result, his plays are not merely succinct; they have no words at all.

Take *The Weekly Portion*, which Max and Francie saw in a little theatre off Elephant and Circle: Two *yeshiva bochers*, teenage Orthodox boys with side curls and skullcaps, sit in the back row of a synagogue during the Torah service. The old men parade the scroll of the Law around and passionately kiss the ornaments in which it is cloaked as it passes. Turned on by this, the kids start to make out. As the Torah reading proceeds, they make out more heavily. That's it. Sid's most successful play. The only one that's actually been performed. No one who has seen it, or heard it described by anybody who saw it, can forget it.

He and Francie are in Sid's apartment, where Sid lives with his wife, Lindsay, a lanky *shiksa* he seems perfectly matched with. Sid says at the end of each day he marvels that they're still together—going on nine years now. Then he marvels again in the morning. It's like Max's prayer, though Sid's is praise, not petition. The place smells of socks. Washed socks, unwashed socks. It's over a cavernous Chinese restaurant called Tiny's. The sounds of Tiny's rise through the floor and trampoline them on the membrane of floor and mattress. *Ba-boom, buzz. Clang* (comes the Peking duck). When they've had sex a second time, they lie in their favourite way, her back to his front. She reverses into him and he goes in again. She slides under and more or less hoists him. Playfully, as if—hey, what's this going on now? He gives one of the cheeks on her slightly bony butt a little slap, a *thwack*, not as if it's something he's always wanted to do, a forbidden moment, he just sensed she might like it, and after all, they're such good buddies these days, especially in bed . . . She yelps daintily. It's a funny little feeling. He's never thought of himself as a hitter. Except for that stuff with Olivia, which it's better not to think about. More of a yeller, like his dad, in those daily morning shriekfests. Yelling doesn't leave bruises, so you're never quite sure it happened, except you reverberate all day. He thwacks her again, she yelps, then again, harder though never very. She's laughing, he is too. Who knew? As he comes, he shouts. Well, why not? Same kind of thing. A shout for a yelp. They're in a zone. The electric light from the street reflects off the dark walls, catching random socks, and his cry deepens as it emerges, coming from farther down his throat, his chest, the diaphragm now—as though he's poking around with a flashlight, a spelunker, curious about what else might be in there. It gets lower, not just a growl, toward a roar. They're pretty damn delighted. *I mean, did we do that? All by ourselves? Hardly.* It's as if they've been joined by a playful third party. The host. The MC. Some underemployed actor you hire to turn the kids' birthday parties into a real hoot with a clown suit and balloons. They do it again, a ridiculous number of times even for them, him tossing his head back and flinging it forward. Getting rid of—stuff. Feeling pours out like liquid. I mean he's a yeller, anybody who knows him, knows that. Ask poor Olivia. Ask Noel. "Stop yelling," Noel once said to him on the phone, when he hadn't even raised his voice. He protested. "Even when you don't yell, you yell," Noel barked back, and it had the ring of truth. But this yelling is different, it's a celebration. Francie jerks with each *thwack* like a joy buzzer. Then they lie in silence, the third party paid and departed—but please return, oh do. Below them, Tiny's thumps on.

Later, they descend to the restaurant, inside the echo chamber rather than bouncing above it. All the orders come covered in glowing orange sauce. Shrimp, broccoli, whatever. The menu calls it sweet and sour. Tiny's serves the best Chinese food in the north of England, Sid told them. He talks; no, he babbles like a brook, an English brook in an English poem in a Canadian schoolbook (so the poor colonials got a taste of the real thing), about how much better our planet could so easily be for its all too often luckless inhabitants. He doesn't mean any system is ideal, he's no perfectionist. It's just that there's no need for life to be as hideously inhuman as it is for so many, among whom a small improvement would mean an immeasurable difference. It's within our grasp. She beams at him. He glows humbly in her esteem. "What I adore about you," she says, "is you are such a Keynesian"—a word he taught her.

He always thought of it as sheepish and unadventurous, a

source of embarrassment. He'd like her to tell him more, though it would be too simple to simply ask. He wants to know why she thinks it's all right to be so . . . politically uncomprehensive. "All the boys I know who are political," she says, "*shout* all the time." Tonight's theme is shouting. She elaborates. "If they're Maoists," she says, "or Trotskyites." Yes, yes, he nods. "Anarchists, De Leonists," he adds to her list. He knows the political and economic screamers. He secretly admires the De Leonists. Perhaps there are thirty of forty in the *world*. They don't just shout, they break things. You know it's them because everything comes down to breaking things. She laughs. Sid took him to a play by a De Leonist playwright. It ended with the actors smashing the set.

He tells her about his dad, who rarely yelled at his son directly yet who became, they would say in a later age, collateral damage. "But you do shout," she says. For a freaky, scary moment, he thinks she means, like father, like son. But she means upstairs. "No, but I shout love," he says, laughing out of control, though it's absorbed in the din of the restaurant and the glowing orange of its specialties. She's looking strangely at him, so he tells her about a goofy poet he knows in Canada, their shared homeland, Milton Acorn. She can't believe the name of a *poet* in *Canada* is Milton . . . *Acorn*. His eyes tear up at the thought. If you're walking down a street and hear the smack of head on lamppost, he says, it'll be him. No need to look. He once saw this guy try to read a poem in a bar. Its first line was, "I—shout—love!" The poet got to "looooovvvve" and couldn't stop shouting it, so he ran out of the bar and into the street as if his mouth was on fire. People saw him vanish up Spadina Avenue with the word still trailing from his mouth, as if he was searching for a trough. "Anyway," she says, "You are a radical—in sex."

"At least," he says, "I don't always have to worry about whether I have the correct line."

When it's her turn, she takes him meandering around her past to places they've never gone. Somewhere comes a stay in a psych ward at the Clarke Institute in Toronto. Bedlam for the well-heeled. They were *ridiculous*, she laughs, those doctors. She got out of there damn fast. He doesn't follow it up with his normal persistence, the style of the engaged observer that he's cultivated for so long, the journalist at a press conference when some *dyn-o-mite* slips out and the government officials are looking around as if, *Uh-oh, hope none of these reporters caught that.* Why would he, with one he so adores, at so complete a moment? Doubtless it was all, as she said, ridiculous.

Olivia calls from Vancouver, where she's begun her new life. Post-marriage, post-Max. They drove out together, a final marital gesture, then he returned to London and she got on with it: good job with the city parks department, doing what she can to improve the perfect coastline of English Bay. Lives in Kits and has become a player in the local women's movement, since she's determined to wring what wisdom she can from their period of foredoomed wedlock. There's even a new guy. Max found out when he called one day to confirm details about their amicable divorce. In Canada back then, adultery was the only excuse; you had to prove it and if you did, the marriage was terminated by act of Parliament. "Mr. Speaker, I'd like to bring to the attention of this House, a hussy in Vancouver who has been getting up to hanky-panky. . ." He phoned all the way from London to give her the number of a Vancouver PI he'd hunted down. He always handled those tasks, even from halfway round the globe; Olivia considered it a guy thing, like changing the tires. Her mission was to phone the PI and arrange to be discovered in bed with a "co-respondent," another roust in the house, really, permitting the parliamentarians to proceed with the matter. That was when a guy answered. He handed the phone to Olivia. She knew by the crackle of the overseas line it was Max, her ex-to-be, and slid effortlessly into caught-and-guilty mode. He didn't want her to feel bad. "I guess we're even now," he said, meaning something or other, maybe the bank teller she had roiled his life with during their token separation. They both relaxed. It was really truly over.

This time she's calling to say she'd like to divvy up the money in their joint Canadian bank account, the one with the cheques that came at the time of their wedding, along with innumerable hot trays. He tells her to take it all; with his economic savvy, he figures there's almost nothing, and how often do you get to make a grand gesture that will cost you fifty cents? A day later she wires him. Turns out there was *another* account from wedding gifts, it's a mystery how it got there but it contains a fair stash, and she's sending him half. He decides to take the small bounty and use it to move to Paris where he will author a great study on the damage debt is doing in the developing countries. Something worthy will at last emerge from the debacle of his wedding day. Why Paris? It somehow seems closer to the colonial world with its endless rumblings and grumblings. There he will put his ear to the post-imperial ground. Francie is moved by his ambition and idealism, not to mention his mighty intellect—I mean, a whole *book*. But, um, what about me? They both agree there were no obligations in this—well, you can't really call it a relationship—and besides, Paris is near.

It's not original. Young North American goes to Paris to write! Maybe that's why he avoided it during their London years, his and Olivia's. They made one trip over, during the May '68 uprising. He went reluctantly in order to confirm his conviction that revolutionary change is a dead end. (But if he believed that with real conviction, why did it need confirmation?) The French Communist party, he observed with mild satisfaction, declined to call for a revolution, so the workers did not join the students in the streets battling the helmeted CRS in their baleful vans—though the workers did, it's true, occupy their factories. Then at the crucial flashpoint, it all got stuck and petered out. What a waste of energy and potential, he felt. If that sounds patronizing, well, those weren't easy years for a young man to be a gradualist, an *étapiste*, as the French radicals said in their smug way. At least the failure of the revolutionaries meant he didn't have to rethink his position. Altering your intellectual framework can be such a drag, especially after you spend years of seminars and research constructing it. By then, it's pretty much equivalent to who you feel you are. You wouldn't be just shifting a few ideas, you'd be reconstructing your very *self*, that's the trouble with being an intellectual: you are what you think.

In '68, Olivia had wanted to wander the city and breathe in its eternal bits. He said no, they came to see revolutionary politics in motion, he was there to learn, not holiday. Then she dragged him into Notre-Dame and she couldn't get him out. When she finally did, they went to the Jeu de Paume and she couldn't get him out again. He wouldn't even leave the little sailing pools in the Tuileries; they were so . . . *parfait*. Paris was, he had to admit, *pas mal*. It was as though he lost track not just of time but of the history he'd come to encounter. Innis too became fed up with history at the end of his career. The old master by then was sated with history, he'd done it better than anybody else, and now he wanted to spend a little, um, *time*—beyond history—in the realm of the eternal.

Max felt he could live in this city. Not with Olivia, though. Here was a place to walk the streets alone. Well, so was everywhere. But here, the women looked right back at you. Often, they even smiled. It was no country for married men.

He sublets his (formerly their) London flat and moves straight into a fifth-floor walk-up near the Place de la République. It belongs to Guy-Paul. He only meant to stay till he got oriented and found a walk-up of his own, but Guy-Paul insists. Guy-Paul was one of Jenny's lovers in Cambridge, she introduced them, and he has the plummiest Oxbridge accent Max ever heard till Francie happened into his life. What is it with foreigners in England? There's a toilet *à la turq* at the end of the hall and one floor down: two ceramic imprints of oversize feet on the floor and a hole between them. They prefer to pee in the sink.

Guy-Paul has always found Max wild and free because, when you ask how he is, he might answer, "Lousy" Guy-Paul says, "That is so *Américain*." Europeans would never. No way. That first night—single in Paris at last—they walk down to the river along the Boul. St. Denis. And oh the hookers, "the *putes*," as Henry Miller called them in his wild and free books about Paris in the thirties. So very unapologetic. Out in the street like everybody else, like the cops and booksellers, doing their business. You've got your student types, your model types, your . . . hooker types. You can hardly tell the shoppers from the people just cutting down St. Denis to meet a friend for dinner, as he and Guy-Paul are, over on the Left Bank.

The friend they meet is Guy-Paul's old girlfriend, Anne, from the south. She pronounces the *e* on the end of it. Ann-ne. He finds that awesome. Awesome Ann-ne. After dinner they take a bottle of *rouge* to the river, hang their legs over the embankment, and drink. Then they traipse up to the elegant apartment of Guy-Paul's current mistress, an older woman, that is, in her mid-thirties. They all spread out on her big bed and, at some point he barely notices, Guy-Paul and Anne disappear, leaving him on the mattress with the mistress.

Late next morning, he makes his way back along St. Denis toward the walk-up. The *putes* are out again, the day shift. He glances in the window of a patisserie, there's a scrumdelicious strawberry tart. It costs three and a half francs, which doesn't seem very expensive. And it looks great. On the other hand, he isn't really hungry, he just had a fine breakfast *chez* the mistress. He moves on. There, on the other side of the narrow street, leaning against a wall, is a brunette, great leather pants. He doesn't know what she would cost, probably not all that much at this hour, the traffic isn't heavy the way it was last night. Hard to say no. On the other hand, he isn't feeling horny, it was a lovely, largely sleepless night. Ah, so this is the meaning of Paris, all appetites converging. . .

He does his work on a nifty little cream-coloured portable typewriter he bought in Knightsbridge before he came over. It's the image of—well, to be precise, it *is* the very machine Rip Torn swings as he swaggers through Paris as Henry Miller in a new movie version of *Tropic of Cancer*. They updated the setting to the 1960s. It's amazing how *technological* he feels with that little beauty by his side. Think of it now: metal keys slamming into an inky fabric ribbon and onto sheets of paper manually rolled in one at a time. The equivalent of a butter churn or flail, stuff they have in the museum of agriculture in Saskatoon under a little spotlight, to remind school groups how primitive farm life once was. How prehistoric it will seem some day, far sooner than he could have imagined. Technology is always the joker in economic analysis. Each one feels so natty and modern in its time, you have no idea how urgently it's waiting to be replaced.

He's flailing away at the Millerwriter when there's a knock on the door. Someone has scaled the five flights. He opens. "Hi. I'm Rhonda," she says. "I'm a writer too." A few years ago he saw a play at the Roundhouse in London that opened with one character answering a knock at his Paris walk-up to another who says, "Ernest Hemingway? Scott Fitzgerald." Maybe she saw it too. Back in the real world, Rhonda explains, she's a psych prof at the University of Wisconsin; here in Paris, she's a writer. She tells him this as they stand in the doorway, he hasn't even invited her in yet. Now *that's* American: the full life story while you wait for the next bus. By the time the bus arrives, there's nothing left except small talk. She tells him she's working on a "cycle" of poems. She's trying to stretch her resources in order to extend this sabbatical, so she's inscribing the cycle on sheets of toilet paper, one stanza per sheet. It's not as peculiar as it sounds, if you think about French toilet paper in those years: stiff, light brown stuff, and probably better suited for writing. Canadians and Americans used to ship themselves huge cartons of Cottonelle before they came over on hardship assignments like foreign correspondent or junior year abroad. Plus she figures it will be a quirky addition to her collected papers when she donates them to some university archive in exchange for a tax write-off, especially if the damn thing never gets published. "It's money, honey," she says as he stares at the "manuscript" in her string bag, among the onions and Camembert.

"I want sex the way a man wants sex," she tells him inside, as they toke on a joint she produced. She is Guy-Paul's main source of dope, something she assumes Guy-Paul mentioned when he warned Max she'd be dropping by, which he didn't. "Voraciously, like Krushchev." Inhale. She has a thing for the poor, deposed Soviet leader, who went for a summit to the U.S., with sidetrips to Disneyland and the Grand Canyon. As he stared into the canyon, his translator asked what it made him think of and he answered, "Sex. Everything makes me think of sex." He had lots of issues on his plate at the time, Rhonda points out: nuclear war, internal dissension, crop failures in the Ukraine— and he gave due attention to each, but everything made him think of sex. "He was a real peasant," she says. Inhale.

Rhonda doesn't affect him sexually, not from the second he opened the door, but who understands these things—even a recently accredited womanizer. There was a young Parisienne weighing out hamburger behind the counter in the *charcuterie* yesterday: pulling a few strands of hair off her shiny face, checking the scale, mopping her brow, and brushing back more sweaty strands. She likes sex more than anyone else back there among the chops and hocks, he thought. The basis of being sexually attractive, he concluded, in anthropological mode, is liking sex yourself and projecting it. But Rhonda clearly likes sex, she's still talking about it. Back to the theory board.

She sponsors him as her guest at her weekly writers' circle. It meets at the posh American Centre for Art and Culture, doubtlesss one of the CIA conduits currently being denounced in the French press, which are meant to counteract the vile influence on European opinion of Picasso and other commie dupes. (Sartre is viewed by the CIA as a straight-up, *conscious* Moscow agent.) You don't have to be a conspiracy nut; the funding program was revealed in a secretly funded CIA journal. Its editors were shocked. Hard to know what the CIA gets out of this writing circle though, or the "writers" either. Every poem, novel, and play opens, more or less: "Here I am sitting on the bed wondering what to write about next." You Can't Leave Home Again, thinks Max, picturing the lost generation of writers who called Paris home in the thirties; do they now kvetch on the porches of retirement homes in the American Midwest? Rhonda introduces him as another writer; it makes him queasy. He tells them his book is mostly numbers and charts.

It leaves him feeling nostalgic for Canadian culture, such as it is; next day he finds his way to the embassy. He's leafing through the *Globe and Mails* in the waiting room alongside visa appliers and people who lost their traveller's cheques. He meant to go straight to the Report on Business, he really did, but finds himself checking the standings for the Leafs. (It's the early years of the Ballard era and all hope has not yet been extinguished.) "Excuse me," says a Canadian voice. He glances up, ready to explain he's looking for the financials and sometimes they slide inside the sports during the long descent into Orly each morning. "Got a match?" she asks.

She's from the Peace River country, she tells him in a café up the street. She went to school there, then teachers' college in the Okanagan, then taught kindergarten in the Pas, in Manitoba. You roamed the West like the buffalo, he thinks. He feels a certain yearning and loss, though he's never been in any of those places. He can see her as a kindergarten teacher. Miss Brooks, like the radio show he used to listen to, with Mr. Boynton, her heartthrob, and Mr. Conklin, the principal. She left the Pas, she says, because the only men available to date were miners, Mounties, and hockey players. Then and there he wants her, now and forever, at this moment anyway. *So* Canadian. So *home*. She rings the same bell Francie did. What is it with him and Canadians? You really can't leave home again, even if your home was a shithole you couldn't wait to abandon. She's working as an au pair here in Paris. He ought to say, You're pretty old for an au pair—she's in her late twenties—in the same voice Groucho used in *A Day at the Races:* "You're pretty big for a pill yourself." He saw it at a petite cinema in Montmartre. Paris is old movie heaven. Old *Hollywood* movie heaven. He's worked his way through the Marx brothers and Bogart since he arrived.

They have dinner near the river, and kill another *vin ordinaire* on the embankment. Then they wend up St. Denis to the apartment (Guy-Paul is staying at his family compound on the Left Bank). They occupy the little bedroom and she leaves rather than staying the night. Three days later, she knocks on the door while he's hunched over the Millerwriter and tells him she just left her au pair gig because she got a secretarial job working for a Texan who's designing one of the North Sea oil rigs. "I didn't really want to sleep with you the other night," she says. "It was too fast." Now is different. They don't bother with the small bedroom. They lie on his sleeping bag on the cushions in the centre of the airy main room under old *Figaro* front pages that are plastered across the ceiling. Four days later (Guy-Paul has returned and Max curses himself for his homelessness), they head over to Rhonda's place near the Bastille. He knows Rhonda is *à la campagne* this weekend and she once said he was welcome to use it if she was away. He feels around the doorway but there's no key. It's on the third floor—or fourth, however the hell they figure floors—facing an inner courtyard, but the kitchen window looks slightly open so, balancing on the railing, he hops across the open space, manages to cling to a shutter and clamber down, then opens to her from inside. Errol Flynn or what? Afterward they go to a bistro for rabbit and frites. He loves rabbit. He can't believe they eat rabbits here. Nobody minds, nobody winces. As he babbles about underdevelopment being the actual if not conscious *policy* of the West toward the Third World, she mumbles, *"Je t'adore."* It may have been that leap across empty space. No one has ever said it to him in French. She sounds so awkward. You can take the kid out of Peace River but you can't extract Peace River. When Rhonda returns, she is furious that he broke in. "But you said I could stay there when you're away," he argues. *"En principe,"* she says, using one of *la belle langue*'s slipperiest phrases—in theory. Can be she jealous? Rhonda doesn't admit such things. She rarely admits anything. *I'm sorry* doesn't exist in her vocabulary, and *thank you*, only rarely. They don't speak for months.

He maintains his cover story—I'm here to write. He has the Millerwriter to prove it. He taps out something each day. Eventually there will be a monograph; later, a book. But he suspects a hidden motive beneath the plausible veneer.

When he left Olivia to begin her new life in Vancouver, and started back across the Rockies, his poor little car sputtered into silence at the top of a modest rise in Fernie, B.C. Fernie, City with a Future, read the sign on the outskirts. He knew no one here, and even those he didn't know were asleep. He was marooned in the dark, surrounded by mountains, lonely as he had ever feared life could be. He released the emergency, gave a little heave, jumped back in, and coasted to the bottom of the hill. There his guardian angel had placed an all-night gas station. He spent the next hours with his guardian angel, known as Vince—sewn across the pocket of his monkey suit. At midnight, when the car gurgled back to life under "Vince's" calm urging, he realized he would be all right. That was what he needed to know.

He has a fondness for songs with the words "all right" in them, they stick to his mind like burrs. "It's all right now, it's all right now, Never thought I'd make it but I always do somehow . . ." sang Randy Newman. Or Bob Marley: "Don't worry 'bout a thing, 'cause every little thing's gonna be all right. . ." All right in French is *pas mal*. He can convince others (he hopes) that his motives are mature and professional: a thesis (in London), a book (in Paris). A shrink he consulted once, after listening for an hour to his ambivalence about Olivia, said, "So you want to fuck a lot of other women." But lurking farther below, barely suspected even by himself, he needs to know if he'll be all right.

On a rainy day, he goes to the Louvre. You can only put it off so long. He meets Paige, in front of the Mona Lisa. She has the determined chin of a birder and a chest that hangs on her like a shelf. Amazingly, they are alone with Mona. Where's the milling crowd at any hour he's been warned of, the one you need a periscope to see over, like the mobs at Queen Elizabeth's coronation when he was in grade five. (As he walked into class, Miss Scott was writing the words to "God Save the Queen" on the board. They still rhymed! "Send *her* victorious, happy and glorious. . ." It was his first inkling that history can happen in your own lifetime.)

They pick each other up. Paige is from Montana so they have something in common: the North American landmass. It's raining outside, so instead of wandering or sitting in a café, they go to an afternoon flick at the theatre in Montmartre: it's *Royal Wedding* with Astaire and Jane Powell, not Ginger Rogers, but still from Fred's golden, i.e., black and white, period. Not his finest, people say, but no matter, since it's the first Astaire for each of them; and the first sample from any brilliant *oeuvre*—like your first truffle—will always knock you out because it reveals a potential you never suspected might exist. They dance out the door, across le Marais and up Rue de la Bastille to Guy-Paul's. He tries to discuss the movie but she says she couldn't concentrate very well, once they began playing with each other in the dark. He doesn't get lost like that. He stays split between the ecstasy of touching and being touched back on the one hand, while firmly holding onto the other experience, the manifest one in sociologese—which would be *Royal Wedding*—as if he wants to have an alibi ready in case a sex cop (*Aha, I thought that's what you were doing!*) storms in and charges him with falsely being at a movie.

They're all over Guy-Paul's mattress on the floor of the little bedroom when he becomes aware of a thunderous pounding, like a military barrage just before the infantry advance. It's the front door! He flipped the deadbolt when they entered, not considering that Guy-Paul himself rather than Rhonda the writer or some messenger with a *pneumatique* might show up, here at his own apartment in the middle of a weekday. The pounding is insistent and finally overcomes their absorption. He grumpily rises to admit Guy-Paul, who is with Ann-ne. He introduces everybody (Paige is exquisitely *deshabillée*), and they all go for a kir, the Parisian working man's drink that hasn't yet crossed the Atlantic to the wine bars of Toronto and New York. He doesn't know if Guy-Paul will expel him from the walk-up forever and forget their friendship too. That night he lies alone on the cushions in the middle of the big room, looking up at headlines on the birth of NATO, and hearing the sexual sounds of Guy-Paul and Anne, from the little bedroom. Next day, after Anne has left, Guy-Paul thanks him extravagantly. It's the best sex they ever had, he says, and the only, since their first months together as students years ago. "Why thank *me?*" asks Max. "It was the atmosphere when we came in," says Guy-Paul. "The room was drenched with sex, neither of us could stop feeling it, and it was still hanging there ready to drip on us when we got into bed last night. Thank Paige too," he says, "if you ever see her again."

When Noel hears his old buddy is in Paris, he's over there like the Concorde. He never cared much for London, though he visited dutifully a few times during the Marriage. But he's now become a gourmand, as well as a *connoisseur du vin*—twin titles he wears like boxing crowns from different divisions. Max is touched, thinking back to the kid who lived in the fifties equivalent of a monster house and whose spending habits even as a child were the embodiment of conspicuous consumption. He's managed to retain some of that lack of couth, even in his new worldliness. "This is the third-most expensive Chablis in the world," he announces to Max and Guy-Paul, pointing to a label at a little *boîte* near Châtelet that he's taken them to; he copied the address from the in-flight magazine.

Guy-Paul, a non-practising Trotskyite, may be unimpressed but Max is willing to hand it to his lifelong pal. The trick about living a life isn't where you arrive, but where you came from to get there. In Noel's case, Max knows the point of origin. Noel has moved from a Corvette a year, to some of the cruder fine points of food and wine. Don't knock it. And his journey clearly isn't over. He says he has helped fund a little voluntary agency back home that works with street kids, and been drawn into broader questions of social justice and economic equity. "You start donating a few spare bucks and you end up wondering if you shouldn't just go down to city hall and blow everything up," Noel says over a post-meal Armagnac. Maybe he's met some De Leonists along his way. Even the stuff about high-end Chablis doesn't seem offensive; by the time they finish, they couldn't distinguish a *nouveau* Beaujolais, to which they move, from Newfie screech. Dollar value is a reasonable basis for judgment.

"Why don't you give me some of your money?" Max asks Noel, saying something he's often thought. It must be the money the wine cost that's talking. "Why should I?" says Noel. "Because I need it and I don't have it and you have it and you don't need it," Max says, wondering if he's just made a breakthrough in economic theory, or then again, maybe not. He'll know better in the morning. "If you give me a bunch, I can stay here and finish my book, instead of going back to London and hunting for fellowships." Noel is scornful. They chase the topic around during more aperitifs, and suddenly Max finds himself in a rage. This happens in his life, usually with women or service people, but Noel can stand in. You know he's losing it because "fuckin" becomes every third word in his discourse. It's a sixties thing; a way for bourgeois types to show they're grittier than they seem. Noel does it back. Guy-Paul steps in to settle the argument. "What your childhood friend argues is logically impeccable," he tells Noel, like the Cambridge fixture he once was. Then he turns to Max. "And you are totally nuts. Because the world is not logical." Max can work with this. "*Ah-zo,*" he says, conjuring Sorstad, "but should not the rational become real?" To which, Guy-Paul says, "Should has nothing to do with it. It isn't going to happen." Noel leans back and marvels to be here in Paris with one old and one new friend. Later, Guy-Paul insists on stopping in a working class bar for a kir in solidarity with the proletariat. The barman is telling some Moroccans he won't serve them. When they finally head for home, Max peels off; he's going to drop in on Guy-Paul's former mistress, Madame as they call her, like a character from *The Three Musketeers.*

He returns in the early morn, tiptoeing in so as not to wake Noel, who is up and reading the headlines on the ceiling, since his sense of time is still over the Atlantic. "I'm worried about you, old son," he says, forgetting they're in France now, not England. "You seem to be overdoing the sexual action." When Noel got in from the airport yesterday morning, Max introduced him to Paige on her way out. Then, when Noel returned from a stroll in the afternoon, the belle of Peace River was leaving. Noel has never shown a strong sense of moderation in this area himself, but he pulls unexpectedly into the conservative lane. "It's like fine wine," he says. "You can't simply pile them up indiscriminately. You have to stop and savour." Max thinks of last night's procession of vintages, rear-ending one another like cars in a fog, like Godard's famous traffic jam in *Weekend*. But the contradictions of Noel's life have never made good conversation; there are just too many. Noel has trouble keeping track himself. He's just switched shrinks, from a behaviourist—"He had only one trick: the double bind, so it had to explain everything you did"—to a neo-Freudian—"There's really no other kind, post-war"—and ordered a complete set of the Old Man's works, clothbound, from the Folio Club, the literary equivalent of a wine importer. He plans to work his way through them, one day.

"Your idea of how to deal with a problem," says Max, "is buy a book and let it sit." Noel concedes. On the other hand, who needs to read Freud, if you've lived through the collected repressions and avoidance of a guy like Max since you were both kids? All you need is a few concepts like repression and avoidance along with one he recently acquired—*acting out*. "Bottom line," concludes Noel, using a term which will become the battle cry of his generation a few decades hence, though here it's meant to touch an economist's troubled heart, "you'll never get your book done if you keep banging your guts out."

Here Max knows Noel is dead wrong, even if Noel is the guy who kindly, generously, introduced him years ago, against his will, to essential notions like boners and breasts. Because you can *always* find time for sex. Max has been doing it since the Marriage ended. Noel thinks today was a rarity. He fears Max is working his way to physical collapse and mental breakdown; maybe moral catastrophe too: for certain the sad end to a promising career in economics. Perhaps he thinks of this as an "intervention," and tried to enlist Guy-Paul on their walk home last night, the other friend of Max's he's met here, not counting the daisy chain of sexual partners who spin through the door. He seems not to know how sex can *energize* every compartment of your soul, especially if you've spent a lifetime till now pushing it under. There's no lack of energy, only scheduling problems. It's logistics that rules in this realm, not cost-benefit, because there's no cost and it's all benefit. The sole time you lose is the hours you'd have sat in front of the keyboard or over a book pondering Keynes's refutation of Malthus or Boehm-Bawerk on the close of Marx's system, while stuffing your errant thoughts about sex back into drawers they keep exploding from. You can work ten times as efficiently, who knows how, you just do, because it's sex and it's worth it so you make it work. You want something done, find a busy person. You want something written, call a sex maniac.

Francie follows Noel. Max doesn't mind breaking from his complex schedule; she's just over from London for a week and Paris will still be full of possibility when she's gone. He's not compulsive, eh? Just, maybe, a touch driven. Healthy driven. He'll resume the varied agenda when she leaves. Who knows, maybe that's why he moved here from London. The two of them were getting a little thick, like that note she left about him always winning. What if she occasionally won a round, would it have started to bother him?

She still has the tassel of blonde, it still moves him in a deep place. She adores the walk-up. Good. He was worried she might think it was carrying the anti-establishment thing too far. They hang out with Guy-Paul and Anne, they walk, and walkand-walkandwalk. Encouraged by her delight in the pad, he acquires an old Deux Chevaux from Guy-Paul's sister, Hélène. Takes it off her hands for almost nothing. Some problem about needing to clear more parking space at the family compound, where Hélène and the many sibs hang out, each with their own *appartement*. That's why Guy-Paul can glory in the walk-up: there's always a private and very bourgeois pad at the family homestead he can revert to. Several times a year their dad, the ambassador, comes home for a consultation at the Quai d'Orsay and Guy-Paul pays fealty. Last time he took Max along, who met Hélène, took her out to dinner next day, and wound up on the couch in her place rather than weave his way back to the *République*. After he'd found repeated excuses to wander past her bedroom or into it, she wearily said, "Oh, climb in here with me." (Everyone in the family speaks perfect English. As he joined her in bed, he said, "You speak better English than me." "Than I," she corrected.)

For Francie's last few days, they take a little hotel room on the *rive gauche*, then he drives her to the boat train in Le Havre. They dawdle in a town on the Normandy coast. It's late and all the hotels are booked, but they meet a local high school teacher in the *supermarché* who invites them to his place, they have a meal with him and his wife, also a teacher—the pair are tickled to have exotic foreigners as their guests—and bed down in the guest room. In the middle of the night, groggy with *vin ordinaire* and feeling Milleresque, he staggers to the toilette, takes a wrong turn coming out, and tries to wiggle into bed between their hosts, thinking it's Francie and wondering how she's spread out so extensively. "*Mais qu'est-ce que vous faîtes ici?*" yelps the wife. He returns to Francie and falls asleep.

At the boat train, she's nattering, they both are, and she mentions Curzio, who she chanced into by absolute utter accident on the tube in London. You know Curzio—her absolute heartthrob of an Italian businessman from when she spent that winter in Firenze, and who begged her to stay but whom she's totally lost contact with and then there he was on the same train in the same car, wouldn't you know, playing as always the role of the tempter. As she steps onto the gangplank, Max says, utterly surprising himself, "I love you." You could knock him over with a feather. These are words he has assiduously not spoken since the Marriage. He feels a band ought to strike up, a tinny one, from an English music hall, just offstage—*Tararara boomdeeyay, Tararara boomdeeyay*—or the one that blared out of the wings on the old Groucho Marx TV show when you said the magic word and a stuffed bird dropped down on a string with a little scrawled word in its beak. "Scram, boid," Groucho would say as he handed fifty bucks to the contestants.

Then, without knowing why, he's back in London. He's low on money, it could be that. And it turned out he could get the flat again, his and Olivia's. Before he left for Paris, he walked into the pub up the street and more or less whispered it was available. Takers rose from every stool, like a Gilbert and Sullivan chorus, any of them would have moved in before closing time. Out of professional solidarity, he gave it to Ozzie the Aussie from the OECD and Ozzie's new Irish wife. Right after Francie's visit, Max called Ozzie, a systems analyst, and asked in a dreamy way if there was any chance he could get his flat back—as a Canadian native tribe might open negotiations with a local government by asking for the return of Vancouver or Quebec: an opening ploy that would end with some hunting and fishing rights plus a lump sum in return for abandoning all other claims. Those London flats move glacially, the way people in Canada put their tickets to the Leafs or Canadiens in their *wills* so the heirs won't have to fight for them in court. He'd only *left* it five months ago. But Ozzie said he'd just fallen passionately for an OECD econometrist in Vienna and was taking a post there—a demotion in career terms, therefore proof of true love, what other evidence does a scientist need?

Max asserted a claim to repossess and refused to dicker over anything except timing. Then he called Francie, said he was returning, and asked her to move in with him. When she did, he knew it was a mistake, though not as fast as he knew at the wedding.

This time it takes a week. Maybe that's progress—a concept almost always more trouble than it's been worth historically. He just knows he isn't ready. Not after the dark years of his sexual silence. They were nobody's fault, but they *happened*. The women of the world are out there, like Sidney the solicitor. He met her waiting for a job interview. (Sids and Sidneys come and go in his life at this time.) He tried his various turns on her— the self-deprecating stuff about Canada, the passionate but realistic commitment to social betterment through intelligent economic planning, the intense interest in her biography. She replied absently. She strolled across the room to check a notice on the board. It wasn't the challenge that moved him, it was her indifference. It would be his shield. How much can someone hurt you who barely acknowledges you? She might reject and ignore you, then it's over! It's not pleasant, you're bloodied. But it's nothing compared to the damage Francie's casual remark about running into Curzio did. In his *mind*. Had the encounter been accidental, as she claimed? In that case, was fate working against him?—for surely once she has gone to someone else, he will miss her unbearably. Not having her is one thing; someone else having her is sheer damnation: the absence of her passion and respect (and the tassel of blonde) will tear him to bits. Better if she vanished altogether, not that he wishes it. But if news of a fatal accident had come to him in Paris—that she'd, say, fallen in front of a train that day on the tube just before she saw Curzio, or even, God forbid, been pushed off the platform—well, he'd feel sad, he'd mourn, he'd bathe in regret and probably guilt. If, however, she met a former lover by chance in the same context and ended up returning to his bed, a momentous torture would begin and who knows if it would end. The night Rhonda took Max to her writers' circle, she read what she called a "hurtin' pome"; it was in country-and-western mode. The title was: "Cuz It's Three Parts Missin' You and One Part Pride." He told her afterward that she had the proportions exactly wrong.

And what if Francie was faking? How likely are you to run into someone you know on the London tube: all those lines, multicolours on the ingenious maps, multiplied by the number of stations per line, and trains and cars per train. He knew probabilities and stats; he'd made himself an expert in order to give his arguments a sheen of credibility in the debates over social and moral priorities in economic planning, as if it wasn't all really about justice—which it was—but about quantifiable *facts*. He knew how unlikely it was to run into anyone you know on the subways of London or New York, as opposed to Toronto or Montreal. That's why people feel a licence to wig out, which they wouldn't in the streets or transit systems of their hometown. They sit confidently on the train, babbling or drooling or wearing three hats, one on top of the other. Did she invent the part about it being an accident and actually call Curzio, go to him, give herself as only she could so achingly? The thought broke him down. He'd be almost asleep, and think it. He was suddenly totally awake. He'd turn on the light, read, turn it off, think it again. Or maybe it wasn't too late. Had she called and seen Curzio but not yet slept with him? He didn't exactly want her himself, except maybe once in a while; that is, when he wanted her. But he knew with certainty that he didn't want anyone else having her. Like all of us, in other words, he had his problems learning to bear the beams of love. And like most of us, he thought of these spasms as his alone. Asking her to move in was an effort to staunch the flow her passing comment opened, or forestall another cut. Nevertheless, or maybe therefore, once she's in, she has to go. He tells her. Yes, it's too bad she just moved in. The fights begin.

They have a scripted feel, despite the unquestionably spontaneous, thermonuclear quality of each battle. This must be what actors experience when they're doing a lacerating scene, like the brawls in *Who's Afraid of Virginia Woolf*, for the hundredth time. Very powerful, yet he feels detached. As if there's a third party in the room while they squabble and howl, toss things, and sometimes swat or scratch (he swats, she scratches). But now the third party isn't a hired birthday clown, he's a bandleader. He stands to the side or out in the hall, head cocked to catch the unit of dialogue they're heading into—there's always an element of improvisation in the performance, so he can't just put his head down and keep his eyes on the script. His baton poised to lead the band into a number as soon as he catches the cue. The swelling "No Other Love Have I" from Richard Rodgers' score to *Victory at Sea*. Cutting through the crap with, "Is That All There Is?" Or "Strike Up the Band," acidly commenting on his own absurdist place in the farce.

Sometimes they feel they can't continue; the bandleader himself falters. Then they coach and prompt each other, for they have no one else:

"I can't. I can't go on. No more—"

"Yes, you can! Do it!"

"All right. I'll try. Gimme my line, dammit!"

MUSIC UP AND UNDER.

Followed by a plot twist: great sex in the middle of hate and fury, for instance, better than ever, even for them.

He's stirred awake by the muffled rap of the knocker. *Good thing I woke up or I might not have heard it.* She's been gone now, minus some odds and ends she left here, for a month. He's resumed the life he'd have had if he never made the mistake of asking her to move in. He wrestles a shirt over his shoulders and goes to the door. He hates undoing the buttons, it's a waste of time, like matching your socks. He wonders if it's the social worker with henna in her hair who moved onto the third floor this month. That redness is intriguing, it's still not the commonplace it will become. Yesterday she asked him for information about buses, papers, local pubs. Maybe she's dropping by to see—

It's Francie. He hesitates behind the chain, then slides the door in and releases it. *She's a person, she's a human being, a decent guy would let her in.* She forgot her stupid map. It was on the wall over her desk in their, now his again, bedroom. "It isn't here," he says. "You took it, along with the desk." She says, "Well I don't have it." He steps into the kitchen, puts a pot of water for coffee on the burner, and reaches for the instant. Ah, England. They just don't get it about coffee. She's rummaging in the bedroom, as if he's hidden someone there who he brought back from the pub last night. She sounds frustrated. Maybe he flushed her down the toilet, the popsie from the pub. Now she's by his side, watching the pot too. "We have to talk," she says. "All I want is a talk." She needs to understand why he did it, that's all. ("Explain to me again why we're doing this," said Olivia at the end.) Moved her in, moved her out, so fast. She gave up the nice room she had in the flat with the little old ladies who work at the library, they treated her like their granddaughter. He owes it to her, she says, so she can understand and move on. That's all. "Once I understand, it will be fine and it will be over."

Except it won't. He's certain. He's suddenly yelling about state terrorism in military dictatorships like Chile and Argentina. He read an article in the *New Statesman*, the one on the stands now. Or maybe it was in *Time Out*, an advance story on a coming lecture by a released political prisoner from Latin America. He always feels better when he has a theory to correlate with his panics. The torturer doesn't actually *want* answers to his questions, said the article. If he got answers, he'd have to stop torturing. The point is to achieve total control through unending terror. An interrogation is merely the pretext for the terror. Now how else can you reasonably characterize—I ask you, he thinks, addressing the jury—this insistence on an explanation for what he did? He grants he did it. He concedes it was unjust, hideous, whatever. Why do women always want a *reason*? Why is this woman so much like a man? (Cue the band.)

Aren't women supposed to be intuitive as opposed to rational? Why do they ask for reasons when none are available. Don't they know all the causes of the Depression have never yet explained the Depression—something he and Galbraith both realized after intense study of the 1930s? On the other hand, what if he gave her the one answer that might end the torture session?

I still want the Sidneys.

Then, she'll rightly say, *why did you ask me to move in? It was* your *idea.*

If he tells the truth, the way you're supposed to according to Gestalt therapy, Marxism-Leninism, and a lot of rock 'n' roll; if he says, I couldn't stand the thought of you with someone else, she'll feel crappy and he'll feel crappy. She'll say, *How could you?* and the torture will continue. Unless he says, *I was weak, I was foolish.* But he doesn't think of saying that. She crowds closer. This kitchen feels like the galley on a sub. Both of them hover over the reluctant pot. *Boil, damn you! Let's move on.*

In actual fact, as the English like to say, it wouldn't be impossible to tell the awful truth. But it would be hard to find a way to put it which would neither demean nor provoke her. It would be a matter, that is, of being truthful *and* artful. It would be harder to formulate than most of what he's ever written, or will go on to write, including his efforts to justify continued governmental activism and spending in the midst of the manic Reagan-Thatcher-Mulroney-Clinton-Blair-Chrétien tax-cutting years. At least he had decades to try and put the words together to make that case, and even so, never quite succeeded; here he'd have to finish in the time it takes water to boil. The thought of the effort wearies him, and besides, who knows if the right words really exist, if they'd materialize at the end of the exhausting labour required, if the inputs would be justified by the outputs. It's the kind of cost-benefit analysis he abhors in normal economic discussions but here he is doing it. Still, if he had had faith—

Well, he says instead, sounding weirdly professorial to himself, he doesn't know the reason, he thought he did but he guesses he doesn't and it doesn't matter because what he really wants is her out and that's his right. *That's all I have to say. It's all you get.* It's a bad choice, he should have gone the long, hard, creative route. As he speaks there's no relief in it, for either of them.

At this moment the pot decides to boil. She lifts it from the burner and pours it down his bare front. It hits about waist level and proceeds by the law of gravity down the available indentations, as if he's a relief map. It's stripping his flesh as it courses along, you'd assume. Something gratified spreads across her face. It doesn't seem very connected to *her.* He places one of his palms under each of her lovely elbows ("The elbow is the seat of the passions," the nuns told her before her junior prom. She recalled it for him in Tiny's, the first night he yelled with joy.) and lifts. He balances her slender frame and transports her, like a Giacometti, through the living room, the foyer, the door still open, into the hall, lets her down like a forklift, closes and locks the door, thinking all the while: *I will not lash out again.* Then, safe behind the door, he howls.

By the time he opens the door, clothed, each minute up-and-down of fabric on skin like a touch of the dentist's drill, and lurches into the hall, then onto the street, she's gone. Maybe she's watching from hiding, for a bit more pleasure. He hails a cab; London cabs will cross turbulent seas of traffic to pick you up. He asks for the Westminster hospital and the driver says St. Thomas's is closer. He wails all the way like a siren. Like *he's* the ambulance.

The doctor in emergency who applies the medication and bandages wants him to know this is the equivalent of pulling the trigger. "Anyone who can do this," says the doc, putting her hands on Max's shoulders and squaring the two of them up, "would pull the trigger if she had it in her hand instead of a pot handle." Welcome to the world of womanizing. Maybe, like a luckless investor, he got in at the wrong time.

"You're a bartender," he says to Dougie after the burns have healed enough to let him go out briefly. "I guess you hear stories like this a lot." Dougie shakes his head: *Not really.* "Please," says Max. "Well," says Dougie, who prefers to be called a publican but doesn't have high expectations of his lone Canadian patron, "there was this chickie, Sharon Tate. Got involved with a bloke named Charlie Manson." Then he adds that Francie was in the other night, complaining about how she's been treated. On and on, she did, till Dougie finally asked why she didn't just hire a contract killer to put things right. "Can't cost more than two hundred quid," he said, meaning to lighten things up. "One fifty," she replied. She had checked it out.

Calling the stepmother in Leaside is a bad idea. It takes forever, he does it from the pay phone in the pub, Dougie keeping an eye on the door lest she enter with another bubbling pot, or a gun this time. He barely says, "I'm worried about Francie," when the stepmother is answering through the Atlantic crackle, "We've heard about you. We know what kind of person you are—" What does she mean—a womanizer? The way Harriet the geographer said, during a break in their seminar, "You are such a male chauvinist." He didn't know what the phrase meant, it was the first

time he heard it, yet he sensed a new and destabilizing weapon had
been added to the arsenal of gender war. The battlefield would
never look the same. Or does she mean: You're a dangerous,
bomb-throwing anarchist radical. Or a left-leaning, do-gooder
academic, who doubtless uses drugs. Whatever she means, he's
heard that voice before.

Even when he can sleep through a night again, he's still fearful.
He wakes, gets up, looks around, into the closets, opens the door
to the hall, then sneaks back to his own bed. When he's outside,
he thinks he sees her often, as he thought he saw Alice his cat
everywhere he went in those years. He catches a glimpse, then
she's gone. Of course she still lives in the area, but when they
cross paths head-on, she looks down and strides by, except for
the time she's with a tall, natty black guy, who appears to
absorb her completely. He takes to whirling around, like a secret
agent in a spy movie, and that's when he thinks he sees her—
but she was there and then gone. Or was she? Once he catches
sight of her walking ahead of him, he thinks. Tailing from in
front, like a real pro, the way Quiller does in the Cold War novels
he reads in those years. A Quiller thriller.

In fact, it was only on the Battersea side of the bridge that he
thought he saw Alice everywhere, and in a way it was true. She
did look like every cat in the neighbourhood because they were
all, with the odd exception, related. So he'd be coming home
from a movie or about to check in at the pub to see who'd been
there that night, and she'd cross the sidewalk in front of him.
Not just the same grey-and-white patterning but the same . . .
demeanour. Cocking the head and so forth. So he'd follow her.
For blocks. Calling her name, as if that ever got a response. She's

a *cat*. Besides, he knew it couldn't be her. She hadn't been out-side his place, his and Olivia's, then, briefly, his and Francie's, ever, except for shots at the vet's and the pathetic time he tried to take her for a walk in the park on a leash. If she'd ever made it to the street, she'd have freaked, probably got run over by a big old London bus as it revved for the run up onto the bridge, smushed like Sylvester in the Tweetie cartoons. But he'd follow anyway, just in case it really was her and she'd gotten out, till she lost him in an alley or up a fire escape. Then he'd go home and there she'd be, preening as usual, having beaten him back.

That particular night, he puts his key in the lock and finds it's open. Does anyone not know the feeling? Somebody's been there while you were out. The way you feel these days when you step through the door and the alarm doesn't go off. If you live alone, that is. If you don't live alone and nothing sounds, you just think, Oh, somebody got home before me.

She's been meticulous, and at first he can't tell what was done or taken. The phone line is cut at either end: by the wall and near the phone. His axe, memento of camping trips in Ontario's Near North and ongoing proof to himself that he belongs in a place very different from this, is on the cot in the hall, instead of under it. The TV set, the clunky old Grenada he salvaged off the street: she hasn't smashed the screen, just the cone of the tube in back, the source it shoots—shot—electrons from. And broke only those records he delighted excessively in: Ray Bolger singing "Once in Love with Amy"; Pete Seeger's "We Shall Overcome" concert at Carnegie Hall; Winston Churchill's greatest cuts. The rest are intact. His pants, all of them, slashed across the crotch. And his "journal." Little efforts at popular essays in economic iconoclasm, in imitative tribute to Galbraith or Keynes; plus dia-logues, autobiographical fragments, and retellings of dreams, timid hints to himself that maybe he could go a different path, not just be an academic plodder or a policy wonk. No Alice. But Alice might be hiding, she's always hiding, she's a wuss. Even when he can't find her after a thorough search, he persuades himself she's just found a great new haven. He goes into the hall and Mrs. Oates, dusting off her mat as she constantly does, says, "Oh yes, yes, she was here." Did she have anything with her when she left? "Just a shopping bag," says Mrs. Oates. "It looked heavy."

He goes over to the flat she took a room in after she moved out, up near Albert Bridge. He helped her move, back when they still talked about staying friends through this, and who knows, even getting back together, or moving the relationship to another level. The flat belongs to a guy who works in a group home modelled on the Tavistock Institute—the creativity of insanity and so forth—and the guy's girlfriend. The guy opens the door. "Look man," Max says, in the tribal greeting of the era, "you're into self-awareness, aren't you? She took my *journals.*" He makes it plural, hoping it will sound more injurious. He doesn't mention Alice. Then Francie comes in from the kitchen or somewhere. She stops across the room. The guy just stands there, not intervening, respectful of the situation and the feelings involved or whatever. Tavistock crap. "Francie," Max says, "You killed Alice." He doesn't bother to mention the stupid journal. The Tavistock guy stands there, non-judgmental. Her head shakes slowly like a pendulum, her eyes very wide, even for her. Her arms hang at her sides. They look like pipe cleaners. "I don't know what you're talking about," she says. As she speaks, her pupils move up and down like elevators. Someone is nodding yes and saying no at the same time. As if she's saying: I'm split in two.

He walks up Albert Bridge Road to Prince of Wales Drive. For once, he doesn't see any cats. She can't survive, he thinks. She's

never even been out of the flat. When he gets back to Chelsea
Bridge Road, he keeps walking onto the bridge. Maybe Francie
dropped her over the side into the river, or maybe she let her loose
earlier, and Alice fell down into the park where he likes to watch
the kids in their school uniforms play cricket and try to figure
out the rules of their ridiculous game. For Alice, the park would
be as bad as the river. It would be like setting her loose in the
Congo, an Elsa fate for a city kitty. Her little heart would palpi-
tate in the face of nature raw in tooth and claw and she'd die of
feline cardiac arrest before any of the wild park beasts—the
squirrels, the sparrows—had a chance to attack her. Just before
he turns off the bridge approach to descend into the park, he
crosses to the opposite corner. There is little traffic at that hour.
A garbage can stands sedately, almost full, the open basket kind.
*No, your Honour, I can't say why I chose to cross and look in it at
just that point in time.* It is ten-thirty and the trucks don't come
to empty them till about eleven. He looks down into the trash
and sees the Marks and Spencer shopping bag, and inside it a
grey-and-white furry little . . . torso, inert. Shit. Shit. There's no
recovery from this—not for her, not for him, not for anyone
with feelings. *Mrow,* says the little bundle. She's waited, he has
no idea how many hours. For him, or just too terrified to move.
He takes her home in the Marks and Spencer bag, nodding to
Mrs. Oates, dusting her mat, as he goes back in.

He finds his recently purchased Deux Chevaux where he's taken
to parking it on the street. It's dead (dead too, I almost said), its
battery cables cut at either end, just like the phone in the apartment, and the battery gone, leaving a boxy void. He takes the
plates off and just leaves it there. By the time Interpol trace him,
he figures, despite its global resources, he'll have established a

new identity somewhere obscure like Canada. This is the end of European exile for him and swinging London and the sixties. He packs and they head for Gatwick, he and Alice, where the tacky charters take off. Hang around the check-in and see if he can talk them onto one; he's feeling damn lucky right now, Alice is alive, so is he, and they have a home to go to. Well, homeland anyway. He buys a ticket on Transpo 2000, they actually seem happy to sell it to him. Maybe this is their first flight ever and they're thrilled that anybody wants to give their operation a shot. He lugs Alice to the freight desk, asks about tales he's heard of cats emerging, depressurized, scarified and frozen stiff, at the end of a flight, so couldn't he just treat her as carry-on, I mean it's obvious they're just setting up the airline, so they probably haven't established policy on such matters in rigid form yet. Bad choice of words. They say he wouldn't get her through security, and anyway, those things almost never happen. The almost isn't reassuring, he's starting to feel like he's drawn down most of the luck he has in his account. At security, tearful partings are underway. Couples hug till they practically meld. He is struck by the same-species quality of the attachments. He walks through and out on the tarmac. Travellers still embark and deplane in the open air. As they take the last step up before disappearing into the cabin, they look back toward the friends, colleagues, lovers, waving from the big plate-glass windows in the terminal. He looks futilely into those groupings, like graduation photos, then swings his gaze down till it falls on the baggage conveyor, rising into the belly of the plane nearby. A little black cardboard case with breathing holes and a handle jiggles up it and enters the aircraft at exactly the moment he does. He is not alone.

Transpo's flights leave at midnight and get to Canada a few hours later, reversing the normal pattern for transatlantic traffic. It's the secret of their low fares: too late for supper, too early for breakfast. They fly in darkness all the way, which means a full night's sleep, no wake-up at dawn two hours after you nod off, faced with breakfast. When you deplane in the middle of the night, it's your problem. No movie either. It's a charter.

He has a window seat, worse luck. He likes the aisle, to stretch his legs into and, who knows, make eye contact with a stewardess as she passes. But hell, he's lucky to be on this crammed flight at all. He's a fugitive. He just made it, like the Jews who got on the last train out of Nazi Germany, the proverbial one. He's left everything behind (not much, the car aside). But it felt dicey. He didn't relax till the last passenger boarded and he heard the cabin door thunk shut. He's pretty sure Francie didn't follow him on. He scrutinizes his fellow refugees, whoops, passengers, to see if any are her in disguise. It's paranoia but it's all he has. As the cabin lights dim, he leans his seat back and tries to jam his foot against the window. Oooh—cold. The foot slips and jostles the passenger in the seat ahead. She turns and squints back through the crack between her seat and the window. Hmm. Did he notice her as he sat down but pretend not to, since he is of course traumatized and preoccupied by the hideous and tragic events which suddenly terminated his stay here: the *attentat* on Alice, Francie's tragic descent into madness? He's a man in mourning, his sensibilities a shambles, he's not some sex-obsessed perv always alert for the next opportunity; he just went through a savage passage and is trying to recover in preparation for the rest of a monkish life. "Cramped," he mutters dozily, in the tone of someone making a witty crack. Sometimes you get credit for a joke just by sounding like you intended one.

As the flight hurtles on, keeping pace with the dark—the
Treadmill of Night, he thinks in the giddy state of the one who
got away—his toe, encased in sock, edges tortuously around,
searching mutely, on its own as it were, for some touch of her
in the seat ahead. This requires contortion. He must twist in the
seat, as if seeking a less uncomfortable position, while angling
the toe this way and that, to snake it through the opening and
toward her shoulder or the back of her head. Ah, the backs of
women's heads. There's method in his klutziness. He needs to be
able—should she whirl suddenly, snarling—to look up groggily
as if he had no idea where that toe got to while he himself, the
person proper, was on a toeless quest for some z's. Being who he
is—Guiltman of the late twentieth century—he'd like to make
this claim with plausibility even to himself. He's got the headset
on—Transpo provides minimal entertainment—he's listening to
Lonnie Donergan skiffle with "It Takes a Worried Man"; it's per-
meating his own worried spirit and starting to lift him in spite
of the horrid chain of events which brought him here, "transpo"
him to a happier level, he'll have to pick the album up when he's
back on dry land and see if it has the same effect on the ground
(it won't) when all of a sudden—contact! Uh-oh, too firm? He
freezes, he moans almost inaudibly as the toe backs off. She makes
a little turn toward the aisle—it seems, from where his head is
scrunched against the doily thingy on the back of his seat.
Marvellously, her head remains about the same distance from
his toe. The toe edges over again, a millimetre at a time. Finally
it is there, *he* is there—eyes shut tight. He, it—it, he—presses
on. Contact again. Stays motionless a decent interval. But hold on,
is it contact with her, or with his own sock? He's had these
moments of ecstasy in the past, against the arm of a stranger
beside him in a movie, or under a table, only to find it was his

skin having a tingling encounter with his own clothes, or a table leg. Astounding how sensuous inanimate objects can be, when you're picturing them as a her. Pushing harder is risky, but he gots ta know. She shifts and, hallelujah, her shoulder does not withdraw. This seems to exclude the toe-against-sock hypothesis. Now is the moment of truth—and peril. He knows he shouldn't persist but how can he not? As they continue to roll homeward (sings Lonnie), and the moonlit night rolling with them, toe and the shoulder, then head itself, fall into further, happy, wordless contact. He can't believe it. He's exhilarated. Surely he's deluding himself: it's the seat, it's the miniature pillow, it's a rolled-up inflight mag—anything but her!

As always, a single moment of touch opens into the bottomless well. Plummet with it, why do anything else? Breathe it in with each stagy, sleepy-sounding inhale. He experiences it as affirmation in stages. One: she doesn't reject me. Two: maybe she likes me. Three: she wants me! He's won this bet already, the final result isn't significant. If she were to turn right now and say sleepily, "Sorry, but I'll have to back away at this point," he'd grin like a fool and sleep the rest of the ride like a baby.

When the plane stops in Montreal, the seats beside both of them clear. They've disengaged surfaces. The captain turns the lights on while passengers get off and cruelly—no romantic this pilot—leaves them on the rest of the way to Toronto. Maybe Transpo doesn't have its routines airtight; maybe someone reported the overactive toe in row thirty-seven, window seat. He gets up to go to the toilet. She's sleeping soundly against the window. When he returns, she's reading a magazine. She glances up and meets his gaze as if by accident. He asks if she's found anything good in there. She waves an article about hang-gliding at him. Big new thing. They talk, him in the aisle, till takeoff is announced. No one has got on to take the seat beside her. No one has got on at all, it's three A.M. Locals flying from Montreal to Toronto have slothfully scheduled their trips for the daylight hours. He asks if she wants to spread out in the empty seat or could she stand a little company. Have a seat, she smiles. His heart soars.

They spread the blanket she's been using across both their laps and pretend to sleep. Maybe she really does, he doesn't. Their fingers touch, squeeze—could be just friendly—and relax in each other's palms, still under the blanket. She continues "sleeping," all the way to Toronto. The holding hands find their way into her lap and, still interlaced, start to stroke and pressure her crotch. She shifts, into the pressure. By the time the Thousand Islands are "beneath us, to the left, though you can't see them in the dark," she's squirming. By Oshawa, she's tensed. She breathes in with the intensity of one of the jet engines outside and comes. He couldn't be happier. For her, himself, the endless potential of feeling. He looks around, he'd like to spread the benevolence. A lumpy man across the aisle is scowling, or just sleepless. It's easy to take people as antagonistic but they aren't necessarily. He wipes the supersatisfied expression from his face (he thinks) and runs his eyes across the overhead compartments as if it's his job.

She's going to Guelph, she says, in the cavernous, deserted terminal. Does he know where that is? She's supposed to take a bus or train. He says there's probably a fair gap before the next of either and then they'll be frequent. Meanwhile they could go and relax, get some sleep, ahem, some more sleep that is, in Toronto. They collect Alice and their bags, shake a taxi driver awake, and give him Noel's address. Noel owns a house now, it's in a part of downtown called the Annex. Noel says he's calculated that it's at the exact geographic centre of the city. Max has no key when they arrive and doesn't want to knock. It's five A.M. (A glimmer of light at long last, he'd started to feel like the first humans who ever saw the sun go down, and had no reason to believe it would rise again.) The door has been left open. Noel may still not have shaken his hippie phase. He used to call himself a Digger, after a Puritan sect in the English revolution who shared everything. They tiptoe upstairs, find an empty bedroom with a mattress and sheet on the third floor, and get in. It's pink outside. She crawls over to the window, there's a tiny balcony off it, barely as wide as a person. Down on Bernard Street, a garbage truck lumbers along. She gazes at it like she's on a peak in Darien. He crawls over behind her and, as the sun rises and the traffic wakes, slides his finger into her anus. She shudders, then shakes herself like a cat. Later, they fall asleep.

When it's turned to actual day, Noel looks in. He's on his way to work, whatever that is. He asks if anyone knows where a colleague of his from the office can get an abortion—which is still seriously illegal in Canada and will continue to be so for decades. Max has been back in Canada for six hours, less if you don't count Quebec part of Canada, which he doesn't, but he always gets asked these questions about licentious or illicit activities. Where can I score acid? How do you get an abortion? They asked in London, because he was the wild colonial boy. Now it's followed him back here, as if kinky Europe has passed on some of its knowledge through the return of the prodigal son. It's like sex. Maybe they treat him this way because he's a divorcee already, at such a young age. No one would believe how inexperienced he feels.

When Noel is gone, she picks up the phone to call a cab "Where am I?" she says. *Where am I and who are you?* They go down to Bloor to a place called the Mug. They have grapefruit juice, bacon and eggs, toast and home fries, and coffee, a modest morning meal by English standards but he's re-acclimatized, it couldn't taste better. He can't imagine what she's going to Guelph for. "Guess," she says. "Used car?" he says. He knows a dealer in Guelph named Eeph the Pirate. Sell you a car a year for a hundred dollars, whether you need a new one or not. "I'm going to a conference on rural development," she says. Guelph is known around the world for its studies of rural development. He's glad he didn't tell her he's supposed to be an economist with a special interest in Third World problems. She's delivering a paper, she says. He pictures her with a paper route. They emerge from the Mug blinking into the sun, he balances her backpack on the curb and looks at her. She looks skeptically at the grimy cab he hails, as if she's getting one of Canada's rejects, some kind of initiation rite for newcomers. She doesn't know about the transatlantic gap in taxi standards. He could explain but then she'd probably say, Oh yeah, then what about that spiffy limo we took in from the airport last night? It could take hours to untangle. She'd miss her conference. When he shuts the door and tells the driver, "Union Station," she looks up from the window and says gratefully, "I was afraid it would just be penetration."

If this episode, the plane and so forth, seems a little . . . unfeeling, after the excruciating events involving Francie, well, there is the Alice factor to consider. Alice is alive. That relativizes everything. Nothing could have compensated for her death, at Francie's hands but on his account. Alice is a living albeit furry being, to whom he is attached, responsible, and grateful. Love might be a little strong for the connection, it's not the word he uses when he talks to Noel about it that night. But he says he doesn't know how he'd have borne it, her death, her murder really. Noel is right with him. He says when Pearson, his beloved schnauzer—named after Canada's only winner of the Nobel peace prize—whom he nuzzled like a child and who slept across his feet every night at the end of the bed, when Pearson was run over and he had to bury him—

Max feels chills run through him. "Pearson," he says, "is out there in the kitchen gnawing on a bone."

"A milkbone," says Noel. "But it's not Pearson. He was run over in January, in front of the house. I let him off the leash just before we came back in and he jumped in front of a Volvo. They were his favourites. I thought nothing could ever comfort me, for about three days. Then I bought another one, just like him. I know it seems pretty insensitive, to, ugh, just replace him." He stops as if waiting for somebody to whip him, verbally at least. Max is the only candidate. He declines. "It just made me feel so much better. Almost instantly." He sighs a deep sigh. "We're pretty pathetic, aren't we? We're talking about pets. Imagine if we had children. Do you think it would be even stronger?"

"Children used to die all the time," says Max. "The standard economic theory is that people had big families to maintain the workforce necessary in labour-intensive sectors like farming and early manufacturing. Maybe it was just to fill the horrible gap from losing them."

Two weeks later he goes out to Guelph for a Pirate special. Eeph shows him a car he calls a Plodge. It's a Plymouth in front and a Dodge by the time you get to the trunk. "How many miles has it got on it?" he asks Eeph. "How many do you want?" says Eeph. "Any accessories?" he asks. Eeph snorts. "Mats," he says,

"and sun visors." He takes it and drives straight back to
Toronto. She's not in Guelph any more, her conference ended
and she took a ride straight to the airport. They talked on the
phone a few times while she was here. She said she didn't want
to spoil it. "Well, you've got my number," he said. "I surely do,"
she said.

He lays low for the rest of the summer at Noel's family's "cottage" in Temagami, three hours north of Toronto. It's about the
size of the airport. Noel's dad has sold it and the whole island it's
on to someone who's turning the place into a summer camp for
the arts and sciences. The buyer, who drops by once a week, says
parents will send their kids from all over, by which he means the
U.S. There's a construction crew that boats over each day to put
up cabins, labs, studios.

Noel's dad has kept permanent rights to use the place as part
of the deal and that's where they stay. During the week, when Noel
isn't up, he reads a lot and wanders around, watching the contruction. Curious about the economics of the job, he chats with the
contractor, a bodybuilder kind of guy, who shows him one of the
invoices he hands the new owner every week. It's a remarkable
document, for those who share an interest in economic history.
Listed along with charges for materials, labour, and incidentals is a
hefty entry for "profit." It's done so baldly. Poor Marx, with his
breathtaking discovery of "surplus value" as the wellspring of
profit, hidden deep in the cost of labour where no one but him
had ever located it. You wouldn't need the advances of economic
theory if everybody was as frank as a Temagami contractor.

The night of the Apollo moon landing, he's sitting on the
dock with a big portable radio, the type that still uses batteries.
It seems to fit a cottage. He look ups and listens, the way people

sometimes bring radios to the ballpark or the hockey game, so as not to miss any of the deep commentary on the hidden meaning of what's in front of them—much like surplus value, come to think of it. In mid-August there's a fire at the half-built lunch hall and he helps the work crew fight it till it's beaten. The fire has a personal quality, you can feel its spirit rise and then get driven back. It makes him think about money, and the way Shakespeare personified and gave it a voice in *The Merchant of Venice*. Each night that he's alone in the cottage, he checks through it before turning out the lights, the way he did at his London apartment. If anyone asked, he'd say he's looking around. But of course, he has Francie on his mind. To say he's worried about her showing up would be too strong. What would she do—hire a boat? Swim across? He has no sex up there, masturbation aside, which is a big aside. The contractor's wife works on the site fitfully. She's much younger than her husband and has the kind of attractive malnourished pallor he associates with the English working class in the nineteenth century, the sad, heroic souls described by E. P. Thompson in his seminal studies. He thinks about her when he jerks off. It's the longest he's gone without sex with a woman since he "lost his cherry," as the guys on the site would probably say.

On Labour Day, as they're closing up and getting ready to drive back in their cars—his Plodge and Noel's Carmann Ghia—he blurts that Francie will know he's returned to the city, that he's in range again. Noel says that's ridiculous. "Anyway," he adds, "you can stay at my place as long as you want. We can hire some security goons if it makes you feel better." He never knows whether Noel means these assertions that always involve solving personal problems by spending a lot of money. He agrees—minus the goon squad—on one condition: the minute Noel finds himself feeling cramped and wants to be alone again, he will say so. "Righto," says Noel, trying to mock the LSE years. (Three months later, Noel says he's feeling crowded and would like to live alone again. Max is incensed. He moves out and they don't talk for about a year.)

Next morning, back in the city, with Noel gone to work, Max comes out and gets in the Plodge. He has a meeting at the CBC and an appointment on Bay Street. Time to find work and rev up life again. He's parked in the little lot of the Quaker Society, near Noel's house. He always parks there. A caretaker shuffles out and tells him there's no parking and points at a sign that says, Friends Meeting House Only. "It's okay," says Max. "I was meeting my friend at his house." He's feeling good as he gets in the car. A line like that doesn't come along every day. He turns the key and nothing happens. He looks under the hood, trembling as he searches for the battery, but thank God it's still there. For his money, everything looks normal. He calls the Motor League. When you buy from the Pirate, emergency service is not optional. The guy pulls up in his truck, leaves his girlfriend chewing gum on the front seat, and looks under the hood. The guy grins and says, "Is there somebody who doesn't like you?" He points out that the wires are missing. The battery's there, plugs are too, the points are there, and the distributor cap, but the wires connecting them all have been removed, individually. "Strangest thing," says the guy. "I never saw anything like it."

He calls Sid (not Sidney) in London, where it's still business hours. He asks him to phone Francie's office, just see if she answers and if she does, hang up. Sid calls back and says that, well, it sounded like her. Should he go over and watch when they come out at closing time? No, Max says. It wouldn't settle anything. She could've hired somebody.

Cyndi's Version

~

I met him crossing Canada by CP Rail, as the ads used to say before they started letting the railways die off. Those trips always turned into a party. I saw him looking at me when I boarded in Toronto, on my way to Winnipeg where my boyfriend lived. I could practically hear the bedpost clang in his head. We didn't talk till somewhere between the Sault and the Lakehead. I was sitting alone in the club car, they don't exist any more either. For some reason there was always space in the club car even when the train was packed. I like to think he'd been looking for me since I got on. Of course, he could also have been looking for other women since they got on. A whole parade of us. He asked if I was interested in taking a chance on some company. I have to say it sounded like a line he'd used before, but so what? Actors say the same line hundreds of nights in a row and they can still make it real. What counts isn't originality, it's sincerity. I've done some acting, along with some modelling. When I said okay, he looked surprised, maybe even scared, and definitely grateful. Not just to me. Kind of to the universe for treating him kindly. He sat down with his tuna croissant and asked how things were going. I'd been having a rough time with my boyfriend and also my family. My mother was sick and, as it turned out, dying. I didn't say much about it but he picked up on it. That was unusual among men I knew. He didn't just ignore what I said and start talking about himself. He was curious, almost confrontational, about my life. Like a reporter, the way I picture them. When I talked, he listened. There was a joke in those days: Why do Canadian women like quiet men? Because they think they're listening. It always made me and my friends laugh, although I didn't actually get it. Then he started to fill in spaces that I'd left blank, like what I did between high school and first-year university, since it was obvious I didn't go straight from one to the other. Almost like he'd been taking notes and went checking back over them to see what I left out. That's what I mean about a reporter. Once in a while he'd look out the window and say things like how huge Canada was yet so few people lived in it—travelling by train let you feel that, he said. He talked about some prof, I think he was dead, I don't know if Max had studied with him or just read his books, and how his idea was that the main economic activities back in history like fur-trapping and logging and building railroads—it's amazing how easy it is to remember the details but it must have impressed me, maybe he was just so excited about it that I got into it myself—were responsible for what Canada is like today. Such as being big but with a really small population. He was half trying to impress me and half talking down to me. It doesn't matter, I found it interesting and also that he really cared about what he was saying: the country and what was happening to it. If he'd totally forgotten me and talked to himself, looking out the window while I listened, I'd have liked it as much. Probably more. It's so great when people talk about things they really love. Too many people are just . . . blah. About everything, including their own lives! I am, more or less.

When things didn't work out with Brad, and I was back in

Toronto many months later, possibly as much as a year, I phoned him. He'd given me his number and I kept it. We went to a restaurant, Hungarian. I told him I appreciated that he seemed to care about how things had been going wrong in my life, enough even to give me a little advice. He muttered something modest and I got the idea he didn't recall what I'd been upset about, like my mother dying. That wouldn't have bothered me. But he looked worried, like I would realize he pulled some kind of scam on me. If I'd known him better, I'd have said, Relax, there isn't anything obnoxious about taking an interest in somebody, even if you're doing it to impress them or get close to them. But it made me remember what I really enjoyed about him: it wasn't that personal, probing stuff he did. It was more the things about Canada and what had shaped it and how it could be a much better place for everybody in it. Stuff that had nothing to do with me. Except to the point that I'm a Canadian, which I am. We never met after that meal. I didn't follow his career, but I did notice things about him from time to time. Especially after they got stations like Newsworld on cable. If I was awake for some reason late at night, or woke up and couldn't get back, and I flipped on the set, sometimes I'd see him being interviewed or on a panel. A number of occasions. It's not like I see people I know on TV. I guess it was from earlier that day, I don't suppose they were having their discussion in the middle of the night, I guess it could actually have been from years before. How would you ever know?

Cyndi

Max liked to explain how the train allowed you to feel the staggering *size* of the country—to feel what you couldn't imagine—the way Innis felt it travelling the North by canoe in the 1920s, leading to the awesome Innisian thesis about a staples-based economy and Canada's historic destiny: one far-flung industry—the fur trade—requiring a far-flung and underpopulated land to support it, traits with us ever since, though the fur trade itself is long gone. It became one of his set pieces. He could do it for his students and he could do it lying in bed after sex. Also, the train was a great place to meet women. Not like airplanes. He once read a magazine article called "Ten Tricks to Pick Up Chicks." Tip ten was to board your plane last so you can choose among the empty seats according to who's sitting next to them. It sounded good, but he sliced it so fine on his next flight that he didn't make it on board at all and, since it was last of the day, spent a night in the Montreal airport, scrunched into a vinyl seat, feeding quarters to an unwatchable TV set slung above him.

Cyndi, who he met on the train going west, was Asian, by way of the Caribbean. Her life must have consisted of being approached imploringly by a dreary procession of guys whenever she was alone: in a bar, or the club car. He was reading through his faded undergrad copy of Bacon's essays when she got on, as research into the origins of modern science in the seventeenth century. It more or less jumped off the shelf into his hand, as books tend to do when you need them, just as he left for the train. He was working up a paper on the impossibility of economics ever becoming a precise mathematical discipline but had allowed himself to meander into "Of Love"—*clickety-clack, clickety-clack*, that happens on a train—where Bacon says it's a damn shame that a man, "made for the contemplation of heaven and all noble objects, should do nothing but kneel before a little idol, and make himself subject, though not of the mouth (as beasts are), yet of the eye, which was given him for higher purposes." And there she was—dark bright eyes and a face he could gaze upon forever. Years and eras passing, staring and gazing upon it, as they tracked along the stark shore of Superior. When he found her in the club car, she said it was Cyndi with a *y* and then an *i*. He hated people who spelled their names that way, starting in high school, when Terry's began morphing into Terri's and so forth. But his hardiest prejudices softened and he would grow suddenly magnanimous in the face of a face like hers. Tolerance expands as the heart melts; a quantifiable process, practically a law of physics.

He talked to her about Innis and the staples thesis, staring out at the Shield as he did, as if implying the thoughts were just occurring to him. He felt grubby when he did that: taking the perfect cogent concepts honed by Innis over decades as he burrowed his way through archive after archive, so that Max, his disciple, decades hence, could use them to pry his way into the affections of a Cyndi. He believed what he was saying, oh sure he did, but *why* was he saying it? Even when he unleashed this stuff on a class of economics students during one of his sessionals or while filling in for a prof on sabbatical, he'd have one eye (those damned eyes, as Bacon knew) checking for students he might eventually make it with—following the course and submission of marks to be certain, so no undue influence was exerted. Innis had surely never used the staples thesis to ingratiate himself among chicks he wanted to score with. Innis? Never! But Max? His words were true yet his intention was false; he served with the flame of the impure fire, as some tortured medieval mystic must have said.

She got off in Winnipeg, while he continued to Regina, home of Canadian socialism, where a group of them were planning to found something called the Canadian Association of Radical Economists, or CARE. (When they got there, the Marxists said it sounded too touchy-feely. Max and the Innisians thought ACRE would serve, and had a geographic ring. They settled on Radical Economists of Canada.) He watched her scurry up the platform to the boyfriend she'd fretted about, a hamburger named Brad, certain he'd never see her again. She was too exotic, too delicate, too utterly desirable. They always had boyfriends, who were always ready to offer more than he could. Exclusivity, marriage, kids, or at least sharing an apartment—something he could never picture doing again, after the train wreck with Francie. What did he offer? A night? Then maybe another, but no guarantees in advance. Forget Cyndi, as she would doubtless forget him. By then he was also thinking about a blonde who looked like a fitness instructor and got on in Thunder Bay with a couple of kids. There's something about a brave young mum on the train alone with her kids.

Next fall, in Toronto, Cyndi calls. The thing with Brad the hamburger didn't work out. He commiserates. He feels comfortable with people who feel lousy. He assumes it's the baseline human condition, and is never thrown by it. He didn't anticipate the failure of her relationship, nor those of any of the women he yearns for. After all, the raison d'être of their liaisons is to thwart and mock his need, so why would they tank? She lost his number but found him in the book. It was before he got unlisted because of the insanity with—well, we'll get to that, maybe. They go to one of the Hungarian places that dominate eating on Bloor Street in those years—repositories for the cash and neo-Nazi detritus that fled Eastern Europe in the wake of the Red Army's advance, according to the many Marxists who eat in them regularly. The owner who greets them from his stool behind the counter has the body shape of a cash register, like people who grow to look like their pets. The waitresses wear low-cut blouses with puffy sleeves and high-heeled boots that lace up their calves. No feminist self-denial of the seventies for them. He has asked a couple of them out, but they all live with beefy guys who boost shipments of watches or break arms for loan sharks on the Danforth. More thwarting. The goulash places will eventually succumb to a wave of specialty coffee shops of the 1990s, followed by sushi bars. Many of the neo-Nazi detritus, whom he is destined to meet over lattes in the coffee shops, turn out to be Jews instead.

On their way to a table, they run into Noel, who has finished dinner and is on his way to a movie or something with his date, Penny, the Maoist legal secretary. Penny is utterly severe in presentation except for dishevelled red hair down to her thighs. Some sort of deal she has reached with herself. Noel and Max are still not talking, not since the "breakup." But as they pass, Noel mutters his hearty congratulations.

They don't wind up in bed, that night or any time, probably for want of what you could call a proper date. The kind of thing Noel was in the middle of: he picks her up; they go somewhere for dinner, it needn't be pricey but it would be nice if it required a reservation; then do something after, like a play or movie, plays are more . . . adult. Movies on the other hand are more . . . sexual. No chance the characters on the screen might see your hand meandering into her lap, the way actors on a stage could, and even, if it develops, hers wandering around your crotch, unzipping your fly and so forth. No, no, wait, that wouldn't be a first date. On the first date, you drop her off, with some sexual tension in the air. Say you'll call again, and if the script is working, she says she'd love it. There's a protocol to this stuff. He knows because Rhonda the writer has detailed it for him, practically coached him. He and Rhonda are talking again, after their breakup following the Paris break-in. (His friendships are about as fraught as he tries to keep his liaisons uninvolved.) She called one day from some college in Iowa and said, "I'm following Rhonda's rule. When I can't remember why I'm not talking to somebody, I start talking to them again." She still hasn't finished her toilet roll of Paris poems, but she's parlayed the time there into a position at the creative writing faculty. It's a new program and she's on the tenure track. He's impressed. His own efforts at steady academic work have all failed. Noel said, back when they were talking, that Max didn't look like he wanted a real job.

He and Rhonda speak on the phone after his (only) dinner with Cyndi. "There's a crucial moment on a first date," Rhonda explains. "You have to sense it. For the woman, it's when you lean forward, look in his eyes, and say"—here her voice adopts a southern languor that reminds him of Edna—"'I'm having a *really* good time.' That's the moment," she says. "You can't milk it but you can't miss it. If you get it right, everything you want will follow." She assures him there's an equivalent for the guy.

He tells her he isn't opposed to the rules of dating, but he doesn't think of what he does as dating. It's more like preliminaries to sex. Nor is he against getting to know a woman and talking, in fact he likes to, as he and Rhonda are doing at the moment. But he prefers to get sex out of the way first. Don't you all, thinks Rhonda. Yet there is something earnest in how he says it: maybe he really means it. Maybe, sigh, they all do.

"There is a theory," she says, "that nothing you say matters till after you've had sex." He likes that, he gets it. "Right," he blurts. "Sex clears the decks!" Rhonda furrows her estimable brow. He can feel it over the phone. "Not necessarily," she says. "Sometimes I wish I had a trap door." He is deeply shocked, he feels Victorian. For him, after sex, it is as if the scales of distance and derision finally fall from his eyes and his tongue is unchained. He wants to know all about them. He wants them to know *everything* about him. Let the relating commence.

And then on to the next. He sees no contradiction. "But how do you select the repeaters?" asks Rhonda, meaning the partners to whom Max returns periodically. "That's disgusting," he says, about the term she just used. Rhonda says he uses it himself, she's merely playing it back, it's not a category that's part of her sexual vocab, believe you me. He denies ever saying the word, not that he recalls. Being quoted to yourself is the worst. He just doesn't see why they can't come to bed with you, and date later, it seems more honest. "An admirable position," she says patiently, despite the heavy long-distance tolls which they scrupulously split, even-steven, "but it isn't practical." She can feel him pouting at the other end. "Most women with any substance," she bravely continues, giving him the good advice he doesn't want to hear, "want some kind of commitment."

He hates being called impractical. In the current political environment, practicality is about all he has going for him. He *is* committed, in his fashion. He is committed to truth in his career as an economist, and to honesty in his life as a friend. He is committed to a better world, within the limits, as he honestly sees them, of what is possible for humans to achieve. If that sounds pathetic to radicals like Penny the Maoist, at least he is in the commitment ballpark. And it is certainly practical. Sex though is something else, somewhere else. Sex is what gets you miles away from practicality and commitment. Sex is the reward you reap for being willing to deal with everything else, like your recalcitrant self and the shitty world. Sex keeps you going. It's related to practicality and commitment *dialectically*—

he always feels he should get a prize when that word slides effortlessly into his line of thought ("Scram, boid"). Commitment is commitment and sex is sex.

Once when he dialled information, Max met an operator. Her name was Windi, rhymes with Cyndi. He asked for the research department of a bank and she said, "That's unusual, most people want the loan office." He said he was an economic historian and she said she'd love to hear about it. So they met at her apartment, twenty minutes after work. He assumed they'd move straight to the bedroom but she wanted to go out and really get to know one another. She was a romantic, not a nymphomaniac. For her, meeting over the phone like that was so kismet. Sex wasn't on her mind at all.

Amy's Version

~

I gave him unconditional love. I felt I had nothing else to offer, so that's not as dramatic as it sounds. For a long time I thought I had nothing to give at all, besides my compact body, as he called it. But I found this unconditional love and it made me feel better about my side of things.

It was three and a half steps from the door of his apartment to the wedding-cake bed. There were these twin mattresses below and a queen on top of them. By then I'd have my clothes off, or just my coat if it's all I was wearing. And by then I'd know what I was going to do. I never knew before I got there. I'd slip in the side door, which he always made sure was open, go up a flight, then another, his place was at the top. It was like tiptoeing through the funhouse at the Ex when I was ten—you didn't know what was around the corner, about to fly at you. His door would be unlocked and he'd be in bed waiting. It wasn't arrogant, staying in bed, the opposite really, he was so full of need. He wanted me so much. As if he was afraid to get out of bed to meet me because we might get distracted and waste time talking or raiding the fridge. We were like kids meeting in our secret treehouse. Anyone watching as I went in would have thought, Of course she's going to sleep with him. But it was never clear in my mind beforehand. Not the first time and not the last. It took my breath away. He thought everything took my breath away, but that's not true. Our relationship wasn't *very* out of character for me. It was completely, totally from somewhere else. It didn't belong in my life at all. Most people who knew me thought I was a virgin. Even after Dany and I had been a couple for aeons and lived together and were engaged, they still didn't think we had sex. We could have had kids together and it would have seemed unconnected to sex. I don't think they really believed I had an opening for it. I can see why. In a way it's how I thought of myself.

I don't mean I didn't have sex on my mind. Hah! I thought about it constantly. I'd get on the subway and think about having sex with every person in the car, one after the other. I'd go through them like the customs officer when you cross the border on the bus. When I worked at the Venice Biennale, I'd lock the door of my hotel room and take photos of myself taking photos of myself wearing Italian lingerie in the mirror. I still have the shots. No one has ever seen them. And no one ever will. But there was no way to fit that into my life. My life was my parents, the backyard swimming pool they finally put

in, my sister Jan, her boys. And Dany. The sex things weren't
my little secret. They simply *weren't*, at all, even if they were
part of me somewhere that he—I don't understand how he did
it—slipped into.

When I was little, like many girls, I had a secret friend
who nobody knew about except me. And my friend would
reappear sometimes later in my life, for instance in my Venice
hotel room. Well, that was him. My friend, who I never even
thought of as a he or a she, turned out to be him. He was in
Venice in the hotel with me. If anyone had found out, I guess
I could've said we were double-booked by mistake and had to
make the best of it. Like a chick flick. Maybe it started
because we were both looking at an apartment on Bedford
Road and there was that Brando thing about it. We went in
together and no one knew we were there at the same time.
Three and a half steps. No way out except the way I came,
alone. What I did in the outer world had to be with Dany. I
knew it. Dany was my front door. Every time I went to
Kuwait on a holiday or a school break, he'd ask if I was going
to move there and live with him. One Christmas he asked me
again and I could feel myself thinking no, as usual, and I
heard my voice saying yes. My mind was saying no and my
mouth was saying yes. When I told Max I was going, he got
quiet, then he did that gruff voice they do to show their heart
isn't breaking. There were often long gaps between us seeing
each other anyway. Maybe he told himself it wouldn't matter
whether I was in my little apartment in Toronto with all the
wood and the fireplace, or in Kuwait, so long as we continued
to see each other and have sex. He was already involved with
Deb and the three kids. Maybe that's why he didn't react. I
could tell she was upsetting him, because he kept saying how

great it was and what a good change for him. So a year after I moved to the Middle East, I wrote him a letter.

Amy

The two of them are stalking an apartment on Bedford. She looks like she stepped off a Mr. Sub poster. She was lounging on a rock by the sea in a one-piece, hugging bags of phallic sub sandwich. Then suddenly, perkily, she jumps down and heads off to check out a flat, whoops, apartment, leaving the bags in the sand. Probably the agent should have only let one of them in at a time but they both slipped through. Maybe the idea was to create some competition; this being the dawn of the age of high capitalism. "Hi," she says and stretches it into three or four syllables. She's Amy to family and friends, a generic name of the era. Amy Burt, as in pert. One of those people who can't be anything but friendly. Picture a flight attendant on a picket line after weeks on a bitter strike. Even as the scab stews cross the line, snatching the bread from her and her comrades' very mouths, she smiles and asks if they'd like a Coke, oh, pardon me, leaflet. The world is divided into guests and hosts. He's a guest. She's a hostess. When he sees her, the apartment becomes subplot. Maybe she hears the bedpost clang. Neither are keen about the place, so, like a postmortem the day after the dinner party, they go to a café on the corner to slag it.

It's the year of Brando's movie, *Last Tango in Paris*. Brando and Schneider are both looking at an apartment for rent, and end up balling on the floor. Arty balling, not crass, Russ Meyer-type balling. He mentions it in the coffee shop. She smiles the stew smile and says she heard about it. She teaches junior high. Whew, at least she's not in junior high herself. She says none of her students think she's a real teacher. They think of her as the girl in the Sub poster. He'll have to look at that photo, there's a Mr. Sub down the street, when they're done. He gives her Noel's number and says he'd love to hear from her, that's where he's staying. She sort of squeals; coming from her, it sounds normal. Not a chance, he thinks.

"Amy?" says Noel. They're talking again. It's a couple of years after Max moved out in a snit because Noel asked him to, exactly as he'd promised he would when his good friend moved in. Months passed and, following a version of Rhonda's rule—"You start talking again when you can't remember why you stopped"—they resumed. He's had a series of sublets and apartment-sittings, from which he regularly returns to London for revitalization. As if he doesn't want to acknowledge that he may be home, and this is it. Last time in London, he met Dougie at the pub but kept glancing at the door. "She doesn't come here any more, not for ages," said Dougie, but suggested they walk over to the Bradgate, because for sure she never ever goes there. Plus Dougie could check the brands on tap at the competition (further presentiments of the age of Thatcher). They crossed the High Road, just to be sure, and immediately before they turned in to the Bradgate, she steamed past them, like a mighty ship of the line, looking neither left nor right, leaving dread and reverence in her wake. "Don't say anything, don't even think about it," said Dougie, without turning his head. When Max got back from that trip, he checked in again at Noel's, till he could find another temporary roost. "It's Amy," says Noel, then, "Amy?"

When she looks up at his greeting, he has the sense it's the first time she ever sat alone at a bar. Maybe ever been in a bar. It's based on a snotty set of assumptions about her, the deduction ex suburbia. She doesn't quite squeal. It's soundless. A visual squeal.

She inhales. It fills her eyes, temples, cheeks—they're all waiting on the exhale, which is a long time coming. He says there's a screening (he chose the word deliberately) of a film (also note the diction) from Nazi Germany. He's wanted to see it: *Triumph of the Will*, by a woman (he emphasizes) director.

He's showing a lot of attitude for a guy who would say he doesn't give a damn what she thinks of him. Could he be out to impress her? With what—his feminist sensibility? No reason to think that would move her. A pre-emptive strike to prove he isn't a womanizer—since he apparently is. But why should that bother her? Maybe it's what she *liked* in him. Or is it about his urbanity, his edginess, his downtown, *de la rue* essence? Is he counterattacking her with her suburbanism? Is it revenge on Francie and Leaside, now that he's back in town? Or is it just an any-sided campaign to wear down her resistance, one part of the seduction, always a complex act, as well as a word he claims not to know? She lets the air out of her temples and nods with a big smile. The smile seems to be nodding her. Who could hold anything against this child-woman? Why get aggressive? She hasn't even spoken on this "date." (He never dates. He deplores dating. He already feels compromised by the degree to which this could count as a date. Dates are hazardous—dating back to the prom. Aha! Is *that* who she is: all the cute girls he could never have and never will, no matter how many times he has them? And *that's* why he's feeling crusty?)

It actually is a screening. Not everything is complicated. Sometimes a screening is just a screening. This is no movie and it's not in a theatre. An impressario of the streets named Derek Mack owns a private collection of documentaries, cartoons, early silent films—he advertises them on lampposts and screens them with his own projector wherever he can. This one is in the lounge of a hippie high-rise co-op on Bloor. It's already begun. They grab a little floor—ideal for the womanizer. His fingers meander around on the linoleum, eventually touch hers. The film rolls on. Her fingers don't respond and don't withdraw. He's too fast, he should give her some time, a lesson he doesn't learn for decades. He ought to have counted on Riefenstahl's stamina, whose film on the Nuremberg rally seems to run at the original length. After too many march-pasts, he asks Amy if she's willing to leave. Puff, exhale, nod.

She takes him up the street to an apartment she just rented. It's on St. George, near the one where they met. She hasn't moved in but she has a key. It's bare and woody: wood floors, wood panels, fireplace with wood mantel and pillars. *Last Tango* all over again. They kiss standing up. They kiss leaning against the fireplace. They roll on the floor. She kisses him with that same breathlessness. It touches him, like Francie's tassel. Then she pulls back. "It's completely natural to go ahead," he says. What's the line you're drawing? Talking and touching, touching and talking— where's the distinction? Why stop here instead of before or after? (It's pure Sorstad, this little lesson.) She nods, sighs, and shakes her head with a big stewardess smile. "You're right," she says. They start again, then she pulls back. "You're right," she squeals. "It's just I, just I, I just can't."

A week later, she calls Noel's again. "I'll patch you through," says Noel, who's been falling asleep to midnight reruns of "Hawaii Five-O." He gives her Max's new number. He's moved into a third floor on Euclid, a street name that appealed to the mathematician in him. You have to walk through the Italian family's quarters to get to his. The grandfather, who made the epic move from the old country like a Homeric wanderer, is directly below. He can hear the poor man wheeze and hork. When he drops a shoe, Max waits for the other one. Waits and waits, often. How you hear the noises made by your neighbours has everything to do with how you feel about them. He ushers her up through the house to his place. They pass the old man sitting on his bed, holding a shoe before him, like Hamlet with the skull. He takes her out onto the little flat roof through the kitchen window, his wannabe deck. It's a nice touch—like whacking the headlights of the Deux Chevaux to turn them on. Francie liked that, she thought it was part of his cute Keynesianism.

They kiss. She pulls back. "It's just ridic—" he begins the Sorstad number again, like she hit his replay button: touching and talking, talking and touching, and so on and so on and scoobie-doobie-doo on. "It *is* ridiculous," she breaks in. She takes him by the hand, pulls him back in through the kitchen window. They're in the hall now, by his front door. He sighs the heaviest of sighs, a world-beater. It is sheer acceptance, no one could miss the authenticity, it's Kierkegaardian. I concur because it is absurd. His renunciation is complete, like he resigns from the world. For only when you truly abandon hope, may it return to you as grace. But no guarantees, or the renunciation would be cheap and conditional. As he balances on one foot while lacing up his shoe so he can drive her to the subway with a whole, ungrudging heart, she eases into his back from behind. Like snow, like lava. Reverse of the night of his first kiss in another doorway. He doesn't so much turn, finally, as flow in reverse and then they shuffle toward the bed, clothes being pulled off without urgency, she's so cool and smooth underneath. (Goes with pert.) Then the breathing stuff stops and her pert body goes taut. It has an intensity that leaves him a bit of a spectator. She's way past him, but she pauses and lets him catch up. Keep going for a while. Then they relax and lie there.

When they start again, she kneels on the bed and takes his penis in her mouth. You'd suspect she's done it all her life and probably was born with a highly personal technique. You'd also say it's her first time ever. How else could it be so fresh and inventive? It's hard to remember, in years to come, that oral sex wasn't always common. It was a rarity, especially among the well-behaved middle classes. Something she'd have to be forced into, or he went to prostitutes for, except occasionally, when you were both on a Caribbean holiday and drunk. It had a sense of exception. Then came AIDS and the other STDs, the stuff that used to be called VD, and oral sex came into its own. Its hour struck.

Afterward he drives her to the subway at Bloor. She hasn't moved into her place yet, she's still staying with her parents in the burbs, somewhere between Bloor Street and Hudson Bay. She descends the steps—it has a quality of Greek myth he can't iden-tify—then he drives down to Mars ("Food just out of this world") and parks outside. He knows what he wants with more certainty than he'll ever have about politics or economics: a hot hamburg on white bread with the crusts cut off, covered in beige gravy and green peas on the side. You don't get those anywhere but Canada (and now, with the takeover by sushi and espresso, not even here, much). He's ordered them in Boston, London, New York—the culinary centres of the Anglo world. Of course it's hot, they say, whaddaya think we serve—*cold* hamburgers. They don't get it and there's no point describing it, they wouldn't believe it. He yearned for a hot hamburg when he and Francie were at their happiest. He'd practically draw it: not comfort food, like matzoh ball soup or potato pancakes. Food that goes with the world going well. Harmony food, the music of the spheres turning frictionlessly as background for sex, work, your team winning; walking on the heath at night and suddenly understanding

Ricardo's point about comparative advantage because you grasp what was bothering *him*, so of course he said what he did! Mind, body, yackety-yack, the whole catastrophe, in sync.

They sat in the car a moment before she slipped into the subway. There's nothing as intimate in this society as a moment on the front seat of a car. Time gets shut out, as it never quite is in a building or on a street. He says he hasn't felt anything like the way she melted into him. "I didn't believe it would ever happen," he says, though it's just the third time he's seen her, their second "date." A little early to abandon all hope, but then, he's a catastrophist when it comes to sex. "It had to happen," she says. "It was ridiculous." He asks when she knew. "When you raped my hand in the movie," she says. What movie? he thinks. Have they been to a movie? "The German Nazi one," she says. "By the lady director."

Their relationship unfolds like a join-the-dots puzzle in a book your mum pulls out when you're sick or on rainy days, before video games, except the dots don't connect. He sees her on a Sunday afternoon, they lie in bed on the wedding-cake mattresses, dawdle with the TV on, forget it's there, then slowly tune back in (the halftime show, ads for the pattie-stacker) after coming again. Sometimes she arrives late at night, through the side door that's always open, quietly up past the old man's room, to his unlocked door. He waits, pretending he didn't hear her from the time her car stopped and she opened and closed the door outside. She leaves him at first light, has to be ready to teach her precocious grade eights up there in the land where all kids are gifted. One night of a slow news day he gets a little moment on a local TV show—How the European Monetary Union Matters to Us—so she's there in bed, the one and only time, when *he* arrives. They never discuss where the next dot will come. He doesn't want to know, just needs to know it *will*. He aches if she cancels.

She makes him dissolve. This is not sexual. Maybe it once was but it turns . . . anthropological. With her, he feels Cro-Magnon. Cro-Magnon was the big guy with the heavy, overhanging brow, like an iron plate on his forehead. When Cro-Magnon met Neolithic, smaller and smooth-browed, somewhere on the steppes of northern Europe, he melted and was supplanted, in a stunningly short time, say the paleontologists. Poor Cro-Magnon, Max knows how he felt. Cro-Magnon looked at those smooth brows and thought of his own kids and the kids of his tribe, before they matured and acquired their telltale foreheads. And Cro-Magnon was as putty before the neo's, just the way he was with his children. Reduced. Utterly. The way Max will be by Petey. He will be putty before Petey. He once knew an irresistible girl named Cornelia, who everyone called Neo, because it was all she could pronounce of her own name when she was a little thing.

One Friday Amy has a PD day. Professional development, same as time off. She called to say his bed is her first choice for where to spend it. It's the most aggressive she's been about their . . . whatever. It's as close as she gets to a demand, which is to say, not even. When they run out of ice cream, he goes to the store leaving her orders not to get dressed, under no circumstances, and Noel shows up. He forgot about this: Noel went to get the results for his bar ads today, he said he'd come around afterward. Doing the bar ads is Noel's big concession to rich old dad; Max can't figure out if Noel's loyalty to his old man comes from true filial love or is calculated to keep him in line for the inheritance. But he's failed the exam, sad or glad news, depending. Noel knocks on the door and Amy, wrapped in a sheet, opens it, Mr. Sub style. Noel has no idea who she is. They've talked on the phone once, when she called for Max, who never mentions her to others, even Noel, as she never mentions him. It's not shame, it's privacy, the secret treehouse. Max arrives back at that moment with the mint chip and does the intros. When Amy goes to get robed, Noel says, "I thought maybe you prepared a present for me, pass or fail." That's when he announces his exam result. They don't know whether to celebrate or grieve.

They rarely see other humans when they're together, with exceptions like the bedsheet encounter. She meets Noel again when Galbraith and Milton Friedman are in town. The two of them are touring as a tag team, like G. Gordon Liddy, the Watergate burglar, and Timothy Leary, the acid guru. Together at last, like the ghosts of economics past and future. They're going to debate in the big dining room at the Board of Trade. Grad students inspired by Galbraith at MIT, Harvard, or LSE, or by his books on the Depression and the hideous fifties, have come to cheer. Friedman has a lot of support from Bay Street, including some surprisingly young brokers, but it is long before he got his Nobel Prize and he is generally viewed as an ultra-conservative kook, not a genuine force. Max wasn't planning to go, but Noel's dad bought a table for the event and ordered his son to recruit some bodies. Noel isn't averse, it will please the old man, and anyway, he's thinking about giving the business thing a try, now that he's got law off his plate. He calls Max about an hour before the event and urges him to come. Maybe he wants to watch him react, as he did long ago with the porn book.

    Amy's already on her way over. When she arrives, Max says, "Come with me." She looks absolutely caught in the headlights but he seems to want it so urgently, the way he always wants *her.* She acquiesces. They meet Noel in the foyer. Amy reddens. She didn't know she would have to see *him* again, not ever. He's with Nadine, who is new in Noel's life. "I know you," Nadine says to Amy. "I see you at the downtown Y." Amy crimsons. Noel beams. Something in him likes orchestrating discomfort. He says he and Nadine met one night when he was walking Pearson the Second around the block. She has a dog too. (This was one of the Tricks to Pick Up Chicks, like getting on the plane late.) They had the conversation dog owners always have. Then he said he was walking back, would she join them? She said sure, but suggested they keep going *around* the block instead of back by the same route. The boldness of it won him. "And what do you do?" he says, turning to Amy like a laser. "The tread-mill," she squeals, "or the step climber, some weights. I finish with a swim." It's a dumb-blonde answer, although Amy is a brunette, which is itself a kind of dumb-blonde word, in the sense of not being a word at all. "Teaches junior high when she isn't working out," says Max.

Galbraith is suave and he towers over Friedman. Not that those things matter, it's your politics, your intellectual clarity that counts. Still, it's nice to be on the side of the guy in the white hat. He begins by describing his border crossing where the guard asked the purpose of his visit. "I have come," Galbraith replied, "to nip the flower of Canadian neo-liberalism in the bud." The Keynesians in the audience laugh. "And how long will you be staying?" said the guard with, according to Galbraith, "that unruffled Canadian demeanour I recall fondly." Everyone here knows Galbraith gave up his Canadian citizenship to live in the States. He has been an adviser to presidents and America's ambassador to India. "Twenty-four hours," continues Galbraith, "will be more than enough," and they crack up, even the brokers. Friedman looks up from his notes as if he wonders what that noise was. He is short (but not brief) and awkwardly earnest, when it's his turn. He tells them, as if he's talking about a weather front approaching, that the programs which Canadians assume are inevitable government functions—health care, university education, the welfare system (the Keynesians start to fidget), the police and prisons (some of the Keynesians rattle their coffee cups)—will all be privatized in the future. During question period, Max asks Friedman if he plans on privatizing the armed forces too, which have recently been united in one drab uniform. People chuckle, no one expects Friedman to bother answering. "I've been working on that problem for thirty years," says Friedman, "and I believe it's starting to yield."

Driving back to bed after the debate, he asks Amy what she thought. She says they seemed embarrassed. He thinks she means Noel and Nadine, by her. He tells her she's mistaken, there was no embarrassment, it's in her mind. She was charming. She says she meant, embarrassed by *Galbraith*, most of the people who were there. He doesn't know what she's talking about. "Galbraith is the tall one," he says, as if she's thinking of Friedman. "I know. The one who gave up being Canadian," she says. "He cracked them up," says Max, trying to sort it out for her. "Yes," she agrees, "they liked it when he made jokes, but they didn't like his ideas."

It unsettles him, something about the pure quality of her response. He says Galbraith had to be on track with that audience, he is the representative today of the intellectual current that represents the best of our era, the voice that speaks out for the public, not just some private, interest, and the public good; he's the true American inheritor of the mantle of Keynes (with a quick bio and appreciation) and a special Canadian connection like a cherry on top. Oh sure, you can say government intervention and activism incline to be bureaucratic and unimaginative, no one—least of all John Kenneth Galbraith—would say it represents the final stage. But Friedman? With his private this and private that? He's sheer regression. Back to the jungle of early capitalism and child labour, survival of the fittest and the fattest. It reeks of atavism, clearly it will not prevail, its heyday is one hundred years behind us.

She appreciates the lecture, and adores his passion. "I don't mean they didn't like him," she says. "He just reminded me of my uncle Albert." They are pulling up to Max's place again, ready to mount those stairs and each other. "Everybody loved him. He was a very funny man," she says. "Was there something wrong with him?" asks Max. "He was crazy," she says. "He had been in the war. He was fine when he was being funny. Then," she goes on, "he would start to talk about the war, the officers, how evil they were, and the government, how they steal from us, and how nobody did anything about the awful mess till people like him had to go to war. It was the only way they could get off the dole, and it was the only way to stop Hitler. He would start to rant and rail, my relatives said when he wasn't around." "That doesn't sound like Galbraith," says Max, "though it is sort of what Galbraith would say, in his erudite way." "Oh no," she says, "he wasn't like my uncle Albert. But it reminded me of him."

When they're in bed again, he asks if perhaps *she* was embarrassed. He feels clever, it's the sort of thing a shrink would do, turning the point around. "No," she says, "but I was sad." He asks why. "It was so private," she says, looking around at their nest. "It won't ever be that private again." He asks her about the time Noel came. "That was just funny," she says. "This time was so"—big sigh—"public."

She is virginal, in her fashion, yet there are the men of her life. Thomas: she always mentions him in the context of car and appliance repair. Max gathers they were lovers, but no longer. Thomas doesn't just fix her stuff, he makes house calls at her folks' place and repairs theirs. They call him when anything breaks, though he's no longer her boyfriend. When she says his name, it's with a sigh. "Oh, Thomas." True, a sigh is her universal signature, but it's variable and can be individualized for particular cases. With Thomas, it has a surprising tinge of cruelty. *Oh, Thomas*—who I hurt and continue to—*sigh.*

Raven: hair down to his ass, drop-dead gorgeous. They met on the European backpack circuit, hung out in the Greek isles. She was on her way back from Nepal. She met lots of freaks there and travelled with them. "If they were freaks, I assumed they were fine, any freak was fine with me," she explained, assuming Max—for her the model of a social critic—would approve. Raven smoked dope all day, he was never not stoned. Maybe she tried it with him, maybe she toked up in every valley in Nepal, though he finds that hard to picture, it's not like her, whatever is. But she worshipped his beauty, you can tell from how she sighs when she says his name. Until Dany arrived to beg for her return. Poor Dany—sigh—in his wash-and-wear suit.

He's the constant, the boy next door. He really was. Her parents still live beside his, they chat across the storm fence, invite each other to barbecue or use the pool her folks put in when her dad got the big promotion. Dany and Amy did everything together. By the final year of high school, he was president of the student council, she edited the yearbook. He was the quarterback and she led the pep squad. Of course, they were king and queen of the prom. Everyone assumed they'd marry and have kids, without ever having sex, because she wasn't like that.

Then Dany went on the pro tour. He had a knack for golf. He picked up a driver one day and it felt like a phantom limb restored. That evening he quit the football team, they'd have to find another quarterback (and cheerleader, since Amy dropped out like his synchronized partner). He was nationally ranked, at eighteen he won the championship for his division. He stuck with the tour for a year, then found his place in the world: since he'd come so naturally to this game, he could surely teach others, just by encouraging them to trust *themselves*, as he had. He was a born teacher—of golf, though nothing else. Maybe it was his sunny disposition finding a sunny place to deploy itself out there on the fairway. He wasn't ready to believe in life on any other terms. That time he went to Corfu to beg Amy to leave the guy with hair down to his ass and come home with him, he almost got a little down.

When his knack for golf, or teaching it, turned him into a global corporation, he smiled, as he would when the hardware store happened to have exactly the mop he was looking for, or another kind that was even better. Life dealt generously with him. He went from student to student; some happened to be rich or famous. One said he'd like to invest in Dany's "method," and before long there were eighty-one "Dany Dover Worldwide" pros with headquarters in Kuwait. Well, why not? She'd fly there to see him. Or sometimes to California, where he'd be holding a clinic for movie stars. One day she told Max she was moving to Kuwait. A week later she was gone.

He gets the letter on his birthday, like a card, but it's not. It's written on fine paper, with green ink, in a flowery girlish hand. This is apparently intentional; it matches the style and content. There are thumbnail-scale drawings down the margins, like an illuminated manuscript. It reads:

Once there was a sad knight. He was a knight and so of course he wished to serve the people of his land, fighting their foes, such as want, hunger, lack of education, ill health, and joblessness. He was sad because the equipment he received at the knight-outfitting depot was not well suited to these tasks. His lance wasn't quite long enough to reach into the darkest part of the cave of unemployment and smite the dragons of low wages and rapid technological change coiled in its depths. Its tip was blunt instead of long and spiky so that, when he poked in as far as he could, he might annoy and inconvenience the monsters but was never quite able to finish them off. The beasts, true to their unnatural nature, had the ability to regenerate limbs and other appendages which they lost, and so continued to wreak havoc among the peasants and labourers. (And students.) He found that his armour, when tested in battle, contained flaws, doubtless due to the incompetence of the armourer, although the knight, in keeping with his noble nature, never blamed others for his defeats. He carried on, travelling the kingdom in a lifelong quest to fulfil his mission of solidarity with the helpless and oppressed, heedless of dangers to himself.

(I never thought, he thinks, reading it, that she noticed what I did and thought. Her esteem is on the verge of making him think better of himself. He shakes it off.)

One day he came upon a maiden wandering lonely in a glade, looking for a place to rest. Though he did not know it, she had turned away from her family and lifelong friends in search of—well, she forgets. Perhaps a wildflower, or a grove or crevice in which to rest, or an errant ball that rolled off the field of play. "You are most desirable," he said, in the way others had often said to her that she was most beautiful, or most kind, or most cheerful. This touched her heart, in a place others had not. (For this purpose his lance was adequate.) Then he rode off, but time and again he returned, with the hope he would come upon her once more, and he often did.

Then came a day on which she knew they would part, and not meet in the future, for it was her leaving this time, not him. "You have given me my body," she said. Well, actually, it's what she wished she had said.

Deb arrives from Winnipeg with the three bears a week before the letter. Deb hadn't said she was coming, and he didn't say they could live with him if she did, but he does his best. She's working already, she always works, she's a baker, or an apprentice baker, or an assistant, something that includes union wages, but the only job she could nail fast was on night shift at a bakery in a part of the Annex the old rail line still runs through. So the three bears, ages three, four, and five, are arrayed on the wedding-cake bed under the duvet, like pastries in an oven while she works and he watches them, transfixed. Then he shakes himself alert and pads back into the living room. He takes the birthday letter from Amy he still hasn't had a chance to read. He's almost finished it when he hears a sound from the bathroom and in walks Petey, the three-year-old, like a Christmas present, with his beautiful blond bangs shorn straight across the top of his forehead by a scissors he found there. He grins dopily. He thinks he's balding now too, just like his mom's new boyfriend who they've come to live with. If something catastrophic happened to this kid's parents, and Max found himself transported in front of, say, a family court judge with the opportunity to take full charge of this incredible creature for the rest of his life— *But you have to decide fast, no chance for tortuous dialectics on the subject, my good fellow*—he would answer, Yes, your Honour, in an instant; he wouldn't hesitate or need time, even though the decision would overturn his life and mean the end, in almost all the ways he's come to treasure it, of his womanizing. The letter in his hand never really registers.

Amy visits, though. Nothing ever ends. Years later Deb and the three bears have come and gone, moved on, or back, as Deb puts it, to the ancestral home in Iceland, though she and her parents all grew up on the Prairies. Dany Dover Worldwide is now located in Florida. More central, said Dany's backers. When he watches "Miami Vice," or the Orange Bowl, or some tropical storm bearing down on the Florida Keys, he thinks of her. She comes in summer, when Dany teaches at a lodge in the Adirondacks, or on holidays when she flies in to see her folks and Jan and the boys. Sometimes she calls. Sometimes, if he senses she's in town, he phones her parents' number and asks if she's there or they're expecting her. Or hangs up when it isn't her who answers. When he asks her to come and see him in his new house—a small semi, a starter house, as the sexy (in that suburban, queen-of-the-cowboys, you-can-look-and-drool-but-don't-mess-me-up way) real estate agent called it—she sighs a great sigh (which he misses, and yearns to hear again), and says,

"Ooookay." For her, the routine doesn't change in its essentials. She drives her dad's retirement Buick down and parks two blocks away, to give her time, as she walks toward him, to find out what she's going to do. To get the message from . . . message central. She stands on his porch, rings the bell, he comes toward the door, getting bigger through the plate glass, looking as if nothing in the world will ever matter as much as her stepping into his arms with a big exhale. He has no inkling of this drama.

One day—it's Christmas or Easter, a visiting time—he calls her parents' and she answers. There's something in her voice. "Would you like me to come and pick you up?" he says. They've never done this, she always comes to him, it changes everything. He meets her parents and they drive away together, downtown. The process has been interrupted. She will not wonder as she approaches his door, awaiting the call from message central. No leap into his arms, or bed, because they've defaulted on the approach. The approach has been cancelled. No approach, no liftoff. They both feel it. He parks near Honest Ed's and suggests they go for a walk, like survivors of war in a bitter landscape. He asks, with fear and certainty, if she'll move back here and live with him, as she would have once, when she wrote the letter. He hadn't anticipated saying this, but out it popped. She sighs and talks about Arthur. Arthur? What happened to Dany?

She hasn't lived with Dany for years. She stayed with the company because it was her home. Having him next door was what mattered, not having him. Dany has moved on, he married a flight attendant, but all the pros and the staff say she's nowhere near as nice a person as Amy, to whom they're devoted. Arthur has been her roommate since the breakup. Just roommates, just pals. Last winter, when she got sick, he nursed her. The night her fever broke—this was really sick, he gathers—

Arthur told her how he felt about her. He said if she wanted, he'd never mention it again. For months, she's held back—waiting, she now realizes, for this moment with her big Canadian secret. They've been walking and walking, both hoping perhaps to walk their way back into the treehouse. They're all the way to the lakefront. Joggers. Gulls. Now that he's asked, she can choose. Is she just waiting for another message, or is she, this once, deciding? She'll let him know when she knows. *He* sighs. "Okay," he says. "I'm putting kids on the table." She smiles a smile to make the sky wince. "It would be a tragedy of historic proportions if you never have kids," he says. They part, for the first time since the night in her bare new apartment, without sex. He doesn't hear from her. Weeks later, he phones Denver for her decision. The company has moved to Denver. But he already knows the answer.

Deb's Version

~

I admit it was his reputation as a womanizer that appealed to me. I think I'd been interested in the idea for a long time, to try it out. When we were introduced, he looked at me, but not in the way you get used to—like he wanted to lick me all over, or undress me—but looked at me with this, this keen interest, very sincere, like he wanted to know who I truly was. And also like a kid paralyzed in the malt shop who can't decide between the rainbow parfait, the chocolate shake, and the banana split. He went ridiculously slowly, I thought, given the reputation, but reputations can be misleading, I've learned. I told him to stop talking about everybody else we knew because what I wanted to talk about was this thing happening between the two of us. I could see it stopped him cold. That was good because I felt some power of my own, yet he was still this notorious womanizer. Things aren't so simple when you're a feminist like me.

I didn't expect to hear from him after the night at the run-down hotel on the lake in Toronto. But he called next day when I was back home, and he flew out the following weekend. I was shocked, even though it was going the way I'd more or less—I wouldn't say planned but fantasized. Stewart had already moved out again, as soon as we got back. I took the kids over to my mother's. Then I picked him up at the airport in the VW van. I would have liked to vacuum it but there wasn't time. Anyway, I thought he might find it charming, just as it was, with the kids' stuff and the crackers. Some working-class realism for his broad-minded tastes. I asked him to drive. I told him I liked the way he whizzed me around Toronto in his clunky car. I said he drove like a New York cab driver (the one time I was there). He said it was like a London cab driver. Look, I was impressed by him knowing the streets of Toronto. Zip here, whip there. I'd be completely blown away by somebody who could navigate London or New York. Then we headed up to Lake Winnipeg. There are so many places there you can visit, swim, camp.

We made it all the way to Hecla Island and crossed on the causeway. It was hot. We drove around till we got to the far side of a cove where there weren't any swimmers. We didn't have bathing trunks, so we just went in. We wore our shirts. Tops covered, bottoms bare. That lake is incredibly shallow. Far out, where the water finally rose above our thighs, I settled in his lap, facing him, and I pulled him into me. The sun blasted straight into my eyes. We slipped sideways and went under as we came, together. When we surfaced, I was facing the tiny little bathers on the other side of the lake, or the bay. "Hey," I yelled, "What, no applause?"

We made our way sideways like crabs back to the beach eventually and up to the van. I felt like an ad for a nudist camp. Just unbelievably full of sexual health and happiness. The ads, I mean, not the actual camps. I once worked at one, I was the lifeguard. Believe me, they aren't like that. We dried off a little and got back in the van. He looked great. He felt for the keys and they weren't there. He did the usual male slap-around: pants, shirt, back pockets. A woman would rummage through her purse and the guy would roll his eyes or make jokes—why, because he has pockets and she has a purse? Pardon me, but I don't get the difference. Then he did it again and then again. Then he dropped his head hard on the steering wheel, like it had turned into a dead weight. I was shocked by the clunk of his forehead where it hit but he didn't even react. Then he glared out through his lids onto the lake: that long slow slope of beach into water that took us so much time just to get to waist level. They were out there somewhere, he said, talking more to them than to me. *You're out there, aren't you?* They'd been in his shirt pocket. He didn't want to leave them in the car or on the shore with the rest of our clothes, he said. I don't know why—in case a bear or a deer grabbed them and drove away with my van? Maybe he just didn't know much about life outside a big city. There were parts of him I didn't anticipate.

Then he banged his head on the wheel. Didn't just let it fall, banged it purposely. And again. Bang. Bangbangbang. He started talking, not to himself, not to me. It was like he was broadcasting, as if the steering wheel had a mike built in. *I'm an idiot. I hate myself. Anybody who doesn't agree with that is an idiot too.* And so on. I'm not repeating it exactly. I could but that kind of thing tends to turn me off. Whining instead of butching it up. On the other hand, it wasn't what I'd been expecting from him and it had a certain surprise value, which I liked. *Why don't I quit, give up,* and so forth—and he kept going and going as if he wouldn't stop till he was interrupted by some outside force that would let him off this babbling hook he was on. I put my arm across his shoulders. He was still kind of bumping his head every few seconds on the wheel. "Jesus," I said. "Take it easy on yourself. If you beat yourself up like this over some little thing anybody can do like losing the keys, what the hell do you do when you really fuck up? I hope I'm around to pick up your pieces when that happens." I felt his whole body settle, from the shoulders down, like a suit slipping onto a hanger. I told him we'd just had historically great sex in the lake. It was better for me than being in the Mile High Club, which I was not, and who cared if we had keys. We'd work it out. We weren't exactly lost in the Sahara. That's when he turned his face up to the side I was on, still resting it on the steering wheel. And he looked so incredibly relieved. And grateful. More than anything, grateful.

If I was going to write one of those How to Be Happy in a Relationship books that they sell up by the cash, I would have one piece of advice based on that experience. Don't freak out when somebody bangs his head on the floor. Or the wall or the steering wheel or wherever he does it. People bang their heads. I've seen it all my life. Mostly guys. It's better than putting their fist through the door. Or the wall. And even that isn't so bad. As long as they don't put it through you or your kids. They roll around on the carpet and scream. One guy I knew dragged his fingernails across his forehead and left three parallel grooves, bleeding. That was a bit over the line. I happened to have some vitamin E ointment in the bathroom and I gave it to him to rub into his grooves. The thing that made me more patient with Max was that I didn't expect that kind of behaviour from a famous womanizer who wrote books. Or at least articles in the paper. Maybe he hadn't written any books yet. I don't think I knew anyone who'd even written an article till then. He came from another tribe than me and he completely baffled all my expectations. It made me curious. I would have had less patience with somebody from my own tribe. Or species. But why should that be? It's just as interesting when anybody freaks out, if you disengage enough to see how weird it is. Maybe it isn't what you signed up for, but it's interesting. Also, it gave me a sense of power compared to him, which was satisfying. "How are we going to get out of here?" he said.

As if that was a line in a movie, a guy saunters across the front windshield of the van like the cavalry coming over the hill. His name is Charlie. He's a van man too, he's from my species, the wife and kids are in their van, just over by the road, he's come to check the lake. Is it okay for swimming, safe for kids? The safest, we both say, it's all beach all the way out as far as you can see, and we kind of squeeze each other's hands about our little joke below the dash where Charlie can't see it. And by the way, does he know anything about hot-wiring an ignition? I ask. "Oh yeah, yeah, sure," Charlie says. He was in the Canadian forces, it was no big deal, peacekeeping on the Lebanese border. You learn a lot about keeping your vehicles going when you're out in no man's land. He tells us to get off the front seat a second. He ducks under the dash, pulls, twists, cuts, ties—and lookit, there she purrs. And we drive off for the remainder of my dirty weekend.

Deb

He finds the confident ones, like the needy ones, hardest to resist. "Look," she says when they first meet, squaring up and staring him in the eye. It's the lingo of a straight-talkin' broad. It's how Ann Landers always starts her tartest replies to people who write her for advice: "Look, buster." Or "Listen, toots." They're jabbering in the lobby of a hotel where the native rights conference is happening. He's booked on a panel. "Look," she says. "Never mind your friend Noel and whatever happened with him. That was last year. Something is going on between you and me and that's what I want to talk about." Oof. Takes his breath away. Just call him Toots.

Looking back, he can't say if something was going on or she created it by invoking it, the way lots of things get started. Create, then relate. He knows Noel slept with her last year when she was in town with her husband, Stewart, for the same conference, it's annual, since last year. Stewart is native *and* a lawyer, this event was made for him. They met Noel, who had finally passed his bar ads and was trolling in the law for a specialty. He thought he'd check out land claims. His dad said not a chance, till he heard there was big bucks in it, then he was all for it. (You never knew with Noel's dad whether he was being provocative or just crude.) When they got back to Winnipeg, Deb told Stewart about her tryst in Toronto, giving them something to discuss during the awful Winnipeg winter, says Noel bitterly. "I was set up," he goes on. "Don't get sucked in the way I was."

But what *is* happening? Is he reacting to her breasts? She must be used to it. Guy's eyes slide down, back up, down again. One of the things you do when you're trying not to. *Because* you're trying not to. Like words you want to avoid. You want not to offend the blacks in the community council that invited you to speak on economic challenges of affirmative action. So you hear yourself saying "denigrate," a word you've surely never used before. You could have tried for a *year* to find an excuse to say denigrate and not succeeded. ("Scram, boid.") Yet he hasn't noticed a big sexual subtext between Deb and him, at least not till now. Then, when she says it, with such cockiness (whoops, there's one of the words), he's reluctant to deny it. "Those Pisces are so confident," says Rhonda when he reports on his new relationship. "Virgos like you and me—they overwhelm us. It's no contest."

"Deb Downey," she said with a firm handshake. "Sounds like Blondie Bumstead. I hate that name." Max feels about her as Guy-Paul must feel about Max: so free to be frank. She says she hated being Debbie in high school. She went to Deb after her consciousness got raised: Deb, firm and fast. She's thinking of reverting to Arnasson, her dad's name, it's true, and he was a lout, still is, but it's more her than Stewart's name will ever be. She produced the three bears—age three, four, and five—as Downeys. Native people really care about keeping their line going, she says, more than Icelanders like her. Not that there are so many Icelanders but at least they've got a country, a great place she'd like to visit some day, so at least they don't live in a paranoid state of being responsible for the end of their group identity. "Stay right here," she commands, while everyone who came in for the conference is lined up to check out. He takes a seat. She strides past three or four times, trailing the agitated lawyer hubby, eating his liver for being in this predictable situation again, who can say how often now. Then he's gone and she's beside Max on the sofa, like it's their wedding photo. This is a person who gets things done. "Let's not stay here," she says, peering around distastefully. Max doesn't want to take her to his place, that was last year's scenario with Noel. So they go to the Seaway, on the Lakeshore. "Believe it or not," he says as they check in, "this wasn't always a seedy place."

"I'm just a mousewife from the Prairies," she says with his cock in her mouth. "I don't live a glamorous life where I know people who get interviewed on national TV." It occurs to him that Stewart must get interviewed once in a while, but the thought passes. He drives her to the airport in the morning and watches her in that pointless, moony way through security till she passes from sight behind a bookstall. Then came the phone calls—it must have been the early days of direct dial because it seemed so surprisingly *easy* to get on the line with someone a thousand miles off—then he flew out for the weekend. She met him with the van.

On the drive back from Hecla Island, with lots of time to catch his flight east, she says they'll stop in Gimli to see if Ole Olasson is home. She doesn't ask; that wouldn't be Pisces. Since Ole is retired and eighty, he's nearly always there, or en route to and from. He could be at the Icelandic Club, or the Northern Lights tavern down by the harbour, or at the legion. But in actual fact, he's home. Because she called him before they set out on this jaunt and told him to be there then. They pick him up and drive to the tavern.

Ole grew up in this place. He never wanted to fish, though

he helped on his dad's boat like everyone else, when school was out. His dream was to be a cowboy, to "go west, young man." He says "cowboy" in a way that makes Max think not of guys with gunsight eyes and quick draws but merely young men, sometimes grown old, who work among cows for a living. He joined the cowboys' union, Ole adds. At first that sounds like some gesture at political wit: like introducing a speaker on a panel "to my far left" or "way over on the right." But Ole means it, there was a cowboys' union. He did some rodeo riding too, but he broke his hip, and they also organized a rodeo workers' union. It was "very close to the party," says Ole, and there were big battles with the rodeo employees' "association," a typical company union, which "all the men" knew was under the thumb of management and the cattle bosses. In fact, says Ole, it was the rodeos that made him a Marxist. One of the bull riders converted him. For bull riders, it was flirting with destruction out there every day, he says, just like it is down in the mines, and once you'd been trampled or crippled, the bosses would toss you outside the arena and look for new "meat" to put on the bulls. In those days, the thirties, it didn't take much to convince a young guy of the merits of Marx, or at the very least socialized medicine, now bowdlerized into universal health insurance. Then he rode the rails out to B.C. and did some logging in the woods near "Rupert" where R. B. Bennett's government put him in one of their "slave labour" camps—actually there are no quotes around any of these terms when Ole speaks them, just as there are none around the concentration camps he refers to where left-wingers like him were rounded up once the war (*the* war) began. Why was he rounded up? Well, he says, take your pick. There were the sit-down strikes. There was the Spanish Civil War support committee. There was the "On to Ottawa" trek in '35.

Max is good and curious now. "You weren't related to Rusty Olasson?" he says—a legendary organizer of the trek whom Max heard a paper on at a labour history session of the Learneds the year they were held in Halifax. "He's me," says Ole. "I'm him. We all got an English nickname along with our Icelandic one, because our parents thought it might be valuable when we went 'out' among the Canadians. I used it the time I was organizing in B.C. because I thought it might confuse the horsemen . . ." Max sees Deb glance sidewise to see if he knows this term for the Mounties. He can picture angry, exasperated young guys piling on top of boxcars and following this bony, mouthy man through the Rockies and across the Prairies in order to confront the smug bastards in Ottawa—if the horsemen hadn't broken up the party in Regina.

"So what is your notion of social class?" Ole asks, sitting there under the striped umbrellas on the patio, the goldeye fleet bobbing just beyond the chunky array of beer steins. The way you'd ask somebody if they believe in God or the afterlife. "Hm," says Max cleverly. Social class doesn't enter systematically into his way of seeing society. It's risky to admit in this company, but he does. Ole will surely view it as dangerously individualistic. Or shallow. Deb is attentive. "But," he goes on, shifting into his existential gear, which is all he's got at such moments, "I have always felt there are people nearby in the world who produce things that serve my needs while I provide nothing equivalent in return for them." He feels like it sounds mealy-mouthed and wussy. Soft Keynesian. Ole says, as if he's grasped Max's obtuse phrasing with no problem, "Always? Even when you were a kid?" Max says especially back then. Ole says, as if he's now over on Max's side of the social divide, "Well, that makes sense, since being a kid means getting looked after by others; but middle-class people normally lose that awareness when they grow up, although the working class never ceases to deliver things to the bourgeoisie as if they're needy, dependent children." He is undisconcerted by Max's existential gambit. It seems to energize him. Maybe he's intrigued by a different way of going at the good old questions. Spend your life fine-tuning a particular analysis like Marxism, no matter how superior you're sure it is, and you may be diverted, at least, by something different. You might find it a blessed relief. Like a Bible scholar who discovers a copy of the Bhagavad Gita or a Mickey Spillane that somebody else left on the train. Ole's curiosity—his delight even—seems to shade onto Deb. She stops looking like a marine about to step off the assault boats, screeching at the enemy. Ole says, "Tell me more." Max says, "It's a feeling, that's all. The workers are the people who have to provide for themselves and for people like me. Food, clothes, shelter, cars. The bourgeoisie, though I don't use that language much, are the ones who expect their own basic needs to be supplied by others while giving back little or nothing in return. So I try to write and think about things that aren't just useful to me and people like me, though it's pretty dreamy to expect workers will read a statistical analysis of the relative values added by domestic versus foreign-owned firms. Theoretically at least, I can tell myself I've put something on the table, sort of, in return for the food, shelter, and clothing laid out there for me by the workers." He smiles shyly: "the workers" isn't the kind of language he uses much either. It has a forbidden quality, he can taste it like good dope. "Have you done a statistical analysis that deals with foreign versus domestic value added?" says Ole. Max nods and says he'll mail it to Ole when he gets back home. That would be tomorrow.

Ole, it emerges, is the patron saint and leading light of the

Red Maples, a loose organization with a radical outlook that links folk, Deb among them, mostly on the Prairies and in B.C. Well, this is news, she didn't let on she was a card-carrying anything, just your basic politically conscious working-class mousewife. The Red Maples hold meetings, they collaborate to develop an "analysis"—the word irritates Max but he guesses that would be his problem, not theirs—of what Canada is and needs from the standpoint of "the workers." Why does the word sound so argumentative? *Workers, eh? Wanna make something of it?* Because it is, to a guy like Max and his ilk. But one look at old Ole and there isn't any doubt. He is a worker. The oral-history fanatics and documentary filmmakers must have worn a path here, at least Max hopes they have. The guy won't last forever, though he looks healthy as a horse, the ones he rode on cattle drives and roundups, not to mention the broncs he busted. Max asks what their analysis has yielded. If he can make peace with "worker," maybe he can coexist with analysis.

"Canada is still a colony," Deb answers like it's her catechism. Jesus, she's into it, as if she's been saving this item, setting him up with the mousewife stuff, then wham—Let's see how you handle my analysis of neo-colonialism. "Metaphorically, you must mean," he says. Whoops, he may have insulted them, minimizing their hard-won result, but really, how can anyone call Canada an actual colony? Ole doesn't sweat it. "Well, tell me this," he asks, amiable as a bear trap up here near the treeline. "If you say Canada is no longer a colony, then at what moment in its history did it become an independent nation?" It's a good point. Max leans back with his beer and grants their argument— it's one of his strengths intellectually: he's never surprised when someone else can teach him something. Ole and Deb want him to know how the insight emerged full-blown in a group discussion of Lenin's *On Imperialism*. It was an *Aha!* moment, like ones people in the progressive education movement live for. They can't even remember who said, or asked, it. Famous Sudden Insights: $E=mc^2$; *The medium is the message; Canada is a colony!* Not all inventions and discoveries can be patented, this one was an anonymous collective job, which pleases them. As they're leaving the pub, Ole says, "How's it look?" Maybe he means the town, the harbour, or the sunset. "Same old tub of shit," says Deb. "New paint job," says Ole. "He keeps it in shape." They're talking about a boat. When they get in the car Max says he didn't know her father lived here, they could drop in on him. "He's a prick," she says, "and we don't have time for the fight."

On the drive back to Winnipeg in the dark, they take the old road along the shoreline, passing through fishing towns with their tied-up boats. "My lake is bigger than your lake," she says, meaning Lake Ontario. She's not just making a joke, it really is. He asks if Stewart is part of her and Ole's group. She says he has been but there's a scoff in her voice, a scoff like a cough. Max says it must be good to have an aboriginal person in those discussions. "He's a lawyer," she says. Max, a fellow professional, shifts uncomfortably. "There are always problems," she goes on, "with the petite bourgeoisie, they're allies but unreliable." When they join the larger highway at Selkirk, she slips off the seat, unzips his fly, and sucks him. He is curious about whether he'll speed up or slow down when he comes, but he loses track as it happens. One of the problems of the participant observer. She stays there a while, seeming pleased. "You're my first Keynesian," she says from the floor. "No kidding?" he says. "You're my first worker."

The house they return to after their weekend in the Sexy Islands, as she calls them on the drive back, is definitely, definitively, working class. There are a few stairs up to the three bedrooms (the two boy bears share one), but nothing that defies basic-bungalow status. Split-level to him requires more pretension: like Noel's dad's sprawling new digs on the Bridle Path, where it ranks as one of the more modest abodes.

Deb's neighbour Sally, from across the vacant lot—a developer, some guy with no bank account but a wad of cash in his back pocket, held onto it for years, planning more split-level bungalows to gouge hardworking working folks, then decided against it—brings a bagful of bagels from her shift at the bakery, which Deb helped her find after she lost the good job at the produce plant that closed down as a result of new technologies in long-distance transport of fresh fruits and vegetables. Max has studied the economies of moving produce and concluded they are basically false, like most such "economies." It would be a good point to make, but he can't find a way in that wouldn't make him sound like the man from the moon. It was a good job, Deb and Sally say, because it was a union job, so you got dental. Right, dental. Obvious, though it wouldn't have occurred to him. Everybody needs dental, specially if you have kids, as these people all seem to. The one time he thought about having a kid when he and Olivia were still together (still *married*, bizarre thought), he knew, crazy as he was, it would be insane. He had a flash (which he has never shared, and never will) of himself in a state of abnegation and torment, grabbing the baby by the heels, swinging it like some guard at a concentration camp, and smashing its head into a—

"You an organizer?" says Sally, and his being swells in an unexpected reaction. As if he got stung by a hornet and found out he's allergic. No one ever took him for a union organizer— like Joe Hill or Ole "Rusty" Olasson—truth is he can't name many organizers but that doesn't matter, it's as romantic, it seems to him, as rodeo rider. You might take Max for a professor, a surgeon or doctor, even a network anchorman, the normal ragtag professions, but not someone who goes about alerting the underclass to their potential power. "No, I told you he's an *economist*," Deb says to her neighbour. "I think she thought I said you were a *communist*," she chortles, turning to Max. "Did you ever hear the one about how Che got to be finance minister after the Cuban revolution?"

She has to pick up the kids soon, but she'll drive him to the airport, it's on her way more or less. In other words, the effort will be Herculean and she's up to it. But before that, Harold Evanshen drops by; she mentioned that he might like meeting her new friend Max, or vice versa. Harold is her old buddy and a comrade in the Red Maples. He says he went to community college here, then transferred to UBC in Vancouver, where he studied genetics with David Suzuki. The man himself: science for the masses. But Harold decided academia was bullshit and dropped out to take a factory job where he could organize the workers for the revolution. He says this in a dry way, like: The Blue Bombers are playing the Eskimos tonight. These people expect a revolution sooner rather than later, if they just put their backs into it. They use definite articles ("the" revolution) the way the bourgeoisie goes through hair-care products. In the current Zeitgeist, it's Max who feels embarrassed at not routinely using the lingo. He read an article about Canada in the latest *Harper's*—not in some left-wing rag they force on you on a street corner—during the plane ride out here. "Quebec could become the Cuba of the north," it said. Sid wrote from London recently and asked if he could recommend anybody to write for *New Left Review* about the Canadian Revolution, or might he do so himself? People often take him for a leftist, the way they assume he can score acid for them, or an abortion.

Suzuki reamed out Harold, right in class, for quitting to join the working masses, because he had a bright future in genetics, he had a feel for it, said Suzuki. He wasn't disparaging the revolution, or those who joined it; his point was that many could go into the factories and organize the workers, but few had the potential to serve by developing genetic science in a way which would benefit all humanity (or mankind, as Suzuki probably put it in that early phase).

Max feels more à la maison, here in proletarian suburbia, with Harold, a guy who knows the difference between Hayek and Polanyi, or could sort it out if he doesn't, than with Deb and Sal. He and Harold speak the language even if they don't share a stance. Harold asks why Max isn't a Marxist and Deb perks up. It's an odd era, when you look back from later ones. The question wasn't why you would be a Marxist, a Maoist, or a revolutionary. Those choices *didn't* need explaining. It's why you *weren't* that you had to justify. You didn't feel you'd belched or farted when you said something left wing or just egalitarian. The *range* of political viewpoints had been enlarged, briefly. It was the glory of the 1960s, which lasted from about 1968 till 1971.

He and Harold cover the ground amiably. Harold seems ready to extend goodwill to any guy who's sleeping with Deb, perhaps he's always wanted to himself. Whoops, says Harold, he's gotta go (as if he read Max's thoughts and would rather not deal with them); he's drawn the graveyard shift at the meat-packing plant. It occurs to Max he doesn't know the difference between night shift and graveyard shift. He always assumed they were the same, to the degree he considered them at all.

It isn't as if he's never thought about workers, he thinks on the long dark flight home. (Taking the train back appeals to him, in theory. But it lacks the attraction going west to east that it has on the way "out." Coming back is something to get over with, like the day you decide to close the cottage. Everything else is shot. You can try swimming, you can sit on the dock. You might as well just pack up and leave.)

He believes labour is the source of all value. That isn't Marxist; it's pure Adam Smith, classical political economy. Marx merely added the stuff on exploitation and *surplus* value—enough of a refinement to roil the world in violence and dislocation for 150 years. In his writing and teaching, he always strives to treat the workforce as more than a "factor" of production. The language of the social sciences is one big tool of dehumanization. Workers are not a factor, they are the human essence at the core of that grim abstraction, the economy. He bridles at theories like Schumpeter's, which put the entrepreneur at the centre, or the sources of capital and finance like bankers and the decision takers in upper management. It's absurd to locate the "human element" of an enterprise that employs hundreds of thousands of distinct individuals—in a few executives and bean counters. They are also people, that abstraction known as a workforce. Each is the centre of his and her cosmic drama. This is his notion of existential economics, something he's never yet had the nerve to put in writing. To the management types in HR, they may be a number and function. But the worker on the line or nurse at her station feel a different burden, as searing as that felt by, say, a hockey player veering in alone on goal in overtime. It's not just a matter of whether he will or won't score. At this moment, this is the meaning of his life, a moral responsibility, not some input leading to an output. That applies to worker *and* winger. Still, even as he thinks about the existential quality of economics, he can hear the abstraction. Abstractions piled on abstractions, the life of the mind. He can't think of any workers he actually knows.

Maybe that's why he resists the sort of "analysis" that Ole, Harold, and Deb are devoted to. It's so very . . . Leninist. Sure, he analyzes, does it all the time. "Have you ever had an unanalyzed thought?" Rhonda once asked him. But not in their sense. His analyses are tedious, unresolved, irresoluble, an end in themselves really. I analyze, therefore I am. Theirs is the opposite. They would say what he does is *over*analyze. For them, each problem in life and politics has one and only one solution. Get the analysis right and the answer will pop out. Get the *social* analysis right and the revolution will pop out. No, he guesses, he doesn't really belong in that world of certainties and action based on them—

"Sir," says the stewardess, pardon, flight attendant. "You'll have to place your seat in the upright position." They're landing in Toronto. It's not often he loses himself completely. You gotta attribute it to the combo of left politics and oral sex, mingling in memory. He shifts his seat up energetically. She tapped him on the shoulder. Was that necessary, or a message? They did have that chat when he was waiting by the Occupied/*Occupé* washroom and she was draining her wretched Air Canada dinner. He was telling her about a little pasta place above a realtor on College Street he recommended during her stopover. Well, yes, he is an economist, so he can vouch for the value. No, he wasn't in Winnipeg on business. Aha, he thinks, a class difference: the bourgeoisie does "business," the working class . . . works. He was visiting friends, he said, and discussing how the world, um, works. He wonders if she'll slip him a matchbook with her name and hotel written on the inside cover as he says thanks on his way into the terminal. That's how you should treat working people: thank them, even though you've already paid for their services. It reflects the contradiction between use value and exchange value, as Ole and the comrades would say. It wouldn't be the first number he's been given by a flight attendant. Well, okay, it'd be the second.

He's settled back in, the direct dials to Deb continue. They've been anchoring him, a new feeling. They make him feel he has a soulmate, someone who really understands—at a safe distance. So he can continue womanizing—which also anchors him. One night, he's in a reggae club. Reggae was the music of liberation in those years, as rock was its sound in the sixties. Reggae added a global grace note to the Americanness of rock; that's global as in,"Workers of the world unite"; not, "The markets never close," or, "We'll move the plant to Malyasia if you ask for a raise." The headliner tonight is from Trinidad. He's singing The Mighty Sparrow's song about an intruder in the Queen's bedroom:

> *Philip my dear, last night I thought was you in here*
> *Where did you go, missing out all the action*
> *There was a mon in me bedroom*
> *Enjoying the view. . .*

He misses the familiarity that marks the English attitude to royalty, *their* royalty. Therefore theirs to disdain. Unlike Canadian respect for the royals, proving only that *we*'ve never felt *en famille* with the institution.

> *Puttin' on the royal costume, tryin' out the royal perfume*
> *I'm telling you true. . .*

The only person he doesn't know at the table is Elyse. She's clearly from the islands. Tight curly black hair, dark eyes, a complexion that mixes all the shades which have commingled there since, as Deb and the comrades might say, Columbus and those other imperialist bastards lied and bullied their way in. She wears a halter top and shorts that are pure Daisy Mae, if anybody remembers Dogpatch in the comics. Her legs don't end till about her armpits. He introduces himself across the table. She laughs—not just at this, at everything—and answers with the island lilt. It's impossible to hear anyone except, intermittently, the person beside you. Maybe he could reach her calf with his toe under the table, she's directly across, he can guesstimate the distance. Instead he mimes an invitation to dance. They go onto the floor and do the Failed Conversation: He shouts, she nods, she shouts, he nods, they both shout, "Can't hear a thing," and laugh.

He big just like you but younger
He strong just like you but harder. . .

He drives a bunch of them home from the club. One reason he owns a Pirate special, despite the aggravation, is so he can drive people places. It may not be "Solidarity Forever," but it counts, he hopes. He no longer has the Plodge. Eeph replaced it, first with a Pontiac Stratocruiser that had murderous tail fins, and now this Mercury with a roll-down rear window, ideal for transporting planks. He hasn't figured out any other use. He collects their destinations and contrives a route that will leave Elyse till last. He's heading down Vaughan toward St. Clair—of course she lives in one of the black neighbourhoods—when *pop*, he gets a flat. While he's changing it, she stands behind him and says,

"You really don't remember?" The island lilt is gone.

Ouch. "Where you from?" he says. "Saskatchewan," she says. "Saskatchewan?" he replies. "It's out west," she says. He concentrates on the lug nuts. One of them is tight as hell, it won't budge. "I'll show you," she says, stands on the tire iron with both feet, and bounces. The nut gives way with a squeak. She's from Saskatchewan all right. She's still balanced on the tire iron. Her hips are about the level of the street lights. They get back in and he's starting to turn the ignition. "'Cool City,'" he says, like someone waking from a coma with your loved ones all around. He could mean Saskatoon but he doesn't.

"Yes," she says, as if he can go on to the next level. Canadians have a touch for game shows. Alex Trebek comes from somewhere on the Prairies. "At the *Sun*," he says, slumping, as she steps down from the tire iron like the hostess who displays the appliances you're playing for. She got his name from somebody, maybe Noel, or someone who knew Noel, since everyone did. "Cool City" was a weekly feature she wrote for the entertainment section of the *Sun* on people who made Toronto cool. Or neat. His cachet? He left Toronto a mousy backwater and returned to find it a truly newly, gasp, world-class place. The format was Q and A: What do you miss about London? What did you miss about Toronto when you were there? What was your favourite TV show? What restaurant or food that you couldn't get in London did you fantasize about? (Swiss Chalet barbecue chicken.) He asked her questions back, in his fashion. So what's it like working there? Not so good, she said, unless you're ready to play the bimbo, but it served her purpose. Which was? Gathering material for a screenplay on the urban treadmill—it was her "working title"—the endless, pointless, titillating, grating lives of people in the city. It didn't sound so bad. Writing a screenplay wasn't as offensive as it became later; those were days when you overheard café conversations that were *not* about making a movie. She needed a photo of Max, which she had to take herself, and quick as a bunny he said why didn't she drop over. Had they slept together? Did he start and she didn't respond? Or she responded and then pulled back? Or went to bed with him and left? Or stayed for breakfast? He's been in places with half a dozen women present he could have asked the same questions about. Like tonight. When did he stop keeping count of the number he'd slept with? Fifty? Hundred and fifty? For sure before a hundred and fifty.

"What about the island stuff?" he says as she tells him to keep going past St. Clair. Her place is down near the art gallery, not far from his. "I've been playing that role every day for two months now at this factory where I work," she says. "It started out as a weird thing to do. To see if I could. Now it's sometimes easier to keep it going after work than to switch back. My friends are used to it."

"So maybe they thought I knew?" he says hopefully. "Could be," she says, with a friendly smile. "Hey," she adds as they're passing the El Mocambo, "let's go see Elvis Costello." He doesn't know the name, she tells him it's a very cool singer doing his first gig in Toronto. Sadly, they can only get a table downstairs, and Elvis is upstairs, so they talk some more. She tells him she left the *Sun* long ago but kept freelancing there—a story on parrot smuggling, people who've gone back to live with their parents, she specializes in quirky. Quirky wasn't stupid until it became so . . . conventional. A couple of months ago, some friends from university who were working for a small union and getting paid in government youth grants asked if she'd apply to work in an electronics-parts assembly plant they wanted to organize. They needed someone inside to identify key people, gather names, numbers, etc. Well, that'll be different, she thought. There were Caribbean workers among the many immigrant groups assembled by the owners. She was just back from a holiday on St. Bart's, had a great tan, and could do the voice. It was the pretend part that appealed most. Maybe she'd end up writing about it. It might make a movie—remember that book, *Black Like Me*? He gathers "The Urban Treadmill" has bit the dust. "How's it going?" he asks. It's going okay. But it wears her down. He wonders if it's like acting. She says she guesses it is, as though everyone asks that. Except you can't ever step offstage, where the stage manager hands you a glass of water till your next entrance.

They've left the El Mo and are parked outside her place across from the art gallery. Front-seat intimacy. He puts a hand lightly against her forearm. It's awkward but not aggressive: a wordless question. He doesn't mind raising the issue directly, he can discuss and analyze anything, as we know, but sex isn't really about talk, it's about skin. If you ask directly, he's learned, if you put the possibility in words instead of touch, then it's as if you've already moved past it, onto the abstract terrain of language, the way economists do with the economy. Let it be decided on its own terms: touch to touch. Anyway, a rejection is a rejection, the particular method doesn't really matter. She pulls her arm back gently and says, "You know if this signing-up thing gets going, we have to move fast. Would you help? Maybe you could use it, like, research, and write a paper on it."

"You mean be an organizer?" he says. Yeah, okay, count him in. He doesn't know if it's because it really could be research, or to impress Deb, or to keep the thing with Elyse going.

This is when Deb arrives with the three bears. He didn't know she'd bring them, but come to think of it, he didn't know she was moving here. She said she might visit. Now she's standing in the hallway outside his apartment. "There's no pressure," she says, with three kids and six suitcases beside her. God knows what the old man on the second floor made of their procession past his door. He says they can stay with him a while. She scores the night job at the bakery. She goes out to work while he reads the kids *Mickey in the Night Kitchen*, with the bakers who look like Laurel and Hardy, their favourite book because of what their mama does. He loves it as much as they do, or more. One night Petey wanders in with his hair cut so he'll look like he's balding too. Max considers it the high point of his life, at least so far.

But he tells her it doesn't change the stuff about sex, that he's non-exclusive. Sure, she says, that's what she likes about him. No bourgeois property bullshit applied to wife and family—even if his politics is pretty questionable. Only one thing, what about the sheets? She asks about this more than once, she doesn't want to get into his bed and roll around on someone else's "skin flakes." He's a bit perplexed, it has an unproletarian sound. Nobody else ever asked about skin flakes, but nobody else is his anchor, and moved here because it's where he is. The others come and go, they don't have the right to raise the sheets issue, if it ever occurs to them. Maybe it has. He tells her not to worry, implying he'll either change them or wash them. It's one of those conversations that don't go well.

A few days later he gets home and she's gone. As he's looking around feeling surprised and relieved, she phones. She's taken an apartment in the Beaches with the three bears. It's great, she says. He hears the kids shrieking in the background and feels bereft. She did it in about twenty minutes:

saw apartment, signed lease, moved in. That's how she oper-
ates: pure will, force of nature. Nothing is planned, she erupts
from time to time. That's how things in her life change: volcanically. No other way seems reliable in her mind. If she does-
n't act volcanically, she'll never accumulate enough energy to
move at all. Does he want to come and see it? See me? See the
kids? He gets in the car and drives. Drives and drives. She seems
farther than she did when she was on the Prairies. Which she is,
by certain calculations. Getting to her by phone was almost
instantaneous. This takes far longer. By the time the kids are
asleep, it's late, they're both tired, it's her night off. She tells him
she's planning to open a specialty dessert shop, to tap the trendy
tastes of the Toronto bourgeoisie. It's part of the eruption phase
she's in. She's accumulated a little capital—as Marx would say—
maybe Max would like to make a small investment. It'll give her
independence and she won't have to crawl around taking orders
from some vile boss. It occurs to him that she'll be a boss herself, but he doesn't raise it. She just moved out and he misses the
kids already. They crawl into her bed. After, he says he'll drive
home and sleep there, for some reason or other. On the way back
along the Gardiner, the city to the right, the lake on his left, he
has the conversation they didn't have. She has a right to be her
own boss, and the boss of others for that matter. Even Lenin—
think of his New Economic Program—said after the Russian
Revolution, What this country needs is a little capitalism. At
least the skin-flakes problem has been shelved.

He goes to the launch party for a knock-off line of multicoloured
watches. It's a start-up by Clifford, who is Max and Noel's drug
dealer—as in grass, cannabis only, full stop. Clifford took his
profits and bought a Canadian franchise from the Swiss firm

that produced the watches. He knew the seventies wouldn't last forever. But the American franchisee combusted on learning Canada would be carved from his fiefdom, because Canada is *always* included in the U.S. market, and the Swiss caved, cancelling Clifford's franchise. Max explained to Clifford that this is the nature of the Canadian economy, it's a dependency. If Clifford showed any real interest, he'd proceed to Innis's thesis about empire. Clifford said, Well then, fuck it, he'd create a stand-alone Canadian firm and compete with the Swiss and Americans and everybody else. Noel said he'd do the legal paperwork, he was still looking for a specialty. He also volunteered to throw in a hunk of his dad's money. Max is so sure the whole pathetic effort will tank that he buys a watch he doesn't need at the launch party with money he doesn't have. And meets Charlotte, the last WASP. Button nose, cheekbones built to last, modish coiffe with blonde streaks.

She is there, like Liberty in Delacroix's painting, inspiring the mob yet not of them. She asks what he does. He says he's a freelance economist. Funny, he never said that before. He has noticed, or others like Noel have noticed for him, that he hasn't settled into a career niche. The university, Bay Street, the unions. He says no one made him a decent offer, but maybe he isn't looking. Maybe he's the occupational equivalent of a womanizer, it's his personality: promiscuous in general. He always liked the idea of freelance writers, though that doesn't really fit. More like freelance in the auld sense: medieval knights who wander the countryside, offering their services. Of course it's the birthday letter from Amy that spurred this thought, but he hardly recalls it, it came just when Deb and the three bears did.

He gets Charlotte's name and gives her his number. Three days later, when she hasn't phoned, he looks her up and calls.

"That's funny," she says, "I'm looking at your number." He says, "Yeah, sure" and she says, "Really, I'm looking at it right now," and reads it to him. He wonders how long she's hovered over it.

After dinner they go to his place. He's moved again, to Huron Street. He likes the reference to native peoples. He makes his direct approach, since he knows no other; they nuzzle, she pulls back and asks him to phone a cab. When he calls next day she says she was about to dial him, as if pondering phone calls is a career choice. She puts him off for a month, then they have dinner again and she says she'd like to go to his place. They have what he thinks of as a WASPy time in bed, he asks her to stay over, adding he doesn't always make this offer, and she requests a ride home. Not a taxi this time, personal transport.

It's a high-rise north of Eglinton. They sit outside in the dark. He asks which is hers. She points to the top floor, fourteen, really thirteen. Only in (North) America. She seems to be thinking intensely, the way she must when she's on the verge of a phone call, then asks if he would like a colour TV. There was a guy, see . . . She used to live in rich, WASPy Markham with a husband and kids. Then she began having obsessive sexual thoughts about her t'ai chi instructor; then she met this Armenian businessman who lived out there too but who co-rented a downtown apartment with his buddies where they took women they were having affairs with. She was different, he said. He was going to leave his family and she would leave hers. So she did and he didn't. Max looks up at the thir—fourteenth floor. He bought out his buddies, she says. The first time he came to visit after she moved in, he brought a colour TV and plunked it down like a job description: you are to sit in this sterile place and await me. "Okay," says Max, "I'll take it." She doesn't ask him up, she lugs it down herself.

Just a few months back, he turned down a colour TV at reduced cost that Noel's dad knew about—salvaged from a fire in a mall owned by a guy he did business with. Smoke damage, that's all. There you have Noel's dad. Loaded, but assumed you'd prefer a finagle to a gift. Noel took a set for his kitchen, he already had one in the living room and the bedroom; Max declined at the time. He wasn't embroiled in consequences of blood or inheritance. But he regretted it, especially while the three bears were there. And now here's a giveaway. Within a week he's hooked. The thing about colour, which you can't know if you didn't grow up with black and white, is the sudden and unexpected *depth* it lends TV. The three bears start spending more sleepovers, though not their mom. When he sleeps with her, it's out in the Beaches. He feels he's turned into someone Deb is wary of, then someone she is plotting against. Is he paranoid? Who knows, maybe this is what relationships are about. A certain hostile edge. Keeps up the interest. He doesn't hear from Charlotte for a long time.

Finally, six months later, he's at lunch with her. "The bad-news meal," Rhonda calls it. "If they plan to kiss you off. Cuz everyone has to go back to work." Hmm. In fact, she did invite *him* here. They're at a chick restaurant: you never come away feeling full. "I can't see you any more," she says. "And you need to give back my TV." The Armenian lover finally left his family and moved in with her. As she speaks, there is an abundance of feeling in her voice. His first words after he settled in were, "Where's the damn TV?" Surely he noticed its absence during his many visits. Maybe he assumed she had stuffed it in the closet, or got the super to haul it down to her locker. Or tossed it off the balcony like the opening shot on SCTV. Maybe he didn't want to open the subject, and hear her opinion of the message that came with the set like a closed caption. But now he's in, and he wants his set.

Max is thinking about what to do for a TV. It's late to call Noel's dad and ask if the burnt crisp specials are still on offer. He can hear the old man. "You damn liberal do-gooders, you're all the same. You think the world was built to serve your timetable. You think inventory doesn't have to move? What the hell did you learn about economics at Oxford?" Meanwhile she's talking about a trip. Her prize is taking her to the land of his ancestors, which you can't find on a map because of their great historical tragedy. They will visit the sites of his people's martyrdom. The WASP queen tours the valley of ethnic death. She's on her way out now. She graciously paid the bill up at the door when she went, ostensibly to pee, just before coffee came. Of such subtle stuff is lunch made. "Hey," he says as she gathers up her gloves, "what does this guy do anyway?"

"I told you," she says, which could be true, "he owns a factory. Dynamet Electronics."

That night Elyse calls. It's been a while since reggae night. "Hey, mon," she says, "we're ready to start signing people up at Dynamet. Are you in or out?"

"I thought I recognized the name," he answers. "I'm in. Tell the brothers and sisters."

He's planning to make the long trek to the Beaches to see Deb and the kids tonight. He hopes the union gig will impress her. Or just touch her. That's his ardent wish, to touch her. She has this hold on him. What others think of him matters, but she's on a special level. It must be her diabolical confidence: to be liked by someone so imbued with certainty would mean you are truly worth liking. On the other hand, there's Deb's new plan to join the bourgeoisie and open a cake shop, or should that be shoppe?

Is it already too late to impress her by enlisting in the workers' cause? When he tells her about Dynamet, she's enthusiastic. She wants to hear about the organizing drive as it proceeds. What about that other thing? Oh, the pastry biz? Nah, she'd hate it. She's already forgotten it. Why? She doesn't ever want to become one of them, it's too satisfying to loathe them with zeal and righteousness, there's something so pure about hate, she says.

The change in his life is exponential, like an economy reaching the fabled "takeoff." It's as though he acquires another life, alongside the one, or ones, he already has. Each evening he turns into the Organizer. He speeds across the top of the city in his latest Pirate special, a rusting Honda Accord—Eeph has branched into foreign wrecks and amalgams, anticipating globalization, as if he is piloting a pod launched from the main ship. It hovers above a strange new world: the planet of the workers. He visits various populations below. At one end of his course, a colony of Italians sent to inhabit Mississauga from their original foothold in Little Italy. "Hi, my name is Max, I'm from the union. Is Franco home? Franco? Hi, how's it going up at the factory? Come in? I'd love to. Some of your own homemade wine? Great. . ." Then dip down the Don Valley Parkway to the Danforth, visit some Greeks and Macedonians, and God forbid you confuse them. "You think I'm *Greek!*?" Maybe the guy you're looking for is at the barber shop on Pape. In there it's a rowdy seminar on politics, words stopping just short of blows, as if the Greek civil war never ended, the one Harry Truman funded to stop Communism in its tracks, and Stalin sold out in return for the status quo in Eastern Europe. "Son of a bitch, Stalin, but really, in his position, what else could he do?" says the guy getting a trim. Max departs feeling as enthused as

Byron, who left his own cushy life to join an earlier conflict in Greece. Cut back to a low-rise on Vaughan, from the days when builders (not yet glorified into contractors and ages before they became developers) still named those places themselves. Max always charts his course, using a Perly's guide, to start at the periphery and work his way to the address nearest home. At first it was a relief to be back and stop on Bloor or College, as if he could remove the oxygen pack and breathe air made for his species. But this changes, to his surprise, as if he is acclimatizing, growing new organs that were stunted because they were unnecessary for the life he lived in the past. He starts to feel at home out in the galaxies, yakking with the locals, after all they are humanoids too, seeded in different parts of the universe by a wise generation of intergalactic travellers aeons past, he saw it on a "Star Trek" rerun late one night when he was so excited about his new life that he couldn't sleep.

Why is he so at ease among these people, chatting in their kitchens or on their porches during summery Toronto nights? Of course his family were once immigrants too, but only in the trite sense that everybody was, except native people (unless you buy what the right-wingers in poli sci say: that Indians have no basis for land claims because they also immigrated across the Bering Strait when there was nothing on this side except saber-toothed tigers and glaciers). But these are new, true immigrants; he is older stock, and always felt well apart from the workers. Whoops, lookit that. *The* workers, no quotes. It just happened.

There is a change in his daily, more or less, rages. The Cadillac dawdling in front of him as he races to knock on the door of one last worker before they've turned in, that brakes to a smug stop at every nuisance intersection of a residential street—it isn't just the sanctimonious back of the driver's head which infuriates him as the back of slow drivers' heads always do; this is a *boss* slowing him down (another word that has lost its quotes and doesn't know where to find them), in a Caddy it's gotta be, the cutthroat owner of some factory squeezing his Marios and Surinders, or one of the drones who work for the bosses, shaving tax returns for them, closing the purchase of their cottages in Muskoka, checking their cholesterol every three months so they can stay in harness and keep screwing all the hard-working souls in the plants—

Sometimes he meets a Paulina on the Danforth or an Annamaria in Little Italy. The daughter of workers (Paulina) or a worker herself (Annamaria), and they make his heart go pit-a-pat, just like the women in the bars or seminars. Elyse has identified Annamaria as the potential leader in the plant. As he pulls up at her address, he just knows she is in her fifties with lots of kids and a moustache. But of course she's twenty and exploding with vitality (same thing for him as sexuality). She's been in the plant since she was fourteen. Isn't that illegal? They sit in her living room with her parents and sisters buzzing around. He feels a rescue impulse: Let me take you away from this life, the dignity of which I've spent all my evenings for weeks now extolling to you and your fellow wage slaves. But who would she be if she wasn't installing radio faces at Dynamet—a media researcher? a grad student? He can't construct the conversation at the end of which they'll be in bed and all over each other.

Then comes the "famous lull," as the experienced union people call it, as if it's an element of mass culture like Dylan or Trudeaumania. They're short a handful of names to apply for certification to the Labour Board and the sign-ups go dead, all on a Monday night. He tells Elyse there's no way it can be typical, much less predictable. There are too many independent variables.

He's built a rough model and run what was quantifiable through it: number of employees, size of workforce, timeline of the campaign. You can't replicate the graph, even roughly, for every union drive. Yet all that they say will happen, does. His evenings turn into conversational torture. He returns to the same Uncertains again and again. They're polite, they work on a picnic table they're making, watch an Argo game, open a beer, reminisce about the old country—and never give him an answer. "You know what I'm saying?" says Marek from Zagreb. "You're lonely here," he says. "Lonely?" says Marek. "Ha! If there was a path across the ocean from here to Croatia, I'd walk there right now."

He races to Deb's place that night. He's timed it so he can catch himself as he drives on a pre-recorded radio panel about social transformation in revolutionary societies. He doesn't know much about such places so he's winging it. You do that on media. You never say no or they won't call again. Cuba and China aren't exactly models of Keynesian economics, but then he's not a model Keynesian in his current version. He listens to himself explain alternate methods of organizing the rural masses: inspirational leadership in the case of Cuba, mass mobilization in China. Sounds perfectly doable. Meanwhile September is rushing at them and they can't even get a certification vote. He sits outside Deb's apartment until the show ends. It would be crass to go inside and turn it on. When he enters, she says, "You sounded smart. How's the campaign going?" He glows. Oh, and her plan for the pastry boutique is back on. Um, what about your class hate? He doesn't ask. Who can keep track?

Next morning at home, Charlotte phones. Charlotte of the colour TV. "Why are you trying to ruin my life?" she says. Does she regret not seeing or sleeping with him since their lunch at the chick café. Does she want to come over and, um, talk about it?

It's you and your damn union. Edgar is insane over it. Edgar? Who finally moved in and demanded his TV back. Edgar? Well, it was something else in Armenian but they anglicized it so he could go to Trinity College at the U of T, then business school in the States. He had great plans for the company when he finally took it over from his tyrannical founder father, around the time they went on the Armenian pilgrimmage. Now some union is closing in and the old coot is issuing threats and denunciations from his retirement on the gulf coast. He should never have let his overeducated son take charge, this union crap was unthinkable when he ran the place, the workers respected him, hadn't he worked as hard and harder as they ever did, and didn't they know it? If they had a problem, they brought it to him, man to man, settled it like members of a family. No labour-relations crap or personnel-management techniques that look good in a textbook.

As she rambles on, he thinks of the Chiclet teeth, the blonde streaks, the uselessness of academic theory when you're actually dealing with the real world of work and the economy. He says it isn't about her, it has nothing to do with them, this could have been any paternalistic family-owned company sweating the hell out of its immigrant workforce—

She's hung up by then. He sees her years later. She honks and waves as she drives by in a shiny little car as cute as she is; he looks up as he's getting into his own, a Saab, his first new car ever. He's moved on too, everyone does.

Then the company makes a mistake. It could be Edgar. Or his dad. Or Edgar's dad operating inside Edgar's head, which is known philosophically as the cunning of history. They fire Annamaria, on flimsy grounds. The workers head for cover, the union files a complaint at the Labour Board, the process slides into even lower gear. Max asks Noel if he'd like to work on the case. Noel has been edging his way into practice by lawyering part-time at a community legal-aid clinic. Noel says, "What do you think the law is—a corner store where you can take your pick off the shelf? A licorice here, a yogurt, some dish detergent? You think you can just do a labour case out of nowhere? Can you do economics like that?" He sounds like his dad. Max, chastened by the example of someone taking his chosen field seriously, arranges to do a late-night TV opinion piece on the union drive for a show called "Commentary," to take advantage of his professional, um, advantages. He tries to sound as academic as a bibliography. "To many, Dynamet Electronics might seem to be a success story of Canadian business. Yet it is currently embroiled in a labour controversy that raises troubling questions for economists and citizens alike. . ." He feels as if he's wearing somebody else's clothes. What would the guys on the Danforth who mistook him for a genuine organizer think? Meanwhile, Noel has seen a photo in the paper of Annamaria and decides to help out after all, pro bono, as they say on American lawyer shows. It will be Noel for the Oppressed, like "Judd for the Defence." To everyone's astonishment, the Labour Board rules in favour of the union and orders Annamaria rehired. Maybe they're dazzled by her too. It's just a regulatory board ruling but Max feels like his team won the Stanley Cup. The day after, when you would have the victory parade, he meets Edgar, sort of, at last. They're in a corridor at the Labour Board, Edgar is with one of his lawyers. As Max goes by, trying to read the ROB on the run, Edgar says, "If it isn't Canada's hottest late-night TV star." He fervently wants to answer, "Rough night, Edgar?" Lines like that don't often come when you need them; they're always late, what you should have said. But he calls on something Ole and the comrades would call revolutionary discipline: the ability to forgo personal pleasure for the sake of a political goal. He walks on down the hall. The workers take due note of the board's decision, and the astounding fact that ownership doesn't always get its way, the laggards sign up, and the union is certified.

Next day he drops by Edeble Sweets to tell Deb. That's what she calls her new dessert business: Edeble Sweets, the Pastry Boutique. It's in a coach house off Bloor. She takes that restless energy—the anger, the politics, the hefty analysis, the rage against dad—and converts it all into action. That's her secret. Maybe she figures she'll sneak around the class lines and launch an attack from the rear. Her friend, Harold Evanshen, put up the money. He's been dabbling in the health-food biz, based on the knowledge of plants and herbs he picked up back in the Suzuki days. He started a line of vitamins and additives with his name, Harold's Wholesome Supplements, and his headshot right on the bottles. Deb asked and he wrote the cheque, it got her started. The location isn't ideal, she'd like to have a storefront for drop-in traffic, but right now she's concentrating on catering parties and supplying restaurants.

As he enters, he passes a dapper man with a familiar face and a benign expression, on the way out. "Hi," says Max. The man *beams* back. It's like edging past the Buddha in a hallway. A moment later Max feels like a fool. It was one of those faces you recognize from their photo in the paper (at the top of his columns) or guest appearances on TV. They seem more familiar than your neighbours or, sometimes, your family. It was Robbie Carignan. "His suits are finer, his writing is wittier, his women are more spectacular!" Max heard that on a talk show. If you read about a young beauty in his column this week, you can bet you'll see him out with her next week. Montages of Robbie's women show at the photo galleries. They say Robbie has never met a beautiful woman who didn't have, in his instant estimate, great potential for journalism. They show up at his newsroom regularly with the article he urged them to write the other night at the party, the bar, or in the theatre lobby. He lets his editors deal with it, then takes them for a drink. The point is: Robbie is a *real* womanizer. Max shudders as he looks around the boutique. Deb is across the room, nearly obscured by an array of chocolate.

She's delighted he came, she says, not breaking pace from the baking and supervising. Two women follow her instructions closely, he tries to think of them as workers but they look more like employees. He waits four or five seconds, and asks what Robbie was doing here. She shrugs. Shrugs are killers. Might as well just plant that dagger in my neck. She says he wanted to see the operation, as if he's the health inspector. "We're friends," she adds. "Didn't you see what he wrote about me?" It's up on the wall, the endpiece tacked onto one of his columns, which often seem to run out of steam. "Comin' on Strong" is the head; it's about "IncreDeble Deb" and her funky coach house start-up with the great treats, a formula just right for T.O. Within days, the chauffeurs from Rosedale will be dropping by in their limos to pick up orders. Haute Toronto loves to be told what it likes. She takes a call from a customer and explains that yes, the micro-pizzas are expensive, that's because they're labour intensive. The customer seems delighted to hear it. Max asks if she wants to get something to eat, a stupid question considering the batteries of food around them. She says there's a nice place across the street, he can wait for her there, "Oh, and take something to read, I'll be a while."

He enters the café and there in a corner, ensconced like a

Mafia don in one of his fronts, is Robbie. Max has never been here and he's sure Robbie hasn't either, yet he somehow has taken over. They could put a plaque above his booth: Robbie's Roost. Apparently that happens if you're famous. He's reading a paper, which surprises Max. Robbie's columns sound as if he never reads anything. Maybe long ago, he kept up, but now his stuff is all name-dropping, of politicians or getaway resorts. He looks up without raising his head and calls Max over. He seems to say, *Siddown, kid,* though probably *kid* is implied. "How do you make a living?" he asks Max. Wow. He was expecting Robbie to say, "Stay away from her." Or, "How long is your schlong?" Actually, Robbie is quite short, Max noticed it in the hall. Sort of like Trudeau, Canada's all-time top-ranked womanizer, who was amazingly short when you saw him among normal humans. It's not a bad question, after all Max is an economist, whose opinions Robbie seems hazily aware of. In fact, Robbie seems hazy on most things. It's not noon yet but Max realizes Robbie is drunk. He tries to explain how he makes his living, though he's hazy on that himself.

The waitress comes for his order and Robbie flirts without saying much. She's blushing, she's practically crossing her legs and he's barely spoken. "Very smart," says Robbie when she walks away, as if she could run the IMF or the World Bank. He should know, he's been everywhere, Lebanon most recently, Max thinks he recalls reading about it. Robbie says yeah, it used to be one of the great places. You can *ski* there in the afternoon and then hit the clubs after dark. But the insane politics of the region have turned the place to chaos. The Israelis are bombing and the refugee camps are in turmoil. Max asks hungrily for news. "I met a high school teacher from Smith Falls on the plane over," says Robbie. "I said, 'Let me show you Beirut by night.' Jesus, can you believe I said that? And she bought it? At midnight there we were, in the pool at the top of the hotel." Max leaves before Deb arrives, if she ever does.

The organizing drive morphs into first-contract bargaining, almost a year of pointless aggravation. Max misses it because he takes a contract in Saskatchewan where the NDP government needs a study to justify public auto insurance, in case they decide to create it. NDP strategists across the country have decided auto insurance is a magic potion for voters. He's up against a respectable Marxist economist with an actual academic position, so of course the socialists take Max, the moderate Keynesian, in order not to seem like dangerous radicals. They are unaware that he has transformed into the Organizer. He feels like Clark Kent, using Superman as his secret identity. He tells Deb it's ironic: now that she and the three bears are in Toronto, he's going out where she used to be. She says Saskatchewan isn't Manitoba. Like most easterners, she adds, he sees the West as a single neighbourhood, a suburb of Ontario.

The day he moves into his minuscule office in Regina, he meets his supervisor: Stewart Downey. Deb's estranged hubby. Papa to the three bears. Stewart took the job here in the AG's office, when his lovely little family went east. He wasn't involved in hiring Max and he's been assigned the auto-insurance brief since then, so it's all coincidence. They have a businesslike conversation. Max is still in class-struggle mode; he expects a fist to fly, or an epithet. Instead he learns that Stewart is a true *professional*, maybe the first Max has met. He is commited to his job, the way other people are to saving runaway teens. He tells Deb about it on the phone: now he's direct-dialling home all the time, a strange experience. She says Stewart chose to be a lawyer, not a native, because he doesn't like doing law that reminds him of who he really is. Stewart, in conversations with Max, says he didn't want to be a one-dimensional man. He won't do land claims, he doesn't do native self-government. He does law. It's the same thing that Deb said, but completely different. He and Max never discuss her or the kids, which Deb says is sick, and male. Eventually Max submits his report. Public auto insurance is doable and desirable: exactly what he was hired to write, yet he arrived at it independently, using scholarly tools. The government thanks him for the report, and does nothing with it. "That's the left," says Deb. Go to a lot of bother, make sure everyone is exhausted and miserable, accomplish nothing and everyone is happy.

Elyse calls just after his return. She's scored one of those government youth-training grants her friends all have, and moved on to the union staff. She's dropped the island voice. "Bargaining just broke down," she says and they're officially, legally on strike. The union is loaded with efficient, idealistic young women like herself, but those darned workers say they'd feel better if they had a man with them on the picket line. Some of them asked about the organizer named Max. He feels a delicate tickling below, like long, careful fingernails stroking his balls. He prepares to turn back into the Organizer, like a werewolf.

The first morning on the line he's clueless. He's seen movies about strikes, but they always seem to walk in careful little circles, maybe so the camera won't have to reposition too often. He's at the warehouse, a few miles from the main production factory, him and a dozen guys, men only, the dirty dozen. When the company van starts out, they block it, they try to talk to the driver, a luckless Newfoundlander, who continues to inch forward. Max backpedals as the van advances and, in a burst of creative militancy, bends the wiper out of shape, then jumps aside as the van roars off. By lunch a patrol car has taken a position across the road. Two cops come over to usher cars and trucks through. In mid-afternoon another cop car slinks in and they all have their first tussle. Max feels as awkward as he did at the camp social. Hand-to-hand combat (unlike mouth-to-mouth) hasn't been part of his training.

Everyone grabs a partner. Romir the stationery engineer, who was in the border police in the Punjab, squares off against one cop. He places a hand on the cop's shoulder, points the other in his face, and says, "You. Stay here." It works. It must help to have been one. Others make up their own steps. As the dance unfolds, Max moves about trying to calm things, till the melee dissipates like morning fog on the lake. Then it starts over, with the next vehicle. He is a man in action, yet a peacemaker, like a U.S. marshal in the comic books he used to buy. It's as if there's somebody else walking at his side now, everywhere he goes, it could be that marshal. One night he's coming out of a movie— he thought it would help to do something familiar and passive; a parking-lot attendant steps from a hotel lot and stands with his back to the pedestrians, holding out an arm to let the cars of diners and moviegoers flow into the street while the mere walkers wait. Max reaches out, presses the guy's arm down as if it's a lever, and walks by. The crowd follow. The attendant just stands there. It's as though the touch barrier has been broken. Ever since he survived the breakup with Olivia and turned into the Womanizer, he's wondered what forbidden terrain would come next. He thought it might be gay sex, but it never happened. Hard drugs? Or fighting? You hit somebody in the face, they hit you back. Another boundary crossed.

Next day Elyse comes up to the line and says people in the

office think he should make a report to the local cop shop, for the record. They leave the shipper called Zizi, whose real name is Papa, in charge of the line. They go to the station and wait a couple of hours, typical bureaucratic procedure, he observes. It could be unemployment insurance, could be waiting for building permits, or a censor's office somewhere in Eastern Europe. In such situations, he calls on his years of graduate training. Every trick and strategy helps. He doesn't know how people without higher education survive those lines (he underestimates the power of the workers' patience). When they finally see the captain, Max talks fluidly, making points about zealous, discriminatory police behaviour, backed up by examples, with corroborative details. Driving back to the line, Elyse says, "You are so not a worker."

At the end of week one, he and his comrades leave the line and head down to a meeting at the so-called union hall, a cruddy second-storey office at 2545 1/2A Oakwood, a humiliating address for a fighting organization: "1/2" is bad enough; "A" puts it beyond the pale, whatever a pale is. He's got five of them stuffed in his Honda. At Lawrence and Dufferin they stop dead in rush hour. It's steamy. He looks around at the people in cars: some like him, that is his other self, the professional; others are businessmen or office workers. He can't shrug without everyone in the car having to rearrange themselves. They've been fighting together for five days, backing one another, laughing, "holding off the forces of the state," as Deb would say. "Do you know how much money you lost since you went on strike?" a cop taunted Zizi, while Max was off haranguing the captain. "I know," Zizi said, "but I think for the future." He reported this proudly to Max. There is no one in the world he'd rather be with.

After the meeting, he drives Elyse home. They sit talking, the art gallery out the rear window behind them. The thought of touching her hair passes through his mind as if occurring to somebody else. He's the Organizer now, not the Womanizer. He's telling her how he felt in the traffic jam. "I know," she says, "I miss it, now that I'm in the office." Miss what? "The contact," she says.

That weekend is Noel's birthday. He takes a select group to dinner at prohibitive cost. Each guest represents a period in his life. It was Nadine's idea. There's a vintage wine for each phase. Max has phase one. Representing a later segment is Aubrey, who lives in Manhattan and works for a talent agency there, so he meets lots of stars and lets you know it. Noel met him through Nadine, they all holiday together in the Auvergne or the Loire or someplace you can impress yourself visiting wineries. Unfortunately, Max is across from Aubrey. A conversation happens, like a bad accident. It billows around the strike. It's about lives that count and lives that don't. Labour, and those who exploit it. The wine flows. Aubrey is "sensitive," in the technical sense. He feels people's pain and so forth. They're on bottle six or seven, or on into the house brands. Max is ardently describing Annamaria's bravery in taking on a company that pretty much raised her and employs her entire family, what the workers (no quotes) have been put through with the scabbing, the security thugs, etc. "I can feel her pain," says Aubrey. "Here," says Max, in the only phrase he recalls afterward, "feel some of your own." He flicks a backhand, palm open, across Aubrey's gob. Words have consequences, those consequences can be physical, people should know it, or learn it. Somehow he weaves home in the Honda. It's one of those drives you don't deserve to live through.

"You were brilliant," Noel calls to tell him when he wakes up. Max wonders what he said. "But there is a problem," Noel continues. "You broke Aubrey's bridge, it's worth three or four thou in U.S. dollars. Plus the guy could sue for assault, widely witnessed, which you may not need at the moment." Under Noel's coaching, Max sends a tiger plant care of Aubrey's aunt in Forest Hill, where he stays when in the city. Seconds later, Aubrey phones, ecstatic. "What a rapport you and I have. We are like Gide and Proust. I can't wait to get back to tell my men's consciousness-raising group in Manhattan." Aubrey has simply refused to acknowledge that somebody bashed him in the face last night out of distaste, it must have been due to—profound respect! No wonder Americans are the new masters of empire. These guys don't know how to lose. Aubrey is anxious to meet to talk it through. "Me too," Max says, "but there's this picket line, unfortunately. Next time you're here . . ."

It's Monday again and they're into the third scuffle of the day. The plot unfolds. Everyone has his lines. But Constable Cooper, the cop in the car since day one, puts a thumb lock on Max and spins him. Somehow Max knows it's called a thumb lock. He howls. This enrages the picketers and the pace of confrontation quickens till they are in a serious battle. Instead of calming the situation—his chosen role—he stoked it. Could this be his reward for lecturing the captain last week? One last whirl, like a do-si-do, and he's flat on his back, atop Constable Cooper, who's beneath him, also turtled, on the driveway, thumb lock finally broken, saying, "You're under arrest." Max says, "For what?" over his shoulder. "Impeding," says Cooper. "I never heard of it," Max says scornfully. "And obstructing an officer in the course of his duties. And resisting arrest," says Cooper, rising to all fours.

They bust the whole line, thirteen guys. At the station, Cooper sits Max down and gets out a yellow pad, like a laywer or steno. He starts asking questions. "Do I have the right to remain silent?" Max asks. Cooper says, "You've been watching too much American TV," and keeps posing questions. Max says, "You didn't answer me." "Yeah," Cooper says, "you do," and asks more questions. Max requests a phone call, something else he probably got from the cop shows. They point at a pay phone. He puts a dime in, calls the union, and gets Elyse. He asks her to phone Noel and say his friend is in jail, he thinks maybe Noel is at his dad's "cottage," fishing.

Cooper says they're going to put him in the cells, where the dirty dozen already are, then they'll let the others go and "visit" him when he's alone. Cooper's partner and some other cops nod. They look like they're trying to look scary. They take him to a cell across from the guys. Divide and conquer, like the Romans. He wonders if cops read the war journals of Julius Caesar as he did in high school. They're all Max's age or younger. Latin was still available when they went through. Now you couldn't get Latin if you begged and pleaded. The guys see him drooping and try to cheer him. Romir swings from the bars like a monkey. A while later (they've taken his watch), the others are released. He sits wondering what a man of action does when there's nothing to do but wait. He saw a movie with Kirk Douglas in a jail cell. He was about to get beaten by the sheriff, so he wadded Kleenex into tight rolls and stuffed them in his nostrils and cheeks. It was a little obscure but he decides to try it. He's begun wadding when Noel bounds through the door in a fishing vest, flies askew, waving a bail order from the sole JP in Metro who wasn't in bed yet. The cops who said they'd come to rough him up aren't even outside pouting as he and Noel leave. Maybe they've gone off shift.

He messes up at the trial. Noel asks him on the stand what he thought Constable Cooper meant by impeding. He's supposed to

say he has no idea. Full stop, shut up. Noel has instructed him
on this. There's a case from the Supreme Court of Queensland in
Australia in 1896 that might, maybe, save his ass, *if* they set it
up. That's how the law works. Your best chance against a cop is
always some legal quibble, never mind what really happened.
This is the game and we are going to play it. That's why Noel
bows to "your Worship" when he goes in and out of the court.
But Max's other self takes over. He gives a little lecture dissect-
ing the term "impeding," as it went though his mind flat on his
back in the street. Noel keeps his face straight but his strategy
has been torpedoed by his client.

The judge seems asleep anyway. He only stirs once, when
Noel calls Rhonda, who flew up from her creative-writing program in Indiana, to be a character witness. There's been a change
in her life, she tells Max outside the courtroom. She wrote a piece
for a small women's journal, for no money, about her theories
on men and women. A New York editor spotted it and got her to
turn it into a self-help manual called *Oh for a Trap Door*. Sales
have been, she says, ahem, brisk, especially in the airports,
where businessmen buy it. "They like the fact that I like men,"
she says. "But you want to drop them through a trap door!"
says Max. "Only some," she says. "They always assume they're
the ones I want to keep." She has a signed copy for Max. Noel
joins them. He met Rhonda in Paris and didn't like her much. He
regards the book with amazement. "This is you?" he says.
Nadine has just read it, she adores it. "But, but, but"—like an
outboard—"but *you* can't be famous!" On the stand, he introduces her as the famous author and asks her about Max's reputation for violence. She says he's very non-violent, he's known
far and wide for that, even in the face of mighty provocation—
she's starting to roll, and can't be held back, it's the storyteller

in her. "In fact, your Honour"—she uses the American term, but everyone is tolerant—"somebody once poured boiling water on him and he didn't retaliate." That's when the judge rouses. "Was it really boiling?" he says as if hailing her from dreamland. "Well, it had just been on the burner," says Rhonda, "immediately before. And," she adds, "he pays back money when he borrows it, which can't be said of everyone."

He gets three weeks for impeding, obstructing, or whatever. The judge says he has taken into account the fact that Max, unlike the workers he was arrested beside, knowingly turned his back on his privileges of upbringing and education. *Three weeks for betraying your class*, thinks Max, like a card-carrying Red Maple. As he passes from the courtroom, he sees Deb. He keeps scanning. He sees Elyse. He mouths "car" to her. It just occurred to him: If you lose, they take you straight to jail, what happens to your Honda? They cart him around for a few hours, alone in the back of a paddywagon. Are they lost in traffic? Or do they want to keep him out of reach till it's too late for Noel to arrange bail, at least overnight, maybe the whole weekend. So Cooper and the boys can pay their visit. At a light, he looks through the mesh, the sun starting to slant down, at the oblivious souls crossing on green. They have no idea how blessed they are, just waiting for a red to change, then it changes, then you go. He reaches the Don Jail about ten at night, they put him in a cell with no wiggle room and a straw mattress. He feels like the Count of Monte Cristo.

They wake him and take him downstairs just as he's nodding off, having finally given up hope of falling asleep. Noel, the miracle man, has a bail order. They each have a hissy fit about the trial. ("You didn't have to treat it like your damn orals. You just had to say you didn't know what impeding meant. . ." "I need

reasons. You should have told me the strategy.") Outside Deb is
waiting. She says she's come to drive him home, meaning his
place, it's an executive decision, Pisces all the way. But maybe
she'll come in, spend the night, he'd like that. He asks who's
with the kids. Harold, she says, her silent partner in the café. He
moved here from Winnipeg. He lives in a condo overlooking the
lake. It used to be the Palace Pier, where couples like his parents
danced during the war. "I'm going home now," she says, dropping Max at his door. "I'm going to sleep with Harold." He
wonders if she means it.

Six months later, the Mistral is screaming down a hillside in
Provence. Rhonda is yelling too, you must, to be heard. "Facts?"
she shrieks. "There are no facts. No, wait. There is one fact—*it is
all fucked up! That is the only fact!*" They've finished dinner, the
sun is setting on day four of this wind, normal here, even if it
drives everyone mad. He said casually he'd go into town tomorrow to watch the game between Poland and Zaire. Zaire is this
year's sentimental favourite at the World Cup. There's always a
sentimental favourite. Oh, and while there, he'll mail a letter he's
been writing for several days now to Deb. He just wants to get
the facts straight about what happened because—this is when
Rhonda detonates: "Facts?" she howls. "There are no facts. . ."

 She cooks dinner on the hot plate each night, he washes. He
wouldn't mind cooking but she hates to wash, and this is her
place, she has rented it every summer and now she has bought
it, with the advance on her next book about men and women.
The businessmen in the airports can't seem to wait. One of them
flew to Indiana in his private jet to take her to dinner in Chicago.
He was a real trap-door candidate, most are. She invited Max,
rather than any of them, to join her here, *affolé* as he was not so

much by his trial as by his endless trials with Deb. Rhonda asked him last summer too, but he said no, Deb and the bears had arrived and moved in, then left, he was trying to sort it out. "Ah, you're getting old," Rhonda said. But she went up and testified for him at the trial, including the finer details—the boiling water—and this spring invited him again. The Mistral makes people crazy. Last night after cleanup, they watched the sun descend and he toured her around the dial of his TV at home. Two is the provincial educational channel. Three is Global, known as the Love Boat Channel because it runs so many crappy U.S. shows. Four is multiculti. Five is PBS, the American education station that routinely guilts Canadians into sending donations so they can "support public broadcasting," which they've been doing since their own CBC hit the airwaves back during the Depression, which is six, next up the dial. Seven is CITY, a local little chatterbox of a station . . . Actually, he's not circling his dial, which few use in the dawning era of cable; he's describing the buttons on his remote box which are worn down from over-use. Some won't even stay depressed any more. He enumerates the raggediest. . .

It didn't bother her, it went with the wild wind. The letter is different, that isn't harmless. It will keep this fetid thing alive, give Deb something to feed off, which means feeding off *him*, and even if he doesn't mind the pain, even if he *likes* it, which she sometimes thinks, at least he should give her, Deb, a chance to slide off the hook. Rhonda pushes hard, as if she's concluded he's hopeless. It touches him. He shouts, above the wind, "*Okay, I won't mail the damn thing!*" They're kind of silent then, and the wind stops. Down and out fast, the way little kids like to leave the family dinner at Christmas or Thanksgiving. No loitering, no small talk in the hall; when you go, you go and you're gone.

They drink another bottle of rosé. People used to drink a lot of rosé, just like *rouge et blanc*. He asks her many questions about her writing, no need to shout now, as if it's serious stuff, as if he never went with her to the writers' circle where the poems and stories all began: "Here I am sitting on my bed wondering what to write about. . ."

It gets dark oh so slowly. They stretch out on the stone patio and look up. Blue serge sky with stars starting to peck their way out. They lie like the hands of a clock at ten-thirty. He reaches back and takes her hand lightly. This could be friendly. They touch each other's hands, outsides of hands, wrists. You can go a long way between friends and not get tense. Eventually they roll in toward each other, collapsing the clock, and still relaxed as two old pals, start to hug and kiss. Very languid, even literary, as if they're in a short story, wondering what will happen. They loll, feeling each other all over. A truck rumbles by down the hill and breaks their bubble. He says he's going to bed. She stays on the patio.

She comes into town for the Zaire game. They watch without paying attention, as if they're still waiting for the truck to pass and let them get on with it. He says he's terrified of losing their friendship, she's meant so much to him, and always will. He adds that he thinks they should leave last night where it ended. She says okay, no problem. He's sweating this, waiting for her to bring up the many times he's spoken about sex not being an impediment to friendship, like a good meal or a conversation, it can come and go. Talking and touching, what's the diff, yadayadayada. She says nothing. On the way back after the game, he says he'd still like her to come to Canada with him, as they've discussed, en route to Indiana. They can rent a place in cottage country, or go see some Shakespeare or Shaw, or drive to Montreal. He can show her a good time as she's done for him. She says she realized a few days ago that she can't, she thought she mentioned it, she has a manuscript due, a short story collection, and she's still intent on proving she's a real writer; that's the paradox of her life today: She has to churn out the gunk to make time to write, but the more she does, the less writing time she gets. End result: she'll stay here.

"She can push my buttons," he says, meaning Deb. "I don't want to go back and face her alone."

"I know," says Rhonda. "I wish I could come along and hold your hand."

(Rhonda's version: The only part of relationships I've ever had confidence about is when *not* to get into one. I just know, I always have, it's like an alarm goes off. The minute we touched, it started ringing. If he hadn't pulled back, I would have. I can think of better things to have great instincts about.)

He catches the train in Cotignac. It comes through about ten at night and the conductor says there are no seats. Maybe by Lyon. He's thinking about going to the Louvre or the Jeu de Paume. He might meet someone who will want to see Canada with him. If not, he can route via London, try the Tate or the National. For some reason, every plan he concocts is based on a museum. Linger around the Turners, it wouldn't be a total loss, even if he doesn't solve his facing-Deb problem. The conductor waves from the end of the corridor. It's like standing-room at a hockey game. You slip the usher a two-dollar bill, he lets you sit in one of the empties at the end of the first period.

No, no seats yet, but here's a mademoiselle who speaks English. Her hair is blonde like the straw in a Constable haystack.

She sits on her trunk and he sits on his knapsack. Some day he will come to Europe without a knapsack. She wears a baggy sweater and she's American. She's been in the Aegean with a businessman from Torino. It's one of many visits she's made to see him, though he never went to meet her family in Oregon. They planned that but something always came up. It's hard for him, he has a daughter, who's twelve, it was never convenient, so she went there. But this trip, on Hydra, Lycra, one of those islands, she felt he likes it this way. His young American. She comes, meets his friends, it's warm, she goes. She told him it was unacceptable. As a gambit, that's all, she wanted a conversation. But he wished her luck and congratulated them both on how adult they'd been. "No tears, no fuss, three cheers for us," she sings softly in the corridor, against the clack of the wheels. She twirls a finger in the dim light. Oregon will be lonely but Oregon is home. Canada, he says, is on the way. Here, this is Newfoundland, where he's planning to visit. It's very picturesque. He draws a rough map.

From the end of the corridor the conductor beckons. They manoeuvre their luggage through some cars. He puts them in a compartment with two sleeping nuns. At Dagenais, the nuns rise and shine, and exit. They're alone now. They doze on each other's shoulder. *Bang.* The door flies opens and the conductor sticks his head in like Señor Wences on "The Ed Sullivan Show": *'S okay? . . . 'S awright.* Then he's gone. Light shows on the horizon, like the flashlight of a kid reading under the covers. His head is on her chest, she's helping him undo her buttons, and—*Voilà!* She has this amazing bra with circles cut out of the cups. Her breasts glory there, like the prize in Crackerjacks. "I bought it for him," she says, "but I didn't put it on till I left." He must get the stricken look on his face, as if he has something to apologize for. "Oh no," she rushes to say. "You looked so happy. I wish I had more than two of them for you." *Bang*, the conductor is there again. They both toss him a look, and he doesn't pop back till it's time to announce the *gare*. From a phone booth, they call the airline. They're all over each other. Her hair in his face and mouth, sweet like hay. How does he know the taste of hay? Maybe those summers at "the lodge." Lying in the farmer's field down the road with eight-year-old Weegee, twice his age, the farmer's kid. He never knew another Weegee. Maybe Weegee is his Rosebud, a word he mutters autonomically, not knowing whence it comes. Eyes shut, he talks to the ticket clerk. They can't move his reservation, the clerk makes it sound as locked in as D-Day, but they can book her for St. John's two days after him. She can join him to visit Norman, the perpetual post-doc fellow at LSE, who's doing research in a dying fishing village. And it will stage the return to Deb-range, slow it down to bearable, he hopes.

Two days later the driver of a logging truck drops him at the turnoff to Chancy Cove, Bonavista Bay. There's a gas station and pay phone. He calls the Paris number of the girl with straw hair, her aunt's place. She says she's not coming. Who is he anyway? Did they really meet on a train? As if someone drugged her and she woke up. "Oh my God," he says, "There's a whale!"

"I suppose he's riding on an iceberg," she says.

"To be honest," he says, "I can't even see the ocean."

"None of this is me," she says from the Old World. "Meeting you here, saying I'd meet you there. Then going back on my word."

About a mile down the sideroad, he shuts his eyes and tries to taste her hair. It works. He hopes Norman and his girlfriend—Norman always claimed a girlfriend but no one has met her—are in the village. He has the name of a fisherman whose place Norman stays at. There are no phones in the village. "The wife is interesting," said Norman. "She pictures alternatives." The restless rural wife. Sarah Miles in *Ryan's Daughter.* A pickup picks him up. They rattle down the tickle, as the driver calls it, and around the bay, as they say, which opens before him. Floating out in the middle of the water is an ice-blue mountain.

The driver drops him in some mud and points up a hill. There are no street names or house numbers. Norman isn't in but there are kids, and the interesting wife. She slices some lunch meat from a can and offers it. Takes another can and pours Carnation in his Nescafé. He asks how things are. She says nothing to suggest a restless soul. He says he'll look around when Norman, as if he'd been observing through a one-way mirror, bounds in and says, "Follow me, and bring your backpack." They head down to the dock to meet the boys . . .

Most of the boys are pretty old. They greet Norman and the new arrival the way Samoans probably dealt with Margaret Mead. They grunt answers to long questions about the catch, the new technologies, the death of the old ways, changes in the community, attitudes of youth. They give you what you want, it's less trouble. "I'm curious," he says to Norman when the boys go home for dinner. Norman furrows his brow, ready to discuss folkways in crisis. "Where do we sleep?"

Norman stays in the house they came from, it's part of his research. There's room for Max in the van, with Felice the putative girlfriend. Norman leads him past a store-cum-house-cum-post office. There stands the van. Norman points and heads back, as if he doesn't want his role as participant-observer compromised by unnecessary contact with his tribe. Max knocks.

"I can't do anything with you," says Felice that night, as they lie in the van's two bunks, her upper left, him lower right. "I couldn't do it to Norman." Max says, "Uh-huh," like one of the boys on the dock. It's dark. They're quiet for about the time it would take to fall asleep. She sighs and drops an arm down. "You still up?" she says. He swings around to sit. There's about a cubic millimetre of squalid air between his knee and her hand, and zero tension. It's been decided. There's more sex in the morning.

Around nine, he dresses and heads for the dock to check in with Norman. "It's up to you what you say," he mumbles on the way out. "But I won't say anything. I consider this between you and me." She looks at him as if he's a lab specimen. "Are you nuts?" she blurts. "Why would I say boo-all? And I'll kill you if you breathe a word. And Norman will kill himself." As he steps out of the van, she says, "I'll see you tonight."

"Okay," he says, "just between us." As he passes the storehouse-post office, he glances back at the van. It looks like it's dancing a rumba. And she can't be doing more than getting dressed and making the beds. Everyone in the damn village must have seen it jump.

The night before leaving, he dreams he is telling someone that Keynes was the greatest economist since Adam Smith. Ole Olasson, the cowboy of Gimli, sulks away and sits with his back to Max, or the dream camera. "You're not very nice," he mutters. Max (in the dream) knows Ole is hurt because Ole thinks Karl Marx is the best. Then Keynes himself says, "I am not the greatest economist since Adam Smith. I am Adam Smith," which

Max suspected, because Smith, with his strong moral streak, never trusted capitalists to behave well. Keynes simply drew the policy conclusions from that distrust, 150 years later. Next morning in the fog he catches his flight home.

He arrives at Pearson like a refugee fleeing to his own land. Felice said sorry, there was no way she could leave Norman to bodyguard her new little sweetie's return home. She said they'd call if they come to Toronto, the three of them can have a nice dinner. He said, "You're making it sound like Canada is another country from Newfoundland." She said, "Well, London is closer than Toronto." She sounded like she'd measured it.

He skulks into immigration and then customs, expecting to be taken aside, interrogated, and sent to the official refugee detainment centre on Margaretta Street, the same building he escaped to when he ran away from home at age eight. He drove by it once, out of nostalgia. It had been taken over by the federal government. He's surprised when they wave him through. He snatches his backpack off the carousel, casually checking outside to see if Deb's there. No sign. What if he doubles back upstairs to the departures level, just to be extra sure, then takes a cab. It may be paranoia but there's no one around to notice, what the hell, indulge yourself. It means going up the down escalator, but no flights seem to be arriving at the moment, so he does, and slips onto the arrivals concourse.

That's when he hears his name, screamed over and over without any breaths in between: "*Maxiemaxiemaxiemaxie* . . ." And here's Petey, four by now, running madly at him, arms flapping, somewhere between the waddle of a toddler and the gorgeous gait of a gazelle-child, then falling into his arms. If he were going to die, this wouldn't be a bad time. Close behind are the other bears and Deb. She has a fistful of tickets, boarding passes, a tote bag stuffed with toys and kids' books over her shoulder. They're leaving for Iceland, she says, in two hours. She heard he might be back today, Noel told her. But, um, what's he doing on this level, isn't arrivals below? Good question.

Over lunch, or snack—airport meals are so indeterminate—with the kids scaling him, she says it was time to see the ancestral homeland. Children need a sense of their roots, she says, their language, folklore, geography. He looks at these three little Indians. Even blond Petey has the cheekbones and gaze of his dad, who is a respected elder of his tribe. But she'll give them roots, whether they need them or not. How long will they stay? She shakes her head, it's wide open. She's brought everything that matters. She flutters the boarding passes, there are many baggage checks stuck on. There's a women's party in Iceland, she says, it's the official opposition and will probably be the government after the next election, it's the only place in the world where women have claimed their rightful place in social governance. What about the pastry boutique? She sold her share, the place is thriving, the money she made will finance the trip, or relocation. She's erupted again, and she's going to the home of eruption, a genuine volcanic island. He says he'll wait till their flight takes off, as if he fears it's an elaborate dodge, with costumes and props. She shakes her head, they see him off, out into the fumes of buses and limos. He's thinking: What happened to her intensity about class and country? Can you just drop those passions and switch to ethnic or gender ones? He envies her flexibility. He doesn't know if he likes it but he envies it, as they wave goodbye and his bus pulls away from the curb.

Elyse's Version

~

There was a thing he did with his face when we had sex. It expressed some kind of effort. As if he was trying too hard to look as if he was feeling something. I mentioned it once. I thought about it, I didn't want him to feel criticized. He took criticism hard, like most of us, but worse. He wasn't thin-skinned, even though his line of work got him into conflict situations all the time. I wasn't critical. I wanted him to relax and enjoy himself and not worry how I felt about how he was feeling. He didn't say anything. It wasn't our normal animated post-sex conversation, about the Leafs or whether stagflation actually existed. We both thought it didn't. We talked a lot, in the times when we were having sex and also when we weren't. I hoped he'd see my comment as good-hearted, or useful anyway. I don't think he did.

I once said I didn't understand what I was doing with him. I think he took that too seriously too. We were at a hockey game and at the end of the first period he asked if I wanted to leave and go somewhere. He meant, to have sex. I was surprised. They were his tickets and he held onto them right through the awful Ballard years. He was a true fan. A *Leafs* fan, if you can believe it. It was like deliberately shooting up with cancer cells. I looked at the ice and asked if he really wanted to leave. He said, "Oh, yeah," as if it was *sooo* important for me to know how much he wanted me. We ended up at his place or mine, or in my car or his, me on top or him on top, or both of us finding ways to roll back and forth. I should have got used to it, because it happened every time, that urgentness. But it always seemed fresh, which makes it sound like the produce section at Dominion. "We're fresh-obsessed." When I got a chance to suggest we have sex first, or ask if I could stay over with him before he had a chance to ask me, which wasn't often, he always seemed surprised I could want it as much as he did.

Anyway, it's true I didn't understand what I was doing with him, but I've never understood much of what I do, and don't expect to. Even if this was weirder than the rest, it was still in the same ballpark of living my life and not quite getting it. I think that's how most people are. If I was any good in politics, which people say I was, it's because I had a knack for talking to people where they lived or worked on the basis of the assumptions they made about themselves. Because they were the same ones I made about myself. A lot of politicians don't think that way. They feel they're on a different level, far above the crowd, like Remax.

He was different. He thought there were answers you could "arrive at." Like staying on the train till you get to your destination. Or going from level to level in a TV quiz show, till you reach the sixty-four thousand or million dollar question.

I don't mean he thought he *had* the answers. Just that they existed and he ought to be able to figure them out. One reason he beat himself up so often was for not being bright enough to do that. So when he messed up, it was always as if he'd made a *mistake*, he hadn't got the answer right, which is a horrible way to feel. People who think there *are* no answers are another category. They're apoliticals and become your basic nihilist hedonists or reactionaries. I've dipped my toe in that. I just can't pull it off. I don't have the personality to truly not believe there's nothing to believe in.

I'd say he was more confident about sex than other things. More at home with it. It made more sense to him than other things. Even though doubt was never far off. Maybe that's what I saw on his face when we were having sex. A happy hope that he was getting close to the truth, along with his usual doubts.

I think he was an idealist about sex and I was an idealist about politics. Though sometimes it would be vice versa. It means you think you can achieve the ideal in this thing, so that's where you put all your marbles. Being thwarted idealists—*"forlorn* idealists," he once said—may have been what we liked about each other. Or recognized.

Elyse

The appeal doesn't happen for years, lots of time for the prospect of prison to fester. He saw *Fortune and Men's Eyes*, a Canadian play by John Herbert, when he was in London. It would never have been produced in Toronto back then, it was too raw. The rape scene in the cell smacked him the way the rape scene in *Two Women* had, as if his sexual "ignorance" would always be with him, like an appendix or tail, something he couldn't evolve out of. He asks Marty Davis, who teaches an extension course in economics with him and who earned his M.A. doing seven years in Kingston Pen for armed robbery, what to do if somebody comes on to him inside, the way Rocky does with Mona in the play. Marty guffaws. They're lined up for coffee at the break, like guys at mealtime in KP. He must look hurt because Marty says, "I just mean you're not exactly their cuppa." Max asks why. "The size," says Martin, backing off as if he's going to draw a quick sketch of Max, and jostling some of the "kids" they teach, most of whom are older than either of them. "The baldness," he says.

"The stubble. But sure," he adds, willing to accommodate a ridiculous hypothesis, "it could happen." Max looks relieved. Marty says, "If it does, I'd just turn around and punch the guy in the face. Mind you, some of these girls have friends."

It's nice, as his mother would say—"That's nice, dear"—that his little moment in publishing comes now. An anarchist named Laszlo who runs a small press called Firebrand Books—in honour of Olde Toronto's radical editor and first mayor, William Lyon Mackenzie—has heard of Max's report on auto insurance for the Saskatchewan NDP. It's been over a decade since the surprise notoriety of the Watkins Report on Canadian economic sovereignty. That didn't just sell, it exploded. It led to imitations and critiques. Laszlo tells Max that "the people" are ready for another round of economic truth-telling instead of the daily bullshit in the business press. He asks Max to tackle the currently faddish notion of stagflation—simultaneous inflation and stagnation, a concept that will have the staying power of stonewashed jeans. For Max, it's a challenge, since standard Keynesianism claims the two can't coexist. Laszlo says this will add a *frisson* of personal drama to the book, making it easier to promote. Will its author emerge from his intellectual joust with the hard-edged reality of stagflation, his Keynesian identity intact, or will his *Weltanschauung* shatter like a chrysalis to reappear in some bold new theoretical form? Laszlo has the verve to make this sound not entirely idiotic. And how wonderful to be courted by a publisher!

Laszlo takes most of his meagre arts council grant and publishes the result in paperback only—so it will be accessible to the masses—with "lots of activity on the page," that is, charts and graphs, plus a blurb from Watkins himself on the back. It sells out its modest printing, though unfortunately Laszlo lacks the "cash flow" to reprint. By then, it has garnered a few nominations for awards, including Ontario's Trillium, which the publisher seems to covet (oddly, given his anarchism). Max even has a few moments on the national media before the real producers start telling the chase producers, "Not him again. Get somebody *like* him."

The awards dinner for the Trillium is held at St. Lawrence Hall, all white and gold. Max and Laszlo go together. The underpaid serfs of the publishing world battle for position at the tables of fruit and cheese. The non-fiction prize is five thousand dollars, a bundle in the heyday of stagflation. It comes from a beer company. He's sure his book doesn't have a chance—one of the other nominees is a study of civil wars throughout history that was deliriously reviewed in the *Sunday Times*. So he has convinced Laszlo to make a symbolic political gesture with the paltry thousand bucks that also-rans like them will split. When the chair of the judges' committee, a septuagenarian book critic, announces that, against all odds, his book indeed has won, there is only one speech in his pocket, so he gives it, gamely trying to soften his denunciation of bourgeois critics, since they've had enough of a lapse in bad taste to select his book. How it must have shone. The prize money will go, he says, to a penurious guerilla publishing collective in rural Ontario that produces nothing but attacks on Northrop Frye, Canada's famed literary critic. The paupers of publishing are stunned that a Canadian author has given away five thousand dollars: they gasp, they cry, they roar a mighty cheer.

As he sits down, the cheers and tears still ringing in his ears, the aged reviewer scuttles over like a crab, bends and whispers, "There's been a terrible mistake. The book on civil wars is the actual winner." He shares this with the room. The real winner, a history prof migrated from Dortmund after the war, takes the cheque for five grand directly from Max's fist and tells the crowd he's going to buy a sailboat. Max gives his speech again, for less money. As he leaves the hall, he flings the framed award for runner-up into a bin of the beer company's empty stubbies, also gone with the era. When he gets home he puts on the long johns Amy gave him the birthday before she sent the letter: it has little red maple leafs sewn on plus the number of a Chinese place they always ordered from. He flips on the TV and phones Elyse, who arrives in ten minutes with a bottle of Bacardi blond, her brain-clouder of choice. She undresses. They fall asleep to "Monday Night Football." Hours later the news wakes him. The anchor is doing his closer: "On a lighter note, an economist and author was given an award tonight, then had it snatched away. . ." He wakes Elyse so she can hear him moan. "Cut the crap," she growls into the pillow. "You smell like a rose. You gave away five thousand bucks and it didn't hurt a bit."

"It's been a *stupendous* delay," says Noel, addressing the judge. "Five years. I hope, My Lord, I never see its like again." Noel makes it sound as if he and the judge are making history together. He has mastered courtroom suckholing and his clients are grateful, or should be. He's made his decision. He will be a lawyer, though not the fee-seeking corporate missile daddy envisioned. He'll be a criminal defence lawyer, and fight the punitive forces of the state. Daddy can't object, his boy has a damn profession.

With that watershed behind him, Noel became a success almost instantly. He seems to understand criminal law as if he dreamed it up himself in a past life. Now people treat him like an all-purpose maven because he's brilliant at this one thing. He pronounces on nouvelle cuisine or Basque separatism and they applaud every pseudo-insight. "You don't know anything *except* criminal law," says Max. "You're an idiot savant." Noel replies patiently, the way lawyers read from a factum on appeal, knowing they will not be rushed. "I didn't ask for it," he says, "but why shouldn't I enjoy it?"

He has no strategy yet. "That 1896 Queensland thing was feeble," he says, "even if you had remembered to say what I told you instead of trying to show the judge what a bright boy you are." So what do we do now? frets Max, thinking about *Fortune and Men's Eyes*. "In the language of *your* chosen field," says Noel, with that recently acquired authority he wears so well, "now we massage the numbers."

First he gives Max one of his three-piece lawyer's suits to wear in court. That morning, Max waits on his apartment steps for a taxi. He's learned not to drive to your own trial. As he gets in, the driver turns and says, "Where to, sir?" He can't remember anyone calling him *sir* before. Inside the courthouse, he asks the kindly old commissionaire at the bottom of the escalator where 3C is. "Up two flights on your right, sir," says the vet. Outside 3C, he stands talking to Noel, who says his plan is to "wing it." The way the flying aces did in the First World War. Noel looks that debonair, he should be wearing a scarf. The Crown walks past, looks Max up and down and seethes. "He knows what we're up to," says Noel. "Nice suit."

As the Crown makes its case, Noel observes, sketching notes on a legal pad. Literally sketching. Boxes, circles, arrows, dotted lines. Like he's designing a . . . battle plan! The Patton of the courtroom. First rule: be flexible; deal with what you're given, not what you'd like to have. What are they given? Constable Cooper, the ample cop Max was sitting on when arrested. Max considered changing the real story, the truth of it is *so* implausible. Noel says no. He says normal people—like the two of them—fuck up when they stray from what happened. It takes a lifetime of training to deceive. You must genuinely feel a lie and the truth are functional equivalents. "They may indeed be," adds Noel, shifting into litigatese, "but those of us with middle-class backgrounds have been imbued with the opposite prejudice." There it is again, such authority when he speaks about law. The guy his schoolmates used to call Howdy Doody (Max was Dilly Dally) goes away somewhere and an old soul occupies his place. It's like being represented by the Delphic Oracle.

Lying is not required. Constable Cooper says he can barely recall that day five years ago. He's not the same lard-ass cop who sat on Max. He's been through the wringer of a public investigation into police brutality that resulted from a series of news reports. It had nothing to do with the strike. It harked back to Cooper's days at the notorious District 71, where he became known for using the claw on petty-crime suspects: a metal pincer they clamped around a guy's balls. Cooper wasn't a central villain—he was built for comic asides like the roadway bust—but he's now famous in the way journeyman pro athletes are. Penalty killers, utility infielders. Cooper was named in the final, damning report. Then the government, having proven its probity by holding an inquiry, showcased its pro-cop side by laying no charges. It was masterful. So Cooper is back in harness, but a different cop, he knows what it is to squirm under a harsh cross, and seems to sympathize with Max. Sorry, he just can't remember. The Crown seethes some more. Noel moves for dismissal. When that fails, he brings on the character witnesses. "They're making him out to be some kind of a saint in there," Max hears a cop say during the break. The Crown makes the error of trying to cross-examine the character witnesses. "You never do that," whispers Noel, "this is amateur night." The profs, brokers, editors, who have heeded Noel's call—plus loyal-and-true Rhonda—hand the Crown his head.

The verdict is a conditional discharge. Noel is pleased. "When you win overwhelmingly," he says, on authority cruise control, "and you undeniably deserve an acquittal, they grant a discharge." Max asks what a discharge is. "No one knows," says Noel. "But you can apply to the Governor General for a pardon." "Why do I need a pardon?" says Max. "Why do you need a discharge?" answers Noel. "You don't, it's what you get. That's the system." Max asks what a pardon means. "No one knows that either," says Noel, "because even when they give it to you, they can take it back if you're convicted for something else." Max says that's irrational. "Trust me," says Noel. "I am writing the definitive text on sentencing. They will be studying it in law schools long after I retire. It is my sinecure. I trust," he adds, as they exit the courthouse, "that this marks the end of what I have heard you describe as your workerist period." Max says he trusts so too; he's firmly back in the land of Keynesian moderation and half measures; he'll settle for an improved but imperfect world. He asks Noel what that fling with class struggle was all about, as if he too has come to believe Noel has the answers. "I was planning to query you on that topic," says Noel. "Will Your Honour please direct counsel to answer his client's question," says Max. He's feeling pretty light out here as dusk falls on Queen Street "It's 'My Lord' when you get to the appeal level," says Noel, "but I do have a theory: you got your wires crossed. For a time there you were acting in politics with the extremism you normally reserve for sex." He's about to get into his BMW, the one that costs more than the houses most people live in, when Max remembers he doesn't have a car. They drive away together, like the Lone Ranger and Tonto.

Since the GG at the time is Ed Schreyer, another former NDP

prairie premier, Max hastens to write. Pardon me, Ed, he says, more or less. You're excused, says the Governor General in an attractive document that arrives a year later, suitable for framing. Max puts it in the bottom drawer of his dresser, along with the decree nisi from the divorce (*nisi*, from the Latin for "unless," meaning, "unless you don't pay your lawyer," he assumes). He forgot it was there till he bent down to deposit the pardon. They nestle together solemnly.

Elyse isn't at the appeal. She stopped working for the union, as he did, right after the strike. He has now definitely achieved the status, in his mind that is, of being the world's first freelance economist. It must be career decision time for his generation. First Noel, now him. Miss Calloweth, their guidance teacher who administered the Kuder Preference Test, would feel vindicated. She made them stick pins into a sheaf of multiple-choice pages and, with the resulting profile, deduced their career choices: become an architect in Max's case, and something so humiliating for Noel that he has never revealed it. The point is, they finally *have* careers. With those sixties people, you were never sure they'd get there. They could have expired just doing their thing. As a freelance economist, he will take a part-time consultancy with the Bank of Canada, or CIDA. That can lead to a trip to Honduras or Sierra Leone to study the efficiency with which aid is being used. Then some sessional teaching. A contract with a public sector union, or the Autoworkers, or Steel, if they're in a "progressive" phase. Maybe they want a study on casual labour as it becomes the dominant form of hiring. A book for Laszlo if he can wangle a grant, or a report on a manuscript for a university publisher. A dab of journalism. Freelance as in phallic, as in the knightly lance, whence the term. He might be able to get on the tenure track, if not at a top-level university then some-where like Brock; or nail a full-time job with benefits at a union or a bank. Something in him would rather not, he prefers it out here in the labour market, like a wage slave in the bazaar— *buy me, buy me*—like the guys who stood with him on the line. He misses organizing, the way you recall a great trip you once took. He associates it with Elyse. "I heard she's into animal rights," Noel tells him.

Eventually she calls. It's a Saturday around five, one of those truly dead times. He says he isn't doing anything except waiting for the hockey game on TV. She says she wants to give him the notes she took at the original trial. It wasn't easy. The cop on courtroom duty said writing wasn't allowed. They went out and argued till a lawyer for another striker went by. Legal aid wasn't as stingy then. The lawyer took over Elyse's side of the argument and she walked back in to take more notes. A lot of politics is about persistence. Eventually they get tired of giving you a hard time. Or maybe they decide to respect you at a cer-tain point, after they've counted down. Max says she can bring the notes now. She sits in the funny wrought-iron chair that opens like a man-eating plant. He's across from her in a rocker that Amy re-covered, then gave him when she moved to Kuwait. Elyse says she's joined the Animal Rights party. Ah, so there's a proper party. They have an office, maybe they run people for office. He asks how it's going. "Like a trip into hell," she says with contentment. He thinks of the time he toured a smelter in Quebec. Pools of molten aluminum on the floor, puddles a worker could step into, just a slip is all it would take; skeletal cabs skittering along tracks on the ceiling far above. It's life and death in here every minute, the guys said, the fires of hell lighting their proud faces. He's thinking: How can you put those people, the workers, the ones we made "contact" with, on the level of cats and budgies? He doesn't need to say it. Even if everything that crosses his mind didn't show on the TV screen of his face, this is Elyse!

They're at opposite corners of the living room by now. He moved off the rocker onto the couch—a box spring topped by a mattress covered with a bedspread and cushions. He's pretty much pinned between it and the slope of the third-floor roof. She's pushed the man-eating chair back till, if she went farther, she'd be in the kitchen. There's a silence they become aware of. She says it isn't perfect—he's not sure if she means the party or the room. But she's going to try and make it work. That's reasonable. No Keynesian would approach the world otherwise.

He says he'll make tea, recalling she's a tea drinker, which is unusual among those he knows. Could be her social roots; her dad the dysfunctional accountant from England, her mom who took her to high tea at the Four Seasons in Yorkville. They even sent her to BSS. He can picture her in the uniform, the shoulder straps outlining her bust. She still has friends named Biz and Sissy. She follows him into the kitchen and stands against the counter. He wonders again how she can turn away from the workers and replace them with lab mice. He wants to be subtle here, he doesn't want her to feel attacked. "How do you stand those people?" he says. She laughs. Everyone knows there are nutbars in animal rights. "It's my party and I'll cry if I want to," she smiles. It's something the sad young people in the Communist party like to say. "I think they remind me of my family," she goes on. "They try to be so controlling, so certain of their superior values." So she feels right at home. Hmm. "You go through that shit again," he says, coming to peace with her choice, "of being in a family. But at least this time it serves a purpose." She's near enough that he can stretch his hand sideways

RICK SALUTIN

and touch her arm, then, when she continues to lean, move on to her breast. He's always liked her breasts. *Quelle surprise.*

The roof of the bedroom slopes even more sharply than the living room. It's like having sex in a tent. After they fuck, or screw, or ball—the words remain problematic: making love is too heavy, having sex sounds evasive, intercourse is clinical—she slips down and sucks him, as if she senses exactly where it all leads in him. "I've never felt better," he says as she does, trying to be both scrupulously honest and effusive. She asks if she can stay the night. She always asks, which he finds very respectful, just the way she sucked his penis. Some time later she calls and leaves a message: she's moving out west. That must be why she brought over the notes. He assumes it's about animals. Cattle? Muskox? Buffalo? The elk in the Rockies. The jolly coho of the Fraser River?

There's a teensy item in the paper under News Briefs, which could be called News You Can Live Without. "Animal activist elected mayor." Wow. It's always fun to see somebody you know, or knew, in print. More than seeing them on TV, which is less serious and permanent. Print is for the ages, even when it wraps the garbage. Next time he's in Vancouver on a stopover he calls Surrey City Hall and leaves a message for the mayor. She calls back, saying it would be hard to meet after work; she has to be somewhere. He says he can meet her, wherever it is—the pound? She says it's a picket line and gives him the address. Ouch.

It feels like going to your high school reunion: what do you wear? When he arrives, he looks around for the guys he was in jail with, Zizi, Surinder—as if the working class is as compact and incestuous as the intelligentsia. Elyse is talking with a clump of them. Nodding, explaining. Assuring and encouraging. He moves nearer. Some of the buses they used to make in the plant—or assembled from parts shipped from elsewhere, Canada's odd notion of industrialization—are parked behind a wire fence. He listens, the observer again, the Organizer is no more. The new owners are winding the place down, what can you do? "We should just turn around, bend over, let them do what they want to us, and hope we're still here," says a worker. Well, what do you expect during a recession like this, the Winnipeg General Strike? Anyway, there were doubtless strikers in Winnipeg in 1919 who wanted to quit. She shakes her head as if she understands. They gather for the inspiring speeches.

"Brothers and sisters," she begins. Everyone does in these situations, he's done it himself. It always sounded odd, from his lips to his ears. She looks . . . great. Wow. It isn't just her features: the cheekbones, the high forehead. It's her bearing. Posture even. Shoulders back, head raised. It accentuates every-thing fine about her. She's so *happy* to be here. She looks like Wonder Woman, from the TV series or back in the comics. (He didn't buy those on his Friday trips to the corner store, yet they passed through his hands: her magic lasso, the diaphanous plane she flew, her jut-jawed pilot boyfriend.) These disheart-ened strikers are thrilled to have her with them in their duress. Oh God, he'd have thought in the old days, if you'd let me have her just once.

He feels honoured when she turns to him after the speeches, still surrounded by grateful strikers, and smiles. As if Galbraith walked over to shake *your* hand in a roomful of prominent col-leagues. He doesn't know if she has time, there's a coffee shop over in that strip mall—"Sure," she says. There's no defensiveness, she has been her best self, just now, he saw it, they all did. She has nothing to prove.

"What does any activist do?" she says across the formica. "The best you can, under the circumstances." But, he thinks, running for office? She reads it off the forehead TV. It began, she says, with substitute canvassing for a friend who was sick one night. And bang, he gets it. The contact. It brought back the contact. Maybe you've been told by the campaign team to just get a quick read on the voter and move on, but a conversation starts, and before you know it, the family's going to bed and you're too late to door-knock anyone else on the street. How much of the contact has he had since he became a full-time freelance economist? She'd be so damn good at it. Good at what? Not politics. The contact that politics allows. Elections as an excuse for people to discuss politics with each other.

So, he assumes, doing the interview thing, the next step was to run for office? "Not really," she says. Someone she had canvassed with called about a problem, it was more than a problem, it was a stinking mess, literally. A tire plant had shut down in the area and kids were getting nauseous and there were fears about pollution and contamination and what did she suggest. She didn't even live there but she got involved, then mired. People trusted her. They asked if she'd run for something, maybe Board of Ed. But she didn't even have kids. City council then. She had just agreed when the mayor had a heart attack and there was no one obvious to take over, so before she'd even been a council member she was running for mayor (not of a big place like Vancouver, just this suburb), and it was like she was born for it. Born to run. It makes micro-sense, like the rules for calculating UI eligibility or the gong going off in Tiny's for Peking duck. She is the most natural political person he's ever known, in the most conventional sense of politics: running in elections, shaking hands, fixing potholes and deadly pollution, assuring people that someone capable who cares is dealing with things that affect their lives in common.

"What about the animals?" he asks. She got out of that. She got involved with animals because the issues were so clear. The hell of it and so forth. But she missed the people, and the people who worked with animals weren't the ones she missed. He asks if she has a pet, or ever did. No, she says, if she had, maybe she wouldn't have got into animal rights. She asks if that sounds dumb. "No," he says. "If I had ever done a real job, maybe I wouldn't have needed to be an expert on the economy. Are you married?"

Of course, the ring is prominent. His name is Tom, he's a bus driver. A bus driver? Well, not like a city bus, taking tickets and handing out transfers. He's an intercity driver, long distance, mostly to the Interior and back. The glamour of being a truck driver, but with interpersonal skills required. No kids yet, that will come. Max says he'll be at the hotel tonight, working in his room, if she has any time. Her eyes register how the same that is of him: *I'm there, come if you want, it's as much as I'll venture.* "Do you miss your old life?" he says. He could mean Toronto, or being young. But he means sex: not knowing what—i.e., who— will be next. It seems vapid compared to the journey she described. But he can't imagine life without it.

By the time he gets back to the hotel, she's left a message: she thinks she can come between nine and ten. He's surprised. He goes down to the pool and does a ridiculous number of laps, as one does in a hotel pool. You spend more time turning than swimming. She hasn't shown by ten, then ten-fifteen. He wouldn't call, not just because of Tom, but because it isn't what he does. Yet she is so solid; if she says she'll be there, even *thinks* she can, she'll come. And now she's a public servant: one of the people that the people count on. Maybe he got it wrong, maybe she meant the lobby. But then she'd phone. It wouldn't hurt to go down and look. If she's not there, maybe someone else will be. There's Roslyn behind the desk, with the name tag, maybe she's on nights: "My name is Roslyn. How can I help you?" When does her shift end? Would she like to meet in the bar? Or come up to his room?

The elevator doors open onto the lobby like a curtain, "discovering" two characters: Elyse and the house dick. They are across the lobby. He has to be the house dick, he couldn't have become anything else, the way hockey refs are never failed players, they've been refs all their lives, even as toddlers they had ref personalities. The dick and Elyse are arguing vehemently yet with a controlled calm. He can't hear them but he can almost see the spit between them, the way you can at Stratford. Or the WWF wrestlers who express their feelings in gestures so broad you miss nothing, not the least nuance, even from the top of SkyDome. He's saying she has to leave. She says she's getting on that elevator to visit her friend. Max draws closer. "Yeah," the dick says, "'visit' your 'friend.'" You can hear the quotes in his voice. It's his idea of subtle. They look up and see him. Her eyes tear, she's so humiliated, it's the shame of a child. "This is my friend," he says. "She came to visit me." The house dick rolls his eyes. "I'm going," she says. "I'm leaving." And she does.

"Come on, buddy," says the security guy when she's gone, as if they're two fellas moving on to the next scene, same play. "You and I both know she's a pro. All it takes is a look." Max thinks back. She was wearing a tiny skirt and a blouse with lots of cleavage, also heels and makeup. Her hair looked shiny and wonderful. It was the Elyse he met at the reggae club, the one who drove the young workers in the plant nuts. The chick from the islands who loved to have a good time. You can't blame the dick for not knowing she was his ancient comrade-in-arms, now the mayor of a nearby industrial suburb.

"Don't worry about it," she says next day when he calls from the airport. She sounds like she's on another continent, in another life. The dead timbre of *don't worry about it* will never leave him; he can call it up for the rest of his life, easy as dialling a familiar number, or the straw hair of the girl on the train in his mouth, or the night looking through the leaded glass at Olivia's. He says he feels horrible, he thought of decking the security man—just for old time's sake. "You shouldn't take this stuff personally," she says, as if it is all, sigh, just another man-ifestation of the political struggle. He says he wasn't, it was her who must have taken it personally. "The personal," she says with conviction, "is overrated."

They drift by each other during the great free trade melodrama of the 1980s. It is a good time for him. The old issues on which he always wobbled have become irrelevant: socialization of the means of production, worker control, the withering away of the state. The country (and soon the world) are on a straight eighteenth-century agenda: free trade, comparative advantage, tariff reduction, protection, industrialization. What the world needs now is a sensible rebuttal, within the limits of the possible, to the claim that free trade and its smarter cousin, globalization, are inevitable. For the coalition of unions, academics, artists, and other nostalgists who huddle together against the mighty corporate and media forces manning the free trade battleship, a Keynesian is as much economist as they require. There is demand, he is supply. As for Elyse, she is no longer mayor. She lost the job after a term. She had to go because anyone could get through to her as quickly as the big boys; probably quicker, she would say. All the parties, the NDP included, secretly agreed on a single candidate to displace her. She fell in among feminists trying to create an alternate model to capitalism—a modest enough project. They work on the local level and issue their own currencies: Victoria dollars or Prince Rupert rupees. Kamloops cash and so forth. Some people actually use them. If economists operated like lawyers, Max and her could become partners and open a firm. They see each other at rallies and gatherings of the anti–free trade coalitions. He'll wonder, during coffee break, if she'd like to go out after the meeting. It's like asking for a first date, every time. She always thinks carefully and says yes. He would shrivel up if she didn't. They drive somewhere (he brings his car to meetings; the coalitions have no expense money) and engage in the ancient practice of necking. He plays with her till she comes, she does the same with him, or they struggle into the back seat together. That's when she says, "I have no idea what I'm doing."

The night of the big defeat, he slips away from a grim party, borrows a cellphone (they had the heft of mortars then) and calls her home in B.C., where life sounds eerily normal, or just three hours earlier. "We deserved to win," he snuffles. She laughs. "We did," he protests. "Deserve," she says, gently as therapy, anticipating Clint Eastwood as the doomed gunfighter in *Unforgiven*, "deserve has nothing at all to do with it."

Her death doesn't make it even as a news brief. By then she's been out of politics for long enough to be forgotten. He hears about it from Noel, who has the knack for gossip. He once asked Noel how you find out gossip, what do you say exactly? "You say," Noel said, "'What's the gossip?' I hear," he added, "that she had joined the cotton battens." Max gapes. "The happy-healthy-holies?"

She committed suicide. That doesn't make it more newsworthy. In those days, the media shied away from suicide. They reported it as "died suddenly" or "of unexplained causes." If they were more daring, they said, "by her own hand." At least that made the event a personal choice, a final act of freedom, of a hopeless sort.

He goes to Vancouver for the funeral. Lurking in the side aisle of the temple—if this was a church, he'd be hiding behind a pillar, but here he's barely concealed by a frond—he feels like the Other Woman, ashamed but can't stay away. It isn't the three *h*'s after all; it's a Vancouver version of the cult. The devotees, as they're called, wear pastel leisure suits with scarves. The centrepiece is a canopy. Tom, the long-distance bus driver, gives the main tribute. He covers the political aspect, her activism, and so forth, and the final move they made together to this temple and their fellow devotees. When someone dies, their most recent stopover suddenly becomes their lifelong destination, as if they wouldn't have moved on had the cancer or bullet or undertow swept them away just then. He talks about the thing that drove her from one cause to another, as if it was a malady that never got diagnosed. The priest, or whatever he is, says the four winds come and they go. It has a meaning we don't understand but we trust the plan, or the winds. Afterwards, in the parish hall, which is not what they call it, Tom introduces himself. "I know you from TV," he says, as if Max has a weekly series. If he'd known Max was there, Tom says, he'd have asked him to speak. "She considered you her best friend. She called you her fellow traveller. I don't think it would be wrong to say she loved you. I don't know if you knew that. Will you come to the Residence after this? Others she was close to will be there."

Other fellow travellers. They're having fruit juice and that strange good time people have at funerals which makes them wish out loud that they did it more often. She had a room upstairs in this stuffy place where about a dozen of the faithful must keep each other going. Like any modern conspiracy of belief. You pretend to take me seriously and I'll do the same for you. It doesn't have to be a cult, it can be an academic discipline like economics or a political party. Tom asks if he'd like to see her desk. There was no note, but he found some stuff in it, a stack of pages in dialogue. He leaves Max and goes back downstairs.

It's an unfinished screenplay. He sits down in the wonky blue swivel chair she must have used. It doesn't swivel, it tilts dangerously one way, then another. The bearings are totally shot. Or non-existent. Whatever it is that keeps a swivel chair true. The script isn't "political," as some of the folks downstairs would say. It's not *The Return of the Secaucus Seven, Harlan County*, or even *Nine to Five*. You could yank it inside out and metaphorize the hell out of it, but it remains a ditzy little romantic comedy, that's its genre. There are a few "political" references, like shards of pottery from an earlier layer in a dig. But this is Tracy and Hepburn, Doris Day and Rock Hudson. A pure vein almost, except for those shards, and damn funny. He remembers how funny she could be. It must have been about the five thousandth time they slept together that she finally let him see the real thing—not the authorized leftist jokes but the ribald, basically witless, um, wit. Thigh-slappers, not zingers. Why are women so stingy with their humour (except, he suspects, with each other)? Anyway, this is it, at long last: "The Urban Treadmill." Did she put it off because she wanted to do "serious" politics instead of shallow cultural impressionism, or because the whole earnest thing of her life bored her and her heart belonged to sitcom? To love and laughter. You shun it, then it worms its way into your desk drawer and hides, waiting for secret meetings with you. You have to sneak time for it. You can't justify it to the people you feel close to. As a student, he always felt fraudulent when he said he was going to work, then ambled off to read a book. Maybe it's how novelists feel when they're "working" on a novel. Who really works? What is real work? When was the last time he met someone who actually produced something useful? That's the kind of thing he and Elyse talked about. In the middle of a bright idea about it, he'd be all over her and her head was thrown back and she was panting. Then they'd talk about it some more. He pages through the screenplay, chuckling, till it peters out in the middle of a plugged toilet scene. Peters out, get it? "The thing about Vancouver," says the frazzled chick who's the central character, "is that it manages to be faddish without being trendy." Downstairs the comrades and ex-activists, the brothers and sisters, the loonies or moonies, clink their glasses and cluck. He closes the screenplay, leans back, then leans forward and starts it again.

Marguerite's Version

~

I didn't want him to torture himself over how he was with me. It wouldn't have made me feel better, because I didn't feel bad. He was a little odd that time, but not truly creepy.

When he started in, as soon as I got into touching range at

the bar in the Chateau, with that urgent, needy look in his eyes and the tight voice, like it was coming from somewhere else— no matter what sensitive, comforting things came from the mouth—well, it was unsettling. But I wasn't repelled. It was unfamilar, in my state of grief and mourning, that's all. I was still having hallucinations about Anton—I'd see him on a bus that passed, though less and less often. Or the back of his head going around a corner. So I didn't exactly want Max to stop pawing me, if that's the best way to describe it. I'm sure I could have made him stop. That's why it wasn't menacing. In fact, it was reassuring, although that's hard to explain. After he left my place, I went back to bed and lay there. Not thinking. With no thoughts at all. For the longest time. It was great—I had nothing on my mind. Then I realized what had gone missing, the thing the silence and emptiness was replacing. It was gone, and I hadn't even known it was there: a jangly, hissing undertone. It had been in my head since Anton died, as if the radio is playing but it's not quite on the station, so you hear static, interference, and it's so irritating that if you had a gun, you'd blast the goddamn set, except you can't turn it off, especially since you don't even quite know it's the thing making you crazy, like the disturbing element in a dream which you're unable to identify. It turns out to be the fact you don't know it's just a dream. It was only when it ended, that I realized it had been there since Anton died! It was like Sleeping Beauty and the kiss that woke her up, which may be goofy but not, as I said, creepy.

I can see how it upset him. He's a sensitive little fellow, when you come down to it, despite being a large-sized adult, with professional accomplishments, and a lengthy list of sexual adventures that Anton and I, as a very settled couple, enjoyed

dragging out of him. It was the usual division of labour, he
might say, between married couples and their single friends.
Each side gets a little supply of what they need. A fix. That
random sexuality of his gave us a boost. The way he wanted
me, you could see it across the breakfast table when he stayed
with us, or as he was hailing a cab after we'd all been at a
movie. If I was sitting between them in a theatre, it was like a
magnetic field between our fingers; the more we held them
apart, the more you felt the pull. Anton was my husband, of
course he felt it too. There was a choice: get offended and
threatened, or enjoy it. It's amazing how much wider your
range of options often is than you think. These are things I've
understood more clearly since Anton died. Once, when nothing
much had happened between Anton and me for a long time,
we took him with us to a cocktail party down the street, mainly
other academics. They found him kind of exotic, the economist
with no job or desire for one, and he flirted with everybody, in
that excited way which he'd have objected to if you called it flirting. That night at home, with him asleep on the couch, Anton
and I had sex like we did on our first date. The only time I ever
did that and then I married the guy. Ah, me. (Maybe he wasn't
asleep, maybe he heard it all, or we were hoping he did, to add to
the mix.) I'm sure he paid a price for what he considered callous
and voracious behaviour, not just that time with me after Anton
died, but maybe every time. The toll must add up.

There was a contradiction, he might have said during what
he called his "workerist episode," between the sensitive man
who worried about being bad and the guy who womanized like
crazy. I once asked him about Casanova. I haven't read the
memoirs, there are over a dozen volumes and only academics
read them, I would guess. But I speed-read a book by a feminist

Belgian shrink *on* Casanova. I needed to evaluate a dance project based, the company claimed in their application, on the famous lover's "amorous exploits as a metaphor of dance." This shrink said Casanova's secret was taking pleasure without shame or guilt. That's why he didn't call his memoirs "Confessions"—because he didn't regret anything. Nothing to regret, nothing to confess. When I told Max about it, he said, "I don't think I'm that kind of womanizer." He sounded like Eeyore. I said that would come as a big disappointment to women like me, since we always hoped he'd write about womanizing so we could finally understand it. He said his friend Rhonda the Writer told him the same thing. She'd been waiting for the book since they met. But he turned out to be Casanova with a guilty conscience, which is no Casanova at all. He got that stricken look, so I said, "Listen, bub"—adopting a tone I knew he admired—"the only book on womanizing I *want* to read would be by someone like you." And he got the grateful look instead of the stricken one. They often rotated, the two looks. He always had some look on his face. He would make the worst poker player in history. But to give him his due, and the lambasting he normally felt he deserved, it could have been awful at any other period in my life.

Timing matters. Some heavy, inexplicable sex isn't a bad way to come out of your most intense period of grieving. Sex can keep you going, its mere possibility can actually prevent you from ending your life—which isn't something you can say about a lot of things.

Marguerite et al.

The three of them meet at the Stupids, an annual week of academic meetings and jabber. Officially they are the Learneds and

Canada is the only place left where the disciplines hold their conventions jointly, as if university specialization and departmentalization are momentary trends. Innis, who till his death lamented the fracturing of political economy—that grand old tent for fine minds from Adam Smith to Marx—into poli sci and ec, would approve. In his own time, he was a one-man band at the Stupids.

Max is there because maintaining a quotient of academic respectability is part of his job description as freelance economist. It helps keep the sessional appointments coming, and an occasional guest professorship. Some day—dream on—maybe even an honourary doctorate. He is there as commenter on a panel about Anton's recent book, *The World of Work in Nineteenth-Century Small-Town Ontario*. It challenges the staples thesis: Innis's claim that manufacturing was always a poor cousin in Canada to resource extraction. Max and the others will attempt to rip the argument, or the book itself, into tiny discredited bits. It is considered a great honour for Anton. It's the first time he and Max have met. Marguerite is Anton's wife, she is in the second row and actually seems to enjoy the panel. She makes eye contact with Max, like the defendant's wife in court, trying to create a relationship with the foreman of the jury. On her own hook, she is a "senior arts administrator," she has a degree in it and travels the country evaluating dance companies in light of their grant applications to the arts council.

Marguerite is classy. She looks like the women in the Holt's catalogue, or the ones who get it in the mail. Somebody with her own business and a car like a Lexus that can only be serviced by a special garage downtown. Fritz, Max's German mechanic on Dundas, wouldn't know what to do with a car like that, any more than Max would know what to do with Marguerite. He wouldn't pray to God for *her:* the clothes, haircut, smooth skin, like stuff you'd order from Holt's too. He had a roommate named Gerald back in second year, before he crossed the sexual-knowledge barrier, when he was still Adam in the garden. Gerald came from Tanzania, and grew famous among faculty wives for his sexual prowess; they passed his name around. They'd call Gerald on the floor phone down the hall, then he'd wander back to their room and ask Max if he had any *rahboss?* Max would ask him to repeat the word, Gerald would increase the volume, as one does on long-distance calls in a foreign language. Even if they had managed to translate *rahboss* into "rubbers," Max wouldn't have known what it meant. So Gerald got the faculty wives and Anton, well—

Anton is the kind of guy who gets a Marguerite, not because he thinks he deserves her, but because he believes he has the right to try. The truth, unsuspected by Max, is that those ethereal women are human too, they want love like the rest of us, and Anton is a decent soul, a mensch among the tenured barracuda. The research he does is mainstream, as is Max's, but academically more stolid. He writes definitive studies, not expanded reports to deadline with half an eye on some media exposure. His point of view is humane; his methodology, first-rate. A Galbraith of the middle, like Galbraith. And he has Marguerite. Because he does and Max doesn't, Max can relax with her, as he will when a woman says, "I'd like to, really would, but I can't." As he did with perfect ponytailed Edna, before the dark downfall of prom night, when he overreached. Marguerite is Edna reissued. The three of them stay in touch. When Anton takes a chair of something in Ottawa, they meet more often. Then Anton dies, fast. He goes into hospital after supper with a stomach complaint. By morning he's gone. Lots of talk about missed diagnosis.

Nothing comes of it. Just like that. As the old guys say in the sauna, Ya never know.

Next January Max is in Ottawa one perfect winter night. Perfect for skating on the canal, though nothing else. He has come to address a dinner club of journalists and bureaucrats who meet upstairs in a Chinese restaurant. They're called the Marco Polo Club, to show what keen intellectual explorers they are. Or maybe it's after the decor on the walls. He'll go anywhere he's asked, so long as they pay expenses and book a good hotel. He adores good hotels. If they try to put him somewhere grotty, claiming it's atmospheric or they don't have a budget, he'll top up what they pay and book in at the Chateau. There's something *just* about using everything at a good hotel, from the toiletries to the bathrobe, a foretaste of economic plenitude and redistribution: to each according to their inherent human worth. After the talk, he calls Marguerite. She sounds tired but glad to hear from him. She'll meet him for a drink.

He pushes, from the second she joins him at the bar, starting with the double clutch on the hug. His knee keeps pivotting into hers. He draws her backward toward him as he helps her on with her coat, furtively (he deludes himself) nuzzling her hair. His conversation, meantime, comes from some other, compassionate place. How hard has it been? Does she have moments when she breathes easier? It'll take a year, people need to see the seasons revolve, each in turn, when they've gone round once you can start associating the mood outside with other emotions than you felt last fall or Christmas, this is Canada, the seasons change, it works for us and against us. He loathes himself in this mode, it can't be him saying the sensitive stuff, it's ventriloquism, a voicebox like a toy has, attached inside the badgering sex-obsessed lout he really is. It's not even strategic. If he really wants her, then solicitude and tact without the windmill of hands and knees would work better. He sees her home in a cab.

There it gets worse. She invites him in, doubtless, he thinks, in the hope of transmogrifying this groper into the sensitive friend in mourning which his words and their shared past keep intimating. Now it's like Greco-Roman: you attempt to pin her, she keeps trying to slip your grip. Gradually the pace slows. She struggles less; he speaks, mutters, *Good, that's good.* Then they're in the bed she shared with Anton, while he slept on the couch, he's in her, they lie a decent interval, he looks at the ceiling despising himself, he slinks back to the Chateau.

He opens the mini-bar in his room, damn the prices. (He wrote a guest column for *Toronto Life* on super-exploitation at the mini-bar, under a pen name, Economicus, hoping it would turn into a monthly gig, but it didn't.) He drains the little bottles of booze like Gulliver. Seduction isn't all they'd have you think—the Millers and Mailers—even at the moment of triumph. A woman sometimes succumbs, not to your brilliant conquest; she just finds it easier to fuck the guy, than struggle drearily on. Rhonda once told him that. "Women even marry guys," she said, "because they won't leave you alone. You marry the jerk to get rid of him."

He turns on Letterman, mutes it, and jerks himself off. Tries to sleep. Jerks off again. Considers calling Marguerite, flicks on the sports channel. There's a hockey game from Vancouver, second period. Praise God for time zones. Well, you can't score if you don't shoot, he thinks, hoping to drift off. That's what the boys say. Of course he's not one of the boys, never was, bellowing in the locker room about getting laid. They used to mute the sex talk when he was in earshot. It was that radar everyone had about him and sex, except Noel. But it's true—about shooting.

What always amazes him in great hockey players isn't how much they score, but how much more often they nearly do. It's hard to bear almosts in such quantity. Normal people would spend the rest of the game moping over how close they came. It's the ability to fail that distinguishes the great ones, not their success, even Gretzky, who missed more than anyone, precisely because he scored more. You can actually quantify it, the miss/score ratio, as he once did in an article for *Quest*, a short-lived mag for Canadian men. What you can't quantify is the toll it takes. He often fails to score himself.

He starts to replay his life as a womanizer, like counting sheep. Then he replays the replays. On TV, Howie Meeker is analyzing the highlights of the last period. He reviews the lowlights of his career as a womanizer. What about the students in the half course he teaches? Economy and Society. There's always someone to look at in there, kids who need to pick up a half credit to complete their degree requirements. Rhonda told him one night in Provence that her profs always peered around in the first class of a semester, checking out the cute chicks. "It's horrible feeling your prof's eyes slide over you and keep going," she said. It sounded hideous. Ever since, he's tried not to and surely failed. The kids in cinema studies, like—what was her name?—Cordelia, have great terminology, they make economists look illiterate. He had to move around to keep her in view. She sat in the back. If anyone in front leaned forward to make notes, he'd lose his eye-line. Students come to see him after class, or at the break, with problems. *My landlord is kicking me out, he says it's because his family is moving in . . . I got fired for joining a union at the theatre where I'm a bartender, they won't even give me severance.* People still approach him for advice though now it's about fighting the system, not where to score acid or get an abortion. Go talk to this guy at the *Star*, he says, or somebody in some union. And let me know how it goes. When they let him know, he suggests they go out and talk about it. Especially if the term is over. No hefty ethical dilemmas then. The grades are already in. When that final sheet of marks hits the registrar's desk is the magic moment. He feels bad about just *teaching* that course. He's got other sources of income. Why doesn't he give it up to the surplus Ph.D.s who camp around universities, like Third World peasants in shanty towns looking for work in Lagos or Rio because their parched little farm was taken over by a monoculture to provide burgers to McDonald's or beans to Starbucks? He's been teaching it so long he has virtual tenure for a half course. The university would have to pay him severance to be rid of him, and it's not worth their trouble. Around here is where he ends the lowlights. Or the TV just switches off, he may have set it on Sleep.

So really, what's the difference between him and the louts beside their lockers? Yeah, sure, he's a feminist. But he yearns to fuck the buns off the Sunshine girls on page three just like the boys do, he just doesn't drool about it over brews after the weekly shinny. They at least get points for honesty. It's like the homeless guy he sees on a bench near home every morning, wrapped in a mouldy sleeping bag—looking much the way Max feels in the king-size bed at the Chateau right now, missing the point, if there is one, of his obsessed, disjointed life. If he was back in his own place feeling this dim, he'd pad downstairs and shiver on the brown corduroy couch that's starting to resemble an archeological dig, layers of earrings and bracelets representing different metallurgical eras, embedded in the cushions and upholstery, as he dozes badly until the seismic thud of the *Star* landing on the porch stirs him and he uses the world's woes to drown out his own. No real difference, there or here, him or the homeless guy, as the whole thing devolves—the thing of his life, whatever it is—like an illustration in a physics textbook, toward chaos and incoherence, libidinal entropy: the sex drive fragmenting as it extends and with each one-nighter, dispersing more widely, while it simultaneously runs down, runs out. Nothing is more typical of this phase than the inability to remember names, and whether or not. He recalls, with a jolt, Rhonda saying she wished she had a trap door after sex. He would use it for himself. He finds it a bit scary, so he acquires a bit of a girlfriend.

Her name is Ellen. She's a bonds analyst. They meet at a party. She is funny and perky with a gap in her teeth. He asks if she'd like to come back to his place. She excuses herself and huddles with Lenore, the hostess. Then she returns and says Lenore recommends going but alas, she can't, she has a new boyfriend, at least she thinks she does, in fact they may move to Montreal together. Kind of Lenore. He once spent an afternoon with her at the beach on Toronto Island. Lenore put him off all day. But when she dropped him at his place, she didn't lean away and they ended up on his bed for a lovely hour, then she went off to meet the entertainment lawyer she's now married to.

A year later, around the time it gets a bit scary, Ellen calls. The boyfriend is over, she's back from Montreal, and Max is the only man she's ever met who was willing to just be her friend. This puzzles him, maybe she's thinking of someone else. She reminds him that they spoke on the phone before she left, from which she concluded he was willing to just be, etc. That's why she's calling, would he like to see her? Never give up, he thinks on the way, nothing is ever over. He rings the buzzer and she says she's on her way down. When the elevator opens and she steps out, his little heart does nothing. No skip a beat, no pit-a-pat.

He's looking through glass doors and across a lobby, mind you. A year ago she took his breath away. They drive to Fran's, he has a hot hamburg, drives her back, and they sit outside. It's late (Fran's never closes). A cop car stops and shines a light in their eyes, asks some questions, and moves on. It draws them together. He reaches over, after a while he asks if they should go to his place. She says, "If you'd asked me at Fran's, even before you put on the moves, I'd have said yes, and saved us time."

That's how she becomes his girlfriend, in his fashion. Not just a "repeater," in Rhonda's offensive term, though not quite what others mean by a girlfriend either. He includes her in a way he hasn't done since the Marriage, they check in daily by phone, as couples do. But he tells her never to just drop by, always call first. It cuts through her like an arrow, which he doesn't notice. After a few months, she says she's taken a posting in Calgary, where her firm, like others in the dawning age of oil boom, is moving its head office. Calgary will be the Toronto *and* Montreal of Canada's economic future, she says. She talks on about it, waiting for him to interrupt and ask her to stay. Her best buddy, Donald, she says, who works for the same broker, is out there. She'll stay with him at first, till she gets settled. That's when he asks her to move in— for the six weeks till she leaves. To her, it's not much. But he makes the offer with fear and trembling. It's the first time he's done anything like it since the Francie catastrophe.

Six weeks after she leaves, she's back. She just arrives, the way Deb did, though not at his door. She didn't know she'd be quitting her job till this morning. Donald, her great buddy, freaked out. He's been freaking out with increasing frequency ("Get it?" she says. "*Freak-wency!*") since she arrived. That morning, driving her to work, Donald stopped, got out, and ran around the car shrieking at her. He did the same thing in the office. This part Max knew because she phoned, shell-shocked, right after. She told him she didn't know if she could handle it. She didn't say she'd quit, she said she was thinking about quitting. He heard himself making a speech at her, there on the phone: You have to stand and fight, this is a battle on behalf of all women in the workplace. He made her sound like Annamaria, who started the organizing drive at Dynamet. *Pauvre mec.* In truth, he simply doesn't want her back, now that he's begun settling into his old life. Having a girlfriend is okay, he gave it a shot, but the logistics of womanizing while you have a girlfriend can be so difficult. So when she asks straight out, he says no, she can't move back in; it's not because he doesn't love her, it's because he doesn't approve of her politics!

Since nothing ever ends, at least not when it should, they try to pick up the pieces of the "relationship," as people have started calling what happens between an unmarried couple or, increasingly, married ones. They go to social events and take a Caribbean holiday in February's darkest hour. They sit on the beach and he tells her about women he has come close to coming close to. She looks as from afar, picturing him unfolding this list to someone else a year from now, with her name added. When summer comes, she travels to Europe alone, and returns to announce there is somebody else, shades of Olivia's London bank teller. Well, he's not exactly a teller. In fact, he owns a bank. He's a merchant banker. She met him in Toronto, at a little party at Max's place. *That* guy? The earnest Scots nationalist who revived the local economies of forlorn parts of the Highlands with his personal fortune? Max *liked* him, he invited Canadian economists and activists to come and be inspired by the little sweater factory that was humming on Skye, or the Gaelic college on, on, one of those humps of rock and moss. Ellen swears nothing "happened" till they met again in Edinburgh. Naturally, Max immediately wants her back. He sends a vast number of bouquets to the office. He tries the poetry again—twenty years after Olivia. He mopes for a full calendar year, till the seasons have revolved, etc. He beats himself up, as only he can. He takes full responsibility—and *more*. Full responsibility is nothing compared to the blame he feels he deserves for the botch he's made of his own life and the deep, unjustifiable suffering he's caused in hers, now that he's reasonably confident he will not succeed in winning her back.

Rhonda, who catches most of the grief because she has the emotional equivalent of a trapper's mitt, even Rhonda is appalled. She wants to scream, *Enough already*, the way she stopped him mailing the letter from Provence by yelling like a sergeant. But this time his anguish is awesome, it's practically religious. It's the unbearable pain of the first Easter Friday before the earliest Christians—who didn't even know that's what they were—got the good news that their Lord would rise again. They believed it was over, all hope lost, the chance for redemption had been but now had passed—exactly as he feels. The trouble with faith, she tries to tell him, as with passion, is that it's based on very little. Therefore it is almost impossible to refute. He's sobbing into the phone long distance as she says this. And yet, he burbles back, replaying his rewrite of her hurtin' pome, if Ellen's damn plane had gone down in the Atlantic on her way home to give him the bad news, he'd have felt sad for a day and carried on womanizing. It's not the being rejected, it never is; it's the being replaced.

He often has a sense of doubling during those years, as if his life is on a loop. It repeats itself, first as farce, then as more farce. The way Francie doubles with Deb, or the girl with the straw hair doubles with the toe-girl on Transpo 2000. They are repeaters, in Rhonda's term, which she claims she got from him (and maybe she did), but in a different sense. They recur in his life like archetypes in Frye's *The Anatomy of Literature*. He meets a Danish editor in Budapest, both of them on assignment, him for a series of radio docs—there was money for such things then. They go to a nightclub that is pure Havana of the fifties, he strokes her hair, which seems to strike her as quaint, much like the chorus line and cigarette girls. "I think I'd better take you to bed," she says with kindly Scandinavian ennui. They spend the night in her room, on one of the twin beds nailed to the walls like berths in an ocean liner, though they are both large and Western. Next morning they congratulate each other for manning the space so well. Then she doubles, i.e., becomes virtually identical in his mind, hard to tell apart or recall separately, though there are no overt similarities, with an American he meets in London on the return leg. Then triples, or doubles again, with an Algerian dancer at an annual theatre festival held in Toronto exactly once. When he thinks back to any of those women, they shade into the others, like blurred vision.

These are days and years, starting to grow into decades, when the students, media interns, summer hires at brokerage houses, and civil service placements run into one another. Meld into somebody named Jennifer or Lisa, who once worked at an ad agency but went back to university because she couldn't bear the inability to talk with co-workers about books and movies that mattered to her. But then academia got her down with its technicalities and bibliographies so she ventured into media, which seemed suddenly to be the force shaping all life on the planet; perhaps by working inside it, she could penetrate the fog

RICK SALUTIN

or teach others how to defend themselves against it. Then she switched to a government job, since you can't regulate in the public interest unless you're a part of government, not to mention the security and union wages; plus every few years she signed up to work in an idealistic election campaign, hoping to revitalize the calcified forces of power—frequently returning to live in her parents' basement in Scarborough so as to save the money that enabled her to pursue these worthy ends. He phones Jennifer, or Lisa, who he met in one or another of those places, to ask how things have gone since they last talked, whenever it was, and might she like to get together? "You sound sad," she sometimes says. "Are you all right?"

Noel has acquired a baronial pile in Forest Hill. The old man finally kicked, leaving their relationship, or lack of it, still unexploded, and freeing up some of the family cash, or loot, depending on how you view capitalism. Noel and Nadine, with their first kid on the way, hold a pile-warming one night, also to honour a special guest, the new minister of justice in the new federal government. "I hear he's an intellectual and ethical vacuum," says Max. "I don't know where you got that idea," says Noel, who is Max's source. "He's decent and a little insecure." Noel loves being an insider. He seems to have acquired his dad's social status as part of the inheritance. The place is laced with faces you sort of recognize. A man in a pompadour cruises by holding a drink. Noel gives him a broad smile, and a courtroom-style bow. "Who is that, some kind of agent?" asks Max. "In a way," says Noel. "He's the head of the police union. I'm representing a few of their members." Max nearly carbonates his drink. The holdup squad, explains Noel, are in deep shit again. The very guys who were targeted by the brutality inquiry that held up, you could say,

244

Max's appeal for so long. "They were impressed by my work on your case," says Noel. "They want you on their side next time they're caught working somebody over," says Max. "Are you saying they don't deserve decent representation?" asks Noel, using an argument that's beneath him. Max isn't going to win this one, and doesn't really want to.

"You are a contrarian," says Noel, edging onto smoother terrain. "I am not, I'm a Keynesian," says Max. "My point exactly," says Noel, as if addressing the bench. "Who else would have become a bedrock Keynesian during the biggest Marxist revival since the Russian Revolution? If Keynes ever comes back in fashion, you'll cross the floor to join the Marxists, as long as you're the only one still there." Max asks if that's why Noel is working for the cops, to establish his individuality? "Maybe," says Noel. "Maybe that's all everyone wants to do. Mark out a space which is yours alone." It has an oddly thought-through quality for this vacuous setting, as if Noel suddenly decided to present a new and compelling proof for the existence of God.

"Hey, you," says Robbie Carignan. Max hasn't seen him— not in the cuddly flesh—since the run-in at Deb's Edebles. Robbie introduces a stolid woman about his own age. "This is my wife," he says. "We're getting married next week. I'll send you an invitation, both of you. . ." Max says, "You betcha, Robbie. We'll be there, we'll go anywhere we're invited." Robbie beams as if this is a bon mot almost worthy of himself, and steers his wife-to-be away. "She's his first wife," explains Noel, Noel-in-the-know, "from their university days. They had a bunch of kids and a divorce. They're getting remarried. It's a trend. I read about it in *Vanity Fair*." Max says, "But he's the playboy of the Western world." Noel shakes his head sadly. "No more. He had his prostate out. They stayed best friends all these years. She got him through the operation. Things change," he concludes as if he's just nailed the landing on his argument about working for dirty cops. Max doesn't know if he has, or if a lawyer just learns to treat everything that happens as if it bolsters his case. Noel has already turned away to greet the publisher of the *Globe and Mail*.

Max surveys the complacent gathering: the new minister, Noel's pregnant bride, their unborn child. Hard to imagine all this striving exists just to establish a little sense of self. He hasn't seen anyone he'd like to meet here, but sometimes when you head for the door, they find you. His hunting instinct, never all that strong despite his reputation, has been waning. He feels a tap on his elbow. She's about his age and has the most severe bangs he's ever seen. "I'm Inge from *Inge*," she says. "So *you're* the well-known iconoclast." He lowers his eyes to indicate modesty, and wonders if Noel was right. *Inge*, she explains, is the name of a new magazine for hip, aggressive urban women. He hasn't seen it because it's not on the stands, she says, it's controlled circulation, a neat new idea that lets you avoid being read by the riff-raff who drag down your ad rates. Plus it hasn't put its first issue out yet. Would he consider writing for something so commercial and trivial? "How much does it pay?" he asks. A thousand bucks for nine hundred words. "Will tomorrow morning be too late?" he says, using one of his audition lines. She smiles with appreciation more than amusement. She says she'd like him to write for a feature called Despatches from the Front, based on a book about the war in Vietnam one of her sub-editors claims to have read, except the front here is the gender wars.

He decides to do an analysis of Tarzan and Jane. That ought to be trivial enough, and he always liked Tarzan. When his mum took him to his first ape-man flick, Tarzan and the Nazis, he came out doing the Tarzan scream and didn't stop for weeks. As he matured, he held onto the attachment but took it in another direction, took it to the limit, in what he thinks of as his unique methodology. He read the Edgar Rice Burroughs novels, with the original Tarzan, such a far cry, ahem, from Hollywood's primitive hunk. The "real" Tarzan was an English aristocrat, sat in the House of Lords, gave speeches there, and when he returned to his jungle, ahem, roots, he reverted to the call of blood to rule there too, an aristocrat even among apes and cannibals, proving the superiority of his race. It was all, we can thus conclude, about imperialism's mythagogic roots, not that you would want to actually say mythagogic in the pages of *Inge*, or her presence. Jenny of Cambridge had a theory about the noble savage who populated so much of late nineteenth-century British culture. He was, said Jenny as if it was too obvious for words, the emergent working class, the proletariat of Victorian England's dark satanic mills. Hmm, but what would that say for the gender wars: that they are inevitably imperialistic? That there must be a loser and a victor? It makes him uneasy. It isn't quite working.

Something else is tugging at his sleeve. He's always wanted to use Hegel's concept of master–slave, it's the kind of casual reference he thinks of as his trademark in the media, where he plays the academic card, just as he plays the pop card in the academy. It's a living, barely. But that conceit doesn't quite work either, so he goes back to Hegel. Hey, maybe he never read this section of *The Phenomenology*, it doesn't look familiar. Or maybe he's changed since he read it, so that the guy reading now is seeing it for the first time. The passage unsettles him: the hideous imbroglio seems even worse for the master than for the slave, the fellow with the power has *no* way out. He digs further, into Kojève's commentary on Hegel. No help there, it's harder to understand than Hegel, even in German. He always found German thinkers more comprehensible in their own language, despite his limited linguistic grasp, than in English translations. Whew, this feels like hard sledding. He knows less about what he wants to say than he did on the night of Noel's party. The column is starting to take longer than some books. Monographs anyway. But that's not his real dilemma. Short ought to take longer than long. Brevity makes you get to the point, which is hard and exhausting, long lets you loiter around the edges. He seems to know increasingly less about what he thinks on this subject. And the subject is merely Tarzan and Jane!

Has he become incapable of triviality? That would be a bummer. Must he invest everything with deep meaning and dilemma? He seems unable to let anything pass without making a fundamental critique, questioning its assumptions. Then backtrack to your original impulse, those Hollywood movies and Tarzan's manic scream, the one he used to do in the house, on the streetcar, cute as a button. Tell the tale, give it a personal hook, readers love that stuff. It feels nice and familiar to him, the scream, but, when you start to think about it, too familiar? Tarzan didn't scream at Jane, it wasn't part of their relationship, as it was at the core between his parents. Was he appropriating Tarzan's fierce yell back then, in childhood, to prepare for his own victims, come the moment when he too had someone to growl and howl at: Olivia, Francie, Ellen? This isn't working either. It won't go where he wants it to. It's all turning toward power and its misuses, toward politics in the broad sense, but that isn't what he means by sex and gender. For him, sex is the blessed escape, the R and R you need to keep on plodding up the hill of the rectification of social injustice and inequality. That's the distinction he's drawn. He hates that thing leftists say about the personal being political. Politics is political and sex is not, sex is his promised land, Garden of Eden, it's outside the sordid realm, even if it can get sordid too. That's why he's a mealy-mouthed Keynesian, not a ranting Maoist. He knew those vessels of economics and public policy would not contain the hot-eyed visions poured into them, they would crack and shatter, they were meant for more moderate ambitions. But sex was something else, it could sustain the ardour and hope, despite, despite—all his experience of it so far? . . .

Weeks later, far past his deadline, when Inge has substituted another contributor for her first issue, he hands in the piece. She edits and sends it back within forty-eight hours, totally rewritten. The words and phrases actually changed! No one has ever done this to him before. He feels cheap and violated. He calls her, sputtering. She says they should meet, it's just a proposal on her part, a draft that can serve as a basis for discussion, why doesn't he come to her apartment this Friday for dinner. Huh? She doesn't want a column, she wants a relationship. She's Tarzan and he's Jane. Has he finally met a manizer, patiently plotting and pursuing her prey? Did she ask the Lord when she saw him at the party, Just give me that haunted-looking guy, I won't ask for anything else.

The column never appears. Something's going amiss. He doesn't feel all right, and he has no idea if it's gonna be.

On his way into Ottawa's forsaken train station, returning to Toronto, he meets Maggie. As he passes, she's saying goodbye to her dad, who looks like a retired fireman. "Now you be good, Dad," she's saying. It is angelic. Low-key, Ottawa Valley, same thing as angelic. She comes and sits beside Max on the bench when Dad has gone back out to his car, and says she once heard him speak at a public forum, she doesn't remember what it was about, could it have been a funny name like Innis? Maginnis?

Just like that, no coying around. She noticed him when he went by, as he noticed her. She's a nurse, in palliative at the moment, stressful as hell. She'll stick it out till she can't. No ethical razzamatazz, no identity acrobatics, she does it because it's right, for as long as it's bearable. He administers the biographical quiz and fills in most of the blanks, by the time they pull into Union Station. She seems happy to take the questionnaire, and intrigued by his interest. It's New Year's Eve and she comes with him to a party at Noel's (Noel congratulates him on her), then home for the night. Sometimes she works weekends at a restaurant on Queen Street. He can phone there late, if nothing, i.e., no one, is around, and she'll come by after closing. She becomes his social date for a year: tall, blonde, beautiful enough to intimidate other women he knows and not even mildly troublesome. One evening she appears without calling. His phone has been out for a week. He stands on the porch not asking her in and her face implodes as she realizes someone else is inside. She says, "Somebody else is here." He shrugs, not meant to be hurtful, but a shrug is a shrug. He doesn't know what else to do and has nothing at all to say. The times they see each other grow further apart, then not at all.

So it comes as a shock when he receives a personal bulletin: MAGGIE IS WHAT YOU NEED TO HEAL THAT PANG STOP DON'T LET HER GO. He is in Fredricton at a conference on Atlantic Dependency. He didn't know he had a pang but, hey, it's worth a look. He listens for it and, damn, there it is. Pang. He just finished the twenty minutes of challenge and provocation they invited him to provide before they break for drinks. He was glancing around the room in case there's anyone to ask to dinner. You never know. That's when it comes—bingo, message for Max. He decides to make a dash for home. With luck, he can connect to a flight in Montreal that will get him back in time for a public lecture by Lew Lapham at the university, where she might be. It's the kind of improbable place she shows up, as she did for his talk on Innis. His plan is indirect, cumbersome, uncertain, and frantic. He could just phone and say he was wrong to let her drift away—if he was somebody else and always had been.

Lapham has flown up from New York, where he is editor of *Harper's*, and has published a few pieces by Max, who admires him. Lapham is a late-century journalistic version of Keynes: patrician, progressive, and in no way radical. Too much breeding. It makes him a pariah in his own country, and a prophet with honour in Canada. Max rushes in late, his bag on his shoulder, and is rewarded with the slightest nod from Lapham at the podium, already in discreet rhetorical flight. No one else would catch the look. His eyes start to sweep the room for Maggie and then they go *boing*, back along their trajectory, like a cartoon, to a redhead in the front row. *B-b-b-boing.* Popping out of his head like twin telescopes. Oh my God, he prays, if you will let me have her just once, I will never ask you for anything again, and this time I really mean it.

After the lecture he arranges to meet Maggie, who was so near him in the back row that he missed her when he swept the room. He'll see her on the roof of the Park Plaza, where Lapham and others are going. Then he goes down to say hi to Lew. The redhead is there, cross-legged on the floor, at the feet, unbelievably, of Laszlo, his once and, you never know, future publisher. Laszlo may have come to offer Lapham a contract. He'd have the stones. Perhaps Lapham has something uncollected—his dry-cleaning stubs, his tax returns—that no one else has asked to publish. The redhead is importuning Laszlo, Max can overhear it: could she *please* come and work with him, learn from him, all of life's career paths seem laggard and drear, but publishing, ah publishing, in it there is still hope, faith, and meaning. She talks about it the way people in other fields think of medicine, especially if they don't know any doctors. Laszlo introduces them. "Aha," she says. "I've heard about you!" It sounds trashy. If it was good, she'd just say, I've heard *of* you, wouldn't she? The three of them walk to the Park Plaza. Laszlo looks outflanked. He had other intentions for this evening. She is wheeling a decrepit bike.

They step onto the roof, Maggie looks at him, then at the redhead, and her face collapses in silent surrender. It may sound cowardly, but it's merely astute, proof she knows him better than he deserves to be known. At the end of the evening, he and the redhead walk Lapham to his hotel, then she walks Max home, her bike hobbling alongside like a wayward child (it turns out she has a little boy, Harry, but he's down in Windsor with his dad), and comes in. They go directly to his bed, an answer to his prayers exactly as they were phrased. Tonight there is a god. He promised to drive Lapham to the airport next morning—there aren't many he'd do that for, maybe Innis, maybe Keynes, and both of them are dead. So he's up at five-thirty, back in the bedroom at ten to seven and she is, thank you, God, still there, everything kind of darling, front and rear. About three weeks later, it seems to him, they get out of bed. He remembers nothing else. That's how he meets Eva, the adorable flake, who occupies the next four years. It's remarkable how far three weeks of great sex can take you.

He never thinks of Eva as the adorable flake till it's over. She is, you could say, adorable in the moment. She bubbles with vitality like a brook, then goes sour as if you turned over a coin. She scores great jobs at will, but, in weeks, grows disillusioned and loses interest. It's always about her boss, who is always a man. She is exhausting, which is enough to keep him in the game, and *so* frustrating. He's not being fair, she never promised to be more than who she is, an adorable flake. When she stays with him after that first stretch, during holidays that Harry spends with his dad and grandparents down in Windsor, Max frequently explodes in anger and frustration. One night she winds up cringing under a table while he howls down at her, louder than Tarzan. He doesn't know what she's doing there, how he put her there, there's no reason, or it's so trivial you'd have missed it go by, yet the gestalt rings with familiarity. After two years of great sex and and humiliation, of her, of him, he asks her to move in, with Harry, as if he's looking for something he misplaced and they are it.

So they do, a year and a half later they move out, and it is as if nothing has changed, or happened. One so mercurial leaves few traces. He never misses her once she's gone, but when he wanders into Harry's empty room, his eyes fill with tears every damn time. It's called grief, says Rhonda. ("And how do you feel about me?" blurts Eva, when he tells her what Rhonda said. "Did she say it's called relief?") What an awful thing he's done, since he knew, as always, that it was hopeless the instant she arrived and began filling her half of the bedroom closet, just as he had after the wedding and with Francie. Before they decamp, he sits Harry down, now a young adolescent, and tells him, "You'll always have a home here." He has helped with Harry's home-work and made sure there were Chipwiches in the freezer every day after school. He feels suicidal about the loss of this child. He wouldn't know what to say if he was Harry. Surely he's placed an impossible burden on the boy. How can anyone respond to such a gush? Harry says, with a simple dignity that reminds him of Maggie, "Thank you."

Coral's Version

~

I truly believe you are the only one responsible for your happiness. I *truly* believe you alone are responsible. It is your
responsibility and yours alone. *You* are the one. I kept saying
this stuff to myself. Over and over. I think he heard me say it
out loud when he came upstairs to see how I was doing after I
moved over into the spare room. *I am the only one who can make
me happy or unhappy.* Like a mantra. Maybe he thought, under
the stress, I was reverting to my ancestral roots, which would
be Confucian, not Hindu. But Eastern anyway. I thought of it
as feisty rather than Chinese. I was not going to collapse.

It helped, in a torture-chamber kind of way, that I felt
some guilt about moving in. We'd been together a while. It's
hard to say how long because, with him, nothing about sex
ever seemed to exactly start or end. It just happened, then
eventually it happened again. Sex, friendship, need. It wasn't
on, it wasn't off, that's how he was with everyone. But with
me, for some reason, it was also a secret. I wouldn't want to
suggest that's because I'm not white, I'm sure it wasn't. He
was living alone, so was I, but we kept it a secret. I think it
helped him get close. I'd say that was the reason. I think he
wanted to get closer than he had in the past, and then again
he didn't. It was and it wasn't. I was and I wasn't. So he
began pulling back. That's when I pushed. I said if we split up
before anyone knew we'd been together, I'd never have the
chance to mourn the end of us because it's as if we didn't exist
to start with. A clever thought, if I say so. I could see he
thought so, he had a respect for intellectual originality, not

just in economics. It was also true, which was a bonus. He got that stricken look, as he called it, or maybe his buddy Rhonda used to call it that. So instead of dumping me, which he seemed to be gearing up for, he asked me to move in. Major victory, eh? I was in and we were "out." Then I get dumped two years later and it *really* hurt.

I was wrong to push. It isn't easy for me to admit that. I have this lawyer personality I switch into when I think I might have made a mistake. I get combative instead of contrite. I can't even recall a lot of times I was wrong, which doesn't mean they didn't happen. I've tried to make a list, as an exercise in self-improvement. You could put the whole list on a Post-it. But pushing him was one. Even so, I'm glad I did.

For the first time in my life I felt I could really be myself with somebody else sitting there. I know that because I found myself saying the stupidest things I ever said, or ever will say, possibly the stupidest things anybody ever heard, if that's not immodest. Like, we were watching the news and I start muttering, "Stinky bumhead, stinky bumhead." I don't know if I meant the reporter or the prime minister or who. To myself like I would if I was alone. I talk a lot when I'm alone. He heard it but he didn't say anything or roll his eyes, any more than if I asked him to pass the dip. Just kept watching TV, eyes ahead. So I did it louder. *Stinky bumhead, stinky bumhead.* Like a Hare Krishna. Those people drive me insane.

You have to be grateful to someone who helps you pull up stuff stuck down in the babyhood part of your mind like a potato. Just lies there with the TV on while you do it. In fact, TV was a key enabling part of the process. I never felt it was intellectually respectable to watch anything except news and nature shows. But we used to watch TV, as he put it, as opposed to watching PBS or CBC, the thing people say when they want you to know they don't approve of TV. TV brings out people's true selves, he believed; like the moment of truth in a bull ring, or the poems you say to yourself when you can't sleep, or what you fantasize about having first when you get back from a long canoe trip. I'd say he had a combative style with TV, a video-watching form of martial arts, to protect himself against the effects other people feared. He was like a car that got Ziebarted on its underside, so you don't worry about driving over the salt and crap. By the end of "The National" that night I was bouncing up and down on the mattress howling it like "Go Leafs go." *Stinky bumhead, stinky bumhead—*

On the other hand, I've gotta admit there's a special incentive in the case of a breakup, to accept blame. Because if you were at fault, it means you were also in control, so you had some power. You blew it, but you had it. That means next time, you just have to get it right. The worst is feeling there's nothing you could have done to make it turn out differently, it was just beyond your control. That really sucks.

Coral

This is a love story, although the love in it comes only at the end, when the two people part, so let's skip the rest and begin there.

"What do you feel," she asks, "about how it's going?" The question emerges from no chain of intellectual or emotional links. There's been no build to it, no apparent deterioration, they still watch TV and delight each other. She's been living here almost two years, it's nearly four since Eva and little Harry, for whom he grieved, left. He could decide to say nothing, or "Nothing," and it wouldn't be false. But he accepts the invitation. "I don't really want it to continue," he says.

She breaks like the little girl Dylan wrote about. That's how he knows what Dylan's line means. Then she gathers herself. She goes up to their bedroom and he hears her moving things to the guest room. She has a daunting way with furniture. He came down for breakfast one day after she moved in, to find the table, sofa, cabinets, and bookshelves all in different locations, rooms and floors. He asked why she did it. "I'm inscrutable." she said, "How would I know? Do you like it?"

After a while, he goes and looks in on her. She's become a guest. He's about to say he's sorry. He knew, as usual, the day she moved in, that it would fail. This news always comes to him the way the news about a death at the Front must have come in the first half of the century. The messenger is walking up the front walk, you can't wish him not there, all you can do is watch him come. In his version, which is farcical rather than fatal, it's the movers who come up the walk, with their useless Ph.D.s in renaissance lit and no teaching jobs, carrying someone else's belongings onto the porch and into his house, then trundle away in their squat truck. He accepted it with a heavy heart, and waited for the end as he'd waited for the movers. With Francie, it took three weeks. He'd become less brave, or more. He endured these errors in judgment a little longer. Eva and Harry were with him eighteen months. "The honourable minimum for a live-in," says Rhonda, "is two years." It's been that now.

"What I wanted most from you," she says, squatting on the guest bed, "was to be yourself with me, whatever that was. I'm not happy this is what you want. But I'm happy you feel you can be yourself. I really am," she adds, since he must be wondering if she really is. When he tells Rhonda about it, she says, "Then at long last, you have known the meaning of true love."

They take amiable walks on College Street. He slides her

toward him. She fits neatly under his arm. It's been a long time since they walked like this. She purrs. They talk as they walk. Sometimes she asks, echoing Olivia, why they're doing it. He doesn't answer so she lets it pass. Understanding has grown less significant, intellect doesn't count the way it did. It's how they're doing it that matters, not why. So that's the way you measure progress over decades: change of an adverb.

"It's actually very, um, lovely," he says with a stammer, at the end of one of their walks. She says she tried to name it when she told her parents she was moving out. She wanted to call it beautiful, but in Cantonese the best you can do is "profound." "English too," he says. There are words for falling in love, for passion, hurt, and despair. But apply positive terms here and you sound like an idiot. Maybe they exist in other languages, the way the Inuit have forty words for snow. When you need them enough, you'll get them.

"Maybe you shouldn't be around," she says, "when I move out. It will be hard on you. Could you get together with somebody? How about Rhonda?" Rhonda has given up teaching and moved here, of all places, to be with a Canadian cameraman she met at the Toronto festival of authors. The other authors don't treat her *oeuvre* very respectfully at those things, and neither does she, but she uses the chance to read from the still-unfinished toilet paper cycle. It makes her feel like a real writer. It didn't hurt that her friend Max happened to live here. Nice to have someone around to gather up the inevitable pieces. She bought a townhouse in the east end, even got landed status, mainly to prove to the guy that she's serious, despite the fact he apparently isn't. His name is Juval, "as in juvenalia," she says, meaning he is juvenile, when he isn't infantile. "I'd warn you to stay away from cameramen," she tells Max, "if you were prone to guys. They can barely dress themselves in the morning, the rest of the day is chaos." They're sitting in her bedroom, him on the floor, her on the four-poster bed where she does all her writing. Juval is away, who knows where or how long. Max says he wonders why he comes to her for advice on these things in the light of her own record. "Because I'm an expert," she says. "We all are, except in our own lives. That's the nature of expertise. You told me so. So what's going on?"

She has a medical appointment later today, she has a few symptoms—the code is pure Women Talk About Cancer—but she wants to hear everything. They drink coffee while the guys with the Ph.D.s lug Coral's furniture back to the van from Max's place, two years after they brought it. That's the day Rhonda says he's finally known the meaning of love. She sounds glad for him and envious. Then she goes to her doctor.

Max returns to the house alone, the bare spaces where her stuff was. There have been times—like his entire life—when he'd get through this by "calling somebody up" and asking her over. Take her to his bed as others take a bottle. Like a baby, or a drunk. When Lily, who I may not have mentioned but who he liked a lot, returned from a housing conference in Africa, he picked her up at the airport and drove her to his place, where she said there was a Slovenian boxboard manufacturer in her life now. After all, Max never said anything to make her think she should count on him. He got through that night, her in his bedroom and him on the couch, by running through the list of women he'd phone tomorrow. He fell asleep with a smile on his face. Either this thought doesn't cross his mind now or he dismisses it. He doesn't wish Coral hadn't left. But he feels her absence, as if he has graduated.

Olivia's Version

~

When he asked me, *decades* later, how I remembered our marriage, I said, "Did you hit the other women you were with too?" I could tell it wasn't what he expected, so that was a pretty satisfying effect. Even though we used to talk so much. Talktalktalktalk—that was us.

He recovered and asked if he'd ever done it with a closed fist, and did he beat me, meaning, I guess, did he stand over me and pummel me. I said I didn't think so about the pummelling, I couldn't remember about the fist. He looked a bit aghast that he had even asked and said of course it didn't really matter, he was sorry either way, but I think he felt he'd scored some points. Open hand, not a fist. You hear that sort of thing in women's groups, or used to, I don't know what it's like now. The truth is, having the shit scared out of you by someone who can pulverize you is what counts. He should know that, he's been terrorized enough in his own life. When we were together, he'd want *me* to do something about his problems. Go talk to the people who were blocking him from getting jobs or appointments he was after, for instance. He wouldn't say so, he'd have denied it, but I felt like I was supposed to figure out how to do it anyway. It wasn't what I signed on for.

I told him the thing I couldn't forgive in *myself* was that I went back to him, after we split. Returning for more. He got that abashed look again, as if he was sorry to ask, but did he ever hit me after we came back together? Suddenly I was being cross-examined. Maybe Noel advised him on it, more likely he just picked it up hanging around Noel. I once heard a lawyer—

not Noel—say cross-examination was better than sex. Of course the guy had never been cross-examined himself. I looked at the floor and said I didn't think he hit me after I went back. "Then you shouldn't have to forgive yourself," he said, "because you didn't come back for more." As if he was Ben Matlock or Senator Sam Ervin, those sneaky-smart country-lawyer types. Brimful of regret for even bothering me with his silly little question; then *wham*. Maybe he suspected I'd been dining out on the line—*why did I go back for more?*—in women's groups, as I had, to tell the truth. He picked up on stuff like that. He was smart, not just about economics, but about people. He read people the way he read books. He applied the same kind of guesswork. It was sexy, it was the sexy thing about him. That "mind." He really seemed to think you could figure it all out, whether it was economics or a fucked-up marriage. Impose order on the chaos. Well, no, not impose. Find order, it had to be there or it wouldn't count. Maybe it wasn't his mind that was so touching, it was his faith.

Anyway, he took one of those big introspective inhales, blew it out, and said, as if he was conceding a large chunk of territory to the enemy, that this wasn't what he'd expected me to say when he suggested we talk about our marriage after all these years. But if that was how I remembered it, he appreciated me saying so, and, um, well, would I like to take my best shot? I said no. He said it would make him feel a lot better. I said, "Then I definitely won't," and we both laughed. I said I knew what we ought to do next is go out for lunch and start over again from a different place, sort of catch up—but for some reason I didn't understand, I wasn't ready to do that. All I wanted was to get up, put on my coat and leave. So I did.

I never had an orgasm with him. He did, of course, starting with those ones against my leg. I never used my hand on him either. He once said Sorstad told him that "the myth of mutual climax" had caused a lot of damage. I imagine Sorstad meant you shouldn't get hung up on the mutual part. He didn't mean you should forget about the other guy *having* a climax.

We used to talk about sex a lot, in a Sorstad way. Sex is like food, we'd say, and who would want to eat just one thing for the rest of their life. I told him that I thought people in a marriage should be able to have sex outside it. I was ironing when I said that and my friend, Cynthia, was at our place hanging out with us. I was glad to have a witness. I watched out the corner of my eye to make sure it registered on him. I was offering it to him as a sort of present, since he was the one having trouble with being married. But really, I'd say now, I was setting things up for myself. The hitting had been going on a while, along with the yelling, usually followed by the self-loathing. It's amazing how almost anything can get boring, even getting the shit pounded out of you, although that's probably an exaggeration, as I admitted to him during his cross.

Then one night I came home late from a life-drawing class at the Centre for Contemporary Art. Extremely late. The tube had stopped running. Noel was visiting us in London from Canada. Noel and I had our own history, but he was basically Max's friend. Noel seemed upset that I'd stayed out so late and he went ostentatiously to bed on the living-room couch once I got back. We went into the bedroom and started to talk. I said I'd been with one of the guys in the class. I let it sit there so he knew what I meant by *been with*. It was my best effort at cruel. He slumped on the end of our bed, his head scrunched, dipping very low between his shoulders. I stepped out of the bedroom into our little kitchen, which was next to it, to make a nice cup of tea to calm myself down. In Toronto, I never turned to tea in those moments. As I reached for the teapot, I glanced through the crack in the door jamb, I could see him on the end of the bed. He looked up without raising his head, and this huge grin spread across his face. *What the hell?* I thought, and then I realized he was sitting in front of the full-length mirror on the door that went to the bathroom. That flat had a floor plan from hell. He was smiling at himself in the mirror. He looked as surprised to see the smile there as I was. He was *happy* I'd gone and slept with somebody else. He looked like he'd just been given his driver's licence and could now go all kinds of places that weren't available before.

But the fights kept on. It wasn't just that he wanted to have sex with lots of people. He didn't want to be married. Sometimes he'd admit it, then he'd take it back. I said if he didn't want this relationship, I didn't either, that was my line, as if I'd been given it by a coach in my drama workshop as an improvisation exercise: I had to repeat it no matter what anyone else in the class said to me. Probably I wanted to get out too. But neither of us would say so. If one of us had, the fights would've stopped, flat, cold, right there. They'd have been unnecessary. It was as if we needed enough pressure to blast us both out of the marriage, since neither one had the guts to walk off with a handshake and promise to try and stay friends. I've done that a number of times since. The hardest thing is saying you want to go. Why is that? Because neither person wants to be the guilty one? Guilty of what? I don't know. Giving up. Not just on the marriage, that particular marriage, but of adding one more defeat to the human stock of failure. Sometimes I feel sad even when I see an unquestionably lousy relationship break up, one that I may have been lobbying against for ages. As if we—I guess, we meaning the human race—blew it again. Christ, I sound like him: theory. It's possible he was just shit-scared to be on his own, although he never gave anyone that impression.

That summer, he took a job back in Canada. Something to do with writing the history of Canadian monetary policy for the Bank of Canada. We both treated it sombrely, like a formal separation, even if it was only for the summer and didn't necessarily mean the marriage was over. I rode with him to Gatwick on the train, we were still being close, being friends, saying this was temporary. When we got to check-in, the clerk said he had too much baggage and he'd have to leave some, so he pulled out a suitcase of books he'd been planning to devour in his spare time. It was damn heavy, heavier than anything else he had, and asked if I'd haul it back and keep it till he returned in the fall. When I got up to the street at Victoria Station, lugging this massive dead weight of books, I must've looked like someone who had just arrived from the colonies, staring around, wondering if I should hail a cab or go back down into the bowels of the underground.

And this completely local guy—working-class bloke with his aim dead set on getting to lower middle—came up to me and said I looked like I needed a place to stay. Tight English bum, shiny jacket, greasy black hair, bad teeth. He said his mother took in lodgers and he'd be glad to carry my bag, it was nearby but not near enough for me to carry—ugh, he tried the bag at that point—all by myself.

And I said yes, I appreciated that terrifically, sounding as Canadian and all in from my flight, as I could. I spent the

summer at his mother's place, pretending to go out looking for
work or sightseeing when I was really headed to my job down
on the Embankment at the housing project, and sneaking back
to my, that is to say, our, apartment, occasionally to pick out
clothes that looked new enough to have just bought them, or
change from my workclothes before going "home" to my
room. It was ridiculous and it involved some great sex. He was
the opposite of my absent husband. If you programmed a
computer to produce Max's exact opposite, he was what you'd
get. He worked in a bank—too, I'd think wickedly, meaning the
Bank of Canada—as a teller. His ambition was to own a pub.
He didn't like the coloureds. He was funny and he adored me.
He ate me, all the time, and he loved it when I sucked him off.
He said I was the best he'd ever known, that before me he
sometimes even had trouble getting an erection. Whenever he
reminded me of that, I went straight down on on him and he
thanked God for this new world he was in. We went several
times to a movie playing that summer called *The Pumpkin Eater*,
about a guy who "had a wife, and couldn't keep 'er."

   At the end of the summer the complex fiction I'd been
maintaining grew even more convoluted. My, er, husband was
coming back—I mean, over, from Canada, I had to explain. I
hadn't hidden that I had a husband, just where he was and
where we lived. I explained I'd gotten a place and a job, and
then I moved into, that is, back into, my, that is, our, apartment full-time. Of course as soon as Max found out about my
lover, and how I wasn't prepared to give him up or resume our
married life, he went just berserk, decided he'd made the worst
mistake of his life, that he'd never wanted anyone but me, and
now he'd gone and destroyed his one chance at true happiness
and driven me to someone else, how could he ever get me

back—you could say it freed his emotions about me up real good. Once I wasn't his, once I was someone else's, once he was living in some shitty little rented room himself, he was at liberty to feel all the love and attachment in the world for me.

I knew it was bullshit, it smelled like bullshit, but after a while the poems, the letters, the flowers started to get through my bullshit-screening devices. Not so much the flowers. I've heard men say you can't go wrong with flowers. I've even heard women say it. But you can go miserably wrong with them, especially if they arrive at work, in embarrassing quantities, and you don't want to explain them to your co-workers. But the letters and poems—the *writing*—was different. "And I will spend a long life wistful/To meet your carnal needs and fiscal." I told him it didn't rhyme. He said it was an off-rhyme. It was the best kind, and deliberate. Dylan had reintroduced the off-rhyme into pop music, he said, after the lock-step rhyming of Your Hit Parade. I said I was waiting for him to rhyme something with "Keynesian." He asked if I would settle for "equal" and "sequel." I could feel the hook sliding back in. I swear I can start getting horny just from reading the opening lines of some novel by a writer I've never heard of, much less my devastated, lovestruck husband. He would sneak into the apartment when I wasn't there—he kept a key, they always keep a key—and found some of the letters from my bank teller. I could see his tears on them even though he denied being there. He'd rent cars on the weekend and we'd drive to Wales or somewhere. Europe is so damn small compared to Canada. In Wales, it was a place we called Betsy Co-ed. I don't remember the Welsh. It freed him in more than one way. He was doing things he'd never been able to do. Being unloved made him bold.

When I told him I'd decided he could move back into our

flat, we were lying on the couch. It's as though a powerful wind went out of me and I sagged down in his lap, head in his crotch, not sexually, but for the sheer, familiar comfort. At that moment, I practically heard a voice say, *But nothing has really changed*. Which seemed wrong since everything ought to have. Maybe if I'd been able to sneak a look up, the way I did through the door jamb, I'd have seen him thinking the same thing. Like that moment he had in the limo after the wedding, which he tells me about as if he's revealing a great secret he just discovered, every time we meet, no matter how many years have passed since we ended it for good and how often he's already recounted that fucking limo story.

When we decided to split a year and a half later, we were back in Canada on a visit. We'd been talking about what to do, though never about what our problem really was. Never mind, it was better than beating the crap out of each other physically and emotionally till there seemed to be no choice. I wanted to live on the West Coast, I don't know why, lots of people went out there, I had never been. And we both agreed: let's do it. So we bought some camping equipment and a car, from some guy in Guelph, instead of a driveaway, which I thought we'd do. It was a little old Saab with a sunroof, the kind you had to add a can of oil to along with the gas every time you filled it up. It was like a sewing machine. It gave us lots of laughs on the way out. He said what the hell, he'd sell it to someone else when he got back. He was very light, not careful and economic, like he was a different guy, going into a new life. We got along fine, same as the time when he thought he'd never get me back. Soon as I saw Vancouver I knew: this is it. He helped me find a place and a job, even a little used car of my own, an Austin that reminded me of London, as much as I wanted to be reminded. The day he left to go back east, and then back to the U.K., he was sitting in that goofy car in front of the eucalyptus outside my new apartment. It was all so mellow and compatible. I leaned my head in his window just before he drove off and I said, "Explain to me again why we're doing this." *Explain to me* . . . Doesn't that say it all?

Part III

YOU COME TOO

I'm going out to clean the pasture spring;
I'll only stop to rake the leaves away
(And wait to watch the water clear, I may)
I shan't be gone long.—You come too.
                        —Robert Frost

Max's Version

~

Our plans aren't going to work out," he said one day as he was waking up from a restless sleep. I asked what plans. Neither of us knew, for a moment, that he was talking about a dream. "We were going to grow up together," he said. "And go skating. You, me, and your mother." Back when the immigrant kids called him the King of Kitzel Park, that would have been in the twenties, and him in his teens. He would glide around the outdoor ice rink on a Saturday night stealing kisses from the girls, so fast no one could catch him and make him—I don't know—accountable. But in the dream, he would take us with him. That was our "plan." Maybe he'd show me how to do it, the heir apparent. And my mom would be part of his whizzy, showy life too. She'd be the Queen of Kitzel Park. We'd grow up together, we'd all get a chance to start over.

From then on, I always asked if he had dreamed. It gave us

something to talk about, and made it less likely we'd fight about how he treated her. He rarely recalled one, and never took them seriously.

Most of those months, he just lay on the bed being more and more the person I'd always known. The petty household tyrant—not so petty when the household is pretty much your world, as it is for a kid and continued to be for her. It was a clarifying experience for me and I was grateful. It left me no opportunity to falsify or sentimentalize. It's good to be clear at the end.

Seeing him wasn't easy but I made myself do it, the way you hang on in a relationship longer than your friends think you should, because you want to be certain you've done everything you can. Or just because he was my dad and there was no one else to do it. One night he summoned me to his bedside and told me to sell his big blue Olds. He was through driving it, he said. He didn't know I had asked his doctor weeks before to phone the cops and say he shouldn't be driving. I didn't want someone's death on my conscience if he collapsed at the wheel, as he had done a few times. My mum objected, she didn't want the car sold. She used to drive—I sat in the back seat shaking as he shrieked her through the learning process when I was a kid. When she went back to work, she bought a clunker with her own money that was almost Pirate calibre. She drove it for twenty years, and when it finally died, he wouldn't let her buy another. Instead, he promised to take her everywhere, which he did, thus regaining some of the control he had lost when she went to work. Now, she said, she was going to renew her licence and drive the Olds when he was gone. He told me again to sell it, as if she wasn't in the room. "That car is half mine," she protested, meaning she'd paid for it and brought in all the other money they'd had for many years. He turned to her and said, "That car is *all* yours—and you'll *never* drive it!" She wilted. He went on. "You'll give me a nice little funeral with the money from it, won't you?" Then he turned to me. We were like a little chamber group with him as conductor.

"What's bothering you?" he said. "I don't like it when you talk to her that way," I answered. "I've always treated her badly," he said, not even angry. It was just a fact. No regret in it. He sounded like a sociologist from the Goffman school describing one of the dramas of everyday life. It shook me, as if a cold wind had blown into the room, along with some snow and evil—if evil is choosing to do what you know is wrong, embracing it, as distinct from what everyone does all the time: messing up because they're confused and then feeling bad about it. Of course I'm no philosopher, just an economist. But that's why I say I was grateful: he helped me figure out how I felt, at a murky time.

Sometimes, it's true, he managed to muddy the water. Once as I left, I asked if I could bring anything next time. "You really mean it?" he asked. I said I did. "Only your love," he said. "Don't push," I said.

Another time he said he was sorry for "whatever" he'd done. It sounded as if he couldn't be bothered looking it up in his memory bank. He just wanted, he went on, to put it behind us. It left me slack-jawed. I once saw a TV host interrupt a furious debate between Israelis and Arabs by saying, "Let's not get bogged down in history." They looked slack-jawed too. "Let me try and explain," I said to my dying dad. "You can't put something behind you that you never acknowledged was in front of you." I did my best not to shriek it at him. "Okay," he said wearily. "Like what?" Now I had to choose the most awful moment in a mountainous catalogue of grievance which had been accumulating since childhood or before. Who knows, maybe I cringed under his howling when I was prenatal. It was daunting. I couldn't request an extension, as if I was back in grad school. I decided to confine myself to one gripe, under the circumstances. I settled on a time in my teens when he rousted me from a deep sleep, screaming that we'd all be on the street by tomorrow and it was my fault. It wasn't. It was probably the loan sharks on the Danforth again and his gambling debts. But he always found something I did that he claimed was the problem. And I bought it. I never tossed his poker games back at him, although by then I frequently drove him there or picked him up. It was *years* till I finally accused him of that, and even then he denied it, like every true gambling man. Oh *no*, he explained patiently, the way he figured it, it all evens out. Maybe *that* stuff was the source of my big sense of life's abiding mystery, maybe *it's* why I laboured so endlessly trying to understand the money markets. I was gathering the tools to prove to him that it *doesn't* even out. Maybe my perplexity wasn't over sex at all. I mean I became an economist, not a sexologist. Keynes was my model, not Kinsey. Maybe I was just trying to bring him down. Most of the time, he was such a bundle of cheer. You know they call economics the gloomy science.

Well, he looked kind of perplexed when I brought up the incident. He said, "I'm sorry"—and sounded as if he really was—"but I just don't remember." At least he didn't say we shouldn't get bogged down in history. Then he brightened up and asked, "Would you like to know what *I* was going through then?" Of course, I said. He launched into a meticulous account of a quarrel he had at work with his supervisor, who plagued him all through his years with the company and refused to submit an expense sheet of his for $72.86. He recalled it to the penny! He was as livid as the day it got sent back to his desk.

It made me feel less . . . morally cocky—which was not part of my dying-dad game plan. So I started thinking of what might make him feel better. "Are you scared?" I asked, as if I got it from a book. He snorted. "What's it like?" I blundered on. "Totally meaningless," he said in a flat tone. He sounded like the impersonal voice of eighteenth-century deism: reason without comfort.

My friends often asked if I had achieved reconciliation or come to terms, some phrase also from books, I assume. When I asked what that meant, it was somehow getting myself to say, "I love you, Dad." Next time I saw him, he was barking her name and snapping his fingers while he pointed at the pillow on the bed beside him like a pasha—it meant she was supposed to deposit herself there. He weighed about fourteen pounds, he couldn't have beaten off a chihuahua, but he ordered her around as if he was the Nazi governor of Warsaw. It made me sick so I said I was leaving, but I managed to add, "And don't check out before I see you again because I'll miss you when you're gone. I don't know why, but I will." It may not sound like much, but believe me, it was the best I could do after plenty of thought. I'd actually scripted it and memorized it. He absolutely radiated in response, he glowed and propped himself up a little as he rasped, "That's a *beautiful* thing to say." He got it, and I melted.

Their relationship was a piece of work. It was a privilege to see it near the end with my adult eyes wide open, as I never could have as a kid living not so much with them as on their periphery (like Canada, or any colony), when most of my effort went into shutting my ears to the outbursts, and the intervals of quiet only meant tensing up for the next eruption. He kept doing it, even when he went into the hospital for a time, with lots of doctors around, whose opinion of him he cared about.

That was near the end. He blustered his way into a private room, after just showing up one morning; then immediately set about getting released so, he explained indignantly, they couldn't pack him away in the dread palliative unit. I'm not sure he knew what palliative meant. He realized it was about death, but he may not have known they were trying to make you feel better as you died. He was that way with words. He once told me over a lunch that all the Third World liberation leaders I so admired were congenital liars. I stomped out in protest (paying the bill as I left). Mum called the next day to say he'd told her about it, and did it make me feel better to know he didn't really know what "congenital" meant.

So he insisted the hospital send him back home where he'd just come from, and she'd be isolated and at his mercy again, as they'd lived for sixty years. It was as if he had a grand plan for his final days which only he could make sense of and he intended to carry it out by force of will, which he did. The doctor, a kindly Scot who had tended to the internal damage and blockages they both had plenty of, tactfully assured him he could go as soon as there was enough home care in place to ensure his fine wife wouldn't be physically overwhelmed by the demands of looking after him. "Don't worry, Doctor," he huffed—but deferentially. "If it comes to that, I have means for dealing with the situation." It was a murky mouthful, but he meant he'd kill himself rather than become a pathetic burden.

It was posturing, it cost him nothing, and there would be no need to follow through. But that one time, with a doctor they shared right in the room, she said, "Can I have that in writing?" I felt like I was witnessing the Boxer Rebellion or Spartacus. The doc blurted, "Pardon me?" But Dad leapt in to take charge. He said, "What my wife means, Doctor, is she's so in love with me she can't bear the thought of me no longer being here." A mutual suicide pledge! That was his interpretation. As if she had sworn to throw herself on his pyre, commit suttee, that ancient Hindu practice of widows, if it ever really happened, who knows, I'm skeptical about myths that cast Third World people as primitives. He said it with such certitude, yet it was completely unconnected to the words she had spoken. I went down to the vending machines afterward with my mum and asked why she put up with so much from him. She said, "Everyone else is going to be on my side. I'm the only one left to be on his." A week later, they sent him home for the final phase, with a modest amount of care tacked on.

A few days later she called and said he was demanding a weapon. It was as baffling as the thing about suttee. He didn't have a gun or a sword. He didn't even have a hunting knife. The closest thing to a weapon was his electric razor and he couldn't shave himself to death. He came on the line and threatened to throw himself out of bed to end it all. But how? He'd twitch a bit on the floor and then she'd have to heave him back into bed. Or get me to drive over and do it. Or the Vietnamese family across the hall who came in each night to cart him out to the couch so he could watch the news. This was the same happy-go-lucky genius of retail who never so much walked as bounced. Like Tigger. Sometimes he'd stride up the street and people coming toward him would start bouncing

by sympathetic vibration. Now a good hard shake was beyond
him. He darkly referred to some pills he had stashed away, but
they were iron pills. If he bundled them up and jammed them
down his throat, maybe he'd gag. I wasn't feeling too compassionate, but on the other hand, he was dying, and he knew it,
and faced it, I had to admit, not gracefully but honestly.
Unflinchingly. So I grabbed one of the many TVs I had in the
house, a smaller set, they'd started to proliferate around people's homes the way computers have more recently. I hauled it
up there with a length of cable, like I was the cable guy. I
thought it might distract him from those bizarro death scenar-
ios. When I lugged it in, he scowled and barked ungraciously
that he'd never allowed one of those in the bedroom, he always
watched TV in the living room, and that was still his iron rule.
His vehemence surprised me. There was a touch of romance,
keeping his bedroom the shrine it was meant to be. If he couldn't
get to the living room, even with the aid of the Vietnamese
brigade, then so be it, no more TV for him. I said, "Look, one
of the few things I admire about you is that you have always
liked to watch the news, it's your way to stay informed as a
citizen, and you deserve to be able to do it." It slowed him up. I
put the set on top of a tall dresser and began stringing the
cable in from the living room. He was grumbling less aggres-
sively but still declaiming he'd die before a TV made it into his
bedroom, when the set clicked on from the remote he was
cradling in his blotchy hand, and just like that, he was flipping
channels, happy as a puffin. It might have kept him going a
week or two longer, till the provincial election when he was
hoping to see Premier Bob Rae get his ass kicked. I promised if
he made it to that night, I'd come and watch the results rather
than take one of the offers I had to go on TV and comment on

the final rejection of the socialist option by Ontario's voters.

He wasn't down on Rae because Rae was left. He hated the guy because he wasn't left *enough!* He thought Rae was a fake, a secret agent for wealth and power. For my dad, the wacko NDP backbencher Peter Kormos, a bike-riding, cowboy-booted, working-class shit disturber from Welland, was the hero. He was only partially conscious as we "watched" those results come in, he was slipping toward the final phase by then, but he stirred himself more than once to ask, "What happened to Peter?" who indeed held his seat despite the tide that almost wiped out his party. My dad always located himself on the side of the weak and persecuted. Go figure. If I owe him anything, it would be an obsession with injustice, based on watching *him* oppress, as we put it in the sixties, my mum. I didn't really enter into the family situation much as he saw it. She was his obsession and prime target, till the end.

I told him that if he kept pushing her as he was, she'd die the day after him. "She has to die sometime," he said without gusto, as if he'd given it some thought and perhaps found it a comfort: So long as she's dead when I am. You'd certainly have to say he loved her, so long as you concede that the word has manifold, contradictory meanings, much like wealth, development, equality, labour, and exploitation.

He never stopped berating her. I told him again, before he went into the final stupor, that it bothered me and I didn't know if I could keep coming and seeing it. He said, with a new detachment, "We're all under a lot of pressure." As if he was moving into the clearing. It was a long way from, "I've always treated her badly." So I seized the moment and asked about the earlier declaration, and if he had *always* treated her like that.

He replied, calm as I ever heard him, that early on he would sometimes explode, as anyone can with those near at hand who love you, and afterwards he'd feel better. She seemed to accept it and he appreciated her tolerance of his rages. "I realized," he said, a little out of breath, "that there were not going to be any consequences." The way Lamarck told Napoleon, who asked about the role of God in his scheme of things, "I do not require that hypothesis." It was the watershed: knowing she wouldn't fight back and wasn't going to leave. It had no downside.

He wouldn't let the curtains in the bedroom be opened. He never had. I found out when I tried to pull them back. I asked why. He said he didn't know, he always hated natural light. In the last phase, his mouth hung open, he spoke incoherently, and couldn't yell loud enough to be heard even in the kitchen. One day she just walked into the bedroom, pulled the curtains aside to admit the light, and walked back to the kitchen where her sisters were having a cup of tea with her. She didn't even look at him. Perhaps it was a relief for him, being unable to harass her any more. He always seemed a bit like a man hoping to make it to the end of his course and take a well-earned rest, though I could be projecting. When he finally died, lying on his side on a rented hospital bed, his eyes and jaw open wide, she went in and made sure. The home-care worker was afraid to, saying she'd never seen anyone dead. Then she phoned me. We sat most of the night waiting for the doctor, who had some other stops to make, and then the people from the funeral home, who took him away. She didn't cry, then or after. She said she kept waiting for tears to come and seemed disappointed in herself. "He always told me that he and I had the ideal relationship, and he expected me to believe no less," she said when I asked if she had any thoughts about what we should put in the obituary notice.

She left, a year later, that crappy little apartment where he kept her prisoner—it seemed to me—for almost forty years. Imagine—in a society where stats show mobility is one of the few universals, based mainly on economic instability. The day we moved in, when I was a teenager, was, I still feel, the worst day of my life. Maintenance was so rotten that the elevator often didn't work and the two of them had to climb six flights carrying their groceries, even when they were into their seventies and eighties. It meant her sisters and friends couldn't come visit with any regularity, which was a way to keep her to himself in their implausible love nest. It was romantic, in a Gothic way. Rapunzelesque. Now she had to get out. She'd been losing pounds for twenty years, taking antibiotics daily to keep whatever it was from finishing her off. Her doctor—the guy who was there that day in the hospital—called her his miracle patient. I knew it wasn't a miracle. It was my dad who kept her alive, bullying her into not dying before he did, since he couldn't have handled being on his own. The guy truly couldn't boil water. Once, when she was in hospital, he phoned and asked if I knew how to turn on the oven.

The day she finally moved out, it took a long time, since the elevator was acting up again. When the movers wheeled out the last boxes, I said, "Okay, that's it, we can drive to your new place." She got up with the implacability she'd had on the day she pulled the curtains back, and strode out the door, looking neither left, nor right, nor behind. The next morning I called and asked how she had found her first night in her bright new apartment. She liked it, she said, she slept well, but it was strange: when she got up and tried to remember the old place, where she'd spent four decades, she couldn't recall a thing about it, not even the floor plan.

His Mother's Version

~

Max finally asked me why I had stayed. I'd been waiting for it.
We were driving up to his cottage, which he had bought a few
years before. It was his pride and joy, the thing he said would
profoundly change his life, he felt, more than anything except
having a child, which wasn't going to happen by this point in
his life. That's why I was happy to help him buy it with some
money I managed to put aside after he left home and I went
back to work. It was my first trip there and we had a nice talk
on the long car ride. It may not have been the most time we
ever spent together, but there's something relaxing about sitting in a car with somebody. I'm pretty sure he feels we didn't
talk enough when he was young, even if I was always "there,"
for instance, when he came home from school for lunch, since
I didn't go back to work till he left home himself. Especially to
do with things that bothered him, like sex, which I felt he was
uncomfortable about, though it was strange, back then, to
think of a mother talking to her son about sex instead of his
dad or an older brother. By that time I guess I had started to
find it easier not to talk than to talk, although I always felt it
was a good thing to do, and I wished I had other people to talk
to me about how my life had turned out. But then when I did
try, especially about sex, it made things worse. Once, Olivia
was on her way up to our apartment, and I said to him, "We
don't take young ladies into our bedrooms with the doors
shut." I know it sounds old-fashioned. As I say, I wasn't used
to talking about such things. It might have been the first time I
tried, ever. He turned and spat in my face. We were in the

kitchen, which was tiny, like the pantry on the old trains used
to be when you tried to squeeze through them while the chef
was cooking pancakes. So he didn't miss. It was a new experience for me. His father yelled at me a great deal, but he never
spat and never hit me. We didn't talk about that either.

So he said, as we drove along, that he understood the pres-
sures I was under while he was still at home, but what about
afterwards, in the 1960s, when I had an income of my own;
and as well, attitudes about marriage and separation had
changed. Surely I watched TV, he said. I read magazines, I
knew there was a new spirit out there, women were doing
things they hadn't done in the times before. Was it just that I
was so stuck in the way I'd been living till then?

I said there were compensations for me that there hadn't
been for him. I think the word shocked him a little. He drove a
while not saying much, we were just entering that part of the
drive where you start seeing all the rocks. Muskoka. It's so
beautiful. Then he asked if I was talking about sex. I said,"Yes,"
a little defensively. It never occurred to me that he might not
know what a big place sex had in our marriage, or even that
we had a sex life. I said it was a terrible shame that he and his
father never talked about sex—"Or anything else," he said, concentrating on the road as if he was expecting something dangerous to come roaring around the next bend straight at us,
even though it was a divided highway. I said there was a lot
his dad could have told him, because he was so good about sex.
He chuckled as if this was just too silly to believe, but seemed
to relax. "Oh no," I said, "He was, he really was." I said before
we got married, he'd read a book on sex, a manual, written by
a clergyman, and then told me what he learned from it and led
me through it, step by step. Still staring at the road, Max said

something like, "What piece of DNA is that encoded in?" He
didn't explain it and I'm not a big asker, like he is. It sounded
as if he had turned out more like his father than he expected.
He asked if his father had been my only lover and I said yes.
He seemed skeptical and asked again in a couple of ways. Then
he asked if I thought I'd been his only sexual partner and I said
I was pretty sure I was. He definitely looked doubtful though
he didn't challenge me or repeat the question. Perhaps his
father once said to him the same thing he used to tell me: that
whatever his faults were, he never fooled around on me. I
never accused him of it, so the denial was unnecessary, and it
did make me wonder.

Then he started quizzing me about sex. I think it helped
that we were in the car, looking ahead, so we didn't have to
look at each other as we talked. I know that helped me. He
asked how often we had sex. Then he said he didn't mean I
should quantify it. Then he said "quantify" was a term they
used in economics. "Yes, thank you," I said. Well, I went on, to
put it in non-quantifying terms—even when Max was in high
school, his father was still coming home "for lunch." Until a
year before he died, in his mid-eighties, it was at least three
times a week. Now he seemed really curious. "Did you ever
have orgasms," he asked. "Always," I said, as we swung past
the Gravenhurst turnoff. "Always?" he said. "Every time?" I nodded, I was enjoying Muskoka out the window. He drove quite a
while. Then he asked what I meant by an orgasm. "An *orgasm*,"
I said, getting a bit impatient. I told him I had just come home
from my first trip since the funeral—I went to the spa in Florida
with my sisters—and walking in the door made me sad. I
thought about him waiting for me when I returned from one of
those trips: he always rushed me straight into the bedroom, first

thing. Max said he never noticed that. I said I wasn't talking
about back when he was a kid living at home; I meant until
about a year before he died. Max shook his head and said again
that he couldn't understand how he had missed it.

When we got to the dock, he asked me to sit up in the
bow—it was your basic cottage outboard—because he thought
I'd feel more secure wedged in there. I've never been very big
and I've been losing weight steadily since about the time of the
funeral, or actually, for years before. It accelerated after the
funeral because, with him gone, there was no one to badger me
about eating to keep my weight up. To bully me into staying
well, as my son would put it. Anyhow, the lake was quite
rough and I bounced up and down like a cork all the way
across. When we reached the dock, he helped me out and asked
how I found the ride. I told him the lake was *beautiful*. I didn't
say anything about the bouncing. I could see him looking at
me and up the stone path to his cottage, far above. I think he
considered tossing me over his shoulder and hauling me up like
he was portaging me. Instead, he went and got some folding
chairs and a pitcher of water, and placed them at various stations along the path. So we took our time getting there. He
was my Sherpa.

When we arrived, I spent a lot of time moving from room
to room and opening closet doors. I was overwhelmed by the
amount of closet space. I think that's when I realized how
closed in I felt all the years we lived in that little apartment. It
must have looked peculiar, with so much beautiful nature outside and the lovely stone fireplace, to keep opening and closing
closet doors. But I found it hypnotic. All those years jamming
things into those few tiny closets. It was a nightmare. But
there were compensations, which there weren't for Max. I saw

him hating that apartment the first day we moved in. He doesn't exactly have a poker face. The air went out of him like a balloon. So I talked a lot about the glass shower door in the tiny bathroom, which we had bought from the outgoing tenant. I guess it made him more depressed. When his dad sat on the couch in the living room to watch TV, Max could hear every motion from his own little bedroom: when he lifted his bum to fart, for instance. (A doctor once told him it was healthy, he said.) Or when he belched. Max rigged a set of headphones attached to the set that he asked his dad to wear when he was doing homework, but his dad tossed them aside. Not at Max, just aside. When we had dinner, we always watched the news, which I think Max liked. His dad considered himself quite a liberal, which may have got passed on. He was even sympathetic to Alex, the communist alderman who we used to share a back porch with long ago. And he supported Adlai Stevenson for president, both times. Our two little bedrooms pressed against each other with just a little wall between and I was a bit surprised to realize he didn't know the kind of sex life we had. I'd have thought it went right through the wall and saturated the whole place, the way garlic and mouldy socks will do.

After I finished marvelling at the closets, I went out and sat on the porch, looking through the curtain of red pines to the setting sun across the water. I didn't go back down to the lake till we left after the weekend, when he seated me a little more sensibly and the water was calmer. Ever since then, whenever I have to take medical tests, which is often, given my condition, the technicians usually suggest that I think about something pleasant. I always imagine I'm sitting on that porch.

~

He's walking up Euclid and he's fifty, the age his century was when he got rousted from his tryst on the couch. He likes Euclid for its associations: Greece, democracy, reason, science; unlike the many streets in the area that recall Olde Englande (Markham) or a cabinet minister from the Napoleonic Wars (Palmerston). Euclid, now there was a numbers man from an era when quantification didn't exclude moral valuation. Ulster. Harbord. Lennox. Herrick. He scans as he walks, that hasn't changed. Noel, who he sees far less now, once told him he looked like a guy with his boat on cruise, staring into the fish finder. There is no such thing as a walk, it's always a quest. There was a film editor, ten years ago he used to pass her. She would smile and breeze by, but once he stopped her and she told him her name, first name only. He keeps an eye out. You never know. His dad peered at women through the windshield till the very end. When he stopped driving, he stopped peering. At fifty maybe, your expectations start to moderate. Yeah, sure. Sure sure.

A woman rides past him on a bike, an old Schwinn. It has big tires and broad fenders. She leans back, grasping the heavy, swooshy handlebars. She looks like she's in a carriage. She looks gay, in the old, irretrievable, turn-of-the-century sense. There are multicoloured spokey-dokes on her wheels. They rattle up and down the spokes as the wheels turn. How does he know they're called spokey-dokes? Where do you pick up such information? Why do you store it instead of something useful like the Kondratiev cycle, or capital's decelerating rate of return? She circles and returns too. She reintroduces herself, since they once met.

Anita. Was married to Noel's associate, Austin, at the bro-kerage, when Noel was still dicking around with finance, before he became Noel for the Defence, which was before he became Noel, mouthpiece of cops and other detestable interests. That's why they don't talk nearly as much, though they talk. He remembers her. Oh God, he doubtless prayed then, how do guys like Austin get women like her? In my life, I'll never know anyone as elegant. Regal like a queen. If you'd let me have her once, Lord, I'll never ask for anything again. But she doesn't look the same. It isn't aging. She's been through something. They cross a couple of those streets named for English shires and lords. She's going to the bookstore just yonder, so she mounts up and pedals on. He marches doggedly ahead, sticking to the route like he's on a mission (which is true—and one day he'll find out what it is). Then he stops, backtracks to the bookstore. She's behind the *M*'s in fiction, holding three thick novels. Looks like Mahfouz, Munro, and Brian Moore? "Is that tonight's reading?" he says. A little joke, or the intention of one. She looks up and nods, it seems they really are. He says he's going to the bistro on Bloor, does she know it? She nods again. If she'd like to when she's done here, she could join him, he'll be on the patio. He hasn't varied the technique: leave it to them. Don't push, minimize your risk.

She nods, noncommittal, just like him. When he's gone, she thinks: I could go the the Y instead, lose ten pounds, then take him up on it in a couple of months. But she's feeling brave, she already made the circle on the street. She pays for the novels and follows in his wake.

The next night he calls and says if she wants to drop by, he'll be in. They start on the deck, on Aunt Mary's hand-me-down, indestructible all-weather patio furniture, straight from the age of the roust or earlier. Then they move inside to the couch, then downstairs to bed—an even flow of an evening, as if they never disengage, not a meld, but a dance. Move closer, pull away, but don't lose touch—that's the rule, like ice dancing, not disco. You get lost in the movement, the contact becomes its own reward, you don't think about an end point, but it draws closer. "Stay," he says. "Stay with me." At some point, "Stay with me" turns into "Come." And again. "Come. Come." Then she says, "You come too," and they do.

From then on, it's not constant, it's fitful. They each have their reasons.

One night, he's in the bath. She slips off her clothes and steps in. But she remains standing, her legs rise up and up, like the colossus of Rhodes, one of those junk references issued to you as you grow up in this society. He doesn't even know what the colossus of Rhodes is but she reminds him of it. It was one of the seven wonders of the world and so is she. Must have been in a book. Or she's the figure in another book, Noel's book when they were—ten? She slipped off her clothes and advanced on him, on them—him and Noel in the den, breasts etc., urgent eager little guys, all of life and sex ahead of them—

She becomes more than a repeater. She becomes the regular repeater, his social date, the repeater of repeaters. When they talk, she has a way of starting a new series with each response to what he said last. He's trying to explain this . . . aptitude of hers to Rhonda. It doesn't go well. This is partly because Rhonda has been sick. It was cancer, that thing she went to the doctor for. She searched the Internet, tried the usual homeopathic and aboriginal concoctions you find there, flew to Mexico to meet a shaman, and got worse. Then she did the chemo and it all went away, she's in remission. She listens closely, with a little parcel of attention reserved to watch for its return.

In ordinary conversation, he tells Rhonda, you start with

statement A, followed by statement (A+)B, followed by (B+)C. Rhonda says she doesn't get it. He expands. Party one states or asks something, party two receives and incorporates that and then responds, throwing it back along with an overt comment on or addition to it. "Can't you just say it in English?" Rhonda says. "Okay," he says, "I say something and you say you don't get it. Just like you just did. The *it* is what you caught from me and then you threw it back to me along with the additional comment that you didn't *get* it." She asks him if this is based on a model from the weird world of economics. He says it's the normal way a conversation goes, it's what they're doing right now, he's simply abstracting it and graphing it. She asks him if he's incapable of just one measly example for a mere mortal whom he's known since the days of the Paris walk-up, or does everything have to go through the roof of theory? It's easier for him, he says, to frame this in theoretical terms, it always has been, she knows that, he's trying to do it simply enough so that it's accessible to a mind like hers—not a *lesser* mind, he hastens to add, simply a more concrete one—"Don't give me a hard time!" "I'm not giving you a hard time," she says, "we're arguing. We're having a discussion like we always do." He says she just did it, she took his "don't give me a hard time," repeated it, and tossed it back with the addition that she's *not* giving him a hard time. His A plus her B. It's what everyone always does, he goes on. He can see her weakening; she hates theory with all her might, yet she can't deny she's beginning to comprehend him. "With her, it's different" he says. Rhonda asks what this woman does that's different. She's feeling competitive, after all she's a writer, wordplay is her métier. "She starts a new series each time she responds," he says. "Instead of answering A with (A+)B, she answers with B, as a stand-alone, as if she's taken notice of A, but left it there and moved on down the line. It's as if the conversation has started again, even though it's related to the old one."

"Then do you answer her with C?" says Rhonda, uncertainly. This is the sign of decades of friendship. She will follow him into this linguistic wilderness.

"No," he says. "I don't have that kind of intellectual nimbleness." She screws up her face. "I find your coinage on the klutzy side," she says, but yes, she follows. "No one I've ever known had it," he says, "except her."

It moves along smoothly till it doesn't. ("When I meet a guy now, I want to cut straight to the bad part because I know it's going to come," says Rhonda, who's on the brink of splitsville with Juval the cameraman. He's just never in town long enough to end it.) He thinks he spies a glitch in her unique combination of worldliness and sensuality, that model on a runway quality, the towering bath person with the most original manner of carrying on a conversation he's ever met. Those elements slip, like the bath towel, and for minutes on end she becomes a gawky teenager, slack-jawed and over-ardent. Where did that come from? It troubles him, and if he is brutally frank with himself, as he loves to be, this is because of how her presence reflects back on him. Something in him wants to be flattered by the company of a regal consort. Her queen to his king; the king he yearns, as everyone does (some more and some less), to be.

It irritates him. He beats himself up for letting it bother him but it does. The relationship falters, she asks what's the problem. He says, haltingly, that he feels a certain lack of sophistication, once in a long while, about her. He meant to be gentle but he failed. He feels like a mechanic who looked up and said, Your engine is shot. But she is unfazed. She doesn't beat him up in return as he feels he deserves. "I am," she says. "And I don't ever want to stop being the kid from Powassan, it's a part of me." It's the most sophisticated thing he ever heard anybody say.

He's picking her up at the airport. She's been in Delhi. He didn't miss her exactly. But he fretted she wouldn't return to him. He's in a controlled panic. He should have made a declaration to ensure she won't step off the plane and announce she met someone new over there. The way Olivia did, and Ellen, after their trips. Why didn't he just say it? Maybe there's a printed form, like the ones they give you to fill out before you clear customs. "I verify I'll be waiting for you when you come back and so I have the right to assume you'll be true to me too, sweetie." He stands with the usual milling throng outside the foreign—i.e., neither Canada nor the U.S.—arrivals gate. He can see over most of them, due to differences in nutritional standards and average height in their countries of origin. That's supposed to change with globalization and the spread of Western living standards, but all the stats he sees indicate an *increase* in the gap between those countries and the developed world. On the other hand, there does seem to be an *absolute* increase of wealth worldwide. Will that tide be enough to raise all ships, eventually if not immediately—

The passengers have begun emerging, one at a time, from the frosted door. There must be more than one flight blending back there, but still, an odd thing is happening. He thinks he sees her, once, twice, many times, he waits for her to look back and smile—and he's wrong, it's not her. This isn't normal. He knows he's not a very visual sort but still. It's the kind of thing they write about in women's magazines like *Inge: Ten Sure Signs You're in Love. . .* One Sure Sign is thinking you see the other

person everywhere. Then he sees her and knows it because—
Sure Sign Number Two—she takes his breath away. She stands
above the rest. She's dark, like the ones he mistook for her, but
her face is luminous; her hair, weightless and alive. How in hell
does she look like this after twenty-eight hours in the custody of
Air India? His little heart goes pit-a-pat. Then it leaps and dips
and somersaults. You're in deep shit, it says to him.

She doesn't do ultimatums. One day she just books a flight to
Finland, where her friend Beryl works as an adviser to the Ministry
of Tourism, open return. Beryl says Finland is like the Canada of
Scandinavia, caught between superpowers and faded empires, the
Soviets and the Swedes. She thinks she'll like it there and maybe
even find work. He doesn't doubt it. He's been to Finland. You fly
forever, get off the plane, look at the trees, and feel like you never
left Canada. "Wait," he says, in the cafeteria on the top floor of a
bank tower. He's writing speeches for the president. "Give me
some time. Not long." "For what?" she asks. "To make you an
offer," he says. "It takes time to prepare a decent offer." They look
around at the hungry bank officials stalking the salad bar. "How
long?" she asks. "Till Canada Day," he says, the creation of one
country from disparate parts.

On Canada Day, he requests an extension. Why? His dad has
been dying, she knows, pretty much since they set the deadline.
The funeral was two weeks ago. Till when then? Thanksgiving,
he says.

On Thanksgiving, lying in bed together, he tells her he thinks
it's time to bite the bullet on this, she should move in. He exhales
as if a rescue crew just removed a fallen tree from his chest, like
a tourist from Buffalo he saw on TV who was impaled by a
phone pole that went through the front windshield of his bus.

The guy never stopped talking to TV crews as they sawed the pole off him front and back, then loaded him into an ambulance. He sounded more relaxed than Max does now. "I'd rather wait till you don't think of it as the equivalent to surgery without an anesthetic," she says, starting a new series. "I'm not sure I ever will," he says. "I think you will," she replies, showing more faith in him than anyone ever has. I'm unworthy, he thinks.

On Valentine's Day, he says, "I want you to move in." Then adds, "I really do," in wonder and awe. Now he awaits the awful moment when she will arrive and he will know, as he always has, that it was a mistake.

Two weeks later, her carpets come. Her magic carpets, as if by their own will, and nothing else. She sent them to the cleaner, then had them delivered to his, and in a tentative sense, her, place. The carpets are more elegant than anything that has ever crossed his threshold. She collected them in markets and bazaars throughout the world. Then nothing. She still has her place, she's there about the same amount as always. Two weeks later, she has her phone switched to his, i.e., their, address. Another three weeks: a small moving truck, the cube, the movers call it, brings some furniture and books. It's brilliant. Who ever moved in, in stages? Who thought of such a thing? The ones who come always arrive *in toto*, on the designated date, and he feels like the German gunners who gazed out from their pillboxes along the Normandy coast on the morning of D-Day to see a horizon obliterated by Allied ships and landing craft. They slink back inside the pillbox, knowing the final disaster has begun. Her gentle transfers continue for months. It's like foreplay—gradualness leading to something but there's no hurry. She knew what he needed. He describes this wisdom to Rhonda, who has another cyst; she starts chemo again on Friday. "You won the lottery!" Rhonda blurts, moved by his fortune rather than her own ill luck. Then she falls asleep in her bacon and eggs. He always forgets it's his joy that his friends prefer to share, not his torment.

If she was a nun, she would wear a cowl, but let a little lick of hair peek out from under it. A nun like that once slipped behind his back in the cafeteria line at LSE, lightly brushing him with her breasts. "I'm sorry," she said. "My pleasure," he said. There was an Orthodox Jewish woman on a kibbutz, he went on a freebie from the Canadian Jewish Congress as part of a group that toured Israel to study "its unique blend of governmental and co-operative ownership models." He still feels guilty for taking the trip. He keeps the gold chain they gave him with a Hebrew pendant meaning *life* in the same drawer with his pardon and his divorce decree. She wore a kerchief, like a Jewish cowl, and strands of blonde dribbling down the back of her neck. That's the mix.

One night she tells him how long she was alone before they met on the street. He asks who she buys the wondrous lingerie for and she fixes him with an odd stare. Well, for herself, you dolt. The nun might have said, For the eye of God. Same difference. It's what you do when you are a sexy, lusty woman, with or without a man. The man is optional. He notices her jewellery gradually, a piece at a time, the way a salesman would bring them out, to highlight them. The ring, then rings, wind up her long fingers like barbed wire. The weighty bracelets seem to levitate around her wrists. Gradually the metal on her multiplies; if she was a charade, she'd be a stylized junkyard. An installation made of judiciously selected scrap mounted on a gorgeous woman. "If it ain't baroque," she says, "fix it!" It's her motto. She didn't wear this stuff when she first began seeing him, she explains, because she thought he would find it shallow.

There's a layering pattern to her, like flights stacked up over an airport. There's the lingerie and glorious jewellery level; and there's the puritanical level: She won't undress with the light on. It isn't *faux* sexy, the stuff you see on Christian TV, the Dale Evans effect: teased hair, rouge, mascara, you-may-look-but-you-may-not-touch. Those Christian women drive him nuts. He once guested on "100 Huntley Street"—he'll go anywhere he's invited, I mean if you'll speak to the right-wing cowboys at the Fraser Institute, why turn down fundamentalist TV?—and couldn't keep his mind off the hostesses. Yet for those women, the Dales, sexy as sexy can be, sex itself doesn't seem to interest them; about sex *en soi*, in the Sartrean sense, they could care less. The look is all. It's a visual. She adores sex. However—another layer—infidelity sickens her. To merely hear of it in others, makes her nauseous. She abhors novels and movies that include infidelity as a plot device—an inconvenience for someone who tears through the mountain of novels and films she does. What a weird pair they make. "Don't you think I'm an odd choice for you?" he asks. Noel once looked up from a book as Max came in with the chic owner of a boutique he met at a book-signing in a mall. "Here I am reading Mao's *On Contradiction* and the two of you appear," Noel said. "I was seeking the secret of the one-night stand," she says, "and I thought I had met the master." She has never had a one-night stand, she adds, she has slept with a limited number of men, whom she tends to marry or live with. "And did you learn that secret?" he asks. "Of course not," she says, looking a little sad. "We're still together. Tell me more sex stories," and he complies. His thousand and one nights, give or take. He feels they're walking an edge together, the womanizer and the sexy nun, hoping not to slip off either side. Is that what it means to be in an, ugh, relationship? The best ones, claimed Sorstad as if he'd done the research, contain an ongoing peril. You're barely okay from moment to moment, and sometimes you aren't. Into this dicey, layered reality, comes Lewinsky and the prez.

They are in bed watching the news when they see Lewinsky for the first time. Those were the Clinton years, when politics was a phantom and business straddled the globe. There was so little for public life to be about that the major political event of a decade was a dalliance, and even that just barely.

They see the president hug Monica. She's in a line behind a barrier. The moment will run and rerun on a loop for a year. Once the Murrican people see what he did—say the Republicans and moralizers—they will turn and whip him like the sexual cur he is. Since the Murrican people never turn and whip him, the clip must be played over, tens of thousands of times, till it sinks in. Which it never does.

She lies beside him on the mattress. It is a modestly sized queen but the space between them grows as the news continues and the clip replays, the way a glacier extends southward, distancing them from each other, though neither moves. She doesn't rise up, balancing precariously, to denounce Clinton and infidelity. But she bristles. She's drifting away and maybe—hard to tell—signalling in distress as her outline grows small. He wishes he could delete the damn item from the newscast. In the future, when media are fully interactive, you won't have to receive current events that can be harmful to your sex life. By next day it's everywhere. It would take an official censor, which you only get in wartime, to scissor out all the articles and photos that come with the morning papers every day for a year; as if a crazy person had gone through them on the porch. Then, after breakfast, he'd have to dash down to her office ahead of her and do the same to the papers there. Next night they go to the theatre. He sees Monica in the lobby. But no one could have got a Monicut that fast. The Monica's must have been out in public for a while, it happens with types, you don't notice them and then you do, everywhere. They're society's screen savers, its default presences.

Well, what is to be done? Should they discuss it? There's not much choice. They always talk about the news. And he's a talker from way back, talk's the constant in his life, it's what he does, put it on the table, whether it's economic misinformation or sex. The French would call him one of the intelligentsia, which is their word for talkers. He could try not talking, but that would be like censorship in the old Soviet Union. It was repressive, immoral, and, mainly, didn't work. The more that was suppressed, the more that was found out. Reverse impact. He went to Kiev to give a paper right after the Chernobyl reactor overreacted and everyone there asked why he had come. He said the radiation experts in Canada told him there was nothing to worry about. They shook their heads sadly and said, "Yes, that's what our authorities say too. It's how we know we're going to die."

But here the subject is fidelity, not merely justice, injustice, or the fate of the planet. Maybe it's better to avoid, and record that as a failure. Failures aren't so bad, some of the finest moments in history are failures: Spartacus's uprising, the Rebellion of 1837, the Paris Commune, the Russian Revolution. He wouldn't have joined any of them, but he admires those who did. Noel and Nadine have been together for years but Noel says they never discuss fidelity. Does that mean their marriage has failed? Maybe the conversation just hasn't happened *yet*. Timing matters. You have to be ready before you attempt to bear the beams of love, especially the big ones. On the other hand, you could die waiting for the right moment. If only Lewinsky had stayed in California.

He and Rhonda, who does not allow the prospect of death to interfere with their ongoing seminar on sex, often discuss infidelity. Of course they aren't *having* sex, they aren't even living together and never have, except for the time in Provence, and she doesn't have an intense repulsion from the very concept. She continues to gather material for her literary *oeuvre* (which she distinguishes passionately from her bestsellers for the meet market)—two novels, one unfinished, a short story collection, an anthology of essays she edited, and the poem cycle from Paris, still under construction. Together, they amount to little more than laying out the conundrum of infidelity in various ways, like overlapping portraits of the same person placed on a floor beside each other. Do you prefer this one, or this, or . . . ? The problem is not telling the truth, she and Max decide one day after chemo, when she is beat, it is *hearing* the truth. One party says, I feel this or did that—adding swiftly—but that does not affect you or my feelings for you. The other hears, I *betrayed you*. Truth is no defence in this situation, nor is honesty. Each person could pass a polygraph on what they speak or hear: a truth and a lie. All in all, most of the time, it's probably better to say nothing. Or to lie, which will be closer to true than the truth. Give this to Lewinsky and the president: they provided the pretext for some interesting conversations.

So Max and Anita blunder and stammer along, atop their mattress, to the news, both trying like crazy and fearing they'll lose everything. He anticipates the worst, it's his nature; her voice is halting and wracked. But as details of the story dribble out, it starts to seem less excruciating, this operetta in the office:

a little grope, a little fondle, some fellatio. No dirty weekends, no Secret Service agents elaborately covering for the boss, as they did in the sixties for JFK. Pissant stuff. The poor klutz never came, not till the last time, and even then only to please her, because she so wanted him to. The essence is always being wanted. *Jenny kissed me when we met—* It's what everyone yearns for. The process plays out over a year, there is no pivotal moment; it's an unrelenting accumulation of the trivial. Moralism and judgmentalism haven't got a chance, the glacier recedes, the mattress contracts, they re-approach, waving cheerily. Lewinsky has let in some lightness to this heaviest of their topics. You couldn't call the way they've dealt with it a success, but it qualifies as a non-failure. Maybe some day they will actually discuss the issue, when they each have some idea of what they actually *think*. But why hurry? It already feels like something has changed for the better, and they did *nothing*.

Change remains the best trick, better than money, better than sex, and he still doesn't know its secret. Given the burden of the past weighing on us, and the forces of the present—markets, weather, self-interest, geography, institutional inertia, sheer timidity—it's astounding that change ever happens. Russia, South Africa, him, her. Why *would* anything change, or anyone? When you're inside, it seems impossible. Then it happens and it's inconceivable that *this* wasn't always so.

It's like motion, which he also finds rationally unpersuasive. The hare, according to Zeno's paradox, can never overtake the tortoise. Even as an undergrad, he knew that was based on a false premise, and if you replace the premise, you lose the paradox. But he never . . . moved past it himself. Maybe he should have taken Intro to Philosophy again till he overcame his problem with change. (And then again, and again . . . he believes in introductory courses, as Innis did: if you truly teach, you'll never get past the first moments of the first course, because everything can be questioned, and should be—) When he was young it was about money: you give the man behind the counter metal or paper and he gives you comic books or gum. This changes to that. It's confusing because he also gives you "change" or "makes change." He's been an economist most of his life and the mystery has scarcely begun to yield. Yet he's always trying to change the world, a bit at a time. Why would someone who doesn't believe in change try to change the world? Why does anyone do anything? Doctors are afraid of getting sick. Teachers don't understand. Economists can't divide the bill at a restaurant. You choose what you do to overcome who you are. Change transfixes him, maybe it's at the heart of his repetitive sexual behaviour. Change daunts him, so he pursues it. And change by an individual is even more awesome than collective change. In a group, you encourage one another. Other groups give you models, the past inspires you—none of it is on you alone. But how does one person move from here to there? He has a cousin named Simon. They meet infrequently and then they talk furtively, like spies at a drop who have to exchange secrets without letting on that they are acquainted. Simon has been planning for years—so many Max has lost count—to leave his unhappy marriage; he often asked Max if he could move in when it happened because he'd need a place to stay if—whoops, he meant to say when—he finally made the move. Sure, Simon. Of course. Then one day the doorbell rings and there is Simon with a satchel, looking like the world has rained and poured on him. He did it!

"It sounds insane," she says. "You're finally comfortable with someone, so you invite somebody else to move in who you don't know, and to stay for twenty years." Except he's wanted a child ever since Deb and the three bears. When Stewart and Deb got their divorce, he asked Noel if he could apply for custody of Petey. Or all of them, in order not to break up the set. If he'd been a woman, he'd have done it long ago. Women tell men they're lucky because they don't have a biological clock. But men don't have a womb either. One day, he has lunch with Noel. Lunch isn't just for bad news, it's good for lots of things. Over lunch you haven't time to debate the sore points that have arisen between you: Noel's work for aggrieved cops, the undertones of anti-minorities, anti-women that have seeped into his approach to his cases, his willingness to represent anyone who can pay his hefty fee. There's barely time for the main item: Will it happen or won't it? He's not optimistic. In their age ranges, the odds are eight per cent. But he checks his messages anyway. Nothing there. When he gets home, there's a little gift box on the kitchen counter. Inside are a pair of tiny mocassins. She must have slipped home while he was out. He collapses onto the kitchen stairs and thinks two thoughts; number one isn't even a thought, it's a religious thing, like Rudolf Otto's *mysterium tremendum* which underlies all experience of the ineffable. What can you say except, words fail? And you can't really *say* that. Thought two is: I gotta get a job. He phones her, then Noel. "Mr. eight per cent, I presume," says Noel.

A girl would be good. He's comfortable with women, he feels like an honourary girl. The implausible postponement of masturbation, the sensitivity thing he does, his dislike of competition (maybe *that's* why he battles feverishly to defeat and destroy the neo-cons)—he'd be fine with a girl. Guys are different. He's never felt like a guy. Guys fish. They talk about chicks and pussy in the locker room. So when the doctor at the amnio tells them it's going to be a boy, he thinks, *Exactly* what I need!

He has many conversations with the little guy, still in his mummy's tummy. Some of their talks are about astronomy, others concern fishing. The little guy seems to need a lot of information. They sit on the dock at night after they come in from fishing and talk about the stars. He can point out the ecliptic: the planets, the sun, and the moon all circle on the same plane, though he doesn't know why and he hopes the question won't get asked. He's often wondered himself. But of course, everything always gets asked.

Meanwhile he waits for the hammer to fall. Surely it will. This time he's really done it.

He goes to the twentieth birthday party of his credit union. He's banked there since it began. Perhaps he's thinking about births, trying to conjure sympathetic juju, something *he* can do in the process. And he wants to start an educational policy for the little guy, maybe he'll talk to somebody while he's there. It doesn't occur to him to just buy the damn policy. He always feels an economic act should be embedded in social connectedness, as if to demystify the abstractions of money and production. It's his version of socialism: being social. So he's at the party.

His credit union is a wretched institution, always has been: inefficient, unprofitable, and sanctimonious. He hates going there because they seem so *proud* of their ineptitude. They don't even have an ABM. They won't let you phone it in. They want you to confront them in all their ineffectiveness, as if to confirm the sheer commitment of banking there, a form of political and financial masochism. But he so likes the idea of co-ops in theory. *En principe.* They aren't top down, they don't require heavy administration and social conflict, the way unions, revolutions, or even elections do. It's not the dictatorship of the proletariat or anyone else. In fact, this one could use a little dictatorship. *Un petit peu.*

Pretty soon everyone has that execrable, after-work, white-wine smell. From across the room, Hildy is coming toward him. Or Hindy. Or Gilda. With a South African accent. He asks what she's up to, hoping for enough information to peg her. Oh, same old thing, she says, no help there. He divines that it's a doctorate in, um, got it finally, sociology. It's kind of nice to meet a sociologist, he'd started to wonder if there were any left. They started to vanish, like society itself, during the Thatcher years. She'd like to discuss an aspect of unpaid female work in rural communities with him, if he has time. He notices a ring. "Sure," he says, "and how's your, um, spouse?" "Apart from him," she says, "you're the only man I ever wanted to sleep with." Well, that's interesting, but he still doesn't know if they did. If he had a computer in his head, instead of a mere brain, he could search her name, if he knew what it was. "I always regretted it," she says. "Then I went home, and for the first time in my life, I masturbated to orgasm. I've wanted to say thanks." He feels like she just pinned the Order of Canada on him. That would make her Governor General. It's surely the nearest he'll come, and better than the book prize they gave and took away at the St. Lawrence Hall. Her smile isn't something she's going to remember to retract and offer to somebody else. "But it's good we didn't," she goes on, "because later that week I found out I had herpes. It was quite a time." And he knows where the hammer will fall.

Who could he have got what from, and what horrible effect might it have on the little guy, where he is now, or when he makes his brave journey down the birth canal into the bright lights of the world? In the last ultrasound, the baby is lounging, kicking back in his womby home. He could be singing: "I'm all right now, I'm all right now/ Never thought I'd make it but I always do somehow." Of course there's no chance he got herpes from Hildy/Hindy/Gilda—he works this out with his impressive brainpower—and passed it on to endanger the baby, *because he didn't sleep with her*. She went home and jerked herself off, or whatever women call it. She thanked him and he should thank her. This fails to calm him. What if he got herpes from someone he *did* sleep with? But he doesn't *have* herpes. He once went three months without sex—his longest stretch ever, since the dawn of history under Olivia's dining-room table—because one one-nighter told him she had herpes—afterward! "You were already inside me and what was the point of bringing it up *then?*" she said. "Besides, I always know when it's coming because I get a tingly feeling in the bathtub, and I didn't." Not reassuring enough. He waited a few months to have sex again, since the books all said you should wait a few weeks for symptoms to appear. The hysteric's time frame: multiply by three. He bolts the stupid birthday party and goes up to Book City on Bloor. He finds the little shelf of books on STDs, extracts a small pile, and ambles over to the history and biography sections to leaf through them, with special attention to index entries on pregnancy. Just like always—look in a book. He discovers what he knew would be there, maybe he recalled it from the previous scare: you can be a carrier without being infected. He must have known that but it lacked urgency, till now, because till now only his own stupid life would have been blighted. But what if he's passed it on? Herpes can blind a child, it says here, who gets infected during the birthing process. He's tormented, he doesn't sleep that night, he wants to avoid sex at all costs, what if she backs into him as she sometimes does and, carrier that he is, he infects her, and it ambushes the baby on his way out? He gets up, boots his computer, and pretends to work all night.

He talks to Rhonda next day. "Well, does she *have* herpes?" asks Rhonda. "How would I *know*?" he says. "She would *tell* you. She'd be in pain, she'd be furious," says Rhonda patiently. "Maybe she's just a carrier too," he says. "Then there's not much danger of infection during birth, is there?" says Rhonda in the same calm voice she used to talk him down from a hairy acid trip one early morning in Paris ages ago.

In the old days, to deal with an onset like this, he'd have "called somebody up," the way other people shoot up, smoke up, or settle in at the end of the bar. Or gone to the track, like his granddad, or Vegas, like his dad. Or just taken a walk, always a quest for sex and solace. Was that what he was doing the day she circled back on her bike? Probably. Not that he's admitting he's a sex addict, or that there is such a thing. It's a notion that's been around lately, people confess and go into twelve-step programs; but he's not convinced it will last, like other concepts and products that seemed inevitable—electronic books, whatever happened to them? Some things only time will tell and other things— not even time. You do have to wonder, though, what happens when your main aim in life is no longer getting laid, and if it ever was? You could design an empirical test, like: Are you experiencing withdrawal? Are you in a panicky sweat all the time? . . .

The birthing room is spare and ritualistic, the bed like an altar, raised and central. She declines painkillers. She wants it to be clear, for the baby and him. The labour must have begun yesterday, when she was propping herself against the walls of the deli at lunch, sliding along to the door. "Have a nice day," said the waiter. The groans get harsher and closer. "I just remembered something," she says. "I'm a wuss. I can't do this." He tries to think of something to say from one of the childbirth books, they must have about a thousand, they're both readers. "Remember why you're doing this," he says. She withers him with one glance, he won't try that again. But it seems to give her strength. Always helps to have an asshole in the group to unite everyone else. "Yes, you can," the nurse says sensibly. "Focus, concentrate, don't try to get away." Some of the books say you should take yourself far off, to an island or distant galaxy, but this nurse didn't read them. Next time a contraction comes she seems to have moved inside, drawing the room with her. The walls are practically bending toward her. He moves back. The nurse withdraws too, turns away and prepares some items on a table; she looks like the priests before Vatican II made them face the congregation. He and the nurse aren't an audience, they're witnesses; she doesn't know they're there, or care, she is self-sufficient. The lights dim, maybe the nurse did it. This is her drama, hers and his, the little guy now en route.

On this cue, the curtain across the door sweeps aside. Enter the doc, like an actor finding his light. He positions himself between her legs and puts his hand under the sheet. He nods. "You can do this thing," he says. He tells her to push when he says, and resist the impulse on her own. It sounds sexual. "Come on, sweetheart, you can do it." There are two of them in the light now, soon to be three. "One more push," says the doc. And then, "This is the last one." She says he told her that on the last push. "If I'd said there are two left, you'd have given up," he ribs her, the way humour often forms a part of good sex. He made me laugh, women say, to explain their otherwise indefensible choices. The top of a head starts to emerge and the doc says, "Wait, stop pushing," and then, "there's a cord." He says this to the student. Huh?

Where did a med student come from? She's standing beside him, must've entered with him. He unravels the cord from the little head and cuts it, then the pushing restarts. She is more wrung out than a human can be wrung. She is ashen. Nothing remains.

He does a kind of dropping motion with both hands, in the basket position, the way Willie Mays caught fly balls, and the adorable little guy drops out, or in. The doc continues the motion, swoooping his catch in an *S*, down and out, then up and over her body, onto her chest and into her hands. Sign here, please. She explodes like a starburst, she radiates like the sun. She is golden. Son.

The arrival looks around, alert and inquisitive. Around and round he gazes, the most arresting moment of his life is already almost over. The nurse, noting his interest, leaves the eyedrops for a while, so things won't go immediately hazy. Enough time for murk and fog in the future. Max holds the baby boy, who already has a name. The name is the hardest thing his dad ever wrote, and he's written a fair amount. Titles have always been hard for him but this was the hardest. How do you give some- one you don't know a name they have to carry all their life? He rains tears down on the wrinkly, alert face. *Owen.* Poor little guy is going to think the male of this species is in a permanent state of weepiness. All they do is cry cry cry.

In the middle of the night, the little guy cries from his crib. She goes to get him, and instead of lying with him on the futon in there, she brings him into bed with them. The three of them fall asleep together.

Something wakes him up, it's a thought. Ideas have always had a physical impact on him, maybe *that's* why he got into his field, whatever it is. The baby is lying *between* them. Who'd have pictured that! A little boy sleeps on his mother's side of the bed, between her and the edge, that's the rule he knew. Behind her looms his dad, Freud's inspiration and probably aspiration. It would never have occurred to him, or Freud, to position the little guy between parents, leaning toward one as much as the other. Yet there he lies, perfectly placed. Freud was wrong about that, among other things, but getting the answers right was not his strength, nor Keynes's. The point is, they asked better questions.

And so, contrary to lifelong expectations, Max is a character in a happy ending. Except everything hangs on where you are when your story ends. So he is at the cottage he adores one day, the sole thing that he knew could alter his life beyond anything except the other thing that has just happened. He is alone on the island, happily storming up and down the stone path from the dock bearing groceries and toilet paper, preparing for his *family* to join him. That night he wakes unable to breathe, a mighty pain in the middle of his chest. It mounts, then subsides. Then it starts again. Between bouts, he gathers a few things, hoping to make it off the island as soon as it's light, by boat, then the car. Maybe he will reach the low-tech hospital in town before it hits again. By morning, he's feeling better. He sets course for home. The pain hits when he fills the tank along gasoline alley, about halfway there, and departs, as if it's toying with him. His doctor schedules a couple of tests. They both think it's indigestion, which the GI confirms, according to the radiologist.

Next day he enters the stress test feeling relaxed. He tuckers out early on the treadmill, but what the hell, he knows now it's his stomach. They do the thallium scan. He lies under the camera feeling unearthly for thirty minutes, then, in great spirits and with a pocketful of Tums, heads back up north. His doctor calls next day and says he's sorry but the stress test was positive. What does that mean, maybe it's as murky as a pardon? Well, there is a problem with his heart, something he and all who have suffered with him through the years will not be surprised at. He gazes through the red pines down to the lake. He has an appointment with a cardiologist. Meanwhile he starts taking some little pink pills. . .

The cardiologist schedules an angiogram at the hospital. Phoning to make appointments looks like the main thing doctors now do. Is there a course they take in med school? The angio is the gold standard, says the cardiologist (Don't patronize me, thinks Max), it will tell him for sure what's happening. It may turn out negative, he adds, the way you would say Christmas might not come in December this year. If there's a small blockage, they will do an angioplasty, it's minor. They send in a little balloon that busts up the plaque and crap, like Raquel Welch who got shrunk in *Fantastic Voyage* and travelled through some guy's body to save his life. Weeks pass before the angio, he feels better, hope revives. They'll find nothing, it was a mistake, probably the digestion, at most a balloon job. He puts on a nitro patch every morning and it gives him a headache.

For the angio, they stick a tube in your groin and snake it up *into* your heart, then flush some purple goop through you. The guy who does it is manic. He chortles and gabs."Will you look at that!" he says to the nurses. "I don't know *what* they can do about it." Max concludes, lying on the stretcher in the hall afterward, that he is inoperable.

So he's filled with joy and gratitude a week later when the cardiologist says a surgeon will be happy to cut open his chest, then shove aside the veins, arteries, and any irrelevant organs in the way. Ah, he thinks, the routine bypass everyone has reassured him about, just like a filling. Well, yes, says the doc, but the test showed something else, a valve. They have to repair, probably replace it. Does that mean going right *into* the heart again? Yes, but it's almost routine these days. So now they're talking about two routine procedures, the second not quite as routine as the first. Don't worry, people say, it's all normal—the way they say at a funeral: *He didn't have anything to regret. I wouldn't mind dying the way he did.* Except if you're the one who's dead. So he waits, puffer at hand, patch in place. Waits and waits.

He is not bitter. He has met his wonderful child, and he has known true love. He won the lottery, nothing says you linger long after you do, everybody goes eventually, that's fine. Except for the footnote re his child not yet knowing him back. Those conversations between the two of them in his head about fish and stars stopped the moment the boy was born. Because, of course, they were really about the dad. Who else could they have been about? Since then it has been about the son, and the reality of *his* experience: inchoate at first, an adorable blob of proto-plasm, flopping and distending like flubber, who soon began organizing himself into a purposive creature, that will eventual-ly be pointed as a pencil. (No wonder people like his dad believe there must be meaning in things like history and the economy.) At about six months, the baby looked up and Max felt him reg-ister: *Ah, so you are the other one.* But he still doesn't talk. Real conversations haven't had a chance to replace ersatz ones. What will they discuss, what end will he, or would he, be required to hold up when they happen? Well, every dad has the obligation to talk to his son about one thing, and that's sex. It may be useless, it may be a waste of time for the kid, who will surely roll his eyes, as well as humiliating for his old man, who must bear the eyerolls, based on the historic duty of each generation to outmode and exceed the last. Max's dad saw himself as a trail-breaker because he stole kisses on a natural ice rink on Saturday nights and the immigrant kids all called him the King of Kitzel Park. Max himself lived through the coming of the contraceptive pill—you go to someone's place for dinner, smoke a joint, and get into bed together the way couples chose a movie to see in his father's time. The newsmags called it the Sexual Revolution, as if there had never been and never would be another. Within years the kids he TA'd for or "mentored"—a new term—were all bi as their sexual starting point; and for those who followed, group sex was a given. The Sexual Revolution started to sound as quaint as courting and spooning and the minuet. It's an iron law of human history. Nevertheless the obligation to speak, remains: you have to offer it because it's what you have to give. But how? In what form? Where to begin? Well, let's consider the little Casanova at age eight. . .

~

What else, what else? (he thinks as he walks, and it's starting to rain). The girl in the rain. Yes. That would be in the seventies; not the cruddy back half, the self-obsessed, disco part that spilled easily into Reagan's and Thatcher's 1980s; but the early years, still warm with the residual heat of Rock and the anti-war movement along with the splendid, delusional confidence that the world really can change for the better in your own lifetime— due to your efforts in solidarity with others. I met the girl with living blonde hair after a concert during those years. I went with Roberta, a Celtic-based folk artist, who introduced us afterward, as we stood among the emptying seats. She was selling tickets for an environmental event. I looked her name up in the phone book when I got home that night. No one had answering machines or services in those days, and there was no way to make a silent call and find out if the message on her line mentioned a "we" as opposed to "I"—not that messages are definitive. A woman might say "we" to fool the home invaders and rapists. Anyway, I never thought you should make people's choices about who they sleep with for them, whether they're part of a couple or not. I'd just have been gathering information by making the call, which never hurts, except when it does.

I called the next night. She didn't react to my name with anything like warmth. I had to explain where we met. Then I asked her over. When? she said. I said, now. I got a brusque no. I could have suggested putting it off till the next night, but she didn't sound like she took to the idea at all. She sounded as if she wanted something more formal: "coffee" or a movie or dinner or a worthy left-wing benefit. A date. It wasn't the sixties any more. We were in a murky historical transition where meeting and going straight to bed was no longer viewed as a brave political act. Not that I ever assumed sex was obligatory. I was always grateful when they said yes. Grateful and *surprised*. But by then it was more or less frowned on. Within a few years the pattern would be described as date rape, especially by feminists. And it used to be called the Sexual Revolution.

We fell into a communications bog. I'd call, she'd call back at a better time, we'd dicker over when and where to meet, it never quite worked, we'd say we'd try again. I had her on a list with other "possibles" I kept in those days. Sometimes it was in my head, sometimes I actually wrote it out. Women I wanted to sleep with; then I could cross them off, or see them again, and sometimes, you never know, someone turned into more. With her, I didn't think sex would happen at all: too much trouble, too much resistance, no enthusiasm, no urgency, just not there. But I kept trying, persistence is a virtue, you never know, it's not right to give up easily. Maybe rejection is good for you. One weekday morning I phoned and she was there. I might have been doggedly going through the list, like a politician rifling his rolodex, just to keep contact. I was too edgy, or randy, to work on whatever jumble of projects and good works were on my other lists. I needed somebody. She said okay, today. It was a first. Maybe she was in a state of urgency too, out of control. Hard to picture. There was a kicker, though. She wanted a picnic. She lived across from High Park. We could meet at her apartment, she'd prepare a little hamper, she called it. I couldn't say no, what would be my reason? But it sounded like sheer time waste. You get caught in these things.

It was fall or spring and storm-clouded by the time I got there. We dodged the traffic across Parkside Drive and into the park. I was feeling pretty sullen, like I knew I was going to be deprived, and she was like a Girl Guide leader, cheery damn demeanour, determined on the outing, whether it turned out to be fun or hell. We settled joylessly on a hill that slopes down to Grenadier Pond and she began extracting items: cheese, wine, a free-range chicken she roasted earlier in the week. The rain started. It seemed negligible and we were both feeling grumpy; making a clean getaway would have been more trouble added to an already unpleasant experience. We moved under a tree while others left the park, just hoping to get the whole thing over with. Then it poured, a torrent of the sort that only became common in the years of global warming. The tree was flimsy cover, but leaving it would have been worse by then. Our clothes got soaked first and then our skin. We huddled, then we cuddled, then we hugged and stroked and rolled and pulled off our clothes and we balled—the word seems to fit perfectly here, for once—while the rain kept coming too.

Then she led me home cross-country—never mind the park's careful paths and trails—to her apartment where we showered and had tea while our clothes dried in the laundry room downstairs. Like campers drenched on a canoe trip warming in front of a woodstove in some cabin we lucked onto. For long after—months, maybe a year—we saw each other. She'd come to my place, since she had roommates. She'd half-heartedly suggest we "do" something, as if sex was nothing. Once, we were waiting for a pizza to come, we were starved, sex usually made me hungry. Looking out the second-floor window, I was behind her, and I went into her again, standing there watching, seeing the car arrive, the delivery guy come to the door, trying to time it to last as long as possible. After, she said she didn't know why she let any of it bother her. Surely this was enough.

But it bothered her anyway and the times began to stretch between meetings. Maybe that was just its rhythm. I heard she moved to the country to raise a lot of peaches—as John Prine sang. Many people tried the country for a while as eras and values altered, though most of them moved back again. I'd run into her, maybe when she came in on market days with the peaches, but she never had time to stop and talk. She'd smile what I took as a conspiratorial smile—Prine again—about our past. Then nothing. Maybe I should have called her. You never know. I can't say why she's on my mind now, rather than so many others. . .

I did see Francie once, ten or fifteen years after our debacle. I was in Ottawa, I think to bid on a small government study that was tendered. I went into a coffee shop to glance through the posting before my interview, and she walked in. She was pushing a stroller with a baby. She went to the rear, right past me, giving no sign she saw me, sat down and ordered. I had to be sure, so I walked back there too and downstairs to the pay phone.

There were still no cellphones. When I returned, she was drink-
ing her latte and reading the paper. She never looked up. The baby
was asleep. It had calmed her right down, as kids can. Ottawa
was a funny place for her to end up, after being so happy in
London, as a transnational. Ottawa is so Not London. Or not so
funny, if you think about where she came from, which is always
a factor. Ottawa is pretty much Leaside as a city. What else . . .

Deb did not become the president of Iceland, and still isn't. The
air kind of went out of her balloon once she got there. Women were
running things as much as men, or more. The whole country was
independent-minded. They didn't take orders from anywhere, not
even the U.S. There weren't a lot of rich folks, or workers either.
You are who you define yourself against. At least some of us are.
She learned a bit of Icelandic and the kids became fluent. But it was
hardly necessary. Scandinavians are very cosmopolitan. Speaking
five or six languages is normal. I've walked into a group of them
talking their own language and they all switch to English without
even glancing up and letting on that they did it for you. When the
three bears got old enough, they moved back to Manitoba. I hear
the little one, Petey, drives a truck. . .

Maybe I should include some advice—isn't that part of what
every dad must leave his son? Okay. Number one. Be patient.
When a woman says no, or not yet, don't pout and feel hurt.
She may mean simply no for the moment. Not quite yet.
Sometimes a rejection is just a rejection—for now but not
always; of your request but not you. If you cultivate patience
(my son) you will treat those you know with respect and yourself with kindness. I wish I had shown more patience myself—
think of all the *other* women I might have had. "That's it?" you
say. "What's number two?" But I'm sorry, there is no number
two. In terms of practical tips, that's it, along with a load of

inconclusive theory. You know me, or I hope you will . . .

I do wonder, sometimes, why I didn't become an anarchist. Kids now tend to be anarchists, I know, if they go in a radical direction. Instead, I spent a lot of my life wondering why I hadn't become a *Marxist*. People often asked about that, so I had to ponder it. Maybe the dogmatism and certainty put me off. The pseudo-scientific assurance of Marxism, built on models like Newtonian physics and Darwinian evolution. Maybe it just was too last century, or maybe I saved my deepest idealism for sex, not politics. I was never a natural Marxist. Maybe I was a natural anarchist. Or a sexual one. Can you be a sexual anarchist? For sure.

Back when Noel and I were undergrads, we went to see Norman O. Brown speak. Brown wrote about what he called polymorphous perversity—every kind of sexualized touch you can imagine: an exuberant continuum of kissing, handholding, stroking, hugging; legs, knees, lips, hair, ears, bums, along with stuff that doesn't even involve touch like looks, voices, and the tilt of a head, all flowing into one another the way a baby experiences it. That would be true sexual anarchism, I humbly submit. You might even still find *Love's Body*, by Brown, in the psych sections of the bookstores, or on the Internet, though other standbys of the era—Fritz Perls, Eric Erikson, Maslow with his "peak experiences"—have been relegated to the libraries and used bookstores. The lecture hall was packed with horny youth, yearning for a sight of the man who wrote, and must therefore incarnate, *Love's Body*. A round, bald little guy came in and people kept waiting for Norman O. Brown, but of course it was him. I have no idea what the *O* stood for. Womanizing doesn't really go with polymorphous perversity, or sexual anarchism. It's too easily classified, filed, and shelved. Its definitions are too firm. If anarchism's time has come, maybe womanizing's time is gone—a thought I have often had . . .

Sometimes I look into your face, my boy—perhaps the only face I've ever looked into unflinchingly—and it fills the cosmos. This effect cannot be constant because one has to see the rest of the cosmos, too, in order to live a life. But looking at your face in those moments has been my only sure way to obliterate the nagging world of childhood and projection, the way I once believed sex could obliterate it, at least temporarily, and know that I am seeing what I am looking at. Those moments are proof that infantilism can be overcome, as Freud prayed it could. Then I know, though I always forget, that almost nothing should be taken personally.

The point is not to be radical—more radical or less radical—as one grows older. Anarchism is nice, not because it seems right but because it seems lively. Eventually you place a larger premium on the ability to be surprised than on the possession of truth.

~

The rain has stopped and he's walking again. Just a short one, around the block. *I have travelled much*, said Thoreau, *in Concord*. Concord's a claustrophobic place, Max used to go there on Sundays the summer he taught at MIT. He'd stand at the foot of the minuteman statue, a John Wayne lookalike, with Longfellow's words on the pedestal: "Here once th'embattled farmer stood/And fired the shot heard round the world." Ah, the panache of Americans. The battle of Toronto in 1837 was bigger and bloodier, so was Batoche, but no one wrote that they were heard round the world. Well, they weren't going to be heard if no one cried them out. Culture is always the decisive force, not economics, wrote Polanyi, who was an economist and no slouch, in the middle of the Second World War, around the time

Max was born. So maybe he bet on the wrong horse. Was he too impressed with the materiality of economics, as he was too moved by the physicality of sex? Would there ever be another womanizer? Was it a quixotic life to set out on? Did it depend on the ongoing degradation of an entire gender, and once they declined to bow and shuffle, did it mean you could no more womanize than you could hold slaves? Who knows when it comes to history? Back during the rise of feminism (and his own minor rise), he'd have bet his all—the Pirate special, the collected works of Keynes, that's about it but it seemed a lot—that there would never be another beauty contest held. Its era was over, its assumptions outmoded and embarrassing, that was plain as the nose on your face. You'd be as likely to see medieval jousts in the future as beauty queens. Now you can go to jousts every night of the week down at the CNE grounds and have your dinner served by a "wench," then put it on your credit card, the way Noel did on their first, um, date.

Maybe he should have it out with Noel again. It's become their intermittent form of contact. Noel has continued to retrench over the years, or maybe just pay homage to his dad. The Gulf War unveiled the new Noel. He declared there was no solution for those people (his terms: solution, those people), because they want what we have and they won't stop till they get it. It wasn't a new conversation between them but now it had gone global, like everything else soon would. "The worst are the towelheads," said Noel. "I don't know why but they're bitter and full of hate. They never seem to know how to make a decent deal and get out of town. In the end we might just have to kill them all." They were on the phone for that conversation, and by the end of it, Max was holding the handset at arm's length and shouting. "You're angry?" Noel howled back, probably on the speaker, as he strode about his office making big circles with his arms: "You're angry? Well, I'm angry too! But this is healthy anger! Do you know what I'm saying?" It was as though the end of the Cold War unleashed something in both of them and they try not to revisit it. Over the months it subsided, now they run into each other, or call on a pretext, have a good gab and after they've caught up, one says, "This was nice. Do you think we should talk about what happened that time?" Then the other says, "We could, or we could just say, 'That's in the past.'" Then the other— the roles are interchangeable—says, "Let's talk about it a little." So they do, till *kaboom*. The truth is when you've known each other so long, it doesn't matter much how you feel about each other. He'd do anything for Noel, but only if necessary.

How calm life would be without expectations. No letdowns, no recriminations. No muss, no fuss, three cheers for us. But without failed hopes and expectations, you wouldn't have Keynes, Innis, Polanyi, Marx, Freud, economics, or science. Without science, you wouldn't have anything we recognize as ourselves and our world. Without science, and his endless struggles for and with it, he wouldn't be him. He'd be—well, who knows? What a lovely thought. He wishes he knew what he would be without everything that has made him what he is. Would you still be you, in the absence of all you've become? He's pretty sure he would. Personality is constructed on some substratum of self. A substratum . . . that is the self?

In London, during his marriage, before he went to the Tavistock and entered therapy, he called Sorstad to say he was contemplating the step and scared shitless. What if he went and questioned all the basics of his life and at the end none of them were left? Who would he be? Would he even be? Sorstad said he understood, making it sound as though he'd taken the dreaded step himself. "And the marvellous thing," said Sorstad, was that after Max had gone and questioned all the pillars on which his identity rested—which Sorstad listed to prove he knew his subject: Olivia, academics, economics, and so forth and so on—in the end all of them would still rest securely in place. It sounded like a guarantee, gold-plated and ironclad. Max took it to the Tavistock the way you'd take it to the bank, where he rummaged through his past and present, and at the end emerged: divorced, an academic dropout full of doubts about his chosen field, who would never gain tenure or even apply for it—plus a host of other losses and abandonments he can't even recall now, yet back then they were *the pillars of him.* What a great experience. You lose it all, and you still *are.* Sorstad called from his Arizona retirement a few years ago and said he had a message he wanted to come and deliver in person. Then he broke his hip so Max flew there instead. They stood on the balcony, Sorstad leaning on his walker, looking out at the mesa. Sorstad said, "I just wanted you to know that the years after sixty-five really can be the best of your life." He didn't say they will be, just that they can. Does that apply to sex? To womanizing? Surely not. "Ah, but don't forget that fine prototype," said Sorstad, choosing his next phrase carefully: "the lusty old man." "There are times it may be better to do it but not talk about it," said Max. "And others," said Sorstad, "when it's better to talk about it instead of doing it." "I hear that was Casanova's choice when he got old," said Max. "He wrote his memoirs." Sorstad nodded. "True," he said, "but the younger generation gave him a hard time anyway, the ones who lived in the castle. They badgered and taunted him. He could hardly get any writing done."

He walks on, it was always the essence of his womanizing. Walking and thinking. Noel saw him from the house on Bernard and said his pal looked like a prowler. Rhonda, may she rest in peace, said the sight of him walking the streets made her think of a swamp, a reptile cruising slime-green waters, just below the surface. He'd go anywhere he was invited, largely on the chance there'd be a woman and they'd wind up, that very night, folded into each other. The events he attended were like stationary walks—parties and dinners, book launches and conferences, rallies and protests. It was always about sexual possibility and intellectual provocation. Walking is moving, he thinks best as he moves (he thinks as he moves). Sometimes all it takes is that first step off the porch. Is it the prospect of sex that lightens and clarifies the mind? Walking is about potential, which means it's about sex and some other good things, always out there somewhere as long as you keep moving. But wasn't womanizing about power and conquest, not freedom and possibility? Maybe it was, maybe it was something else too. When faced with a hard choice, take both, it's amazing how often you can. Some womanizers may be conquerors all the time, and all may be conquerors some of the time, but he's in it mainly to keep moving. When womanizing is to be found only in the dustbin of history, where Marxism already is and capitalism surely will be, there will still be walking.

Of course walking can easily turn to regrets, which is potential in the bad sense: what happened but shouldn't have. Regrets are killers, yet they're impossible not to have, except when you feel good, or *well*, as they say in French, which is the way you sometimes beat regret. It slips aside because everything led to this well state, so what's to regret? The whole cluttered tale gets rectified in retrospect, comes out fine in the rear-view mirror. What could you choose to regret, no matter how insupportable it seemed at the time, since you don't know exactly what brought you to this point? You wouldn't exchange anything, you dare not. Now economics is about exchange, and involves the allocation and exchange of scarce resources, like humour, common sense, love, friendship, useful information, good intentions . . . he thinks as he walks . . .

Acknowledgements

Many thanks to Maya Mavjee, whose friendship I value even more than her immense skill and tact as an editor. Thanks to Bernice Eisenstein, for her engagement in yet another novel of mine, passing well beyond the normal responsibilites of a copy editor; and to Bruce Westwood, for negotiating the deal that made it possible to write the books in the order I wanted to. Thanks also to Nancy White, for her hurtin' song of many years ago, which I have attributed to a character in this book; and for aid on particulars to Anna Coote, Olivia Chow and Dr. Teddi Orenstein Lyall.

About the Author

RICK SALUTIN is a novelist, playwright and social commentator. His work has appeared often in *The Globe and Mail*, *Toronto Life*, *Saturday Night*, and *This Magazine*, of which he is one of the founding editors. He is the author of many books, including *Living in a Dark Age* and *A Man of Little Faith*, which won the W.H. Smith/Books in Canada Best First Novel Award. His stage play, *Les Canadiens*, received the Chalmers Award for Best Canadian Play, and he won the National Newspaper Award as best columnist of 1993 for his work in *The Globe and Mail*. He is the recipient of the 1991 Toronto Arts Award in writing and publishing. Rick Salutin lives in Toronto